What *REALLY* Happened To me?

ELLIE BARKER

By Ellie Barker

The Strawberry Village Series

Do We Really Have to Do This?
What Really Happened to Me?

*For Rob, Arthur, Herbie & Cookie
Just for being you*

x

Vinci Books

vinci-books.com

Published by Vinci Books Ltd in 2025

Copyright © Ellie Barker 2025

All rights reserved.
No part of this book may be reproduced in any form or by any electronic or mechanical means, including information storage and retrieval systems, without written permission from the author, except for the use of brief quotations in a book review.
This is a work of fiction. Unless otherwise indicated, all the names, characters, businesses, places, events and incidents in this book are either the product of the author's imagination or used in a fictitious manner. Any resemblance to actual persons, living or dead, or actual events is purely coincidental.

Paperback ISBN: 9798313646367

For any woman who feels truly lost…
You're still in there,
I promise.

P

Prologue

NOW

Dear five-year-old me

My name is Grace Leven, I'm fifty-three years old and I hate my life.

I'm writing to you because a therapist has told me to do this. Yes, I'm seeing a therapist and yes, I'm fifty-three. I can't quite believe both either, but here we are. I bet fifty-three seems like such an ancient age to you. I know it does me. I'm also guessing you think a fifty-three-year-old should be a grown-up with it all worked out? But clearly, I'm not.

Still, this isn't about me.

This letter is for you.

I'm thinking of you now as I write and am wondering what you're doing. I'm guessing you're probably writing too, in one of your little books. Is it the orange one? Or the red one? You've got your dolls lined up (I'm sorry I never mended Margaret's head by the way) and you're writing an article about them to be published in your magazine.

Your mum – or rather our mum – is somewhere nearby, pottering

1

and singing, asking what you fancy for te. Your dad, if he's not at work, is in his shed, making something. A bookshelf, a wardrobe – something our mum will roll her eyes at, and won't have the heart to tell him we don't need at all.

The house is warm as always, whether it's winter or summer. We're starting to move into the first days of spring where I am, so I'm thinking it's that with you too. Your mum keeps popping into the garden to check on the bulbs; she's never been great at planting them – most end up upside down. But she tries a little harder every year. Your dad will be whistling and asking you what your article is about today. It's so much better than any drivel he reads in the Times, *he'll say.*

You love cooking biscuits with your mum – every weekend you try something else. Your mum lets you decide how many chocolate chips to put in. (Then, when you're not looking, she adds extra so it's the right amount.) Your dad 'oohs' and 'aahs' at every batch – even the ones that taste so disgusting you want to throw them in the bin.

School is going okay. You'd rather be at home but you don't mind. You've made a few friends, which makes it tolerable. Lucy is okay but she always wants to play with your dolls, which you find annoying. The teachers are nice – a bit strict but that's okay. The school dinners are disgusting except on Fridays when it's fish and chips. You have to sit next to Billy Jenkins in maths and he's a pain, but your mum told you to just imagine he's the kindest boy in the world; he just has an act at school. So that's what you do. And then you get to go home.

I chose to write to you first, because I remember you so well. Singing, skipping, giggling – you love to laugh, especially at your dad's jokes, even though they're terrible. I also remember what you told your class when you were asked to share something they may not know about you. You stood up, cheeks pink, unable to look at the big sea of eyes in front of you.

But you got the words out and said…

"My name is Grace. I'm five years old and I love my life."

So, what happened to us, Grace? Or rather what really happened

What Really Happened To Me?

to me? I have no idea, my sweet little girl, but it's time now to work it out – for me and for you.

Speak soon,
Love
G x

Chapter One

"Grace Leven – the woman who proves you really can have it all."

Even as Grace read the headline out loud, she didn't believe the words, nor did she recognise the woman pictured in the magazine at all.

The caramel, highlighted blunt bob was hers. The cream Prada trouser suit they'd gifted her from the shoot now hung in her wardrobe and wasn't dissimilar to the one she was wearing now, as she sat at the very desk in the photo.

But there was something in her eyes. A look she'd never noticed before – one she couldn't explain.

She picked up her phone.

"Do you think they did something to my eyes?"

She heard Polly try not to laugh. "Only you could say that, Grace."

"I look strange. Icy."

"You look like you and you look bloody fabulous. You know it too. You're the talk of the office. It's the first good press Hi-TV has had in months – our very own CEO is leading the way for womankind. You do know you were the subject of Girl's Talk this lunchtime?"

"I heard," Grace said. Her inbox and phone had been pinging with celebratory messages since the article the previous day. It's funny, she thought: the same people pop out of the woodwork the minute there's a whiff of success.

Her assistant Matilda knocked at her door.

"I've got to go. Are we still having cocktails tomorrow?"

"Daphne's at eight. You're buying. You're the woman who has it all, after all."

Grace put her phone down and looked at Matilda, who stood in front of her. She shuffled – and Matilda never shuffled.

"What is it?"

Matilda's cheeks turned a darker shade of pink.

"The board. They want to see you at eight tomorrow morning."

"They do?"

"Yes, first thing."

"Is there breakfast?"

"Yes."

"And why are you looking so concerned, Matilda?"

"It's just, well, you're already back-to-back tomorrow."

"I'm always back-to-back."

Still Matilda stood in front of her.

"Is there anything else?"

"Are you not worried?

Grace raised her eyebrows. She didn't need one of Matilda's outbursts of paranoid emotion just then; they seemed to be getting more frequent lately. If they continued, she'd have to talk to someone, which would be a shame. But she really didn't have time.

I suspect it's got something to do with this." She pointed to the article.

"Yes." Matilda nodded.

"Don't look so worried. They're just relieved the dirty water is passing, so to speak. I've saved Hi-TV's bacon."

Matilda tried to smile. "Yes."

"Is it all of them?"

"All of them."

Grace nodded.

"Have you told them no carbs?"

"Of course."

"So, are we done?"

"Yes." But still, Matilda stood there.

"Is there anything else?" Grace took a deep breath.

Matilda opened her mouth, then closed it. "Have a good evening."

"I will. Thank you. You too," Grace added.

There was a time she'd have asked Matilda about her plans, but that would involve twenty minutes of listening to her ramble about her love-life. Twenty minutes Grace didn't have. She had learned a long time ago to stop asking her assistants about their love lives.

Matilda hesitated.

"What is it, Matilda?" Grace felt the impatience rising in her.

"It's just…I'm sorry."

"For what?'

"For adding to your schedule."

"Matilda, it's not your fault I've got a meeting. Breakfast meetings at Hi-TV are shoe-horned in when they know they have to pat someone on the back. It's about this." She pointed to the article again. The piece in a Sunday magazine had more than done the trick to boost the company's reputation. It was mission accomplished.

Grace picked up her pen. She sensed Matilda wanted to say something else but she neither had the time nor the energy to pursue it further. At last, Matilda turned around and left the office. When had these young girls become so needy, Grace wondered as she put her pen down?

Was she ever that needy in her twenties? Of course she wasn't.

She turned around in her chair, looking through the floor-to-ceiling window. She stood up and looked down at the River Thames. The lights were twinkling now, as the city got ready for the night. She was too high up to see the faces of the people rushing to dinner, or to get home because they were late. She'd be a part of that crowd in a while.

She picked up the magazine again. Perhaps she was over-thinking it. It was her standing there, poised and in cream. As she put it back on her desk, the page turned and a picture caught her eye. It was a picture of a Georgian building covered in roses. She read further. It was called Strawberry House, and it was an advert for a hotel.

"Come and join us at Strawberry House and leave feeling like you again," Grace read. "How ridiculous. Whoever feels like themselves these days?" She tutted, threw the magazine in her bag and turned off the lights.

Chapter Two

Grace: I'm in the bar, waiting. Where are you? X
Eric: Why should I even turn up?

Grace watched her husband bite into his sourdough. The knot in her stomach tightened – the same one that had arrived when she'd reached the restaurant to discover he wasn't there. He hadn't bothered to apologise that he was twenty minutes late. Still, she'd kept him waiting more times than she'd like to admit. He hadn't even bothered to kiss her or greet her either. Still, what did she expect? They'd been married for twenty-seven years.

Besides, the relief of not being stood up by her own husband was overwhelming, especially as she knew eyes were resting on her. It may be Monday night, but the restaurant, with its views of the sky over the night-time City, was packed. She'd been there several times before for work meetings – sufficient background music and ambience to attempt to make it feel relaxed, but eyes darted everywhere except the menus. She knew Eric would love it.

She had to find a way of erasing Saturday night, and another dinner at another fine restaurant would do the trick.

"Why are you looking at me like that? You don't expect me not to eat bread because you're not, do you?"

"No, of course not." She shook her head. She sipped her wine. One glass, just the one. They were, after all, celebrating, weren't they?

"To magazines, and to having it all." Grace raised her glass. Eric looked up from his menu then looked down again.

"If you say so."

Grace put her glass down. She was about to ask him what was wrong, when the waiter appeared.

"Not now." Her tone was sharp.

Eric looked up at him. "Thank you. We're still deciding," he told the waiter in a softer tone.

The young man nodded and walked away.

Grace looked around the restaurant – or dining club, as it was called. The white tablecloths, the hushed voices, the stifled atmosphere. She suspected he'd been told to leave the table many times; her tone was nothing he hadn't heard before.

Eric was still looking at her.

"What? Have I got something on my lip?"

"Don't be coy."

Grace's heart began to race. They were supposed to be celebrating.

"It's not every day your wife is the subject on Girl's Talk."

He leant forward.

"It's not every day your wife screams in your face."

Grace put her glass down and looked around.

"Don't worry, nobody's listening to us. You're not that important."

"I told you I was sorry."

He looked back down at his menu.

"I've been under a lot of stress at work; you know that. All those rumours about Wakefield –it's been a nightmare. Do you know what it would have meant if it had come out?" She whispered now.

"So, it's okay you screamed in my face and shoved me in the middle of Soho? You weren't so worried about people watching you then, were you Grace?" He leant forward. "You were vile."

A sickening feeling crept up her insides.

"I said I was sorry. It was the wine."

"Well, I see it's not stopped you." He nodded towards her hand, as it held the stem of her glass.

She let go.

"I thought we were here to celebrate. It's not every day your wife is on the front page of a magazine."

"I can't just turn it on and off, Grace. Besides, haven't you got an early meeting tomorrow?"

"An early meeting to celebrate my success." She put her hand back on the stem of the glass.

"Christ, you're full of yourself."

The sharpness of his tone startled her and she knocked the wine glass. She managed to stop it from falling, but this time the two men on the table next to them looked over.

She turned her face into a forced smile. "There's nothing wrong with being celebrated."

"If you say so." Eric put the menu down on the plate. They sat for a moment, the silence like a wall between them.

Grace shook her head and sat up.

"I was thinking." Her tone was lighter. "Isn't it time we booked Mauritius?"

"Is it?" He raised his eyebrows.

"Well, you've been wanting to go for ages."

"No, you wanted to go."

"Only because I heard you talking about it, to Pearl."

"I was just trying to sound engaged. It's not every day your daughter calls you from the Indian Ocean."

"How is she?"

"She's great, really great."

"I'd love to speak with her."

"Then make yourself available."

Grace opened her mouth to speak but stopped, a wave of exhaustion washing over her. She drank her wine, ignoring his glance. It was one glass – just one glass.

"I'll have the scallops followed by the steak. Rare – please." He smiled at the waiter. The young man turned to Grace now. Was that a look of fear in his eyes?

"I'll have the kale salad," she told him. "Thank you." She smiled the warmest smile she could as she handed back the menu.

"Wouldn't it help if you actually ate something?" Eric asked.

"Help what?" She knew what he meant, but she didn't want to hear it.

"Your mood."

She leant forward. "Darling, I'm in a wonderful mood." She touched his hand. He didn't pull away but she felt him flinch beneath her. "Look, I'm really, really sorry about Saturday. We all have our moments and that was one of mine. It won't happen again."

"You said that the last time." He sat back in his chair, pulling his hand away.

What Really Happened To Me?

She sat back too. "It's been a tough few weeks. The Wakefield affair," she repeated, lowering her voice. "Pearl leaving, getting the company's reputation back on track." She watched her husband open his mouth – she suspected, to argue. But then he closed it again.

"You're tired," she told him.

"What are you saying? I look dreadful?"

"No, not at all." Grace was feeling the panic rise in her, the same fluttery feeling of dread. "I'm not saying you look tired. You look great." And he did. His short dark hair, his deep blue eyes, his tall frame, his presence – heads had turned, as they always did, when he'd walked through the restaurant earlier.

"But I still think it's time we booked a holiday."

She sat and waited for his reply, but he stayed quiet.

The nausea began to rise in her.

"Eric, please."

"Scallops, sir." The waiter placed the plate in front of him.

"Wonderful. Thank you." She watched her husband pick up his fork. She tried to meet his eyes, but he looked down. Then she watched him eat his food as quickly as he could.

Chapter Three

Polly: Good luck with the meeting this morning x
Grace: Thanks darling. Can't wait for cocktails tonight, even if I am paying x

"Great work out," her trainer called to her as he waved goodbye.

Grace nodded as she caught her breath. The gym was just starting to get busy. There was something Grace enjoyed about being ahead of the race. The four forty-five am starts were worth it, even if her head had pounded like it did most mornings as she dragged herself out of bed.

But by the time she'd met Toby in the park at five-fifteen the painkillers were kicking in. After forty-five minutes of interval training in the gym her head was clearing. The weights had given her the strength she needed, and the sprints up and down the park to finish off had set her up for the day. As she walked back towards her house, she decided not to think about Eric and the previous night. She didn't allow herself to think about how he couldn't get out of the restaurant quick enough, the silent taxi ride home and how he'd slammed the door of the guest room as he'd gone straight to bed.

She opened the door of her house. It was quiet. Enormous, cold, dark and quiet. The silence reached the high ceilings. The large vase of hydrangeas in the hallway did nothing to soften the feel. She must do something about it, one day, she thought again, as she drank water from her bottle.

She walked up the first flight of stairs and saw the door of the guest room was still closed. He must be asleep. She'd book Mauritius later, but for now she must focus. She carried on climbing the stairs, crossed her bedroom and walked into her bathroom, the marble cold under her feet. She welcomed it; it cut through. She stepped into the walk-through shower, turned the dial to freezing and braced herself as the water pounded her back.

By the time the driver pulled up outside Hi-TV at seven thirty-five she'd received four calls. The share price was up, viewing figures for last night's *How to Marry a Footballer* were better than expected and she'd had five offers of television interviews following Sunday's spread. She'd skimmed the papers to discover Hi-TV was scandal-free.

Everything was back on track.

She walked through the revolving doors and into the foyer, ignoring the eyes on her. They always turned, and she was used to it. She was the boss after all, but the polite smile she kept was enough. Small brief hellos, even to Hattie on the front desk. There was a time when she used to chat, but now her energy must be saved. She nodded, smiled and tapped the seventeenth floor. There was the familiar hush in the lift around her, and she knew eyes were looking her up and down. She'd worn her black Chanel dress. It was chic, understated and intimidating enough for the male board. Her feet were already pinched from the heels, but this was part of the job. This was power.

In many ways she found it almost pathetic, how people rallied around her. All because they thought she had the power to make their dreams come true – that she was somehow going to click her fingers and rescue them.

She felt the sigh of relief behind her as she left the lift and walked along the glass corridor towards her office. She caught a glimpse of herself. She looked sharp, poised and ready. Ready to face the board.

Matilda stood up behind her desk. She was looking nervous still. What was wrong the girl? She was really starting to grate on Grace's nerves. She didn't need nerves; she needed confidence and strength. She'd put 'find another assistant' on her to-do list.

"Morning Grace. They're ready for you."

Grace smiled. "My, my, they're keen." She glanced at her watch. It was seven fifty-two am. "Best I be off." She handed the coat she was carrying to Matilda and turned back towards the lift.

"It's on the twentieth."

Grace stopped. "The twentieth?"

"Yes." Matilda nodded and looked down at her shoes.

"Well, they really are pulling out the stops," Grace smiled, not letting the flicker of unease show.

"Please, Grace, come in."

"Good morning gentlemen."

All eight were seated around the table. It still sickened her to see all those men gathered in this way. At least her presence had changed things a bit, but there was more to be done. She'd make sure Polly was also up there soon. She glanced quickly around the stark white room, the floor-to-ceiling glass; the other skyscrapers their only view. It was a rare, clear March day and the sky outside was blue.

Then she realised.

There was no breakfast.

"Coffee?"

"Please. Thank you, Godfrey."

Godfrey nodded to the young woman dressed in black and white who poured a coffee from a silver jug. The hushed chatter in the room continued as there were small nods and polite exchanges. The young woman brought the coffee to her.

"If you could put it on the table, please," Grace told her, as she placed her hands together. She wouldn't show them that her unease was growing by the second.

As the woman placed the coffee in front of her, Grace noticed a trembling in her hands too. How dreadful it was the way a group of men could be so intimidating.

"Thank you," Grace smiled. Her years climbing the corporate ladder had taught her the art of looking perfectly comfortable in an awkward setting. Why it was quite so awkward she didn't know. It was probably something of nothing. She hid her impatience, and picked up her coffee, her hands steady again.

"Great work on the article," Godfrey said, and the men around him nodded, still unable to look her in the eye. She glanced across at the others --Trevor, Jonathan, Rufus. She knew them all well, but none of them looked her in the eye.

"Thank you."

Godfrey nodded. "I'm afraid we have something delicate to discuss."

"Delicate?"

"We've been handed some footage, some very worrying footage."

Her heart sank. "Wakefield, again. I thought we'd put all that to bed." This meeting was supposed to be about her. Her achievements.

"Not Wakefield. You." Godfrey looked her straight in the eye.

"Me?"

"You."

Grace felt a churning in the pit of her stomach, but she stayed sitting upright: she could easily do poise. Besides, there must be a mistake.

"Could you explain please?"

"We've been given some footage, showing you…acting inappropriately."

"Me?" Grace laughed. "When am I ever inappropriate?"

"Saturday night, so it seems. In Soho."

Grace swallowed.

Godfrey nodded to Jonathan, who pressed the laptop in front of him. All their eyes turned to the large screen they used to view programmes. But now it was her face filling the screen – her face and Eric's.

A cold, white, panic began to run through her.

There she and Eric were, as they'd left the restaurant in the centre of London on Saturday night. But she knew the restaurant staff so well, they'd gone out through the back door to save waiting for their coats. There they stood in the street, outside the back door of the restaurant. The moment she'd been hoping Eric would forget.

The room began to spin, and it was as if time slowed down as it continued to play.

She closed her eyes, unable to watch. She knew what was coming. She heard her voice, although it didn't sound like her. It was high-pitched and screeching.

"You fucking bastard. You think I'm going to just fucking take this, do you? Do you know what I do for you? I fucking work all day and you treat me like fucking shit. People like you don't get to treat people like me like fucking this."

She opened her eyes and saw the woman scowling – screeching and vile, just as Eric had said. Her hair was dishevelled, her eyes wide. She was ugly, out of control and a disgrace. Her coat was hanging off her shoulder, and as Grace watched, trying to remain poised, it was as if she was floating, looking down on herself as the whole of the thirty-year reputation she'd worked so hard to build unravelled.

"You fucking arse." She shoved her husband, not once, but three times. "You fucking arse."

He didn't even fight back; he just stood there – as if he'd been expecting it. He tried to walk away, but she grabbed his shirt, the vile, mad woman.

"Don't you walk away from me. We've got to fucking sort this now." She stumbled as she tripped on the step. "Eric. Get back here. Now."

"I think we've seen enough," Godfrey said, and Trevor nodded.

A silence settled in the room as the heat rose in Grace. She breathed as deeply as she could, because somehow she had to find a way of keeping herself together.

"It was a domestic; it's private."

"It was at the back of Giovanni's – you were on public property in the middle of Soho."

"We all have our moments."

"You're the CEO of Hi-TV, Grace. You represent us. You can't afford to have a moment," Trevor said.

"Who did it? Who filmed it?"

"We can't say."

"Why not?"

"The person wants to remain anonymous. But they've made it very clear: if you're not removed from your position, they'll send it to the press."

"What?" Grace felt another wave of sickness wash over her as the words settled. "They can't ask that."

"And we can't afford to have another scandal."

"But this is blackmail."

"Is it?" Godfrey sat up straight. "Is it, Grace? Our values here are family and trust. Our CEO shoving her husband and speaking to him like that," he nodded at the now black screen, "strongly contradicts both."

"I hardly hit him."

"Grace, please."

"You sorted it for Wakefield." Her tone was sharper than she'd wished. She sounded needy and she hated this – her hands were shaking and her throat was tight. This could not be happening.

"There's more."

"More?" What else could there possibly be?

"We've had allegations made of you bullying members of staff."

"Me? Bullying? That's simply not true."

"We've got ten statements telling us otherwise."

"Ten? From who?"

"We can't say. It's company policy, as you well know."

Godfrey looked her in the eyes. "That's what the *Talk to Us* scheme is for."

The very scheme she'd set up. The white heat rose in her.

"But the article? I can't just leave now."

"We'll announce you're taking a sabbatical. We'll say it was always planned. The article was a pinnacle as such, and now you're exploring what next. You are, after all…"

"I'm what?" Grace stared at Godfrey with all the strength she had left.

"Let's just say, it's perfectly plausible." Several of them shifted around the table, unable to look her in the eye. It sickened her even more.

"You'll be on full pay, and of course you've just had your bonus – your generous bonus," Trevor said.

"My *deserved* bonus," she attempted, but her voice was shaking. "You didn't ask Wakefield to leave."

"He's the talent, Grace. You know how it works."

She couldn't take any more. She stood up. "I'll speak to my lawyer."

"Please do," Godfrey nodded.

She stood still. It was as if she was frozen. She dug her nails hard into her hands, telling herself she had to keep it together.

"I think that's everything for now." Godfrey nodded at the others and they all stood up.

"So that's it? I'm out? After all these years?"

"It's just an investigation, Grace – at this stage."

"It's a stitch-up."

"I think that's enough for now."

Grace was about to tell Trevor to stop patronising her, when she felt her legs buckle. She held onto the chair, but she had to get out of the room – they were all staring at her, watching her demise.

"I'll gather my things."

"No need."

Grace turned to see two security men from the front desk standing outside the glass doors.

"You've got to be kidding me."

"It's the only way, Grace. We must be sure you don't speak with anyone."

"I'm not a bloody criminal."

The silence in the room told her everything she needed to know.

"But my coat? My bag?"

"They've both been delivered to the car which is waiting outside for you."

Grace swallowed, searching for air. Matilda must have known.

"Right." She nodded and turned. Thirty years gone. Just like that. She looked down at her shoes as they carried her across the cream carpet, managing to balance on her heels as her legs shook beneath her. But she winced with pain.

"Grace," Godfrey said.

"Yes." She stopped.

"I don't need to remind you, you're not at liberty to speak with anyone at Hi-TV – while you're on your sabbatical."

Grace didn't turn back. She managed a small nod and continued to look at her shoes. One foot in front of another, one at a time. She didn't look up at the two men who were now walking by her side. One step. Then another. Each one dragging her further into the nightmare.

Inside the lift, they had the decency to step aside as

people entered the lift. They said the usual hellos and she nodded, but it was as if everyone knew.

She walked through the turnstiles of the reception and saw the black Mercedes in front of the glass swinging doors. She continued to put one shoe in front of the other.

The two men were behind her as she walked through the revolving doors. The driver of the car jumped out and opened the door, not looking her in the eye.

She got in the car and the driver returned to his seat. She noticed her bag and coat on the front seat beside him. He started the engine, pulled away and in a few seconds, she was gone.

Chapter Four

Grace: Eric, I need to speak with you x
Grace: Please reply Eric x

Half an hour later, the driver pulled up in front of her house. She didn't remember any part of the journey, but there she was.

The driver got out of the car to open the door for her.

"Your coat and bag, Ms Leven." He handed them to her.

"Thank you," she nodded, and opened her gate. She walked along the path to their townhouse, although nothing felt real. There must be some sort of mistake, there would be a solution; there always was. As soon as she saw Eric, he'd know what to do. He wouldn't be mad at her any more not after this. He'd help her. It would all be okay.

She was fumbling for the keys as he opened the door.

"Grace? What are you doing here? I was just going out."

"I've come home. Did you get my message? There's something I need to tell you… What's that?"

She looked down at the suitcase behind him. Had he heard? Were they going away? It was going to be okay. Yes, it was going to be okay.

"I wasn't expecting you."

"You weren't?"

"No."

"What's that?" she repeated. "Are we going to Mauritius?" She felt pathetic, as the words slipped out, heavy with desperation.

He looked down. "No, Grace, we're not going to Mauritius."

The sickness sitting in the back of her throat rose again.

"I wasn't expecting you home; I was going to call you later and tell you."

"Tell me what?"

He couldn't look her in the eye.

"I'm leaving you."

"Me?"

The spinning began all over again. Soon she'd wake up. Soon it would be time to go and work out. This would be over soon.

"I can't take it any more."

"It?"

"You. Your anger. How you are. I need space."

"But you can't."

There was a pause.

"But I can."

"You can't leave me."

"Grace. Please." He picked up the handle of the case and started to walk past her.

"No. You can't." She held his arm and he shook it off.

He kept walking. "Eric. Please, you promised." She walked behind him down the path, despising herself even more with every step but unable to stop. "You promised we'd always be together."

He stopped now. Great. He was coming back.

"This is your fault."

He turned again and started to walk. A taxi pulled up. He was going. But he couldn't leave. She couldn't survive without him. She couldn't do anything without him.

"What do you mean, it's my fault? We're just going through a rough patch. Everyone goes through a rough patch. We can work it out. Let's talk about it. Please Eric."

He opened the gate.

"Eric. Please." Her voice was louder now. A woman walking her dog on the other side of the street looked over at them.

"I need some space." Eric opened the door of the car.

"But where are you going? You have to tell me where you are going."

He sat down in the car and this time he looked at her.

"No, I don't. I don't have to tell you anything. You don't own me." He paused as he held on to the car door. "Grace, please. I'm going."

He closed the door and she watched as the car pulled away and left the street.

She wasn't sure how long she'd stood in the road.

"Everything okay?" The woman who was walking her dog, and whom she vaguely recognised, was standing by her side.

"Yes. Great," Grace lied. She turned around and walked

back along the perfect path through the perfectly manicured front garden to her perfect house. The door was still open. She walked through and slammed it behind her.

She looked up at the enormous cold hallway. The silence rang in her ears. No Eric. No Pearl. The emptiness was claustrophobic and she couldn't move. The panic started to settle like a low buzz. She couldn't go to work. She had nowhere to go. She was trapped. She opened her mouth, but nothing came out, the sickness swirling in her insides.

She looked at the vase on the glass table, the large, magnificent, expensive vase filled with hydrangeas. Eric had bought it from somewhere; she didn't know where – she hadn't taken any notice when he'd told her. She picked it up and threw it, then watched as it shattered all over the white marble floor.

Dear sixteen-year-old me,

As I write to you, I want to tell you, life isn't as bad as you think. I know you feel like your world is falling apart. You didn't get picked for the netball team, you think you'll fail all your exams and you'll never have a boyfriend like all your friends.

You didn't get invited to Debbie Jacob's party at the weekend and you're dreading going to school. It will be all anyone will speak about, and you will feel alone and left out. Plus, on top of all of this, you wish you had thinner thighs.

But what you do have is your mum and dad, who are your most special people in the world. Somehow, they always wrap you up in their love, no matter what's happening outside. 'Come home and be loved' they tell you, 'Who cares what happens out there? This is where you belong.' You sing and dance together and all the worry of that party slips away.

ELLIE BARKER

They'll take you out for an ice cream and remind you, you wouldn't have enjoyed the party, as you're not a big fan of crowds. Besides, they'll tell you, you'll go to much better ones when you're older – and they're right. If I tell you, you will go to countless parties when you're older, with some of the coolest people on TV – people your classmates already watch now – would it make you feel any better?

I doubt it would, but still.

At sixteen, I know everything feels like forever – sometimes it's a wonderful feeling, sometimes it's not. You think you'll always be in the classroom – why do you still have to sit near Billy Jenkins, who is even more annoying now? You also fear that no matter how hard you study, you'll never get an A.

But what I want to tell you is everything you're worried about now will be okay. You won't just get one A, you'll get many which will take you to places you could only have imagined in your wildest dreams. You might never really love your thighs, but you'll find exercise and learn to know what works for you. You'll later allow the hairdresser to cut off your long hair, and you'll be so pleased you did. Best of all, you have your mum and dad. You may be too young to see you, but they can see exactly who you are and what you're capable of – and they're using all their love to help you do the same.

You'll start to put your hand up in class a little more, and you won't feel quite so afraid. You won't get picked for netball, but that's okay – you never really enjoyed it anyway; you just wanted to fit in.

Sometimes, Gracie, it's good not to be picked. The rejection might feel terrible but it's how you cope with it that counts. You're slowly building your resilience, which will become a superpower one day.

If I could tell you one thing now, I'd say just enjoy this time. Enjoy not being an adult, enjoy your mum and dad. Use that unconditional love of theirs like a blanket, wrap yourself in it tight and let it protect you from the world. Not everyone is as lucky as you.

(Also, you'll find out later that Debbie Jacob's parties really

What Really Happened To Me?

aren't that much fun. A bunch of teenagers sitting in rooms, too awkward to know what to say. Drinking vodka, making themselves sick and kissing people they don't even like. When you find yourself at those cool parties in years to come, you'll still always wish you were back at home.)

Worry less and laugh a little more — you have a wonderful smile when you do. This is a special moment in your life, Gracie, which won't last forever. You'll learn later in life, nothing ever does.

See you soon

Love

Gx

Chapter Five

Grace: Eric, I'm sorry. Please tell me where you are at least x
Grace: Pearl, I've left a message for you. Can you call me please?
Mum x

She'd lost count of the number of calls she'd made to Pearl – each one had gone straight to voicemail. She was only four hours ahead in Mauritius – if that's where she still was.

She tried Polly again – but it also went to voicemail.

She looked around her. She sat on a bench overlooking the city, with women and men walking around her. Some walked with others, some were alone. She looked at her watch. It was ten thirty-two. Who were these people who walked around on a Tuesday morning in the park?

Someone. She needed someone.

She sent Polly a text. She was still her best friend, even if she was a colleague.

Daphne's still tonight? x

Grace could see Polly was typing, then stopped. The

desperation took hold again, but then she saw she was typing again. Great.

Sorry Grace. It's all kicked off here. I'm sure you can imagine. I won't be able to make drinks tonight. Hope you're okay. I'll be in touch. Do something nice x

"Shit," Grace said out loud, and the man on the next bench turned a page of his newspaper. Perhaps they were used to people's lives falling apart in the park.

She knew it was to be expected: Polly was head of Daytime at Hi-TV. But what was she going to do? She couldn't bear to go back to the house alone.

Do something nice. What did it mean – do something nice?

Grace looked around. She had nobody else. The irony wasn't lost on her. She'd spent her whole career meeting people – 'outwardly facing', as her job was described. Building relations, making them work – and then there she was.

Bloody alone.

She took a deep breath. She hated self-pity but now she was wallowing in it like a bath. She looked in her bag for something; anything. The magazine was in there still and she pulled it out. She looked back at the article, back at her face.

Proof women really can have it all.

What a joke.

She couldn't bear to look back at herself. The woman with the icy stare, the woman who was supposed to have it all. The lie sickened her more, so she turned the page. The photo caught her eye again. Strawberry House.

Stay with us and leave feeling yourself again.

She looked at it again. The Georgian house was smart, freshly renovated, or so it looked, and she didn't hate it. She searched for it on her phone. The bedrooms were bright; the beds looked large and deep. The exhaustion ached in her.

She couldn't go there, could she? But then where else could she go?

'Shit,' she said out loud, as she pressed dial on her phone.

Chapter Six

Eric: Please. Can you call me? x
Pearl: Are you asleep? If you're not, please call me. Something's happened. X

Six hours later, she walked across the foyer of Strawberry House Hotel in Bristol. A cancellation they'd said – lucky for her.

Lucky was not how she'd describe her day.

She'd never been to Bristol before, but then again, she'd never had such a day before.

She'd returned home long enough to sweep up the vase, cutting her hand as she did. She took the suitcase that sat in her dressing room, waiting for the planned and unplanned business trips. She pulled some clothes from their hangers and collected toiletries from the bathroom. She called a cab which took her to Paddington, then half an hour later she was on a train.

She had no idea what she was doing, what she was

taking with her or what she was even feeling. But it was the silence which was paralysing.

Her phone didn't ring. There were no texts, messages or pings. She was used to the constant trilling of her phone, a sign she was needed and in demand. But now, it sat silent and as if she'd disappeared from life.

She walked across the reception, leaving her sunglasses on to hide her eyes. It was warm, decorated in shades of pink, and there was bustle about the place. She didn't hate it and she felt grateful at least for this. There was a familiarity about it. She couldn't work out what it was, but the warmth was comforting. She looked up at the ceiling, which was gold and painted with roses. It was magnificent, and something she hadn't expected.

She walked straight into someone and the blow knocked her back to reality. Her irritability and her reality.

"I'm so sorry," the man said.

She didn't reply.

"Don't worry – it happens all the time." He nodded up at the ceiling.

Why would she worry? She wasn't worried. She wasn't anything. She looked at the man, his hands and jeans covered in paint.

"Right," she managed.

"Just arrived?"

"Yes." She carried on walking towards the desk. She had no energy left to speak to the hotel's odd-job man. She needed a room and she needed to get away.

"Can I help you, madam?" a woman asked from behind the desk.

"Yes, I've a room booked. It's Grace…"

"Grace Leven? Yes, you called earlier. The cancellation – you were in luck."

Why did they keep telling her how lucky she was? Didn't they know?

No, Grace, they didn't, she could hear Eric sigh if he were there.

Eric. Where was he? Just one text – that's all she needed.

She looked at her phone. Nothing.

The young woman was talking to her about breakfast, housekeeping, a guide to Strawberry Village and something about a place called Dave's Deli. She just wanted her key. Why couldn't she just have her key? The young woman stopped talking.

At last.

"Your hand. Are you okay?"

Grace looked down at her hand. It was not only covered with red welts from where she'd dug her nails in earlier, but the blood had dried from where the glass vase had cut her. She'd grabbed a tissue at the time, but she must have lost it on her way. Her hand looked lacerated and swollen.

Perhaps it was because it was the first time that day that someone had asked her if she was okay, but she felt hot tears sting at the back of her eyes.

"I'm fine. Could I just have my card please?" Grace didn't look up.

"Of course," the woman said. "We're old-fashioned here; still a key." She beamed a huge smile as she dangled it in front of Grace. "Your room is on the second floor. Room 23."

She placed the key on the counter in front of Grace and then leant a little forward. "We're here for anything you need."

"Right."

"Leave your case and we'll bring it straight up."

"It's okay."

Grace pulled her case across the bustling foyer. She wished people would just get out of her way. She picked up her case as she stood at the bottom of the sweeping staircase. If she had been there with Eric, they would have stopped to admire it. But she wasn't there with Eric. This wasn't a holiday, but then, she wasn't there for work either. So what was she doing there?

"I can help." She hadn't noticed the odd-job man behind her. He went to take her bag.

"Please, no. I said I'm fine."

She walked up the stairs carrying her bag with her other hand. She kept her head down, ignoring anyone who said good afternoon. Room 23. At last she was there.

"Excuse me."

What now? She wanted to scream.

She turned around to see the woman from reception. She was holding a white paper bag. "It's from our first aid – a bandage and some cream, for your hand."

Grace stopped – she didn't know what to say.

"Thank you," she managed.

She took the bag, opened the door, leaving her case just inside it, and walked across the room. Then she lay on the bed, put her face in the pillow and allowed the deep, guttural sobs to arrive.

It was dark when Grace woke up. For the first split second there was the delightful moment when she really did think it was all a dream, but then she opened her eyes.

It took her a moment to remember where she was, and she sat up and looked around. The room was beautiful. The walls were covered in antique pink floral wallpaper and the woodwork was painted white. The Georgian windows, the white cotton sheets, the pale pink armchair with tiny red dots and a foot stool in the corner – even in her haze she could see how beautiful it was.

Hand-cut flowers sat in small glass jars dotted around the room, a pile of magazines sat on the coffee table waiting to be read. It was the perfect room for a weekend getaway – but not for a breakdown.

She picked up her phone.

"Shit," she said out loud.

She had no messages. Not a single one. On a typical day her mobile would be ready to burst by now. Advertisers, rivals at other channels pretending to be her friend. The board, the reports, the climbers thinking she held the magic solution to their careers.

She checked her voicemail.

"You have no messages."

Not even someone from bloody HR or Matilda telling her of her evening plans.

"Jesus, word travels fast."

Eric. You can't just ignore me. Please. We need to talk. I love you x

The desperation felt as though it was going to choke her.

Then she added:

We can get through this x

They had to. She had to. This was unbearable.

She rubbed her face and got off the bed. She walked

into the bathroom. There was no walk-through shower like her own but it was still beautiful. It was large for a hotel bathroom; a roll-top bath sat in the middle. She leaned onto the vanity unit and dared to look in the mirror.

The woman staring back at her looked dreadful: mascara streaking down her face, dark shadows under her eyes. She was wearing the same black dress she'd put on that morning, ready for her business meeting, but now she looked as if she'd been to a funeral.

Grace washed her face with cold water, but it didn't make it any better. She looked old, tired and dishevelled; everything she worked so bloody hard not to be. She couldn't stand to look at herself any more, so she returned to the sitting area and opened the door of a large ornate sideboard. There it was, tucked away. The mini-bar. She pulled out the bottle of wine and poured a large glass. She gulped it down and poured another. Then caught herself in another mirror above the sideboard.

There she was again. The women she wasn't supposed to be. The cold glassy stare was still there, like it was in the photo, but this time her face was red. Her Chanel dress was crumpled, carrying all the misery of the day.

She either stayed and wallowed, or she pulled herself together and fought back.

So she took a shower, washed her hair, bandaged her hand and went downstairs.

The same bustle which had greeted her earlier greeted her again. The evening had settled at Strawberry House and she was once again grateful for its warmth. The lamps were on and some light jazz was playing. There were different people behind the reception now, and she saw through an archway people sitting in a lounge.

She'd travelled alone more times than she could remember; she was used to situations of this type. She'd pretend it was another work trip. She'd be fine.

She walked into the lounge and sat down at a table amidst couples and groups of friends. Within a second, a smiling young waiter was at her side. "A glass of Chablis, please." She remembered the 'please' at least.

She pulled out her phone, and tried to think of an email she could send. Her inbox was filled with spam messages – how could she just be erased like this? The panic began to rise: this wasn't a work trip and she wasn't fine. She saw a magazine on the table next to her, and she picked it up.

At the same time as her glass of wine arrived, a man approached her.

"Excuse me. Grace Leven?"

"Yes?"

What now?

"I'm Jack Jones, the owner of Strawberry House. I don't wish to disturb you."

She looked at him, and it was as if he had a knowing in his eyes.

"Believe me, you're not." She stood up and shook his hand. "Would you like to join me, if you have time?" God, she could hear the neediness in her voice again.

"That would be great." He sat down. "I hope everything's okay with your room."

"My room is beautiful, thank you. The whole hotel is beautiful."

"Thank you." He smiled. "We're very pleased with this one."

She looked at him for a brief moment. She'd developed

an art over the years of reading people within a few seconds. The dark hair, the sharp look; he was familiar. She remembered now – wasn't he once described as the most miserable millionaire in Britain? He was *that* Jack Jones. In her daze she'd forgotten he owned hotels – she was losing her edge and she had to get it back.

"Let me guess," he raised his eyebrows. "You're thinking, he looks familiar – I read an article about him once, calling him Britain's most miserable millionaire, and I'm thinking, this is Grace Leven, who I just read about on Sunday. The woman who is proving you really can have it all."

Grace smiled, despite herself. "Guilty as charged."

"That was quite the piece; very inspiring. My girlfriend hasn't stopped talking about it."

"I'm pleased." She was a fraud. She breathed in. Her self-pity was becoming loathsome. "And, well," she nodded around her, "you most certainly do not seem miserable."

"No," he laughed. "I'm not."

"Would you like a drink?"

He nodded to the young waiter. "A beer please, Ollie."

"Your staff here are wonderful."

"Thank you."

His beer arrived and they started to chat. She was used to making small talk when she was Grace Leven, CEO. But was she even still a CEO? It was only a suspension, wasn't it?

"How long has it been open now?" She looked around. All the tables were full, filled with people looking comfortable and at home; it didn't feel new at all.

"Three months this week, and we've been fully booked since. It was lucky there was a cancellation today for you."

Lucky. There was that word again.

"Lucky – that word keeps popping up today."

"Rough day?"

She looked at him. His eyes were warm, and she was impressed by his openness. There was a knowing about him and she liked him. She felt herself relax a little.

"You could say that."

He was about to say something when they were interrupted. A young woman in a short black playsuit, with red lipstick and dark wavy hair, touched him on the shoulder.

"There you are! I'm sorry I'm late." She looked at Grace. "And I'm so sorry I'm interrupting. I'm Lulu. Oh god, you're Grace Leven." She looked at Grace, her eyes wide.

"Yes, I am." Grace nodded as Lulu took her hand.

Lulu carried on shaking her hand. "That article about you was brilliant, just brilliant. You've given hope to us all. Iris and I couldn't stop talking about it."

"Lulu is my old schoolfriend; Iris is my girlfriend," Jack explained.

"I'm pleased you enjoyed the article." Grace felt like a fraud. She let go of Lulu's hand and picked up her wine. "Please join us, if you have time."

"Have time? This is just incredible. What are the chances? We'd just been saying – hadn't we Jack? – it's really impossible for women, even after all these years, and then, there you are, proving it isn't impossible at all. We were so excited the advert for the hotel was next to it, and now you're sitting here in it." Lulu shook her head as she sat down. "Unbelievable. We manifested it; that's what we did, Jack." Lulu waved at the barman, Ollie. "Jack doesn't believe in manifestation." Lulu rolled her eyes.

Grace could feel Jack's eyes on her. He knew, or at least he suspected. Word and rumours travel fast.

"How long are you planning on staying?" Lulu asked. "I'm going to have to tell Iris you're here."

Grace had no idea how long she'd be there, or even what she was doing there.

"Lu, you know better than to probe our guests."

"Yes, of course. Sorry. I'm sorry Grace, that was very rude of me."

Grace shook her head. "It's fine. The truth is, I don't really know."

"You don't?" The waiter, Ollie, appeared and Grace breathed a sigh of relief. "Gin and tonic please, Ollie. Would you like another?" Lulu pointed at Grace's nearly empty glass.

"Yes. Thank you." She took a deep breath – she'd have to say it out loud at some point. "I've decided to take a bit of time off."

"That's great," Jack said. Now she knew he knew.

Lulu looked at Jack then back at Grace. "Yes, that's really great." Her voice faltered. Great –she'd shattered Lulu's illusion too. She decided to change the subject. "So, let me ask, if you're fully booked, why did you place the advert in the magazine?"

"We did it before the hotel opened. To be honest, even we've been surprised at how busy we've been," Jack smiled.

"We were really delighted when it went next to your article though," Lulu said again.

"Are you involved in the hotel?"

Lulu sat back as Ollie arrived with a white wine and gin and tonic. Lulu took her drink. "Thanks Olls." She took a large gulp. "That's good. Oh, I needed that." She put the glass down. "I'm sorry." She shook her head and her big hooped earrings danced from side to side. "I do this. I sound like I've got shares in the place."

What Really Happened To Me?

"Lulu was my assistant for several years," Jack explained. "I've known her since she was five and her dad was my housemaster at school. She's the sister I never knew I had or needed." Jack nudged Lulu's arm. He turned back to Grace. "She runs *The Strawberry Times*, the newspaper in the village, now."

"*The Strawberry Times?*" Grace repeated.

"Jack." Lulu glared at him. "It's hardly Hi-TV, is it?"

"And this is the attitude I've been talking to you about."

"Attitude?" Grace sipped her wine, relieved the attention was off her.

"I took over around a year ago as the managing editor, and let's just say it's been a challenge."

"I'm not surprised." Grace put her glass down. "Newspapers are a challenge these days, no matter their size."

"Yes," Lulu nodded and smiled. "Yes, they bloody well are. Sorry Grace. I've got to stop swearing."

"Don't apologise to me – I've heard worse, I can assure you."

Lulu laughed and so did Jack. A small feeling of warmth rushed through Grace. Their honesty was refreshing. The warmth, the bustle, the atmosphere – all of it felt a little better. She breathed out.

"We're having dinner with Iris in the dining room. Would you like to join us?" Jack asked.

Grace was almost tempted. They were bright, light and entertaining. On an ordinary day she might have joined them. But this wasn't an ordinary day. For a brief moment she'd forgotten it wasn't an ordinary day.

"Thank you – that's kind, but I am planning on having an early night, maybe some room service."

"Of course," Jack said. "The kitchen will look after you,

and if there's anything you want that's not on the menu, just say."

"It's quite the place you have here. It's very, well, welcoming." Grace stood up. She felt her eyes sting with tears, reminding her exactly why she should not join them for dinner. If she was going to unravel, it couldn't happen in front of strangers.

"If you're planning on staying more than a couple of nights, we can arrange something. We have a couple of cottages on the grounds which have just been finished and we haven't let them out yet."

"Yes, that's right," Lulu nodded, meeting Jack's eyes. "They're really lovely too. Sorry, there's me acting like I own the place again."

"Right, well, thank you. Goodnight to you both. It was good to meet you."

"Good to meet you too, Grace," Lulu waved.

Grace walked away, back through the lounge and the hall. The warmth and bustle wrapped around her and she felt grateful for that at least. As she climbed the stairs, she looked back at Jack and Lulu through the arch into the lounge. Another woman had arrived now, and Jack was kissing her. It took Grace a couple of seconds to realise it was the young woman who'd been on reception earlier who'd noticed her hand.

Chapter Seven

Grace: Eric please. You have to speak to me sometime. x
Grace: Eric, I'm not at home if you need to go back there. x
Grace: Eric I've given you space. But please talk to me x
Grace: Eric. Talk to me. Please x

Grace was surprised, when she opened her eyes, that she'd slept. Not only that – she'd slept well. She never slept well. She looked at her phone.

No messages.

She'd sent Eric at least ten messages the previous day, Polly the same. Polly had had the decency to reply once when she was getting into bed that night.

Sorry, day still crazy. Hope you're doing okay x

Her phone beeped, and it made her jump. She felt the relief rush through her, until she saw who it was from.

Are you okay? Were you not feeling it today? Toby

Damn. She'd forgotten to cancel her personal trainer. She replied telling him something had happened and she would not be coming for the rest of the month. She'd paid in advance so she didn't feel too guilty. But then he replied.

I hope you are okay. T

The tears stung again, more that her personal trainer appeared to care more for her than her husband, daughter and best friend put together. The phone beeped again. More hope, but then she saw it was Toby again.

If you can keep exercising, do. You don't want to undo all your good work and it can really help. T

"Really, Toby?" she said out loud. "Exercise can help me get my life back?" But even as she sat alone in the dark, she could hear the self-pity and she hated herself a little more. She needed a plan. She couldn't just sit there and wallow. Perhaps it was one of those signs Pearl was always going on about? The ones Grace normally rolled her eyes at. She sank back into the pillow.

She had nobody to meet, nowhere to go. The emptiness sucked her in like a vacuum. In her haze, she'd packed her trainers and kit as she always did when she went on work trips. Fine, she thought, getting out of bed. I'll go for a run.

Ten minutes later, she'd left the hotel and was running through what she now knew was Strawberry Village. The staff on reception had explained it had always been known as a village even though it sat in a corner of Bristol, and

Grace could understand why. She could smell the coffee brewing in the cafés as they prepared to open their doors; there was a small queue at the baker's and people were leaving the local shop with newspapers tucked under their arms.

The sun was just starting to rise as she ran along the street. The staff had told her to head towards the bridge. She'd nodded, her impatience rising as the two of them had consulted together and drawn her a route on a map. Did they really have to make such a fuss about everything? She was perfectly capable of finding her own way.

But as she ran alone, towards the bridge, as instructed, the doubt began to rise. She wasn't used to running alone or not having any idea where she was going. She was used to Toby telling her to run faster, to do better. Matilda normally had her day planned out for her. Running alone now with an empty day stretching ahead of her seemed pointless.

She turned a corner and saw the bridge and the sight was so magnificent it made her stop running. She hadn't given any thought to what Strawberry Village would look like, because at the same time the previous day she'd had no idea she'd be there. She started running again, one foot in front of the other.

She tried to take in what was around her: the river, the rolling hills, the houses dotted around – but she couldn't think. Her mind whirred in a thick grey fog, despite the clear morning sky around her. What had happened? Who'd said she'd bullied them, and why had Eric decided to leave? She stopped and pulled out her phone.

Eric. Please. I need to speak with you. I need to know what's going on.

Then she had another thought.

Eric. Are you even alive? x

She put her phone in her leggings and carried on running. The voice in her head kept niggling and she didn't like it at all.

It was telling her she wasn't as surprised as she was making out; deep down she knew things hadn't been good for a while. She shook her head. But that was marriage, wasn't it? Who doesn't have their ups and downs? The more she ran, the more the panic rose. This wasn't supposed to happen; she was supposed to be working it all out. She didn't bother to consult the map as she ran down a path, off the main road. She didn't want to be near people; she wanted to be alone. If she could run fast enough, she'd shake it off, it would clear and the answers would come. She ran as fast as she could, imagining Toby's voice shouting at her to run faster, harder, more. She could do more.

Then she tripped.

She hit the ground, and her cheek banged onto the muddy path. For a moment she stayed there. Was this it? Was this rock bottom? The hot tears stung in her eyes, as she pushed herself back up.

"Are you okay there?"

No, she bloody wasn't – and she didn't want anyone else to see her in such a state either. She pushed herself up, her hands shaking. Her palms were grazed and bleeding and the sickness was now swirling inside her. She hoped the man who had called out had gone. But she heard the footsteps behind her.

Damn it.

"This path – it's lethal," the voice said. She forced

What Really Happened To Me?

herself to turn around and look at the man. He had kind eyes and a friendly smile. She suspected he was in his seventies and he stood there with a chocolate Labrador. "You don't look like you've done any major damage."

She shook her head. "No," she tried to say, but instead, her face crumpled and she burst into tears.

"I'm so embarrassed. I don't normally cry in front of strangers."

"Lucky you," the man nodded. "I'm sobbing all the time, aren't I Fred? I'm Bruce, by the way, and this handsome fella is Fred." Bruce tipped an imaginary cap.

Bruce, she'd discovered, lived in a pink house tucked away on the path. He had told her to sit on the tree trunk while he went inside to get her some water. He'd returned with cold flannels, a flask and a packet of biscuits. "Jammy dodger?"

"It's not even eight am," she'd laughed.

"Falls like that call for a jammy dodger, no matter what the time." He opened the packet and held it towards her.

She took one and bit into it. It tasted good, really good. "I haven't had a jammy dodger in years. I'm Grace," she added. "Grace Leven."

"The sugar will do you good."

Grace smiled, despite herself, as she took it. "I feel like I'm ten years old."

"Nothing wrong with that, Grace Leven." Bruce chuckled. His eyes crinkled as he laughed. "We've all got our ten-year-olds inside us, wanting a biscuit and a helping hand. So, no major injuries?"

Grace looked down. Her hands were grazed and on top

of the cuts from the previous day, they burned. But the cool flannels were soothing and the jarred feeling somehow had jolted her back into life. Her leggings were covered in mud, and she suspected her knees were grazed underneath them, but everything was moving as it should.

"No injuries," she said. "Not on the outside, anyway." She wasn't sure why she added this.

Bruce chuckled again. "I get that."

She breathed out. "Oh Bruce, I'm battered – on the inside and out."

Bruce opened the flask and the smell of coffee filtered the air. "Coffee?"

"Thank you," she nodded.

"I've only got black."

"It's the way I take it."

"Well, there you go. It's a sign."

Grace took the cup. "Thank you. You sound like my daughter."

"Not a believer then?"

"I don't know what to believe any more. I'm sorry, I'm disturbing you." Grace had forgotten her manners. Just because she didn't have anywhere to go, didn't mean he didn't. She could never have imagined stopping for a total stranger like this.

"You're doing no such thing. Fred and I were just going out on our walk. We've got all the time in the world."

So, it seemed, did she. The panic began to rise again and she breathed in the cool air.

"Is everyone in Strawberry Village this friendly?"

He laughed again. "Believe me, we all have our moments."

"The staff at Strawberry House where I'm staying – they're friendly too. A young woman gave me a bag with plasters and cream in when I checked in." Grace looked down at her grazed and cut hands. "I'd cut myself yesterday – a broken vase."

"Ah, so that would be my Iris. My daughter. She sometimes helps out on the front desk, but she's a journalist really. She's courting the owner, Jack. Courting? Is that what they say these days? In actual fact they're engaged, so is that something different?" Bruce shook his head.

"I don't know. Is it? I'm so out of touch." Grace looked at him. "Did she tell you she had a raving mad customer?"

"She said nothing of the sort. But she mentioned a guest who'd hurt their hands – which, it turns out, was you."

"It's like a small village in a city."

"Yes, it is." Bruce took a cup out of his backpack and poured his own coffee. "There's nothing wrong with not rushing you know."

"Isn't there? I'm just not used to it. Yesterday, my whole life fell apart." She had no idea why she was saying these words.

"Well, that doesn't sound very good. And then you fall over and end up chatting to a stranger. What a couple of days!" Bruce chuckled.

"This is the highlight, believe me," She sipped her coffee.

"Have you tried writing a list?"

"A list?"

"I find when I don't know where to start, when I'm feeling a bit overwhelmed, I begin with a list." Bruce sipped his coffee. "It's a good place to start you know: the beginning."

"I am used to endless to-do lists at my job." There it was again, the doubt. Did she even have a job?

"Not so much a to-do list, more a thought list. Which

thoughts need looking at, which thoughts are actually true or not. I find it helps me get a bit of perspective."

Grace nodded. She finished her coffee and handed back the cup. The morning sunshine was glimmering through the trees surrounding her and she felt the heaviness lift a little. "Thank you, Bruce and Fred." Fred wagged his tail as he looked up at her. "This has really helped."

"Any time. You know where we are."

"Thank you, and yes I do."

Grace: Eric. Please. Just one quick phone call. It's all I ask.
Grace: Where are you, Eric?
Grace: Pearl. Where are you? I need to talk to you.

By the time she walked through the foyer of the hotel, she'd decided her next plan of action was to call Leonard, her lawyer. She was just pulling out her phone when she walked – once again – straight into a man's chest.

"I'm sorry." She looked up.

"It's proving quite the habit." The man laughed. It was the same odd-job man she'd seen the day before. Her heart sank. While she'd enjoyed speaking with Bruce, she really wanted to get on with her day, which did not include making small-talk with the over-friendly odd-job man.

"And what happened to you?" he asked.

She looked down at her mud-covered leggings.

"I had a fall."

"Are you okay?"

"Yes. I'm okay," she said. "Thanks," she added, to make it clear the conversation was over as she carried on running up the stairs.

What Really Happened To Me?

"Thank you, Leonard."

"For what?"

"For answering my call."

"Of course, I'll answer your call."

"Nobody else will. Not even my own daughter."

"I will always answer your calls, Gracie – and not because you're paying me, before you say that."

Grace felt the tears sting again and she sat down on the chair in her room.

"I'm not going to lie though – I can't see much of a way out of this just yet." Leonard spoke in a low voice. It was a voice which was familiar to her: the one he used to deliver bad news.

"So, you know?"

"Yes, I know, Gracie." She heard him sigh.

People still talked, even when they weren't talking to her.

"Who told you?"

"You know what it's like."

"Yes, I do. You know it's not true. I'm not a bully."

She heard his intake of breath. "Gracie, look, I've known you all of your life, but just for now I need to separate this and look at the facts. The problem is, with one allegation we could argue it straight away – no problem – but ten? This is a serious investigation. The company is duty-bound to look at it, even without the footage."

"So you know about the footage?"

"Yes, Gracie. I know about the footage." There was a pause on the end of the line. "I haven't seen it; I'll ask to see it, as your lawyer – if you agree, of course?" She nodded into the phone. "But I think there we're safe, at least. They don't want it in the wrong hands any more than you do. The company can't take another hit. The share price has only just gone up after Wakefield."

"So, what am I supposed to do?"

"Sit tight."

"Sit tight?" Her voice was high-pitched.

"You're going to have to let them do this investigation."

"But what am I supposed to do in the meantime?"

"You say you're at a hotel?"

"Yes. Strawberry House in Bristol."

"Then enjoy yourself."

"Enjoy myself? Leonard, how the bloody hell am I supposed to do that? I've lost my job, I've been accused of bullying and Eric has left me. How am I supposed to bloody well enjoy myself?"

There was another pause on the line.

"I'm sorry about Eric, too."

Grace nodded into the phone again. She was trying to pull herself together, get a grip of some kind, but her whole world was unravelling. Leonard was supposed to have the answers, he was supposed to tell her everything was going to be okay.

"While we're on the subject, are you happy he keeps having access to all your accounts?"

"What do you mean?" Grace sat up.

"What I say. If you are technically separated, are you happy he is still able to access all the money?"

"But we're not separated. This is just a blip."

Grace heard Leonard take a deep breath.

"We're not going over that again, are we?"

Grace could imagine Leonard shaking his head as he always did. "You know I've always thought it would be better if you kept a private account for you."

"We've been through this." Grace sighed. "I feel bad enough I kept some of the money back from him. I don't like it at all."

"It's for the best; trust me."

Grace's insides tightened as they always did when this came up. She knew Leonard was only trying to protect her, but there was really no need.

An uncomfortable silence crackled on the line.

"Look, Gracie. Maybe this is all for the best."

Grace sat upright in the chair. "How can it possibly be for the best?"

"You've been under a lot of pressure, for a long time. Perhaps you need this?"

"Leonard, please. I don't need this. I need my job and my husband."

"I'm on your side, Grace. I'm trying to help."

She knew him well enough to know he only called her Grace when he was losing his patience with her.

"Well, you're not helping."

"I'm sorry."

"I'm sorry too. I thought you'd be able to do something."

"I will look at everything, I promise. But in the meantime, I say it again, Gracie, please, take some time."

"I don't want bloody time. I want my life back." She managed a goodbye, then hung up before she threw the phone on the bed. She sat back in the chair and noticed the red dots were actually strawberries. Bloody strawberries. What the hell was she doing and what was happening to her life? She put her head in her hands, and pulled at her hair, trying to make sense of it somehow.

She was still sitting there minutes later when the thought came to her. Leonard hadn't said she wasn't a bully. So, if even Leonard thought it was a possibility, and if ten employees thought it too, could it actually be true?

Dear eighteen-year-old me

It's strange, isn't it? For pretty much all of your life you felt like nothing changed, and then everything changed all at once.

You never imagined you'd be where you are now. In your very own room in Clare College, Cambridge, with your very own ensuite. When you visited with your mum and dad you thought the door was a cupboard – you couldn't believe it when you opened it to see you had a bathroom of your own.

When you came for your interview, you had to wait in a room just like this. You sat on the bed, preparing, a constant loop in your head asking how you ever found yourself here? You dared yourself to wonder if you ever did come to a place like this, would you ever even fit in? This was 'proper posh' as your dad said. Your mum and dad sat outside waiting, wondering too – how they'd created a girl as clever as you. They were so proud they thought they might actually burst – and that was before you'd even had your interview.

And you did get in. The day came when you left your lovely cottage, to step into a new world of your own. You stayed with your mum and dad in a little hotel in the city the night before, so you could walk around and find your feet, as they'd said.

That's what you're still doing now, finding your feet – but you're loving every minute. Even the strawberry drink at The Maypole pub – which tastes like milkshake, only this one makes you feel dizzy.

You thought everyone would be really clever and posh – but they're not. Well, they are clever and some are posh – but they're kind and funny, and for the first time in education you feel like you belong. There are some things which are expensive and you wonder how you'll pay. But you'll work at the ball where it costs two hundred pounds, so

What Really Happened To Me?

you get to go for free. This will alight something in you — work, money, how this can go together and you can still see the world. But you're not thinking about that now.

You're too busy thinking about last night.

Last night you went to a party — it was in your halls on the corridor with some stairs. There, standing on one of those stairs, was a boy called Eric. You were too embarrassed to smile, but when he smiled at you, you felt like the most important girl in the world. If sitting next to Billy Jenkins for all those years was the price you had to pay — you would hands-up do it all again. You and Eric spoke all night. He's studying French & German. He's posh — he went to a private school — but that didn't matter at all. You didn't want to be rude to your new friends, but he was just so damn gorgeous, you couldn't walk away. His dark hair, his blue eyes — he looked like a model from a catalogue and here he was talking to you.

You even told your mum and dad about him, and they seemed as excited as you. They came for a visit today and you showed them everywhere — even the step where you saw Eric for the first time. You don't even feel too sad that they've left now. You'll be back home in a few weeks and they'll be calling soon to tell you they're back.

Only they won't, my darling girl.

I wish I could sit next to you on your bed now. I know what happens next, and if I could do anything to change it, I promise you I would. There'll be a knock at the door and you'll think it's a friend — but it's not. Sometimes a lifetime can change in a second, and this is what's going to happen to you. There will be news about your parents and if I could protect you from what you're about to learn I would.

I wish I was there with you, Gracie, to hold you tight, my darling girl. I wish I could wrap you in a blanket of love.

Love

G

x

Chapter Eight

Grace: Eric, no matter what you think of me, I'm still your wife. Please call. x
Grace: Eric, just ring me. Please. It's all I ask. x
Grace: Eric, stop playing games. You can't do this to me. Please x

At eleven-thirty, Grace walked down the stairs. She'd tried sitting in her room and she'd tried watching television. Sitting watching *The Morning Talk* on Hi-TV had only made her agitated. Who sat and watched television in the middle of the day?

"Grace?"

Jack Jones called out to her from the lounge. He was sitting at a table with Lulu and the girl from the front desk – Iris, his fiancée.

"Come and meet Iris."

Grace felt another wave of irritation. She wasn't there on holiday, she didn't want to make small talk and she had no interest in making friends, no matter how kind Iris's father had been to her earlier.

The small voice whispered in her head again. *"Are you a bully, Grace? Are you?"*

She made herself smile, nodded at Jack and walked into the lounge.

"Hello Iris," she extended her hand. "In fact we met yesterday, when you checked me in, and this morning I had the pleasure of meeting your father."

"Yes – he said," Iris beamed at her. "How's your hand?"

The girl's radiance only irritated Grace more. Was there anything this father and daughter didn't discuss? It had only been a couple of hours ago.

"My dad said you had a nasty fall."

More irritation flashed though her. She wasn't some sort of Strawberry Village talking-point.

"Are you a bully, Grace, are you? The voice asked again.

She smiled a bigger smile and held her hand up. "Better. Thank you. You and your father are very kind."

"It's all part of the service," Iris beamed.

"Would you like to join us?" Lulu asked.

No, she wouldn't, but between asking herself if she was a bully, and wondering what on earth she was going to do with her days, she could think of no excuse. Damn, she missed her packed schedule she thought, as she heard herself ordering a coffee.

The only way through this was to pretend she was there on business.

"How long have you worked here, Iris?" she asked in her most business-like and professional of voices. She felt Jack's eyes on her.

"Oh, I don't work here – I was just helping out."

"Iris is a journalist."

"A journalist. Yes, of course. I'm sorry – your father did

say." Grace's insides tightened. The last person she needed to be spending time with was a journalist.

"For *The Strawberry Times*. Iris works with me," Lulu explained.

"Yes, I do. I work for Lu and I freelance as well."

"Iris wrote the piece about me," Jack explained.

Grace nodded.

"And then they fell in love," Lulu smiled.

"Lu," Iris blushed. "I don't fall in love with everyone I interview." She looked at Grace.

"Only the irresistible ones." Jack leant over and kissed her.

Grace looked at them. Young and glowing with love. She needed to get away.

"Makes you sick, doesn't it?" Lulu rolled her eyes at Grace, and Grace tried her best to smile as she wondered if it was too soon to leave.

"Iris is now in demand for big profile pieces – after they saw what she did for my image, everyone wants her." Jack held Iris's hands.

Really. She needed to get away.

"Speaking of articles, the one about you at the weekend was so inspiring." Iris beamed at her again. "Lulu and I couldn't stop talking about it."

Grace cringed.

"In fact, Grace, if you don't mind, we were wondering if we could ask you some advice?" Lulu asked her.

"Me?" Grace sipped her coffee, wishing she could be alone.

"To be honest, we're trying to work out what to do with *The Strawberry Times*," Lulu continued. "I'm just going to come out with it: we're really struggling. Our main advertisers are local restaurants, but their budgets have disappeared at the moment. We can't seem to find anyone willing to support a failing newspaper."

The words were whirring over Grace's head. Didn't they know she had her own life to save? She was used to running a global television company, not some tiny backstreet paper. She didn't have time for this.

She sipped her coffee again. It was then she realised Lulu had stopped talking and they were all looking at her.

"I'm sorry." She put her cup down. "I don't know what to say."

Lulu and Iris looked at one another, and then at Jack, who had sat watching in silence. "We just thought –you know – with your expertise?" Lulu stumbled.

"I run a television channel." Grace was aware her tone was curt, but seriously.

Used to run a television channel, the annoying voice in her head said.

"I'm sure Jack has some good ideas," she added as she stood up.

The three of them looked at one another.

"Yes, but we thought…"

"I'm sorry. I'm sure you'll find a solution, but I really must go."

"Of course," Iris said, and the others nodded.

"I need to make a phone call." Grace pulled her phone out of her trouser pocket and then, before they could say anything else, she walked out of the lounge.

Grace called Pearl again.

"Please Pearl. If you could call me when you get this message?"

Then she called Eric.

"You can't just stop talking to me like this. At least send me a bloody text."

And then she called Polly. The call also went to voicemail.

"I could just do with a friendly voice," she admitted as she left the message. As she stood out in the street, she looked around. Everywhere she looked she saw people with a place in the world: an early lunch with a friend; a business meeting; a home to go back to.

Her phone beeped and her heart leapt.

It was Polly.

I'm sorry Grace. They've told me no contact for the time being. I hope you're doing okay x

Grace felt the tears sting the back of her eyes. She turned around and saw the small local shop she'd seen the day before. She went inside, bought six bottles of wine, bars of chocolate and large packets of crisps. Then she went back to the hotel and shut the door of her room. She sat on the floor of the room, with the curtains closed, and then she drank and drank as much wine as she could, until she couldn't drink any more.

Chapter Nine

Grace: Eric, you can't keep ignoring me like this. x
Grace: Pearl, please ring me. x
Grace: Eric, am I really that bad? x
Grace: Eric, please, I'm begging you x

The next day her head pounded as she opened her eyes. She didn't know when she'd fallen asleep – or passed out, if she was being honest.

Was she being honest? She had no idea.

She looked around for her phone and found it on her pillow.

No messages. No missed calls.

There was a faint buzzing in her ear and her head throbbed.

She had two choices. She could go back to sleep, or she could get up and go for another run. She sank back into the pillows and closed her eyes, but all she could see was Eric's face. The anger, the hurt, the hatred in his eyes. She felt sick.

She got up and pulled on her second pair of running clothes – at least she'd packed a spare. She'd buy some water and paracetamol, then get some fresh air. She could get to a shop, couldn't she? She caught sight of herself in the mirror – the smeared make-up, the grey skin, and the dark shadows under her eyes.

Is this what her life had come to. Running?

"For god's sake, pull yourself together woman. You're a bloody CEO, she told her reflection. "Look at the state of you." She washed her face, grabbed her phone and stepped out into the hall.

This time she didn't fall over, nor did she see Bruce. Just over an hour later, when she returned to the hotel, she was feeling better. The morning was crisp and refreshing, as spring was beginning to creep in. Her head was clearer, and she felt embarrassed by how she'd behaved with Iris and Lulu.

She had a choice, she had decided as she walked back towards the hotel: she could continue down the path of self-pity, or she could create her own agenda for the day.

She searched on her phone for the number of *The Strawberry Times* and called it.

"Can I speak to Lulu?" she asked the man who answered. When Lulu spoke into the phone, Grace stood up, and assumed the poise she had used at Hi-TV.

"Lulu, it's Grace Leven. I'm sorry I was so rude yesterday."

"You weren't really."

"First rule of journalism: don't lie," Grace said into the phone, pushing her shoulders further back. "I wondered if you'd like me to come into the paper later today?"

"Seriously? I'd love that. We'd love that."

"Great. When suits?"

"We've got a meeting at eleven am, so perhaps twelve?"

"Wonderful. I'll be there. See you then." Grace hung up, surprised by how good it felt to have just one plan.

She took a deep breath and sat down on the bench at the front of the hotel. The garden was already beautiful, even though it was only early spring. The beds were full of bushes, with daffodils pushing through – the morning sun shone down on her face and she took a deep breath.

"It's a lovely day," a voice said.

She opened her eyes, to see the odd-job man in front of her, carrying wood.

"Yes, it is." She'd been rude to him the previous day as well.

"You look better."

"Better?"

"We've been a little worried about you."

"We?"

"The staff here. The bad hand, the fall yesterday."

"Right." Grace didn't know what to say.

"We're a nosy bunch, really."

Grace nodded and managed a small smile.

"I'm Harvey, by the way." He put the wood he was carrying down and held out his hand.

"Grace Leven." She shook it. His hand was rough, she suspected from his work. "Are you making something?"

Harvey picked the wood up.

"Indeed I am. It's a cabinet for the lounge."

"A cabinet?"

"Well, it's a fancy word for cupboard I suppose."

"That's very clever."

"You haven't seen it yet."

Grace smiled again. She noticed his eyes crinkled as he laughed. She felt a flush of embarrassment that she'd been quite so rude to him.

"Do you enjoy making cabinets?"

"I love it. It's still one of my favourite parts of the job."

"How wonderful to be so creative."

"Are you creative, Grace Leven?"

The question surprised her and she paused for a moment.

"No. I don't suppose I am."

"Ah, well I think we're all creative human beings somewhere inside us. We'll have to find what you like creating while you're here. Best I get going. This cabinet – or should I say cupboard – is not going to build itself. It was good to meet you, Grace Leven."

"Good to meet you too, Harvey." She waved as she watched him say hello to everyone he passed before he disappeared into the hotel.

Chapter Ten

Grace: Eric - if you'd just answer me, I will stop messaging I promise x
Grace: Pearl - if you'd just answer me, I will stop messaging I promise x

Just before twelve pm Grace rang the bell of the Georgian building which was home to *The Strawberry Times*.

"Come in. You need to shove the door; we're up on the second floor," Lulu called through the intercom. Grace gave the door a shove as instructed and walked up the staircase, where she saw Iris and Lulu leaning over the banister.

"Welcome to our empire," Iris called.

Grace looked up. "Hello ladies. This is quite the welcome."

"Say what you want about the dodgy door, but I bet you don't get treatment like this at Hi-TV," Lulu laughed.

"You're absolutely right," Grace said under her breath as she climbed the rest of the stairs.

"Sorry, it's not super glamorous." Lulu opened the door to the office.

"Another rule: do not apologise when you have nothing to be sorry for. This is a wonderful space." Grace walked in and caught her breath. She counted six desks, all of them empty. But it had the musty smell of a local newsroom, an old feel of anticipation in the air. She liked it at once.

"It's not every day *The Strawberry Times* has a visit from a VIP."

"I wouldn't quite say that," Grace smiled as she walked in. She'd dressed down on purpose, in her navy Sezane trouser suit. Back in her job in London, anything that wasn't Prada felt casual, but now she felt over-dressed.

"Would you like a coffee? We don't have a posh machine, but we do have a very smart cafétière."

"That would be lovely," Grace nodded, and looked around again. "Where is everyone, presuming there are other members of staff?"

"Nigel, our transport correspondent, is out on a train, as you may guess, and Lottie, our PA, is taking her dog to the vet's," Lulu told her. "Would you like to come into my office?"

Grace nodded and followed Lulu into a smaller room with a large window overlooking the square. The desk was also faded, large and brown leather. There were pictures of a man golfing on one wall; Grace wondered if they were pictures of Lulu's father. There were also candles, orchids and multi-coloured notebooks on the desk.

"I bet your office is far grander than mine."

"This is lovely," Grace said. And it was. She didn't add that at least Lulu could see people walking around. Grace's office was so high up, it felt she like was in a different world.

What Really Happened To Me?

Iris arrived with a tray of coffee, cups and some biscuits. "Dave baked them this morning."

"Dave?"

"He owns Dave's Deli, in the village. You should go there." Iris poured a coffee and handed it to her.

"I'm sorry – I didn't ask if you wanted milk."

Grace noticed Iris's cheeks flush with colour.

"It's fine," Grace shook her head. "I take it black. And I've heard about it – Dave's Deli," she added, when they looked confused.

"Everyone knows Dave's Deli here," Iris beamed.

Grace looked at them both, their eyes wide as they stood staring back at her.

"I'm making you nervous. You know there's really no need to be."

"But you're…well…Grace Leven," Lulu said.

Grace put the coffee on the desk and sat down on one of the chairs.

"Look, let's get his straight. Girls – if I can call you that – I may be Grace Leven, but the truth is I have no idea who I am, if I'm perfectly honest." Perhaps it was their warmth, perhaps it was her exhaustion, or perhaps it was being in this musty, fading newsroom, but for some reason she could no longer pretend. "I don't know if I'm allowed to call you girls, I don't know what I'm supposed to do. I don't know where I'm supposed to be. But I do know, there is no need for you to be nervous."

Iris and Lulu carried on looking back at her.

"It's us, isn't it? The newspaper. Well, the mess of the newspaper. We knew we should have taken the pictures of Dennis down." Lulu nodded to the photo. "That's Dennis. He was the editor here before me."

"Dennis?" Grace looked at the man swinging the golf

club. She shook her head. "No, no. I'm not talking about the newspaper, I'm talking about me."

"I'm sorry?" Iris put down her own coffee.

"But you're the woman who has it all," Lulu stated.

"Well, that's the point. I need to be straight with you. I'm not here on a holiday, or a sabbatical. I'm here because I've been accused of bullying by ten different people."

"You have?" Iris sat down on another chair.

Grace nodded. "The board of Hi-TV also has a video – sent to them anonymously – of me screaming at my husband, who, when I returned home from work on Tuesday, I discovered was leaving me." She leant forward and put her hands on her head. "So, here I am – no job, no husband. Not a woman who has it all; more a woman who has lost it all, in the most spectacular of ways. My only friend isn't allowed to talk to me because she works for the company and my only daughter doesn't want to talk to me because she believes I spent her entire childhood putting my job before her. So, if you'd rather ask someone else for advice other than me, I would completely understand." She sat back up, took a deep breath and sipped her coffee, feeling oddly relieved.

There were a few awkward moments of silence as Grace sipped her coffee while Lulu and Iris stared, their eyes wide.

"But that's awful," Iris said at last.

Grace nodded. "It is, really."

A silence settled in the air.

"Ten accusations of bullying?" Lulu looked at Grace.

Grace nodded. "I know I haven't been the most patient of bosses and I don't have as much time as I once had, but have I really turned into a bully?"

Grace looked at their faces. For a moment she saw something register in both of them.

"You're thinking about yesterday, when I was a complete bitch when you asked me about *The Strawberry Times*, aren't you?"

"No," Iris tried.

"Really?" Grace raised her eyebrows. "My first piece of advice is always directness."

"Well, actually yes," Lulu nodded.

Grace sat back in the chair. "I don't blame you. I was, and you have every right."

More uncomfortable silence settled among them.

"So, the article in the magazine was a lie?" Iris asked.

"Not to my knowledge. When I was interviewed, I had no idea about the allegations, or that my husband was going to leave me." Grace paused for a moment. "I mean, I know things hadn't been right, but I thought we were going through a rocky patch, like every bloody marriage."

Grace rubbed her head. She could feel her headache coming back. She picked up her bag and got ready to leave. "I'm sorry girls, this isn't what you signed up for. I shall leave."

"Please don't," Lulu said.

Iris nodded. "Yes, please don't."

"You don't really want me involved, now you know this."

"I'm sure you were just doing your best," Iris tried again.

Grace thought for a moment. "Do you know, Iris? I was. This industry's tough. Whether it's television or newspapers, the media is not for the faint-hearted. It's not a nine-to-five because stories don't happen only between the hours of nine to five, and if you can't take it when you're told no or knocked back, you're going to have a miserable time. I just wanted younger members of staff to be aware of this, and there are plenty of other industries if this isn't for them."

"What are we going to do?" Iris asked.

"We?"

"Yes, *we*. We're not going to let you go through this alone."

"But how do you know I'm telling the truth?"

"You're Grace Leven. I haven't just been following you since the article – you've been one of my biggest role models for a long time," Lulu told her.

"And mine," Iris agreed.

"I'm flattered, really I am, but this is my mess and I need to sort it out."

"Not on your own, not anymore."

"Other than my lawyer, I haven't told anyone this."

"We won't tell anyone."

"I saw what happened with Jack, remember?" Iris said. "There's more to this, just like there was with him."

"This can be our first mission – we need to get to the bottom of this," Lulu said. "We're journalists. Or rather, technically, Iris is. I just took over from Dennis." Lulu nodded to the wall.

"Is he no longer with us?" Grace asked.

"Dennis? God, yes. He calls up every week asking if I've buggered it all up yet. His parting words were 'don't bloody bugger this up'. I leave the picture up there to remind me every day."

"I'm sure you're not buggering it up."

"Well, maybe a bit – we just won't tell Dennis." Lulu smiled a small smile. "And we won't tell anyone about what's happened to you."

"Except Jack – can we tell Jack?"

Could they tell Jack? Could she trust Jack? Could she trust them?

"But the point is, it's a lie," Iris said.

"How do you know it's a lie?" Grace asked. "The video isn't lying."

"You can't fake it for all the years you've worked at Hi-TV; it would have come out before."

"Believe me, I've met people who've faked it for a *long* time," Grace said. "I did shove my husband."

More awkwardness settled.

"We all make mistakes, Grace," Iris said. "I also saw what happened when everything was blown out of context with Jack. This is why we need to find out who is behind this and the allegations. If it is true – well, then we'll discover this. But I don't believe it is."

"Me neither," Lulu nodded.

Grace looked at Iris and her bright purple dress with daisies on the hem.

"That's a lovely dress."

"Thank you."

"She used to wear matching socks, but she's stopped that now. Now she's a grown-up journalist, she needs to be more discreet. Hang on…" Lulu stopped. "That's it."

"That's what?" Iris asked.

"That's what we need to do."

"We?" Grace asked.

"Iris needs to go undercover."

"Me? Undercover?" Iris stood up.

"Not undercover exactly as such, but, well, yes, undercover." Lulu perched on the desk as she thought for a moment. "What we need is for Iris to write one of her profiles on someone at Hi-TV and spend some time there.

That way she can do some digging and work out what's really been going on."

"That's ridiculous," Grace said, but then thought for a moment. Perhaps it wasn't. "What you're saying is, if Iris works on a profile, then she may pick up information which will help me – or you'll discover I'm actually a bully and a complete cow."

"Exactly." Lulu clapped her hands. "But not the complete cow bit."

"Is it illegal?" Iris asked.

"How? You'll write a profile and you'll give someone the wonderful Iris touch. We don't have to tell anyone there is another motive behind it."

The three of them thought for a moment.

"Okay, I'll do it."

Grace smiled. Their enthusiasm was contagious, even for her in her terrible mood.

"Girls, while I'm flattered you're even thinking this, it's not going to happen."

Lulu looked at Grace. "In all due respect, Grace Leven, yes, it is. If there's any sniff of foul play going on at one of our big national broadcasters, it's our job as fellow women in the media to learn what is going on. We need to get to the bottom of it. One minute you're the woman who has it all, the next minute you're being marched out of the company. We can't have women being held up and then ripped apart like this, even if it is a tough industry." Lulu looked at Grace. "You said: be direct."

"Yes, I did." Grace nodded.

"Who would I follow?" Iris asked.

"Polly," Grace said, without thinking.

"Polly James? Head of Daytime?" Lulu added.

Grace looked at Lulu. "I'm impressed."

Lulu shrugged. "You're role models. What can I say?"

"I think it should be a woman, and I'm not biased because she's my best friend – she's the only other woman in one of the top jobs. And something like this could help her with her next move."

"There you go: women helping women. We approve," Iris said.

"Do you always talk in 'we?'" Grace asked.

"Only to role models and people who we think aren't really a complete horror," Lulu said. She raised her mug.

"To role models and women who aren't complete horrors," Lulu said.

"To role models and women who are complete horrors." Iris raised her mug.

"To role models, women who aren't complete cows and not buggering it up, thank you Dennis." Grace raised her mug at the photo on the wall. "Rule number two: just because a man has done a job for a long time, doesn't mean he has the right to make you feel incompetent."

Iris and Lulu nodded and sipped their coffee.

"I like that you called us girls, by the way," Iris said.

"Me too," Lulu added.

"I'm sorry again – you know – for being so rude," Grace said.

"What did you just tell me? Don't apologise when there is no need to apologise. Really, Grace Leven, we expect more from you." Lulu shook her head and Iris did too.

"So, we're on?" Lulu looked at Grace and Iris did too.

As she had no other ideas, and this wasn't a terrible one, Grace couldn't argue.

"Okay, yes. Iris, Lulu – thank you. Let's do this. Women supporting women in media and not buggering this up.

Either I am a complete cow, which Iris will uncover, or we will find out what really happened to me."

Dear twenty-six-year-old me,

Today is your wedding day. It's a day that many young women dream of. A day filled with love, hope and new beginnings. On the outside you're smiling and putting on your dress. But the truth is you, my darling girl, as you stand looking at the girl dressed in a cream dress in the mirror, just want the day to be done.

You're excited to marry Eric and to officially be a family of your own. Leonard has agreed to walk you down the aisle. He's been there for you, ever since that dreadful knock on the door and your whole life change – and so much has changed since then. But this is your chance, you believe, of starting all over again. You wouldn't have chosen this way – nor would you have picked such a big church and venue, but it's like Eric says: he shouldn't have to miss out just because of you.

Eric's family are nice (enough). You've always found them a little cold, if you're perfectly honest. Not that you'd say. You suspect his father is a little disappointed in his son. Eric works in marketing but he hates it really, and never gets a promotion even though he says he tries. His mother smiles too, but it's as though there's not much behind her eyes. She's obsessed with her schedule of golf, crib, yoga, booking holidays and then telling everyone she meets about these holidays. Then, when someone tells her where they're going, she wants to book that too. It looks dreadfully miserable to you and you've often wondered if she ever wanted a career for herself – but you've never dared ask.

There will be aunts, uncles, parents and sisters – the problem is, none of them are yours. There are mutual friends you met at Cambridge, but really, they belong to Eric, not you.

What Really Happened To Me?

You have some people here – Godfrey, who is Director of News at Hi-TV – he has been your mentor since you started at the firm. You suspect he and his wife feel sad you haven't got your own parents here today, but you're grateful nonetheless that they'll be here.

Then there's Polly too.

You've only known her for a few months – she's been your assistant since you became Editor of Breakfast Today – but because you spend so much time at work, she's also become your friend too. You thought it might be too soon to invite her, but she was delighted when you did. Deep down you feel it's wrong that you feel happiest in your work – but it's where you thrive and feel like you belong. What would your mum and dad say if they knew you were the youngest female editor of a breakfast show Hi-TV has ever known? You know they'd be proud.

But then again, you wonder if they were here – perhaps you wouldn't have spent so many hours at work? You don't sing any more, not since that time at university when Eric laughed at karaoke night and said you probably don't want to do that again.

They never told you to stop singing, but they did tell you at night to stop studying. Would they have told you to stop the nights which turn into mornings at work, or would you have listened? Then you tell yourself to stop these thoughts too. You've become good, over the years, at stopping these thoughts that lead you down the 'what if they were still here?' path.

And after today – you'll have Eric.

You still don't know why it was he fell in love with you, when he could have chosen anyone he wanted. You've often secretly worried if he'd change his mind, but after today it'll be official and you'll have a family of your own. He may not love you always in the way you wished he did, he may not like you wearing your favourite perfume, and he may think it's better you wear dark colours at work.

But that's marriage, isn't it?

Compromise. Besides, when you look at his parents you can see why he is how he is. But you think it'll be different when you're married and hopefully create a little family of your own. Everything will be okay. Your example of marriage from your mum and dad was so different to his – and love lives on in us, doesn't it?

Oh, dear twenty-six-year-old Gracie, I wish I could warn you. I wish I could stand next to you in that beautiful dress and tell you it doesn't have to be this way. But I know your determination, while sometimes your biggest enemy is also your greatest strength, and I love you even more for it. Whatever I told you now, I suspect you wouldn't listen anyway, my darling girl.

Enjoy the dancing, and don't worry what anyone tells you, even if they are your new family now.

I think you're magnificent.

Love

G x

Chapter Eleven

Grace: Eric please. I'm your wife. Just bloody call me.
Grace: Pearl, I know you think I'm a terrible mother, but please could you stop ignoring me like your father? x

The next morning, after her run and shower, Grace walked down to reception.

"Can I help you Ms Leven?"

She nodded at the young man. "I've heard about a *Dave's Deli*. Is it nearby?

"Of course." He pulled out a map of Strawberry Village and marked it for her. "Everyone says it's the bacon baps, but I personally prefer his cinnamon rolls." He winked. She nodded and took the map.

A few minutes later she sat down on a table outside Dave's Deli. The spring air had a warmth about it and she closed her eyes for a moment, wishing the gnawing ache in her insides would go away. When she opened them, a man wearing an apron was standing in front of her.

"Good morning, madam. Welcome to Dave's Deli. I'm

Dave by the way, and I'm here to help." His smile was so big, she smiled back.

"Pleased to meet you, Dave."

"I'll get you a menu."

She shook her head. "A coffee, please."

"Is that all? Can I not tempt you with a bacon bap? A cinnamon bun at the very least?"

"Just a coffee please. Black."

"As you wish." He shook his head and disappeared back inside.

She looked around her. The street had the same bustle as the hotel and she liked it. People were walking around, going about their day. But they didn't seem to do it with quite the same edge as people in London. There, it felt like everyone was striding or striving, trying to be somewhere else. She'd never known the owner of a café to introduce themselves.

But then again, she didn't remember the last time she'd been to a café near her house on her own.

A younger man sat down at the table next to her, and she pulled out her phone. She may have been feeling a little brighter, but she still couldn't face small talk. A few minutes later, he spoke.

"Excuse me, are you Grace Leven?"

Her heart sank.

She wondered if she could pretend not to hear? It happened to her sometimes: people would recognise her. It was nothing like Wakefield. When she ate with him, it was par for the course – people walking up to him, acting as though he was their best friend. While she would hate such a permanent invasion of her privacy, he seemed to revel in it. But that was his ego for you. Just the thought of him made her insides twist. Her heavy mood started to weigh her down again and she wondered if she could take her coffee to go.

"It's okay," the voice said again. "I'm not a complete crazy stranger."

She looked at the young man. He had blue eyes with brown curly hair and she was certain she'd never seen him before. But then again, she'd met many people over the years who remembered her while they were faceless to her. This happened, she'd learned early on, when people think you have the power to give them a job.

"You won't remember me, but I worked as an intern for a bit, years ago. I'm Greg." He waved.

She wanted to nod and return to her message-free phone. Then she remembered she was being investigated for being a bully.

"Grace."

Dave arrived with her coffee.

"Morning Dave," Greg said.

"Morning Greg. Your usual, I'm guessing." Dave looked at his watch. "You're right on time."

Greg laughed as Dave disappeared.

"This is the trouble having Dave around the corner like this. I find myself keeping my eleven o' clock slots accidentally free."

Grace sipped her coffee.

"So are you still working in television?" She didn't really want to know.

Greg shook his head. "I decided it wasn't for me."

"So you hated it?"

He laughed. "Yes, I did."

She liked his openness and warmed to him a little.

"And what do you do now?"

"I'm a psychotherapist. I've got a practice room just around the corner."

Grace couldn't think of anything she'd dislike more. Talking about people's misery, trapped in a small room.

"You're thinking how could I leave the world of television to talk about misery?"

"No…well, yes." She paused. "You're clearly good at your job."

Greg laughed as Dave returned with his cappuccino. "Watch it," Dave said to Grace, "he'll have you working out where you've been going wrong all your life in minutes. He's done us all."

Grace sipped her coffee.

"I'm curious – what didn't you like about the wonderful world of television?"

Greg sat back and thought for a moment. "There was so much to like about it: the buzz; the excitement; the world where dreams come true."

"Yes," Grace agreed. "There's that."

"But then I suppose it's just that – the world where dreams come true – for a very small few. The same dreams that can disappear overnight, that are always at the mercy of ratings, popularity or a powerful boss. It felt fake, I suppose."

Grace swallowed.

"Careers could end in a phone call. No wonder everyone was on edge, even the ones you thought had made it. I suppose I wanted something more, something I could build myself, which helped people and was a bit more, well, real."

"But isn't it—" she stopped herself.

"Boring? Define boring?"

Had she really been about to say boring? Yes, she had.

"It's okay – I questioned all this myself. But is it boring? Doing something you enjoy and helping people turn their lives around, if they let you? I have my own practice here and I work my own hours. The insecurity of television, the knowing my fate was in someone else's hands – for me," he put his hand on his chest – "I found that boring. But, I suppose when you are the boss, I can imagine it's a very different experience."

She needed to change the subject.

"So, Strawberry Village? Are you from here?"

He shook his head. "No, my husband, Lewis, who I met in London, grew up here. I fell in love with him and the place, and so here we are."

Dave returned with Greg's bacon bap. It smelt delicious and Grace felt hungry, empty and full of longing all at the same time.

"Greg took over Peggy's rooms," Dave told her as if she knew who Peggy was. "They've been working their magic for years on people in this place."

"Peggy?"

"She was great – a real character here. She died over a year ago now, bless her." Dave stood for a moment, as if deep in thought and then disappeared back inside.

"What show did you work on?"

"*Breakfast Today*."

"And I was?"

"You were Head of Daytime by then; you'd just been promoted from editor of the show."

Grace nodded.

"Did we meet?"

"Once. I sat in on a meeting with sales."

"Right." Grace nodded.

"It's okay, I don't expect you to remember me. There were many of us and only one of you."

"So, how long did you stay?"

"A year. I was a trainee. But one day it hit me; all the long hours and the striving was for a promise of dream which didn't even really exist."

"I see." Grace swallowed.

"I wanted to connect with people. One of the reasons I thought I wanted to work in television was to connect with people. Television programmes are made for people and they were about people. But when I was there, I felt a disconnect."

"A disconnect?"

"Many people I met were more worried about themselves and their own careers than ever actually connecting with an audience. I'm sorry," he added. "I'm not talking about you."

Wasn't he?

"I'm sorry, I hope I have not offended you."

Grace shook her head. "Not at all. It's just I'm more used to people telling me how they've always wanted to work in television and asking me for a job."

"But you're the CEO; you've an incredible job. I read the article about you – you're the exception. You've gone all the way to the top, and with a family. You've proven you really can have it all. So, for you the dream does exist. You *are* the power."

Only she wasn't, and for that reason she could no longer continue this conversation.

"So, what brings you to Strawberry Village?"

"A sabbatical." Her tone was sharp.

She could tell he didn't believe her, and neither would she.

"Ah, there she is. I was wondering how you are."

She looked up to see Bruce, Iris's dad and the man who'd helped her when she fell earlier on in the week. Was there no space in this place?

"I'm well, thank you." She wasn't about to take part in some sort of group therapy session on a pavement outside a deli. She really needed to leave.

"Morning Greg." Bruce nodded at Greg and looked at his watch. "Eleven sixteen; how did I guess you'd be here?"

"I really have to start filling my eleven o clocks." Greg took another bite.

"Does everyone know everyone in Strawberry Village?"

"Not everyone." Dave came out with a coffee for Bruce and Bruce sat down at the table next to them. "But we like to keep an eye out."

She signalled to Dave that she wanted to pay, but he disappeared.

"So, are you recovered?" Bruce crossed his arms and looked at her. The attention was making her more and more uncomfortable. She was feeling hot in her navy Prada trousers and white blouse. Hot, and out of place – and Grace Leven wasn't used to feeling out of place like she did in Strawberry Village.

"Recovered?" Greg asked.

Grace stood up. "I tripped while running; that's all. Bruce was very kind. Now I really must go."

She looked around for Dave. Where was Dave?

Bruce chuckled his chuckle as he sipped his coffee and Grace felt her irritation rise. Why did nobody have proper jobs around here? One where you couldn't just hang around delis in the middle of the morning.

She stood and almost tripped again. She looked down and Fred was looking up at her, wagging his tail.

"I'm sorry."

"Don't mind Fred. He gets in the way."

The whole of Strawberry Village gets in my way, she forced herself not to say.

"I'll buy the coffee, Grace," Greg told her. "If you need to go."

She didn't need charity – she needed the bill. But when she looked inside and saw several customers waiting with Dave chatting happily to them all, she nodded.

"Thank you. I owe you."

Bruce waved goodbye and then turned to greet a woman who was joining him. "Grace, this is…" he began to say, but Grace couldn't meet anyone else. She needed to leave.

"Goodbye Greg."

"You know, Grace, I'm just two streets along." He nodded to his left. "If you ever want to pop in…"

"I don't need therapy." How dare he? She turned and began to walk.

"I was thinking more if you fancied some company while you were here."

Grace stopped. "Right."

"Goodbye Grace."

She nodded, but didn't turn as she walked away as fast as she could.

Chapter Twelve

Grace: Eric where the bloody hell are you? Stop this. Please. x
Grace: Pearl! Please stop ignoring me. I'm your bloody mother. Where are you?

Grace felt a surge of relief when her phone finally beeped as she walked into the hotel.

But it was neither Eric nor Pearl. Instead, it was Lulu. Iris had news and could she meet them in the lounge at Strawberry House in ten minutes? They could come over immediately if she was free.

She ordered herself a glass of sparkling mineral water and ignored how much she wanted a large glass of wine. Daytime drinking? Isn't that what you do when you have nothing else in life? She was still contemplating this as Lulu and Iris appeared at her side.

"We're in, or rather, Iris is in." Lulu clasped her hands together, then she looked around. "Sorry, I shouldn't be blurting it out loud," she whispered in a more hushed voice.

"It's okay." Grace nodded and ushered them to sit down. "That was quick."

Iris nodded. "I'm going to go in as a freelancer. I know one of the editors at Simply The Best Magazine. They were gutted they missed out on your article so they're happy to do this. I've worked with them a few times – they liked the piece I did on Jack and I've done a few profiles for them since. I told Hi-TV they were interested in a commission and I suggested I follow Polly. They jumped at the chance. I suppose," Iris looked down, "I suppose they're keen to do something…"

"After my so-called disgrace, you mean." Grace ruffled again. Still, she reminded herself why Iris was doing this and tried to shake it off. "This is excellent news, thank you Iris. Who did you speak with in the press office?"

Iris beamed. "Thank you, Grace. Someone called Jemima. She also knew my work – not just Jack's profile but some of the others I've written, like the politician who was accused of late-night meetings with an unknown woman who was really his therapist."

"I remember that," Grace said.

"You see, the media doesn't always get it right." Lulu nodded at Grace. "Our Iris is carving out quite the reputation for herself."

"Anyway," Iris continued, blushing, "I suggested it would be good to write about another female after seeing your article last weekend. I told her it had made me wonder about the other women in the company, and how well they progress too. It would be an honour to shine a spotlight on their wonderful working culture which helped women to thrive." Iris clapped her hands together. "I've just had a call from Sophia in publicity to say Polly Jacobs would be delighted to take part. Do you know Sophia or Jemima?"

Grace shook her head. She only dealt with Rupert, who was Director of Press & Communications.

"It doesn't make you a bad person that you don't know everyone at the company," Lulu said.

Grace shifted with more unease. She wasn't sure about any of this now. Was she really being a good friend to Polly by doing this? Is this what friends do? Should she even be dragging Iris away from *The Strawberry Times*?

"When will you start?"

"Monday," Iris replied.

"Monday?"

"Yes, I'm going to go up to meet Polly and then spend a few days with her."

Grace felt a sickening feeling in her insides. Even Polly was moving on without her.

"And this is okay with you both? What about your paper?"

Iris and Lulu nodded.

"Jack's going to stay a few days in London too," Iris said and then blushed.

Lulu nudged her. "You don't have to blush; he is your fiancé.

"Lu." Iris nodded at Grace. "I bet Grace didn't take her boyfriend with her on assignments when she was starting out," Iris said, her cheeks still red.

But Grace wasn't listening.

"It'll be okay, Grace," Lulu said to her. "We'll find a way of filling some of the slots Iris does over the next few weeks, we always do."

Grace nodded. She had to pull herself together. She was Grace Leven, CEO, and even if she was suspended, she must remember her manners. Isn't that what good leaders are supposed to do? Live in integrity all the time? Find solutions? Be curious, not frightened by problems?

She nodded. "Well, thank you, I really appreciate all of this and I'm sorry this debacle has affected you."

"Don't be." Iris shook her head. "It's good for me to do an assignment like this. Believe me, I was stuck in such a rut before I met Lulu and Jack."

Lulu nodded. "She really was."

"They saved me, and now we can save you."

What were they saying? That she needed saving? She was the person who saved others. She was the person with the power, just like Greg had described. Wasn't this just a blip?

"And what about you, Grace? How are you going to spend this glorious afternoon?" Lulu asked.

Grace felt the tightness across her chest.

"Yes, what are you going to do, Grace?"

"Well, I've got several phone calls to make," she saw their smiles falter a little, "and I'd be happy to give some thought about *The Strawberry Times*. Now that Iris will be on assignment, it's the least I can do to give you some backup."

"That would be wonderful." Lulu and Iris stood up. "I've got a lunch meeting with a potential sponsor, but perhaps afterwards we could talk?"

"Well, that sounds promising. A potential sponsorship lunch?" Grace thought of the hundreds of lunches she'd had over the years in the numerous private clubs in London. She'd found them tedious at the time, but now she longed to have one to go to.

"It's a bacon bap at Dave's if I'm honest, but he said he'd help me brainstorm at least." Lulu shrugged.

"I see. Well, it's a start."

What Really Happened To Me?

Grace tried not to look at the glass of white wine being carried to a person on the next table.

"You know, if you have a couple of hours to spare, I'm going to see my dad this afternoon. He'd love to see you again."

"I've just seen him. I too have been to Dave's this morning."

"He has an art studio in the back garden – well, more a conservatory really. We would love you to join us."

Art? "Thank you, but no."

Lulu stood up. "You may say no now, but they get everyone – even Jack."

"Jack Jones?"

"Exactly. I was as surprised as you were." Iris stood up. "I'm off there now, if you change your mind."

Grace looked at the two women on the next table drinking their glasses filled with something white and crisp. A bottle on ice. How it would take the edge off, if she could just have a sip.

Grace didn't know what time it was when she woke up. There was a sharp pain in her head and a buzzing in her ears.

The room was dark; she must have closed the curtains. But when she sat up, she saw it was dark outside. The room spun around her and she felt nauseous. She never felt nauseous. She had to get to the bathroom, but her throbbing head felt too heavy. She'd go back to sleep – she'd be okay in a bit.

But there was a sound; what was it? It was the television, she realised, and it was still on, murmuring at her. She opened her eyes and saw it was one of the late-night films Hi-TV bought cheap to fill the air time.

The room spun again and she closed her eyes. But as soon as her head hit the pillow the nausea crawled up her insides. She pulled herself from the bed and saw the mess. The bottles of wine, the crisp packets, the empty chocolate boxes all over the floor. Her beautiful hotel room looked like a pit. She was just about to turn off the television when her insides started to heave. She made it to the bathroom and clutched the sides of the vanity unit as she wondered if she might actually break. When it stopped, she slumped onto the cold marble floor.

Was this it? Was this rock bottom?

She remembered the painkillers she'd bought a few days previously, and crawled back into the sitting area. Her bag was discarded on the floor and she pulled them out of it, crawling back over to the mini-fridge, where there was some sparkling water. She gulped them down and sat back, another wave of nausea returning. She closed her eyes and prayed it would pass.

The email.

She remembered now. The official email from her company, from Human Resources – that she was suspended on full pay until further notice. Full pay? Was she supposed to be thankful? She was supposed to be doing her job – not sitting here with her life ripped apart.

She looked for her phone and found it next to the wine bottles.

Six missed calls. Her heart leapt. But then she saw they were from Lulu and then Iris. She played the voice message. Lulu's voice pierced the room, asking her if she still wanted to meet, adding that she'd been inspired by Dave. Then another message from Lulu: was she okay? A third one was

What Really Happened To Me?

Lulu suggesting she could come and see her. Would she like to have a drink? Then it was Iris – inviting her over to their house again; the sun was shining and they'd love her to join them.

She forced herself to look at her outgoing calls. Ten to Eric, eight to Pearl, three to Polly. She felt sick again as the memories flooded in. The begging, the pleading, the venting – she couldn't remember everything, but she remembered that. The shame slowly filtered through her.

What had she done?

Her phone beeped again and her heart leapt again.

But it was Iris again.

I hope you're okay Grace and have had a good night. We would love you to come and paint and hang out another day soon, love Iris, Bruce and Fred X

No. She didn't want to hang out. She didn't want to be in Strawberry bloody Village, and no she wasn't having a good night, she was having a disgusting, dreadful night.

She just wanted her life back. She wanted to be back at her desk. She wanted to be Grace Leven again. She wanted her routine, her lunches and her power. What she didn't want was bloody painting.

Her headache was lifting slowly so she crawled back towards the bed, still clutching her phone. She climbed up, pulled the covers over her and rocked herself until at last she fell asleep.

Dear forty-year-old me,
 Today is your birthday and Pearl and Eric are holding a big

surprise party for you – only you know it's happening; you just don't want to say.

There's a lot you don't say at the moment – there's never the right time and if there is, it seems to cause some kind of scene.

You think back to your wedding day – and all the big parties Eric has thrown since. He loves big parties. You don't. He always wants to go to the ones you're invited to through work; you also don't.

But then you tell yourself to stop being so ungrateful.

When you look at Eric and Pearl you feel jealous, and you loathe yourself for that. You often wonder what would have happened if Eric had wanted a career. He'd wanted to stay at home when you had Pearl – not that he'd ever told his parents that. But now, as I look back, I see there was no real discussion – it was as though the decision was already made.

But when you look at your husband and daughter now – as they whisper, plot and plan – you wonder what would it have been like if you'd stayed at home? Or at least worked somewhere part-time. Would you have gardened like your mother? Planting the bulbs upside down instead of the right way up? Would you have baked biscuits each weekend, trying a different recipe every time? Would Pearl have helped, and would you have bonded over putting in more chocolate chips or less? Or a little more sprinkling icing sugar when she wasn't looking to cover up the bumps.

Eric isn't a fan of biscuits so I'm guessing it wouldn't have been the same. He wouldn't have oohed-and-aahed like your dad – Eric is not an ooh-and-aah-er. You can't imagine him pottering in a shed either. Eric is not a 'potter-er' either. His only hobby is golf and hanging out at his club.

You watch Pearl as she shares her teenage gossip with your friend Polly and pretend that it doesn't hurt as much as it does. But it's to be expected, isn't it? Polly may be an editor herself now, but when she was your assistant, she'd answer Pearl's calls and often knew her schedule better than you. Is it any wonder Pearl feels more comfortable with her?

Tonight, you'll act surprised when you enter the house, expecting just a quiet dinner with the four of you. Polly told you she was bringing good wine – she'd love to join to celebrate, and reminds you how lucky you are to have the husband and daughter you do.

You'll watch everyone dance in your kitchen – the large kitchen you didn't pick, and where you never cook. You'll chat to all of Eric's friends, who aren't really yours. You'll wish Godfrey was here, but now your jobs seem too big to be friends. Leonard seems to have slipped away too, just like so much else of your life – you only speak to him on the phone these days.

You'll feel guilty for feeling on the outside when every decision has been yours. But I see now you never asked the question – did I really have a choice?

Love

G

x

Chapter Thirteen

Grace: Eric, please just give me a chance x
Grace: Pearl, I'm sorry x

She woke to her phone ringing.

"Bloody leave me alone," she muttered, but then she saw it was Pearl and she grabbed the phone.

"Darling. How wonderful to hear from you." Grace sat up, put on her best voice and straightened her hair as if Pearl could see her.

"You've given me no choice."

"Darling, don't be like that. How's Mauritius?"

"I'm not in Mauritius, I'm in Cape Town."

"Of course. Right." Eric hadn't told her this.

"What do you want, Mum?"

"To speak with my daughter, of course."

"That'd be a first," Pearl said under her breath.

"I had something to tell you. It's about…"

"If it's about you and Dad or you and your job, I know."

"You know?"

"Of course. Dad told me everything."

"And you didn't think to call me?"

"Let me get this straight; you take no interest in me – you don't even know where I am – but you have a crisis and I'm supposed to come running. Who's the mother here?"

"Please darling, don't be like that."

"I'm supposed to be having time away."

Grace paused. Her head still hurt. Time away that I'm bloody paying for, she stopped herself from adding. Both Eric and Pearl had forgotten to ever acknowledge this a long time ago.

"Your father – where is he? Did he tell you where he is?"

"Is that what this is all about? You've been leaving me endless messages just so you can get hold of Dad?"

"No, darling. Of course, it's not. We haven't spoken in too long."

"And whose fault is that?"

"Pearl, please."

"I need to go. We're at the restaurant. My friends are waiting for me."

"Friends. What friends?"

"Mum, please."

"Well, at least let me tell you where I am."

"Mum, I've got to go. I'm sorry." Pearl hung up.

Grace sighed as she stared at the phone and out of habit checked her email. Her spirits lifted a small amount when she saw one from Leonard until she spotted the word sorry. He was forwarding the Hi-TV correspondence. She sucked in her breath as she read it; it was like being punched all over again. It was official, suspended on full-pay until further notice and if there was any truth to the allegations all costs would be liable to her.

Grace stood on the bridge. She'd taken more paracetamol, pulled on her running clothes and attempted some sort of run, which was more of a walk. Her legs were heavy, and she hadn't gone very far, but at least she'd made it out, she'd told herself. The fresh air had lifted some of the heaviness, but the shame was still there – what had she done?

Had she really been that bad? Yes, she'd worked, but she was the main breadwinner, wasn't she? Isn't that what happened in families? Pearl knew this. Eric knew this. This was the deal. This had always been the deal. Eric wanted to be the stay-at-home father; it had been his choice, hadn't it? Just like where they'd lived, what designers they'd had in the house, what kind of colour scheme they lived in. She'd given him everything he'd wanted.

Grace carried on walking, but she couldn't shake the thought. Her own daughter couldn't stand to hear the sound of her voice.

After all she'd done for her.

She stopped herself. She'd promised herself she'd never say these words. Pearl didn't owe her anything. Children don't owe their parents anything; that's not how it works. Her own parents had taught her that.

What would they make of her, if they could see her now? What had happened to her, since the days of the sweet girl who used to write stories in her coloured notebooks?

And now, on top of it all, here she was, wallowing.

"Let's not be a wallower," both her parents used to say.

She clutched her sides, walked over the bridge and back

along the road into Strawberry Village. She looked at her watch; it was just before eleven o'clock. In her real-life she would have had at least six meetings by now, her workout long done.

The agitation rose again in her.

She walked along the main street, where she could see Dave outside his deli in the distance. She found herself looking and counting. Two streets along, hadn't Greg said? She saw a cobbled street and started to walk along it. It was lined with mews houses, with different-coloured doors. On a different day she would have admired them; she secretly loved these houses when she saw them in London – much more than the looming townhouses, the sort she lived in. But this wasn't a different day. She walked along.

A navy-blue door opened.

"Hello."

It was as if he'd been expecting her.

"Hello," she nodded. Her cheeks flushed and she shuffled. She wasn't used to shuffling. "I wondered if I could buy you back that coffee?"

He smiled, nodded. "Actually, I've just bought a new fancy machine of my own. What about you come in and we try that first?"

She stopped, then nodded, then followed him. She heard the door close behind her and for the first time since she'd arrived in Strawberry Village, she felt safe.

She sat while Greg made the coffee, hearing the machine grinding as the smell of it filled the room. The walls were white, the curtains navy blue and the sunshine shone through. There were some black and white photos framed on the wall, and she could see a small patio with a table and chairs through the French doors.

"This feels more like a holiday cottage," she called.

He leant out of the kitchen. "What were you expecting – a room of gloom?"

Actually, yes, but she didn't say.

He walked out with two white steaming mugs.

"You take it black, right?"

"Do you notice everything?"

Greg laughed. "I'm not some undercover detective, Grace, and this is not a therapy session, just so you know. We are two people who sort of know one another – or rather I know you – having a coffee."

Grace nodded as she sipped her coffee. "This is good."

He sipped his. "It's dead fancy. Lewis made me invest. He's the photographer too." He nodded at the prints.

There was a coffee cup, a view from the bridge and a close-up of a beautiful rose. "They're good," she told him.

"Yes," Greg smiled, "they are." He sipped his coffee again. Behind him was a child's Liverpool kit in a frame on the wall.

"So you're a Liverpool fan?"

"Yes, I am." The silence lingered in the coffee-filled air. "So, how are you finding life in Strawberry Village?"

Grace paused. She could lie and tell him she was fine. She could pretend and she could smile. She could say everything was okay.

"I've got no idea."

A hot tear slid down her cheek.

"It's okay, Grace. It really is."

No, she wanted to tell him. It's not.

"I'm sorry."

"Why are you apologising?"

She'd explained everything that had happened since the Monday when she'd been called into see the board.

"If I'd had the week you'd had, I'd be a wreck. I say you're holding it together remarkably well."

Grace laughed a hollow laugh.

"I'm in my gym gear at eleven-thirty on a Friday morning. I've offended pretty much everyone I've met since I arrived here. My husband, daughter and best friend don't want anything to do with me. I'm hungover and an absolute wreck."

"Well, you're carrying it off nicely – in a true Grace Leven way."

Grace wiped her nose.

"Grace Leven – who even is she?" Grace looked at Greg. "What was I like? When you were at Hi-TV? Please, be honest. Was I rude?"

"Quite the opposite. You gave me a voice."

"I did?"

"I was invited along to a sales meeting as part of my traineeship. You were holding the meeting, talking about the weekly figures. I was supposed to just sit there, and be quiet, but you asked my opinion."

"I did?" Grace repeated.

"You wanted my honest opinion about a show called *Cosy Corners*."

"Ah, the one where they turned tiny corners into wonderful spaces where you want to hang out."

"The very one. It was aimed at the twenty-somethings who'd bought their first flats, spent an absolute fortune on their tiny space and had no money to do anything with it. But I said I thought you were missing a trick for the older market – the forty-fifty-somethings who deep-down didn't really like their big houses and were still crippled by their giant mortgage, and were secretly craving something else."

"That was very insightful." She thought of her own house.

"After that meeting, the producer I'd gone with told me she was impressed. She told the show's editor and a day later I was offered a staff position."

"Which you turned down?"

"I did. But up until then nobody had given me a voice. You, Grace, gave me a voice."

"So I wasn't a complete cow?"

"Not in the slightest. Grace," Greg leant forward, his elbows on his knees. "Perhaps you're kinder than you think you are."

"Then why am I sitting in your office, feeling like a needy child?"

"We are all needy children, Grace." He sat back. "Have you ever wondered if perhaps you just haven't met the right people yet?"

"I'm fifty-three, Greg. I have a job which has taken me around the world. I've met bloody everyone."

She paused.

"I *had* a job."

"Had? You don't know that you don't. There's no point catastrophising."

"But my life is a catastrophe." When he didn't answer, she carried on. "So, is this what therapy is? You leaving pauses for me to fill in, or if I was paying, would we be analysing my childhood?"

"Would it bother you if we did talk about your childhood?"

Grace rolled her eyes. "Oh please. This is exactly why

I've never bothered. I had a great childhood and then my parents died when I was eighteen." She held her hand up as he opened his mouth to speak. "Please, spare me the pity."

Greg looked back at her, but said nothing.

"What? I don't qualify for therapy because I don't want to go over every tiny bit of my past. That's what therapy is, isn't it?"

Greg's eyes stayed on her and she didn't like it. She shuffled, she felt odd – somehow unnerved.

"A little," he said at last, "but we can become too bogged down by the past. I'm more interested in what's happening now."

"Right," she nodded and breathed out. She looked around the room again. She didn't hate what he was saying. "It does feel brighter in here."

"Thank you. It's why I chose these photos. Flowers tend to make people smile; there's always a different perspective," he nodded at the view of the bridge, "and not much can't be solved with a close friend over a good coffee."

Grace sipped hers. "It's good coffee. Your husband has good taste." Whatever this was, she was able to breathe a little more and for that she was grateful.

"Do you have any idea what you will do while you're here?"

Grace shook her head. "None. I started at Hi-TV the day after I graduated. I've never been out of work and I didn't always take all my leave. Since I arrived, I've either offended people or got drunk. I can't seem to do anything else."

She was surprised by her own honesty. "What exactly did you put in this coffee?"

Greg laughed. "Sometimes it's good just to say it as it is – you know; out loud. This is how I feel."

Grace thought for a moment. "I always tell my staff to be direct." She sat back and stretched her legs in front of her. "But that's just it. I have no idea how I feel. I feel numb, as though I'm floating and as if none of this is real. That it's somehow all pointless yet catastrophic at the same time."

"And how long have you felt like this? Since Monday?"

Grace leant forward again. "I don't know."

Greg leant forward also. "Can you think of the last time you felt like yourself?"

She couldn't. Her head was starting to ache again.

"What did you like doing as a child? Can I at least ask that?"

"I thought this wasn't a session." She wanted to leave.

"It's not. I'm just curious."

Grace rubbed her head. "I don't know. It's so long ago."

"There must have been something – anything."

"Writing, I suppose. I liked writing."

"Did you write stories?"

"Sometimes, or I wrote a diary, writing down everything about my day, and I wrote articles too."

"And what did you like about that?"

"Oh, I don't know. I suppose it made sense of everything. I liked writing stories and shaping them in my colourful notebooks." Grace picked up her coffee. "I sound bloody ridiculous."

"No, you don't."

She thought some more. "Sometimes they were about me, sometimes they were about other people. Sometimes they were letters."

"To who?"

"I don't know. I never did know. But my parents would read them."

"And you enjoyed doing it?"

"I suppose, yes."

"Okay." Greg leant forward again. "I'm going to give you some homework."

"But this isn't a session."

He shrugged his shoulders. "Look at it as a taster, on the house – and it's your choice if you want to do this."

"Go on." She was a little curious.

"I want you to write some letters."

"Letters?"

"I want you to write them to yourself – your younger selves."

"But what would I say?"

"That's for you to decide. There's no right or wrong, Grace. Just like when you were a child, you did what your heart told you. Nobody is watching, nobody is judging. You did then what felt right for you. Why don't you do the same now?"

The idea was ridiculous. She'd never do it.

"Let me guess," Greg peered at her. "You're thinking you'll never do it. You're Grace Leven, the CEO. Why would she be writing letters to her five-year-old self? But I'm seeing a Grace Leven who doesn't really know what's happened and how she has ended up here. The only person who has been with you this time, every day since you were born, is you. So only you really know."

"You're good, aren't you?"

Greg shrugged. "Maybe, maybe not."

"Did you ever regret leaving television?"

"Not for a single moment." Greg finished his coffee. "I'm sorry, about your parents."

Grace nodded and stood up. She'd become well-rehearsed at dodging people's pity over the years.

"Thank you and please let me pay for today. What do I owe you?"

"Nothing. I owed you, remember? You helped me get my first job offer."

"Which you turned down."

"That's hardly the point."

"I wasn't always like this, you know. Abrupt. Rude. Unsure. A wreck."

"I wouldn't say you're any of these." Greg stood up and nodded back to the photo of the bridge. "It's all about perception, remember, Grace? Just write those letters, and you might see what I mean."

Chapter Fourteen

Grace: Eric, please ring me.
Grace: Pearl, I'm sorry. Can we try again?
Grace: Polly, will you ever speak to me again?

"Grace." She recognised Jack Jones's voice as she crossed the foyer. "Don't worry; we'll leave you in peace." He walked over from the front desk. "Great news about Iris, by the way," he said under his breath.

She'd forgotten how helpful Iris and Lulu were being to her. She was being rude – again.

"Yes, she really is quite something, as is her father."

"Ah, Bruce? Has he got you painting yet?"

"Not yet."

"He will."

She doubted it.

Jack laughed. "I get it. It makes no sense at first, then suddenly it does. Give it time. Anyway, what I wanted to ask, is would you like to move to our new cottage? You're booked in your room until the weekend, and we've got somebody else going in, but the cottage is available. We weren't sure when it was going to be finished so we haven't advertised it yet. We can move you into it, if you'd like.

Did she like? She didn't know.

"Have a think about it."

She nodded.

"So you've been out running?"

She'd forgotten she was still in her gym wear. She could see from the big grandfather clock behind Jack it was nearly one o'clock and she felt a mess.

"I saw Greg too. Do you know Greg?"

Jack smiled. "We all know Greg. He's great. I knew Peggy very well too. She used to live in the house where he has his practice rooms. It was hard seeing it sold to someone else, I'm not going to lie, but he's done a great job. It would have been harder, I think, to see another family or couple in there, but he's doing work she would have approved of, and that helps."

Grace could see the sadness in his eyes.

"She sounds quite the woman."

"She was," he nodded.

They stood, the two of them, in the bustle of the foyer – the two of them and their sadness. It felt awkward, but at least it felt something.

"If it's okay, I will move to the cottage," Grace said.

A smile returned to Jack's face. "That's great, Grace. I'll tell the staff. Now, if you'll excuse me…" He turned away and then turned back. "You know, there's something magical about Strawberry Village. I've never quite worked out what it is, but it's as though there's always someone here for you the moment you need it."

He smiled and she smiled a small smile too.

"I'm sorry. I haven't really been myself since I've arrived," she called after him.

He stopped. "Grace, you don't have to explain to me; I get it." He turned again. "Oh, and by the way, I've been told to tell you it's darts night at The Strawberry Arms tomorrow night."

"Darts night?"

"Trust me; it's like doing art with Bruce. It makes no sense at first, and then suddenly it does."

Chapter Fifteen

Grace: Eric, message me. Just ring me. Please. Anything? x
Grace: Polly, it would be great to talk x
Grace: Pearl, I'm sorry. Can we try again?

Grace wrapped the blanket around her and finished the contents of her glass. All she could think about was the cold, hard ache which sat in her chest, and she hated it. She felt wired and unnerved. She picked up one of the magazines on the table, and flicked through it, but articles on *'how to get the best out of life when you've gone gluten-free'* and *'why going out is the new staying in'* felt trivial. Everything felt so bloody trivial. What was the point knowing what she was supposed to wear in the summer when she had no life to live?

She turned on the television and hesitated before pouring herself another glass of wine. Just one more wouldn't hurt.

But then she saw the man smiling back at her on the screen, and it was as though the cold ache in her chest started to burn, the buzzing in her ears became louder and all she could do was gulp down the cold liquid.

Wakefield. Christopher bloody Wakefield. It was gameshow night – his chat show was on Saturday. She watched him make the guests laugh as they smiled at him adoringly. He turned to the camera and she knew he had the same effect on the woman bored with her husband asleep next to her at home. His suit was sharp and he was on just the right side of handsome. Not so chiselled that he would alienate, but enough to have the women – and men – around him laughing and feeling like they were his chosen one.

"What about the prostitutes? Are you going to tell them about them? Or the coke? Or the long-running affair with your make-up artist? What does Anne think of that?"

He kept smiling and waving back.

Grace knew his wife, Anne. Not well, but enough from small talk at the events they'd been to over the years – the ones they'd both turned up at out of duty, but were always desperate to leave. She knew enough about Anne to know that she'd given up her own television career as a great producer to raise their two sons. She'd created the perfect home and the perfect family, which fitted his perfect lie.

Hi-TV's lawyers had spent hundreds and hundreds of thousands of pounds on non-disclosure agreements, paying off the women and the witnesses. The photos had been destroyed and the witnesses gagged from talking. The shots of him leaving a hotel with his arms wrapped around a woman who was neither his mistress nor his wife would never see daylight again. He'd been clumsy – or had he? Wasn't that part of it? Men like Wakefield loved the thrill.

There he was, smiling smugly back at her. He was in the

job she'd helped him keep, but now she'd lost hers. She was sitting in a hotel room, broken and alone.

"You bastard," she shouted at him as she threw her glass and it shattered across the floor.

The knock at the door was light.

"Hello?"

"Piss off," she said under her breath as she picked up the shards.

"Hello? Everything okay?"

"Piss. Off," she whispered in a louder voice.

Whoever it was knocked again.

Grace stood up. What was wrong with this place? Did no one have lives of their own? She opened the door and prepared herself to not be a bully as she told the person to sod off.

"It's you?"

She hadn't expected to see the odd-job man, Harvey, at her door.

"Ah good, you're all in one piece."

Grace nodded. "I'm sorry, I dropped my glass."

"Accidents happen."

Grace felt the sting at the back of her eyes. He knew it wasn't an accident and she was grateful for his pretence.

She wiped her face.

"You're working late," she managed.

"That cabinet – I'm obsessed. I'm making it down the hall."

Grace nodded, the tears still stinging.

"Look. I was just going down to the bar for a nightcap

before I head home. If you don't have any plans, would you like to join me?"

She was about to say no, but then she thought of the empty hours that stretched ahead – and drinking alone wasn't doing her any good at all.

"I'm not really dressed." She wrapped the blanket around her.

"That's okay – there's no dress code here."

She couldn't think of another way to say no.

"Okay," she nodded.

"Great, I'll see you down there."

Grace nodded as she closed the door.

A few minutes later she walked into the bar.

She wasn't wearing Prada or any of her work clothes. She'd left her trousers on, which were described as loungewear even though she and the rest of womankind knew they were really pyjamas. But she didn't care. She wanted another drink and at least this way she wasn't drinking alone.

She spotted Harvey lounging back on a sofa, a beer on a table in front of him, and she wanted to run way. She was meeting a man who was not Eric, and she didn't like it. What would Eric say? Then she reminded herself she was being ridiculous: she'd met many men for work drinks over the years.

Although this wasn't work, and she wasn't there as a CEO.

Harvey waved at her, and she decided even she, the woman who was offending most people in Strawberry Village at the moment, couldn't run away at that point.

The waiter Grace recognised as Ollie walked over with a glass of white wine on a tray.

"I can change it if you don't like it, but I told Harvey this is what you tend to order."

"Thank you, Ollie," Grace nodded. "It's perfect." And it was.

"So I see you know the staff. You'll be one of the locals before you know it." Harvey stood up and raised his eyebrows.

Grace didn't answer as she sat down. She wasn't even supposed to be in this world, she was supposed to be in hers.

"I've told the desk by the way. They'll pop in and clear up the glass." Harvey sat back down and picked up his own beer.

Grace was about to protest, but felt too exhausted. "Thank you," she smiled and picked up her wine too.

"Cheers." She raised her glass and he raised his. She sipped her wine, and it felt better to drink down in the lounge at least.

"So do you always come in for a drink after work?" She tried to muster some of her CEO small-talk. She'd been good at that, hadn't she?

"Not always. Sometimes. It depends on the day I've had."

Grace wondered how building cabinets could ever be stressful? She caught herself looking at him. His thick sandy hair flicked above the collar of his t-shirt. He was big, broad and so different to Eric. His jeans were covered in paint, while Eric would never wear jeans covered in paint. Mainly because Eric never painted or did anything around the house, even when they'd had no money.

What Really Happened To Me?

Grace decided it was best she didn't think of Eric. "So how was your day today?" she asked. "How is the cabinet?"

"The cabinet is frustrating; I cannot lie. I had to re-order wood, as one of my measurements was out. But I got a couple of hours in this evening and at least I've made a start. It's that part that always gets me, the starting. But then once I'm off, I'm off.

Grace nodded. "I get it."

"You do?"

"Walking into a meeting – that moment you don't know what you're going to find or who you're going to need to be." She surprised herself by saying this out loud.

He smiled and nodded.

"Exactly. So we all do it?"

Grace nodded and sipped her wine again. She noticed he hadn't asked her what she did for a living.

"Have you always been a carpenter?"

He nodded. "My father taught me. It's been in me for as long as I can remember. A day is not a day unless I've attempted to build at least something."

"And you've worked here since it opened?"

He nodded again. "I've known Jack for a long time now. I've been involved in all his hotels."

Grace looked around – the soft lighting, the pink blossom wallpaper, the jazz playing in the background. All the tables were taken, and a low hum of people chatting settled in the air.

"It's a wonderful place."

"He has a magic touch," Harvey agreed as he crossed his foot over his knee. She looked around again. She couldn't imagine the odd-job person having a drink like this in most places. Stop, she told herself. She was being rude.

"So, what's your passion, Grace?"

She shook her head. "I don't have one."

"What? We all have a passion of some sort."

She shrugged, "Then, my job, I suppose."

"Something away from work."

He still hadn't asked what she did for a living. She wasn't sure if she was irritated or relieved.

"I always work; that's what I do. Well, apart from now."

He sipped his beer and smiled at her.

"What's so funny?" She felt her cheeks go hot. Why was she was sitting there blushing with the odd-job man?

"What did you like to do as a child?"

"It's funny, as you're the second person to ask me this. I used to like to write stories in little books, and read, I suppose."

"And what else?"

Grace wondered if enough time had passed for her to excuse herself.

"Harvey. Grace." A familiar voice interrupted them and Grace turned to see Jack Jones walking into the bar. "I didn't know you two knew one another."

"We don't," they said together.

Jack smiled.

"Are you going to join us?" Harvey asked.

"I'd love to, but I'm already late meeting Iris."

Grace nodded. She knew Iris had been busy that day planning her London trip. "Thank her again for me, will you please?"

"Of course," Jack nodded.

"He's here for me," Harvey told her. "I've got those papers for you; they're in reception." Harvey stood up and walked through to the foyer.

"It's good to see you enjoying yourself."

Grace blushed again. "I'm hardly…" she stopped herself; she was going to be rude. Again. "Your hotel is very welcoming, Jack. Even your odd-job man looks after the guests."

Jack laughed. "Is that what he said? That he's the odd-job man?" He shook his head.

Grace picked up her wine. "Well, what does he do if he isn't?"

Jack laughed.

"Harvey built this hotel. Well, gutted the building and re-built it, and he built all my others too. Or rather, he and his company did."

Grace choked on her wine just at the moment Harvey returned. "Here you are, as requested. What?"

Jack laughed as Grace wiped her chin.

"Nothing, nothing at all," Jack smiled. "Now, I really must be off. And Grace, we can move you into the cottage in the morning." Then after a couple of waves to other guests he was gone.

"I think I owe you an apology."

"Me? However could you have offended me?" Harvey sat back down.

"I thought you were the odd-job man around here."

"Well," he picked up his beer. "I am. What's wrong with that?"

"But Jack said your company built all his hotels."

Harvey smiled and nodded. "Yes, I did, or rather most of my staff did."

"I'm confused."

Harvey sat forward and leant his arms on his knees. "It's a bit like we were saying before. Carpentry is my passion and I've never wanted to let it go. Jack knows this and he's decent enough to let me potter around here when I can."

"So you come in here to make a cabinet, but run a large company too?"

"Yes. Although it's not that large."

"How large is not large?"

Harvey finished his beer. "I think we've got around one hundred staff now."

"One hundred?"

"Actually, one hundred and forty-two."

"That doesn't sound not…not large."

Harvey laughed.

"So, what about you, if you don't mind me asking?"

"What do you mean, what about me?"

"How are you enjoying your time here in Strawberry Village?"

"Well, you know I fell flat on my face in mud, and you heard me break a glass in my room earlier."

"A tough time?"

"You could say that."

Harvey sipped his beer. "We all have them, Grace, and they're not pretty. But this is the beauty of what Jack creates here. Here in Strawberry House you're not alone."

"I'm coming to discover that."

Grace sat back and breathed out.

"What?" Harvey asked.

"It feels good to be surprised. I haven't felt surprised for a long time."

"Well, you're lucky. I'm constantly shocked – especially by my bills."

Grace smiled. "Thank you, Harvey."

"For what?"

"For taking my mind off me."

Harvey picked up his empty glass. "It's my pleasure. Now, could I interest you in another?"

Grace nodded. "Yes, thank you. You could."

Chapter Sixteen

Grace: Eric are you ever going to talk to me again? x
Grace: Pearl, please darling, can we speak again? I'm so sorry. I don't know what else I can say. Hope trip is going well. x

"So, the question is, who is your ideal reader?"

Grace watched Lulu as she thought about the question. "I'm already concerned you have to think about this."

"One with lots of money?" Lulu tried to smile.

Grace looked around the empty office again. She could almost smell the history of *The Strawberry Times*. She was certain there was once a buzz, a hubbub – the sound of typewriters and phones ringing. Instead, now, a quiet sadness filled the air.

Still, Grace felt more uplifted than she'd done since she'd arrived in Strawberry Village. She'd slept well after her two glasses of wine with Harvey, and when she'd woken that morning, she messaged Lulu. Now, with something to do alongside her room change, her day had felt almost full.

As the sun crept down behind the Georgian square, she

looked out of the large window. It was peaceful here – more soul than the view from the tower she was used to working in. Here she could see people and they looked like people – instead of the dots she spotted rushing around beneath her office.

It was quiet and somehow soothing too, and they sat, just the two of them at an empty desk.

"I know the Strawberry House Committee read it."

"And they are?"

"Penelope Fanshaw, Eileen Jenkins, Kenneth Bigsby, Betty Bishop; the list goes on."

"And do you know why they're so loyal to *The Strawberry Times*?"

"They love it here." Lulu nodded towards the square outside. "This is their home and *The Strawberry Times* is part of it. Plus, they eat at the restaurants which advertise with us. "It's not just them, there are lots of people who read it around Strawberry Village, and in other neighbourhoods nearby, but, well…"

"You can say it. As they get older…"

Lulu nodded. "There's no younger audience coming in."

"And you're print as well as online."

"Yes, but the online isn't doing that well. The print and the most loyal of advertisers, like The Strawberry Arms, Dave, Strawberry House – they're who are keeping us afloat."

"I see," Grace said. "So you don't know your ideal reader. You just have a few die-hard readers."

Lulu sat up. "Well, I wouldn't say that."

Grace raised her hand. "Look, you're doing a wonderful job, I can see this. But I'm not going to be of any help if I sit here and only tell you what a wonderful job you're doing, without working out the problem. We need to establish the problem to be able to solve it. Have you any idea who your ideal reader should be?"

"Only one who buys the paper."

"Lulu." Grace raised an eyebrow.

"I know, you think I'm a complete amateur." Lulu sighed as she put her pen down.

"Believe me," Grace leant forward and touched Lulu on the arm, "I've seen people in charge of budgets that would make your eyes water, and they have no idea who their ideal reader is, or what one is."

Lulu smiled a small smile. "Thank you for not making me feel stupid."

"You're not stupid. Look at how you and Iris jumped to help me. I felt stupid, but you two made my misery your mission. That's quite something. You've been true friends."

"We saw Greg, by the way. He told us you were a great boss, he told us how you helped him without even knowing it. You're not a bully, Grace."

It was Grace's turn to smile a small smile now. "We'll see what Iris finds, shall we?"

She looked at her watch. It was five-thirty. Even in the midst of her misery, there was something she enjoyed about having an evening. In her old life, she'd be in the office until at least eight, or if she wasn't, she'd be going to some sort of working dinner.

"I tell you what, what about I buy us a drink and we brainstorm who we think we're selling to?"

"Deal," Lulu smiled. "Only I'll buy. It's the least I can do."

"Darling, I've just seen last month's figures. These are definitely on me."

What Really Happened To Me?

The jazz played in the background of the lounge in the bar at Strawberry House. The lamps were lit and most of the sofas were full.

"I do love this bar." Grace sat back in her chair.

"Jack knows what he's doing." Lulu sat back too.

Grace picked up an olive. "And does he know who his ideal customer is?"

"Jack Jones knows everything. He knows who they are, where they work, what they want and how they're feeling before they've even worked out how they're feeling. The man's a genius."

Ollie placed two glasses of wine down.

"Thank you, Ollie."

"Ms Leven." Ollie smiled and walked off.

"I used to work for Jack as his assistant before I took over the paper. I went to school with Jack. My dad was the housemaster so we've known each other for a long time."

"And yet his knowledge of business hasn't rubbed off on your work?"

Lulu picked up her glass. "I suppose I didn't equate his hotels with the tiny *Strawberry Times*."

Grace picked up her own glass. "But I'm guessing these hotels were once a tiny idea too. His ideal customer was the same then as it is now."

"I suppose. I hadn't looked at it like that before."

"Business is business, whichever industry you're in."

"You see, you're good." Lulu held her glass up. "Cheers."

Grace laughed. "It's just common sense." She clinked her glass and took a sip. "You're more than capable."

"Did you mean what you said earlier? That Iris and I were your friends?"

Grace put her glass down. "I did. I have Polly, as you know, but she's not allowed to talk to me because of everything that's going on. But other than that," Grace's voice trailed off. It was a sorry state of affairs. "I'm the classic 'spent-all-my-time-at-work-and-missed-out-on-everything-else' woman. Polly was my assistant before she rose through the ranks. So it makes perfect sense she became my one and only friend."

"Quality not quantity." Lulu sipped her wine again.

"I'm sure you've got lots of friends?"

"Me?" Lulu laughed. "At least you've got the job, the marriage and a daughter as an excuse. I don't have any of those and I've hardly any friends. Well, Jack, but he's more like a brother. And now Iris. But until I met Iris, I wasn't very good at holding on to girlfriends either."

"Quality not quantity." Grace raised her glass

"Well, I'll drink to that." Lulu chinked hers.

"So, perhaps we should start there. For your ideal reader," Grace said.

"Someone who has no friends?"

"Someone who's looking for something. Community. Friendship. Bonding. You don't even have to live in Strawberry Village to want to spend time here. Look at me. I saw Jack's advert in London and it's the sole reason why I came here."

"Is that true? What was so good about the advert?"

"Well, as you know, I'd just lost everything, and when it promised I'd leave feeling like myself again, I thought that's where I need to be."

"Interesting." Lulu pulled her notebook from her bag.

"So, lonely, lost and unsure what to do next. Lost everything," she wrote down.

"I don't think we have to expect everyone to be quite as down and out as me."

Lulu laughed as she crossed out *'lost everything'*.

"But I do think a lot of women are feeling lost," Grace said. "So you may want to write that down."

"Done." Lulu sat back. "I feel lost all the time, so it's got nothing to do with age. Why are we all feeling so lost?"

"How old are you, Lulu?"

"Twenty-nine."

"But you're not lost. You're exactly where you're supposed to be. You don't want everything to be sorted at twenty-nine. Sometimes it's all about perspective."

"I suppose," Lulu thought for a moment. "But it's bloody exhausting."

"Yes, it is," Grace agreed.

"So, what was it like having the job, house, marriage and family?"

Grace thought for a moment. "You know, you'd think it would feel as if you'd arrived somewhere – like a destination. But," she shook her head, "I never once felt like that. It was always as if there was something I was missing, somewhere else I should be."

"Even when your photo was taken for the magazine?"

"Especially then. I didn't even look like me."

"Who knew? So we all think someone else has it all worked out."

"I'm yet to find the person who has," Grace said, "and I've met many people who've made careers out of convincing other people they have."

"Really, will you tell all?"

"Never," Grace laughed. "But you know not to believe everything you see."

"That I know, but somehow we get fooled, don't we?"

"Yes, we do," Grace agreed and sat back in the armchair. "This is nice. I haven't felt like this in a long time, even though my life is a complete mess."

"Felt like what?" Lulu asked.

"I don't know. Relaxed, I suppose, or maybe if not relaxed then at least a bit less uptight."

"Ah, well, there you are: the magic of Strawberry House is working."

"Perhaps it is."

Grace didn't add that perhaps writing letters to her younger self had made her feel a little different. Lighter, was it? She wasn't sure.

"Why did you work in television?" Lulu asked. The question jolted Grace back to the present, "if you don't mind me asking?"

"I don't," Grace said. "I never set out to work in television. I always loved writing as a child, but then I studied law at university. The long essays appealed and I suppose I thought being a lawyer was a proper job. But then Hi-TV was at one of those recruitment days they have for graduates, and I went to the stand. I'd never considered I could work in television and the woman sitting behind the desk asked me 'why ever not?' So, I went for an interview and I got a place on the trainee scheme, and the rest, they say, is history."

"So you don't regret not being a lawyer?"

Grace thought back to the first moment she'd walked through the revolving doors of Hi-TV. "I thought it was the most glamorous world I'd ever walked into. The buzz, the celebrities. Not knowing who you might bump into in the lift. I never thought it would be possible for someone like me to work somewhere like that."

It had been a long time since Grace had thought about that first day. She looked at Lulu, who was watching her.

"Sorry, I'm being nostalgic."

"Sorry? I was just thinking how incredible it is. You ended up running the company."

"Well, CEO."

"Isn't that running it?"

I suppose in some ways it is." Grace laughed. "Also, Eric, my husband, was very happy for me to work in television," she said, without thinking about it. She thought back to him then, how excited he'd been. He'd always been so encouraging of her career, hadn't he?

"What does he do?"

"He worked in marketing, but when we had Pearl, he was the one who stayed at home."

"You've just gone up in my estimation even more."

Grace shuffled; she was starting to feel uncomfortable again. She didn't belong on any pedestal – not any more. "And why's that?"

"You were trailblazing."

Grace shook her head. "Believe me, it's not as simple as it seems."

Would Lulu still be as impressed if she knew Grace's darling Eric hadn't replied to a single one of her messages?

"The point is, you've shown there is a different way. Just like in the article. Whatever has happened, it doesn't change anything. You have a huge career, a husband and a daughter."

"If only the midlife murder hadn't happened."

Lulu started to laugh. "The midlife murder. That's brilliant."

Grace smiled. "But we're digressing – we're here to discuss your ideal reader."

"It sounds like you know her well. Someone who is lost, who is looking for answers and is wondering if there's been a midlife murder?" Lulu put her glass down. "Can I ask you a question? And you need to be honest with me."

"Go on."

"If you lived here, would you read *The Strawberry Times?*"

Grace thought for a few moments. "Honestly, if I lived here, I would wonder what it was. What is it, really? Is it a local paper telling me what's on? Does it set an agenda for Strawberry Village? Is it online, appealing to people living here, or are you trying to achieve a further reach?"

Lulu picked up her pen and wrote everything down, then looked up.

"A further reach would be better, wouldn't it?"

"Well, that depends. You have a thriving community here. Why wouldn't you want to tap into that? But what you could do is grow your online audience with something which has a further appeal to your ideal reader, something not just about Strawberry Village. More like the themes we just said – loneliness, lost, not knowing who she is."

"Like a column?"

"Perhaps."

Lulu sipped her wine and thought some more. "What about you?"

"What about me?"

"What about if you wrote the column?"

"Me? Why would I write a column?" Grace picked up her glass.

"You just said you used to like writing, and you're the one who came up with the brilliant title – Midlife Murders."

What Really Happened To Me?

Grace choked a little on her wine. "I'm used to handing my ideas over, not creating them."

"Well?" Lulu leant forward. "Perhaps it's time you didn't."

Grace paused. She didn't hate the idea – and this would be a way of helping Lulu while Iris was in London helping her.

"I don't think anyone would want to hear from a suspended CEO." She lowered her voice.

"But if it was anonymous? Nobody would have to know it was you."

Grace laughed. No, it was a ridiculous idea.

"I feel very flattered that you think I could do it, but…"

"At least say you'll think about it."

Grace thought for a moment. "I'll agree to think about it, if you agree to think more about your ideal reader. I want you to write down everything you know about her and then we can find her."

"This is hard, Grace." Lulu sighed.

"Learning something new is always hard, but we can work it out."

"You said *we*."

"Yes, I did." Grace smiled again and sat back. The warmth of the lounge wrapped around her again. It felt good.

"Agreed," Lulu said. "Now, can I persuade you to come to darts night at The Strawberry Arms?"

"Ah, yes, the infamous darts night."

"Twice a week at The Strawberry Arms. Three times, if you're lucky on a Saturday night."

Grace was about to say no.

"*We* can look at it as though it's research if you'd rather?

The whole of the Strawberry House Committee will be there. You can at least see the starting point."

Grace was about to come up with an excuse before she realised that she would have nothing else to do. Except perhaps go up to her room and drink herself into another stupor?

"I've never played darts."

"Well, now is your chance. If Strawberry House is all about feeling like yourself again, perhaps you've always had a deep-down hankering to play darts?"

"I don't think I've ever wanted to play darts."

"But how do you know if you haven't tried? Learning something new is always hard, remember?"

Grace laughed. "I can't argue with that."

"However bad you are, I guarantee you'll have a better shot than most of them. One word of advice: don't stand by the board."

Chapter Seventeen

Grace: Please Eric, just one phone call x
Grace: Darling Pearl, tell me when's a good time and I'll call you x

Grace was just about to follow Lulu into The Strawberry Arms when her phone rang. Her heart skipped a beat.

Eric?

She looked at the screen.

"It's Iris," she said out loud as her heart sank. Then reminded herself how much Iris was helping her. She must stop being so selfish and rude.

"Iris? How is life in London?"

"Life in London is okay," Iris said, her voice faltering.

"Just okay?"

"Everyone's being rather guarded, shall we say?"

Grace nodded into the phone. "That makes sense. Don't speak with the press, unless it's to maintain the party line. Everything is great. This is a fair and wonderful company. I wouldn't want to work anywhere else."

"You got the brief then?" Iris asked.

"Darling, I wrote the brief," Grace sighed. "What about Polly? Is she also sticking to the brief?" Grace pushed aside the guilt she felt that they were using Polly. She reminded herself Iris was a great writer and a profile like this in a Sunday magazine would hugely benefit her friend, even if it hadn't in her own case.

Especially if she was never going back.

A wave of nausea rushed over her and she pushed this thought aside. Of course she was going back. She stood up straight. Enough of this; she was wallowing again.

"I haven't spent quite as much time with Polly as I'd hoped," Iris said. "Aside from the meetings, she spends most lunchtimes and evenings with her boyfriend."

Grace stood still. "Polly doesn't have a boyfriend."

"Well, that's who she says she's with every time I suggest we have lunch or drinks."

"That doesn't make any sense. She's been single for years."

"Perhaps it's someone new?"

"Perhaps." The sickness rose in Grace even more. She was becoming more and more disconnected from her life every day. What else was she missing out on?

"Grace?"

"Iris, yes. Apologies – and thank you, you're doing a great job, I'm just sorry it's a bit slow."

"Don't be. Jack and I are here and we're having a wonderful time. Your office is incredible, by the way."

"It's still empty then?"

"Yes. I only saw it when I went up there with Polly when she spoke with Matilda."

"Right." Grace nodded. Polly and Matilda had grown to know each other over the years; they were just catching up. At least some things were still the same.

"Thank you, Iris. I do appreciate it."

"I'll find something."

"I'm sure you will."

Grace put her phone in her pocket. She wanted to go to the darts evening even less now. She turned to walk back towards Strawberry House.

The door opened and Lulu's head poked out. "Don't even think about it, Grace Leven. I've put your name down; you're officially in the team."

Grace: Boyfriend? Are the rumours true Polly? X

Grace was just about to send the message as she stood at the bar when a tall man bumped into her – or rather his back did.

"I'm so sorry," a familiar voice said. "Did my beer get you?"

"Harvey."

He laughed, his eyes crinkled and his warmth was welcoming. "We really have to stop making a habit of this. Here, let me buy you a drink."

Grace looked around. Not only was her mind now buzzing with thoughts of Polly moving on, she felt even more out of place. Everyone was dressed in t-shirts and jeans, while she was wearing the same Sezane suit she'd worn to meet Lulu earlier.

"Yes, we do," she said. "I mean about the bumping, and it's okay, I'm buying for Lulu too." Grace felt hot and flustered and wanted to leave.

"It's no problem; I owe her." Harvey nodded at the barman, while Grace looked around the packed pub. To say she was out of her comfort zone was an understatement. She couldn't remember ever going to her local pub at home; she was always at bars or restaurants, or more likely a private club. It was just after seven in the evening. She'd never be home at this time, even if there was a place like this nearby.

Harvey passed a glass of wine to Lulu, who was now in deep conversation with a woman Grace didn't recognise."

"So they got you to darts night?"

"I'm sorry." She couldn't concentrate.

"There's a small courtyard out the back. It's hot and very loud in here – would you like a bit of fresh air?"

Grace was about to say no but felt too exhausted to pretend. "Yes, Harvey. Thank you," she nodded and followed him out.

They sat down on a wooden corner seat. It was cold, dark and lit with fairy lights.

"Thank you." Grace breathed out a little.

"There's no need to keep thanking me, Grace." Harvey sat back too.

"Can I ask you a question?"

"Please do."

"Do you ever feel like your whole life is spiralling out of control?"

He laughed as he sipped his pint. "Always. Every single day. It's part of the daily routine when you have your own building company. But I'm guessing you mean something else." He put his pint down.

"I'm sorry." Grace felt needy, out of place and desperate. This was not who she was supposed to be.

"Don't be sorry. I understand. When my wife died, I had no idea who I was. I didn't know what I wanted and I didn't know how to live; I didn't have a clue about anything. I didn't even know if I wanted to live."

His words jolted Grace back to the moment. "I'm sorry."

"Again, there's nothing for you to be sorry about. But, thank you." He smiled his warm smile at her. "Look, I'm not here to talk about my woes, but what I'm saying is, it's okay not to know; it's easier to accept the feeling than to fight it. Fighting it just makes you feel even more awful."

"Is that what you think? That I feel awful?"

Harvey held his hands up. "I'm not here to pry either, but when you arrived at the hotel, you had a cut hand. The next day you walked in covered in mud, and then yesterday…"

"You heard me smashing a glass and shouting at a television." Grace nodded.

"I'm putting two and two together and I'm not the best at maths, but I would suggest you're not having the best of times."

Grace was about to deny it, but what was the point? Her own denial was exhausting her.

"Everything in my life is out of control. I've lost my job, I've lost my husband, my daughter won't talk to me and now my one and only friend has a boyfriend I didn't even know about. Plus, I'm wearing an expensive suit, which is hot, uncomfortable and I feel completely out of place." Grace felt the hot sting of tears at the back of her eyes.

"And on top of all that, you've got to play darts."

Grace laughed. "Yes, Harvey. On top of all that I've got to play bloody darts."

"Oh Grace, it's official: you're in the land of not-a-great-place." Harvey laughed too.

She paused and thought for a moment. "Yes," she laughed. "I am, and hot too, in a bloody stupid designer suit."

She started to laugh and so did Harvey. She laughed harder than she could remember laughing for weeks, maybe months. She laughed so much her insides started to hurt.

The door to the courtyard flew open and the woman Lulu had been talking to earlier appeared.

"Excuse me you two, darts are no laughing matter. You're being called and you're needed, *now*." She peered down at them.

Grace looked at Harvey as the woman waited for them to join her. The two of them started to laugh more and the woman rolled her eyes, as they stood up and went back inside.

When they got to the darts board, the woman passed Grace three darts. "I'd like to remind you, this is serious business."

"Yes, of course. Thank you," Grace said as she took off her jacket. Then her eyes met with Harvey as she took her spot.

Grace managed to hit the board and scored a grand total of forty-three. It was her best achievement in days.

"Grace, I'd like you to meet Penelope Fanshaw. Penelope Fanshaw, I'd like you to meet Grace Leven." Lulu introduced Grace officially to the woman who'd marched them inside.

"Word has it you're big in the television world." Penelope peered at her again.

"I wouldn't say big exactly."

Lulu handed Grace another glass of wine. "You'll need it," she mouthed and nodded at Penelope.

"CEO of Hi-TV – that's fairly large in anyone's books."

"Well, I suppose it is." The woman had been doing her homework.

"And you are the woman who *has it all*, are you not?"

"Sorry," Lulu mouthed.

Grace had for a moment forgotten about the article. It felt a lifetime ago.

"Well, everything isn't always as it seems." There was something about the woman which bothered Grace. Was it her tone or the look in her eye? A woman like this wouldn't normally bother Grace. But here, hot and uncomfortable still, she felt unarmed.

"And your daughter, where is she?"

"My daughter?"

"The one you spoke about in your feature. I'm only repeating what was said there."

"Yes, of course." Grace nodded. She wished the woman would go away. "Pearl is on a gap year; she's travelling. I think she's in South Africa now."

"Think?" Penelope raised her eyebrows.

"Yes. Well we haven't spoken in a couple of days." Grace looked at Lulu, who had returned to her side.

"I suppose a full-time working mother encourages independence."

"Penelope," Lulu said with a warning tone.

"Excuse me?" Grace said. She tried to keep her poise as she got ready to defend. She'd batted away comments like these throughout her career – normally with ease – but tonight this woman and her words were ruffling her and she didn't like it. Turn it back to them; she knew what to do.

"Do you have children?"

"Yes, I do, and I speak to them every day."

Lulu snorted into her drink as Harvey joined them.

"Everything okay here, ladies?"

"Isn't that a little unhealthy, to have such a rein on grown-ups?"

"I'm sorry?" Penelope took a step back.

"I just wonder how healthy that is?"

"I can assure you my children are perfectly healthy."

"If you describe completely mollycoddled as healthy," Lulu said under her breath.

"Grace and Lulu, can I speak with you please?" Harvey pulled them both away. "We need a team tactics talk." He nodded at Penelope and then led them through the crowd. "Have you been Fanshaw-ed?" he asked, when they had reached a clear spot where Bruce was standing.

"I'm sorry, I should have warned you," Lulu said.

"I shouldn't have bitten. I've had far worse over the years." Grace thought for a moment. "Is Fanshaw-ed actually a thing?"

"Not just Fanshaw-ed, but Penelope Fanshaw-ed."

"What's that?" Bruce turned around. "Don't tell me Grace has been Fanshaw-ed?"

"Well and truly," Lulu said.

Bruce raised his pint to her. "Well, Grace Leven, it's official: once you've been Penelope Fanshaw-ed, you're truly one of us."

"To Grace Leven." Harvey raised his glass and smiled at her, his eyes warm.

"To Grace Leven." Lulu raised her glass and so did Bruce. "Welcome to Strawberry Village."

"Thank you," Grace nodded.

"And don't think we're going to let you run away any time yet," Harvey smiled. Grace smiled back, hoping it would hide her fears that not only was she unravelling, but she was becoming reliant on a group of strangers she'd only just met.

An hour later they'd left the pub and Lulu and Harvey were walking with her back to her hotel.

"It's on my way home," Lulu said.

"And mine," Harvey agreed.

"I thought you lived over the bridge." Grace looked at Harvey, but then her phone rang, making her jump. Her heart leapt when she saw it was Polly.

"I'm sorry – I need to take this."

"Of course." Lulu linked arms with Harvey as they walked ahead of her.

"Polly. It's so good to hear from you." Grace was aware she'd drunk a lot of wine, and her voice was slurring, but she didn't care.

"I'm sorry darling, I can't stay for long."

Grace breathed out. The relief of hearing her friend's voice, something from her old life – just anything – was wonderful. "It's okay. I understand. It's just, so much has happened."

"So, what's this, you've heard I've got a boyfriend?"

Grace stopped walking. Polly's tone was sharp. Polly's tone was never sharp with her.

"Oh, you know how the rumour mill works."

"Actually, I don't. Who's saying what about my love life, and what business is it of theirs?"

Grace had to think; the wine wasn't helping. Why did she keep drinking so much wine?

"It's Leonard," she tried. "You know how he loves to gossip."

There was a pause on the other end of the phone. Polly had known Leonard through Grace for a long time; it was plausible at least.

"Well, Leonard should mind his own bloody business."

"So, is it true? Do you have a boyfriend?"

Another pause.

"Polly, I hate us having secrets."

"It's not a secret. It's just, well, private."

"This is me, Polly." Grace heard the desperation in her voice and she hated it.

"Well, yes, I have just started seeing someone. I didn't want to tell you about it as you're having such a terrible time. I didn't want to rub it in."

Grace sat on the wall outside the hotel.

"Oh, darling Polly, I'm always happy for you," Grace said. She hoped her friend would soften. She missed her friend.

"Look, I must go. I'm never convinced these phones aren't bugged, and if they knew I was speaking to you…"

Grace sat up. "Right."

There was another pause. "How are you?"

Grace looked at Harvey and Lulu standing at the entrance of the hotel. They waved and she waved back. "Oh, I don't know Polly. It's all so…"

"Sweetheart, look, I really must go. Hang on in there; it'll all sort itself out. Stay where you are and we'll speak soon." And before Grace could say another word, Polly was gone.

Chapter Eighteen

Grace: Please Eric. Please x
Grace: I love you Pearl x

When Grace opened her eyes the next morning, it took her a moment to work out where she was. The staff had moved her things to the cottage – something she hadn't paid much attention to the night before. Her mind had been too busy going over and over the conversation with Polly. What had happened? What was going on? She'd been shown her new room, but she hadn't really cared. She'd climbed into bed and had stared at the ceiling, her thoughts still going round and round before she drifted off to sleep.

Now, as she looked around, she was surprised, in a pleasant way. The bedroom was decorated in the same pale pinks and floral wallpaper as the hotel room. There was also a beautiful cream armchair, which, when she looked, also had tiny strawberries dotted all over it. It was tasteful, playful, and made her smile, despite her heavy mood. She opened a white door to discover a bathroom, smaller than the last, but still beautiful. A walk-through shower, roll-top bath, white scrubbed planks on the floor.

She looked out of the window at a beautiful walled garden. The grass was well kept and daffodils filled the beds.

The smell of fresh paint told her how new it all was, and as she walked down the stairs to the small lounge, she breathed a little sigh. A small pale pink sofa, a matching chair with a footstool, a television and a cabinet filled with books.

Had Harvey built the cabinet? she wondered.

She walked through to the small kitchen, where she saw a coffee machine. She took a pod which was by its side, and looked around for a mug. The cupboards were filled with white china cups and plates. There was a small basket of biscuits, jams, marmalade and different teas. She opened the French doors, which took her to a small courtyard with a table and two chairs. The cool March air hit her, but it felt good, as though she could breathe.

When she walked back into the lounge with her coffee, she saw for the first time a beautiful basket of orchids. Propped up against it was a card with her name on.

Dear Grace, we hope you enjoy Strawberry Cottage and it helps you feel like yourself again. Jack & The Staff of Strawberry House.

She wrapped her hands around the coffee mug, and breathed in the rich smell. Sitting down on the small sofa, she noticed how a tiny part of her felt a little better. For a brief few moments, she hadn't thought about Eric, Polly or anything else.

What Really Happened To Me?

An hour or so later, as she returned from her run a voice called out.

"I was hoping I'd see you."

"Harvey. Have you recovered from our win last night?"

"You know better than to ask questions like that, Grace Leven." He was carrying planks of wood. "How would it be humanely possible to recover from such a victory? It'll take weeks if not months."

Grace laughed. It felt good to laugh.

"I was hoping to see you," she said.

He put the wood down. "You were?"

"I wanted to apologise about last night. My friend Polly called and I was so distracted, I didn't even thank you for an enjoyable evening."

He shook his head. "It doesn't matter; you've got a lot on your mind. Still, if you describe the local darts night as enjoyable…well, this is worth noting. I think I'll have to get Lu to make it breaking news in *The Strawberry Times*."

Grace laughed again.

"It's good to see you looking…well, brighter." He smiled his warm smile at her.

"I've moved to the cottage; it's beautiful."

"Ah, yes, the cottage. We've all got a soft spot for it."

"I take it you were involved in the designing of it."

"Not so much designing. I'm just told what to do – as long as that bookcase stays upright."

"So is it a Harvey original? I did wonder."

"Indeed it is."

Grace nodded, impressed. She was about to say goodbye when he spoke again.

"Look, this might sound silly, and I don't know what you've planned today, but I've got to go out to see a site. It's in Somerset, and I wondered if you'd like to come with me? Have a change of scene, perhaps?"

Grace was about to say no, then thought about what she had planned for the day, which was the exact sum of nothing, unless she counted more waiting for calls from Eric, Pearl and Leonard, which would no doubt never come.

"Okay," she said.

"Great." Harvey looked surprised for an instant and then nodded. "It will be lovely to have some company. Shall I see you back here in an hour?"

"I'll be here." She waved as she returned to Strawberry Cottage.

Just over an hour later she climbed into Harvey's car.

"Coffee?" He held out a tray with two cups. "From Dave's Deli. And the latest offerings from his magnificent oven. He nodded at a paper bag on sitting on it. "Today's special is pain au chocolat. He hoped he could tempt you; they're still warm."

Grace laughed. "This is quite the service."

"We thought you were used to the finer ways of travel."

"We?"

"Dave and I."

Grace took the coffee and sipped it. It was black, as she'd ordered in Dave's before.

"Do all Strawberry House guests get this treatment?"

"Not all; only the VIPs." Harvey laughed.

Grace looked around her. It was a new BMW four-by-four with leather seats. "This is a smart car."

"It's one of the company's. I still like an old van if I'm honest, but I thought you'd be more comfortable in this."

"It's very thoughtful of you."

"So, I can't tempt you with one of Dave's delights? They're still warm, you know." He waved the bag in front of her.

Grace shook her head. "I've not eaten carbs, in well…" she couldn't remember when.

Harvey laughed. "I can imagine the world of television is like that. A lot of hungry people not eating very much."

Grace nodded. "How very insightful. So, where are we going?"

"We're off to a little village in Somerset where there's an old family home which Jack is thinking he might buy. He wants me to have another look to see what's involved."

"Do you only work with Jack?"

"Not officially, but I work with him most of the time now."

"How did you meet him?"

"I know him through my son, Josh. He went to school with Jack, so I've known him since he was a boy. It was only when he was older and he bought his own place that I started working with him."

"Have you worked on all his hotels?"

Harvey nodded and sipped his coffee. "All of them. Cornwall, Bamburgh, Paris, Antigua."

"Antigua must have been good."

Harvey nodded. It wasn't quite the reaction she'd expected, but then again what did she know? She didn't know anything at the moment. She sat back in her seat and looked out of the window.

"So, have you been to Somerset?"

"Have I been to Somerset?" Grace thought. It often

took her a moment to think where she had and hadn't been. She'd travelled so much with her job, she'd arrive, have whatever meeting it was, then leave. She could barely remember any of the places.

"I think I've been to a private member club in Somerset. Turville House? That was the last one."

"Ah yes, Turville House, I know it well."

"I can't imagine you enjoy places like Turville House."

"And why's that?"

Grace blushed. "Sorry, I'm being rude again."

"No, you're absolutely right. I can't stand pretentious places."

Grace looked around the car again and glanced at Harvey. He was dressed in a smart blue shirt and trousers – so different from the odd-job man she thought he was when she arrived.

"I've been really rude to you, and I'm sorry – for thinking you were the odd-job man at Strawberry House."

"And we've been through this: there's nothing rude about it at all. I *am* the odd-job man – well, between projects, and it's my favourite job of all."

"It is?"

Harvey nodded. "Yes, it is."

"That's wonderful." Grace looked out of the window. They'd left the city now and the busy streets had morphed into open countryside. She stared out onto the endless fields, but an image of her father in his shed came into her mind. The sound of his hammer late at night, her mother walking out in her nightgown telling him it was time to go to bed.

He'd been so happy and content pottering in that shed.

"Perhaps you don't have to be sorry all the time." Harvey interrupted her thoughts.

"Sorry is all I seem to be at the moment." Then she added, "I'm sorry again – now I'm wallowing."

"For the love of God, woman, stop saying you're sorry."

Grace nodded and felt herself cringe. Why did she have to be so needy?

"So, what's your simple pleasure?" He changed the subject.

"Me?" Grace laughed a hollow laugh. "Simple and pleasure are two words I don't associate with my life."

"And why ever not?"

"I don't think you can be a CEO of a huge company and have simplicity and pleasure."

"Well, I'm not sure I agree with that."

Grace shook her head as she thought back to her endless days. "It's impossible: the meetings, the responsibility, the decisions. When I'm not at work I'm either still working or thinking about work, or trying not to think about work. There's nothing simple or pleasurable about that."

"And you enjoy it?"

Grace didn't answer, which surprised her. She wanted to change the subject.

"Do you write stories still?"

Grace laughed. "God, no. I've not written since I was a child, unless you count the essays I wrote at university."

"Do you miss it?"

"I don't know." Grace hadn't given it much thought – not even Lulu's suggestion that she write a column. It all felt a ridiculous idea. She wasn't a writer.

"What did you used to love about it?"

Grace thought back to her coloured books. "Well, I loved the feeling of pen on paper and creating a new world. There was a connection I suppose – something in my mind was coming into the real world. I didn't have much of an audience; only my parents and Margaret."

"And Margaret is?"

"Was. My doll, Margaret. Until her head fell off."

"Poor Margaret."

"Poor Margaret, indeed. I never did mend it."

Grace sat back in her seat. Just her thoughts; being back there now, in her parents' warm and cosy cottage – it was so safe and simple. She felt tears sting at the back of her eyes. She hadn't thought about it in so long.

"I'm sorry. I'm making you nostalgic."

"I went to see Greg." She didn't know why she was telling him this, but she kept talking anyway. "I was wandering past and, you know, he just stepped out." She left out the part where she'd timed it knowing he would.

"Now, here's a coincidence. I also happened to be wandering past Greg's rooms when Alice died. In fact, I happened to be wandering past most weeks for more than a year, if it makes you feel better?"

Grace laughed. "It does."

"He's one of the best. Not that I know any others, but I've heard, you know…"

"On the Strawberry Village grapevine?"

"The one and only."

Grace sipped her coffee and opened the window slightly. The cool spring air seeped into the car and the tightness inside her loosened. They were driving into a small village which had pretty cottages lining the street. There was a small shop where she could see people inside, sitting at tables, drinking coffee.

"Do you know, I am still finding it a wonder…" She looked at her watch. "It's eleven-thirty two in the morning and people are sitting here in this pretty village drinking coffee."

"And what's so unusual about that?"

"I suppose I've spent so many years in London, working in a big firm, you forget there's a whole life which exists which isn't one filled with meetings."

"It is a Saturday, Grace."

"And?"

"Even the weekends, you worked?"

Grace nodded. There was always something. If not some emails to catch up with, then meetings for people who couldn't make the meetings in the week. Grace looked ahead. "Meetings, meetings and more bloody meetings. Followed by lunch meetings and dinner meetings. Then sometimes a late-night after-dinner meeting."

"That's a lot of meetings – what were these meetings about?"

"The Hi-TV brand mainly, whatever that meant – whether it was its relationship with advertisers, or journalists, or hearing how well or not so well we were doing, so I could put a spin on it for the advertisers or journalists." She thought now of all the years, all the energy and time she'd spent, only to be tossed aside, and a horrible taste came into the back of her throat.

"So, does anyone eat carbs in the television industry? Even with all those meetings?"

Grace smiled. She had to stop wallowing. "Not many."

Harvey picked up the paper bag. "Well, considering we're a million miles away from the carb-free land of endless meetings, are you sure I can't interest you in one of Dave's finest?"

Grace looked inside the bag. "They do smell delicious." And she needed something to take away the horrible taste.

He shook the bag.

Grace laughed and took one. "Why not?" she said, as she sank her teeth into the buttery pastry. The oozing chocolate took the horrible taste away, and it felt a relief to have something so satisfying inside her. "This is delicious."

"Life doesn't always have to be quite so hard, Grace Leven." Harvey smiled at her.

"Thank you, Harvey," Grace said, her mouth full.

"For what?"

"For saying that."

"My pleasure, Grace Leven, my pleasure. Now, eyes off; the other one's mine."

"I still don't quite understand why you parked half a mile away." Her heels were starting to rub and once again she felt out of place. She must get something else to wear; she felt even more ridiculous now in the Isabel Marant black dress she'd put on without thinking that morning. Now, as she teetered along the country lane once again, she felt stupidly out of place.

"Sorry, to make you walk like this. I always think the car gives the wrong impression."

Grace nodded, not that she really understood. She stopped when they turned the corner, and stood at the drive of the house.

"Wow." She was greeted by the most beautiful country house. It was two storeys high and covered in ivy. It was white with black windows, and as they walked along the drive, she could see some of them were broken. It was in desperate need of some love, but it was charming, understated and magnificent – all at the same time. The door opened.

"Harvey." A small elderly woman smiled and waved.

"Elizabeth," he called. "That's Elizabeth," he said under his breath.

Grace glanced at him

"And who's Elizabeth?"

"Elizabeth owns the house. And don't let her sweet look fool you; she's a bloody tyrant," he added as they carried on walking up the drive.

"I suppose Harvey told you I was a tyrant?"

Grace laughed and Harvey rolled his eyes.

"I wouldn't say that."

"No need to lie, dear. I am. It's a wonderful compliment."

They sat outside because even though it was March, it was a beautiful day. The sky was clear blue and the sun shone down on them. Grace wrapped her coat around her, and Elizabeth opened a box and pulled out a blanket.

"You're hardly dressed for the country, are you dear?" She placed the blanket on Grace's legs, which made Grace's eyes suddenly sting and fill with tears. It had been so long since anyone had wrapped her warm.

"Mind the cobwebs; the spiders won't bite."

Grace sat upright. She hated spiders.

"But I might, if you freeze to death – bite, that is." Elizabeth met eyes with her and Grace settled again. "There's no spiders, dear; just a blanket of love."

"You see – bloody tyrant," Harvey said under his breath.

"I heard that." Elizabeth sipped her coffee and they all did.

Elizabeth pulled a hip flask from her apron. "Brandy, dear? I find it brings out the taste of the coffee."

"Thank you, but I won't."

"Why ever not?"

Grace met eyes again with Harvey.

Grace held out her cup. "Thank you," she said as Elizabeth poured brandy into her coffee.

"I won't offer you, as you're driving." Elizabeth nodded at Harvey as she filled her own. "Why he insists on parking his posh car half a mile away I don't know. He thinks I don't notice." Elizabeth winked at Grace. "I'll sell this house at the same price, whatever bloody car the builder drives. That old van doesn't fool me."

Grace tried not to laugh.

"So, you've been here before?" Grace asked Harvey.

"Several times."

"I can't keep him away, like the arthritis in my knees – bloody pain." Elizabeth sipped her coffee.

"It's true. I keep telling Elizabeth I'm here because Jack wants something looked at, but the truth is, it's that magnetic personality of hers."

"Don't be ridiculous dear – it doesn't become you. Now, what is it this time?"

"The atrium. He wanted me to see how possible it is to build a pool in there."

"Well, that would be fancy." Elizabeth sipped her coffee again.

"Have you lived here for a long time?" Grace asked.

"Oh, I don't live here, dear. It's far too big and draughty for me. Nobody has lived here for years. It's ever so sad. But my sister could never bring herself to sell it. She said our father would come and haunt us if we did. She was a bigger tyrant than me, but terrified of ghosts. She passed away six months ago, so they'll all bloody haunt me now, but I don't care."

"I'm sorry," Grace said. "About your sister."

"Don't be. She was a battleaxe. I've never lived so much since I haven't had to answer to her every day. God only knows the havoc she's causing up there now." Elizabeth looked up into the sky. "Still, I'm free as a bird now, and I'm going to make the most of it, I can tell you. You can haunt me all you bloody like. I won't care." She looked up, then turned back to Grace. "I'm off on a posh cruise next month and I'm going to learn all about the Byzantine Empire while I stuff my face and get pissed as a newt…and you lot can eff off." She raised two fingers and her cup up to the sky, then turned back to Grace. "Have you ever been to Turkey, dear?"

Grace shook her head. "No, I haven't."

She couldn't take her eyes off Elizabeth. She had curly white hair, big bright blue eyes and a wide smile. She looked more full of life and fun than anyone Grace had met in a long time. Her face was crinkled with laughter lines and Grace found herself wanting to know everything about this tiny woman.

"So, you're thinking of selling to the famous Jack Jones?" Grace sipped her coffee.

"Indeed I am. I've known that boy since he was a baby. He's the only person I'd ever trust with it. But that doesn't mean he still doesn't have to pass my test."

"How did you know him?" Grace asked as Harvey stood up and started to look around.

"I was friends with his grandmother. We grew up together. We were girls about town, shall we say, back in

Yorkshire. She was a right one; man mad. What am I saying? We both were. I'm hoping I'll have a holiday fling while I'm away. Do you think they have Tinder in Greece?" Elizabeth turned to her again.

"Do you know, I have no idea."

"Well, I'll soon find out. I'll find someone – or maybe a few – and you, Free, can say nothing at all." Elizabeth looked up again.

"Free?"

"My sister. Freda. The battleaxe."

"Right." She could see Harvey was trying not laugh.

"Elizabeth, do you mind if I take a wander? I think I'll leave you two to your girls' talk?" Harvey stood up. "If you don't mind either, Grace?"

"We're fine," both women said at the same time. Grace watched Harvey as he walked along the path and disappeared through the gate at the end. She looked around the garden, which was in a much better condition than what she could see of the house. The borders were filled with beautifully cut greenery and shrubs. Large displays of daffodils provided bright clumps of colour. She could only imagine what it would look like in the summer.

"This is a beautiful garden."

"My husband Larry looked after it, before he died, bless him. It was his pride and joy. I've been paying for gardeners to keep it going since. I couldn't bear to see it go to ruin."

"Even though you don't live here?"

Elizabeth shook her head. "Not since I was a child. It always felt like I'd be going back somewhere in time. It was my parents' life, not mine. If I lived here, I'd feel as though I was clinging on to them and I don't think that's healthy – I don't expect that to make any sense."

Grace thought again of her own parents' cottage. "It makes perfect sense."

"So, how long have you and Harvey been together? If I'm honest I hadn't clocked he was seeing anyone?"

Grace choked on her coffee. "We're not together."

"Really?" Elizabeth raised an eyebrow. "But you seem so comfortable together."

"I'm married."

"Is that right, dear?" Elizabeth sipped her coffee and her gaze lingered on Grace. "Well, I got that all wrong. I suppose it's wishful thinking. I've wanted Harvey to meet someone for a long time. It was so awful him losing his wife as he did."

"You knew her?"

"Not really. But I've seen the effect it's had on him, and today is the first time I've seen him smile – a proper one, that reaches those wonderful eyes of his."

Grace felt her cheeks flush and looked around the garden.

"Oh, don't mind me dear. When you get to my age, you lose your filter. So, where is this husband of yours?"

"That's a good question, Elizabeth." Grace sighed. Perhaps it was exhaustion, or perhaps it was because she realised there was no point in lying to this small, incredible woman. "My whole life is a bit of a mess at the moment, if I'm totally honest."

"Well, we've all been there, dear." Elizabeth sipped her coffee and Grace did the same.

They sat in silence, even though Grace never sat in silence with someone she'd just met.

"You know, in my moments, when life is up in the air, I always think it's trying to tell me something."

"But what could it be telling me?"

"Well, I'm no expert, but perhaps it's telling you the one you had didn't belong to you?"

"But…" Grace started, but stopped as Harvey walked back up the path.

"When you're living the life which is truly meant for you, it's funny how everything seems to fall into place." Elizabeth stood up. "But don't mind me; it's probably the brandy talking. Now, Harvey, are you going to tell me how you need to knock even more off the price? Because I've a fist here, and don't think I'm scared to use it."

Chapter Nineteen

Grace: Eric aren't you even curious about where I am or what I am doing? I am still your wife.
Grace: Please Eric. Stop ignoring me like this. We need to talk.
Grace: Pearl Please call. I hope you're having a wonderful time. But I miss you darling. x

"Somebody suggested to me yesterday, that perhaps my life doesn't belong to me."

"And?"

"And what?"

"And what did you say?"

Grace looked outside at the little patio. She was starting to wish she hadn't stopped by to see Greg again. The truth was she hadn't been able to stop thinking about Elizabeth and what she'd said on Saturday and so, here she sat, in front of a distant acquaintance and therapist, trying to make sense of it all. She had to stop doing this to herself. Life had been perfectly fine when it hadn't made any sense.

Grace shrugged. "I didn't say anything; we changed the subject. But it left me feeling…"

"Yes?"

"Unnerved."

"Did it touch a chord?"

"Well, yes. I suppose it did."

"Have you spoken with Eric yet?"

Grace shook her head. "Am I being so bloody unreasonable? It's been more than a week. I've lost my job, I'm being investigated and my husband won't return any of my calls. What have I done wrong? What is wrong with me?"

Greg sat back. "Who says anything is wrong with you?"

"Am I really that much of a monster that my own husband and daughter want nothing to do with me?"

Greg didn't reply.

"I am a monster," Grace said in a low voice.

"You're not a monster," Greg said. "How are you getting on with the letters?"

"Okay. Fine. I suppose." She shrugged again. "I suppose I quite like it. It's making me think of times I haven't thought of for a long time. Parts of me I suppose I thought were gone."

"Those parts haven't gone anywhere. They stay with you, but when they're buried and ignored, this is when the trouble begins."

"Here we go." Grace tried to make her words sound like a joke, but she could hear her sarcastic tone. She really was failing at everything she did.

"Let's take the part of Grace that likes to write," Greg continued. "If you ignore this part for years and years, it starts to become restless and wants your attention. You don't see it as that, but you start to feel disconnected. You think you're tired, or that something is…well…off. But really, it's that part saying 'remember me'."

Grace laughed a hollow laugh. "Well in that case, I think a lot of parts are bloody screaming at the moment."

"And now we're getting somewhere." Greg sat back.

"But that's just it. I don't know. I don't know anything. I don't remember what I like, or don't like. I've got no idea. It's like I've been on this treadmill for so many years, working every day, being the best at my job, doing what I'm supposed to. How the bloody hell am I supposed to have time to think about parts?"

"Well," Greg paused. "You have some time now you're here."

"But I don't want this time. I want my life back."

"Are you saying you're not enjoying anything about being here?"

Grace thought of Saturday, when she'd felt lighter, travelling through the Somerset countryside. She'd laughed a lot with Harvey when they'd stopped for lunch at Turville House and she'd realised how stuck up it was. The service was slow, the atmosphere was cold and the effervescent water, as it was described on the menu, was expensive and flat.

They'd laughed all the way home and they'd carried on laughing when they'd shared a glass of wine and beer in the lounge at Strawberry House. She'd slept better in her little cottage than she had in weeks.

She'd been happy to spend the day alone the previous day, writing her letters, being in her cottage. There was something so warm and familiar about it. When Harvey had knocked on her door later in the day and asked if she fancied a drink to celebrate finishing his latest cabinet, she had been delighted. They'd laughed and chatted and she'd slept well again.

"I suppose it's good to have a change of scene."

"A change of perspective?" Greg added.

"Well, yes."

"Have you thought much about your home?"

Had she? Now she thought about it, she hadn't. Could she really say out loud she'd never really felt like she'd belonged there? That it felt more like Eric's and Pearl's home and she was just an outsider who joined them at the weekend.

"Sometimes," she lied.

"Do you have any photos anywhere of younger you?"

"Of course. At home. Somewhere." Now she thought about it, where were all her old albums? She guessed somewhere in the attic. She hadn't been up there since they'd moved in fifteen years before.

"Would it be possible to get them?"

"I suppose. But that would mean me going back to the house."

"How would that make you feel?"

"Okay, I suppose. It is my house. I know it's empty, as Eric isn't there and Pearl is away.

"I've found it can really help to look at those old photos of you. Those old versions can tell you a lot about yourself, and provide you with answers I can't."

"They can?"

It made no sense to her, but she nodded anyway. She could go back, she supposed. It wouldn't hurt. It was after all her house and she could pick up some less work-like clothes too. It would give her something to do.

"Okay, I'll go back. Tomorrow. What do I have to lose?"

"More to the point, what do you have to gain? You might be surprised at what you find."

Chapter Twenty

Eric: Where are you? Could you just tell me where you are please?
Pearl: I'm still here if you have a moment. x

It felt strange, Grace thought, as the train pulled into Paddington. It had only been just over a week but so much had changed. She'd started to become used to the warmth and the friendliness of Strawberry Village, the staff at the hotel knowing her name, her knowing theirs.

Now, though, as she looked around her, the familiar anonymity returned. The pacing, the charging, the importance of it all. Where was everyone going, and was it really as important as it looked? Her natural instinct was to get into a cab and go to the office, to see what was happening, what she'd missed. But Leonard had warned her against any contact.

"Just let everything take its natural course."

He'd assured her he was happy the investigation being conducted was thorough and professional. She'd wanted to scream – happy? How could he be happy? It was all so bloody ridiculous – but she'd managed to stop herself.

She took a cab and asked for her home address. Even saying it felt strange. Everything felt strange. It was as if she were a visitor in a life she once knew, but now she was existing in some sort of no man's land.

She watched the people around her as they continued to rush and stride. It was just after midday on a Tuesday. In her old life she'd be rushing and striding too.

She thought of Harvey and Lulu, back in Strawberry Village. They didn't rush and stride. She looked up at the skies, which were grey and heavy, and an unease settled in her.

She was grateful the cab driver didn't talk. She wanted to go to her house, get the photos then return to the hotel. It was silly, she thought, coming all this way for some old photos. But she suspected she was also curious to see if her life could just carry on without her. She'd get the photos then get straight back on her train.

Twenty minutes later she put the key into her front door.

The minute she stepped inside she sensed something. She walked through the hall and noticed it was clean and all trace of the broken vase was gone. Maria the cleaner would have been in, so this made sense.

But when she walked into the kitchen, there were cups on the side; the smell of coffee was in the air. Someone was there.

Eric.

She stopped herself from shouting his name. She didn't

want to scare him and make him run away again. All these days, had he been here? All the messages she'd sent, but he'd been here all along? Her heart began to race.

Perhaps there'd been something wrong with his phone. Perhaps there'd been a simple explanation for it all?

She walked up the stairs, one by one. She could hear music playing. The soft sounds behind a closed door – was it the jazz he liked to play? She walked past his office, up more stairs. *Eric*, she wanted to call out. But she didn't.

The unease gripped tighter inside her. There was something odd, but she couldn't work it out. There was a smell which was familiar but different at the same time.

The music was coming from their bedroom, and the door was closed. Perhaps he was taking a shower; perhaps he was using new gel?

She mustn't forget the photos, she told herself. That was, after all, why she was there. Would she even need the photos now, if everything turned out to be okay? If he was playing music, having a shower and back at home, perhaps he was about to call her to tell her he'd returned and so should she.

Eric, she wanted to call out, but still, she didn't. She didn't want to startle him but she didn't want him to run away either. *Oh Eric, I've missed you so much*, she wanted to say. He was here, and it was all going to be okay.

She opened the door.

"Eric," she said, but the words choked in her throat.

Because there was the back of Eric. Naked in bed.

"Shit!" he shouted as he turned and their eyes met, a look of fear in his. And then she saw the reason why. Because there she was – Grace's best friend Polly – lying underneath.

The nausea filled Grace. Her throat was so tight she didn't think she'd be able to breathe.

"What are you doing here?" Eric asked as the two of them scrambled out of the bed. Her bed. Her bedroom. Her unread books at the side.

The familiar smell – it was Polly. It was the perfume she always wore. The smell filled her now. it was everywhere: in her room, in her home, in her bedroom. She felt sick.

"Grace," Polly was speaking. "I can explain."

The room was spinning now. This couldn't be happening really, could it? It was a dream. A nightmare. Her husband and her best friend.

Her heart raced against her chest and a loud whistling filled her ears. Was she going to pass out? She might pass out.

Eric stood at the side of the bed. He was wearing a t-shirt and shorts now.

"Grace. What are you doing here?"

"What?" The words choked in her throat.

Polly was wearing her gown. Her satin gown – the one she'd bought in Paris. Sickness filled her insides, along with a white, hot horror. Her whole body felt as if it might explode.

"Eric," Polly whispered to her husband, and Grace felt even more sick.

"I'm sorry. Did I disturb you?" The words came out in a tone Grace didn't recognise. Her hands were shaking, her whole body was shaking.

"We weren't expecting you back," Polly said.

"We? We? When the fuck was there a we?"

"Grace," Eric said. "There's no need to be…"

"Don't fucking Grace me. I've messaged you every fucking day and you haven't even had the decency to reply. I had no idea where you were or what you were doing and now I know – you were fucking her."

"You need to calm down."

"Don't fucking tell me what I need." She was about to explode, and she needed to get out. She needed to get away.

"You're wearing my gown." She looked into Polly's dark eyes, and her once-upon-a-time friend looked back at her.

"Fucking bastards," she managed before she turned around and slammed the door.

Grace stumbled and tripped out of the house. Her legs were buckling, but she couldn't stop trying to get away. She had never in her life felt she might actually die until that moment.

She stumbled and tripped until she couldn't any more. Her whole body was screaming and she couldn't move any further. There was nothing she could do; her insides started to heave and all she could do was put her head in a bush. If people were walking by, she didn't know and she didn't care.

When at last it stopped, she slumped on the curb, her head in her hands. When she closed her eyes, she saw the two of them. When she opened her eyes, she saw them. The smell, the perfume, the sex, the sound of the jazz; she wanted to vomit again. Was this rock bottom? Was she going to die? Did she actually want to die? Yes, she thought. Perhaps she did.

"Are you okay?" a woman's voice asked her. "Are you unwell? Would you like me to call an ambulance?"

Grace shook her head.

"You live on Appleyard street?"

Grace looked up. The woman's face was blurred.

"I also live there. Three doors along. The same side as you."

She couldn't do this.

"Would you like me to walk you home?"

Grace shook her head.

"I need to get back to Bristol." She managed the words.

"Bristol? Right. Well, is there anyone I can ring?"

Was there?

"Do you think you're well enough to get in a taxi?"

Was she?

Grace wrapped her arms around herself and felt her body began to rock.

Chapter Twenty-One

Eric: Grace, we need to talk.
Polly: Grace, say something. Anything x

"Grace? Are you in there? Please – we're worried about you."

She had to leave Strawberry House. Which part of the 'do not disturb' sign did they not understand?

Since she'd returned three days before, each day there'd been another knock on her cottage door. Lulu. Harvey. Jack. Several members of staff.

She was there to rest and this was a hotel. Why couldn't they bloody well leave her alone?

She would have left, but any energy she needed seemed to have left her body. She lay under the covers, eating small amounts of the food room service delivered – not that she'd ordered it. Even the wine burnt the back of her throat.

She'd kept her curtains drawn, which made her feel safe. Nobody in, nobody out. She had no idea how she'd ever leave again – or where she'd go.

"Grace. I know you're in there."

Great. Now it was Greg, and she groaned at the sound of his voice. The very last thing she needed was a deep therapy session.

"I know you're groaning because you think I've come to do a deep, dark therapy session. But I'm here with treats from Dave's. Here – can you smell these? The pains au chocolat are just out of the oven."

She didn't have the energy to tell him to go away.

"Have you seen the time?"

Grace looked at her watch. It was five minutes past eleven.

"I'm not going away, Grace." His voice was softer now.

Grace clutched the blanket around her as she got off the sofa and moved towards the door. Just moving hurt. Her whole body ached and the nausea was still coming in waves. She opened the door and returned to the sofa.

"Well, you're alive, which is a good start." She looked up to see Greg standing in front of her, holding a tray with two cups and a large paper bag. He also had some tulips under his arm.

"These are from me." He nodded to the flowers. "The rest are from Dave."

"Thank you," Grace said. She felt pathetic.

"Now, I appreciate you're a grown woman and can make your own decisions, but just for this moment, I'm going to draw back the curtains. It's a beautiful, sunny day out there and when you see it…"

"Please. Don't," Grace said. She didn't care that her tone was sharp.

"Okay." Greg nodded. "Do you mind if I sit down?" He nodded at the pink armchair and Grace nodded.

He placed one coffee on the small white table next to the

sofa, then he took the other and sat down. Grace sat back on the sofa, the blanket wrapped tight. If she let go, she wasn't certain she wouldn't fall apart.

Greg took the lid off his coffee and sipped it. The aroma of it filled the air, which was at least better than the stale smell of her misery. But still the smell of coffee made her feel nauseous again.

"So, I'm guessing the trip back didn't go well?"

Grace pulled the blanket around her. "I didn't get the photos."

"It's okay, Grace. It was just an idea."

The silence filled the heavy, miserable air. She heard him sip his coffee and then open the paper bag.

"I caught him. Eric. In bed." The words choked out of her.

"Right." She heard some rustle of paper as he put the bag down.

"Polly. My best friend."

She felt sick again as she heard the words. It was real now.

More heavy silence filled the air.

"I'm so sorry."

She nodded.

"Now I get why you don't want to open the curtains. Bloody sunshine."

Grace nodded again.

"You're still alive then?"

"Yes." Now, she'd said it out loud to someone, it somehow felt easier to sit upright. "Just. I'm sorry – I'm a mess."

"Why are you sorry? You're lovely," Greg told her. "And you're allowed to be a mess."

Grace took a tissue from the box on the side table. A tear slid in silence down her cheek.

"It's good that you're crying. Let the tears come."

"They barely do. I feel numb."

"You've had a shock. You're grieving; this is normal."

"Nothing's normal and everything is ruined. I've ruined everything."

Greg picked up his coffee and sipped it.

"Can I ask why you think you're the one who's ruined everything?"

"Because I have." Grace blew her nose again.

"Why have you ruined everything? You weren't the one cheating. We still don't know if there's any real evidence behind these accusations at work. Who says you ruined everything?"

"It must be me. Look at me. I've got nothing. No marriage, no job. My daughter won't speak to me."

Greg leant forward on his knees. "Look, Grace, this is not the time – and I promise this is not a session – but I'm watching you beat yourself up over and over and you're not asking yourself the one question I want you to ask."

"Which is?" Grace couldn't deal with this now.

"That perhaps none of this has anything to do with you."

She looked up. "But of course it has everything to do with me. It's my life and I've ruined the lot."

"Have you ever been unfaithful to your husband?"

"No."

"Have you ever been disloyal to your friend?"

"No. Other than not being strictly true about the reason why Iris is at the company. But the article is still promoting Polly."

"And you're protecting her, by not telling her the truth."
"Yes."
"So, you've been a loyal wife and a loyal friend."
"I really don't see what you're getting at."
"Your daughter, Pearl?"
"The one who doesn't want to speak to me? Are you going to tell me that's not my fault also?"

"A young adult child who's travelling around the world, who's angry at her mother for not being everything she wished she could be. Do you know how many mothers and fathers I've seen with children thinking the same? You're not the first mother to bear the brunt of her child's anger at life. Nobody's perfect, Grace. We all fuck up."

"But I abandoned Pearl. I left her to go to work."

"You left her with your husband, her father. You two made an agreement that this is what you'd do. You earned money and you provided for her, and you've set a great example – that a woman can build a tremendously successful career. I'm not saying everything turned out as you wanted it to, but Grace, life rarely does."

"I still don't see your point."

Greg paused.

"My point is, when we're surrounded by people who make it feel like everything is our fault, we become accustomed to thinking it is."

"But how could any of this not be my fault?"

"Because, Grace, it isn't."

"Then whose fault is it?"

Greg sat back in his chair.

"Have you ever heard of the term emotional abuse, Grace?"

"Of course I have. Everyone has."

"Do you know what it means?"

Grace's head was feeling like it might explode.

"I don't know. Someone who calls someone names, who is cruel. Puts someone down."

She didn't have the energy for any of this.

"It can be more subtle than this. We call it gaslighting, scapegoating, blaming, manipulation. It can sometimes be so subtle you have no idea it's happening, until you find yourself curled in a ball with no idea how you ended up there. You want to die. You have a white-hot pain in your insides you can't quite describe. You have no idea who you are or what you want. All you can feel is that indescribable pain which is so rigid and stuck and is stopping you from feeling anything else. No joy, no hope, no excitement – just a horrible, aching never-ending pain."

Grace wrapped the blanket around her.

"It's my professional opinion you're emotionally abused."

"I thought you said this was not a session."

"I say this as my opinion. We haven't spent long together, but everything you've told me about your husband so far points to this."

"You're wrong, Greg."

"You live a life that he wanted, and that you work hard for and fund."

"And? It's not uncommon for one spouse to work while the other stays at home."

"No, of course. But when one person is controlling everything, I have concerns it may be abuse. Your daughter has been independent for a long time; adults can and should be financially responsible for themselves."

"That's not what's happening."

"Then I'm wrong."

Greg sat back again.

"Who told you not to eat carbs, Grace?"

"Get out."

"Grace—"

"I said, get out."

She didn't have the energy to shout or scream or anything she wished she could do. She'd just caught her husband having sex with her so-called best friend, she'd lost the job she'd worked decades for, her daughter was on the other side of the world and now this stranger, trying to make out he knew everything about her and her life.

She closed her eyes.

"Get out," she repeated.

She heard him stand up and walk towards the door.

"I didn't come here to upset you."

"Fuck off, Greg."

She heard the door click shut and more silent tears began to fall.

Eric: Where are you, Grace? Where the fuck are you?
Polly: Grace. You can't just ignore me. We need to talk x

The sound of her phone beeping woke her. She must have fallen asleep. Her head hurt and her body ached. It was dark outside.

She looked at her phone and then sank back in the cushions. The irony wasn't lost on her. All those days she'd been desperate to hear from them.

She looked at the mini-fridge in her room. It seemed too far away – even if going over to it meant she could drink wine. She looked back down at her phone, at their messages, one on top of the other, and the nausea rose. Were they together now? Were they laughing at her? Were they having sex? If he was going to fuck anyone in the world, why did he have to fuck her?

She typed in the two words.

Emotional abuse.

Then she stopped. Did she really want this on her search history? Who knew what would happen next. She thought for a moment. She could say it was part of the research for her column, couldn't she? She pressed enter.

She scrolled to find a credible source.

The underlying goal of emotional abuse is to control the other person by discrediting, isolating, invalidating and silencing them. It is one of the most dangerous forms of abuse, as it can be subtle and insidious.

She looked up.

Greg was being ridiculous. Of course Eric wasn't doing that to her. As she lay back down, she tried to push the thoughts aside. Discrediting? Eric hadn't been doing that, had he?

She did a mental flashback. He'd supported everything she'd done. One part of her brain told her Greg had it all wrong, but there was another part – a deeper, darker part which felt unsettled. She wasn't good at cooking and she couldn't organise the house – Eric had been sure to point this out every time she'd made his favourite dish. When she was promoted, he'd told her it was because she was a woman and it had looked good for the board.

He was only stating facts, wasn't he?

She thought of the money she supplied without question. It was only because of Leonard insisting she kept a separate bank account that she had done so. Had he suspected the same? They were just being cynical men.

But still the nausea twisted and turned in her insides and Greg's words whirled around her. The indescribable pain he'd talked about was exactly like the one that sat in her now. It was rigid and hard, and ran up through her back. It was white-hot, yet cold too. She couldn't find the words but it was almost unbearable. She needed to move. If she could clear it somehow, if she could make it go away, she'd be fine. She threw the blanket off and was about to open the door of the fridge when there was another knock.

"Go away," she called this time. She didn't care who was outside.

"Mum. It's me. Pearl."

For the briefest of moments, Grace wondered if she might be asleep – if this was some sort of dream – that in a moment she'd wake up. Was it a sick joke? Was it someone pretending? But she opened the door, and there she was.

Her daughter, Pearl.

"Oh Mum." Pearl put her hand over her mouth.

Grace tried to say something – anything – but she couldn't. She could barely breathe.

Pearl put her head on Grace's chest as she felt her daughter's arms wrap around her.

"I'm sorry, Mum," Pearl told her as Grace let go of her blanket and wrapped her arms around her daughter and they both began to cry.

"I'm not going to lie, Mum – you look like shit."

Grace laughed. "Thank you, my darling daughter – your honesty is a tonic."

"This is good." Pearl looked into her glass. Despite the desperate scene her daughter had walked in on, they'd decided to order a bottle of champagne.

They were there and they were together. It was a start, they'd decided.

"To you. To being here." Grace raised her glass.

"And to you. For being alive."

Grace sipped the champagne and the cold bubbles slid down her throat.

"You didn't think I'd be dead, did you?"

Pearl sipped her own drink.

"Seriously?"

"No. Well, I hoped not. But when I heard about Dad and Polly, I thought that's a lot for anyone to stomach – even the great Grace Leven."

"So, you know?"

Pearl looked at her feet, stretched out in front of her on the sofa. She nodded.

"Your father?"

She nodded. "I suppose he thought if he told me first, it would make it okay."

"That was very noble of him."

"She called too."

The nausea returned. "She?"

"I stayed in touch with Polly – you know that." Pearl looked back down at her feet. "I'd tell her about my travels – you know – the usual. But this time, she called and she acted like everything was okay, like it was the most natural thing in the world that my mother's best friend was screwing my dad."

Grace drank more champagne. She hated her daughter sounding like this – the bitterness and anger; Pearl was always a sweet, kind girl who thought the best of everyone – except for her mother.

"I owe you an apology," Pearl said.

"Me? Why? What have you done? I'm the one who's been the terrible mother."

Pearl sipped her champagne again. "But you haven't, have you? Been a terrible mother."

"I spent most of your childhood at work, Pearl. It doesn't qualify me as mother of the year."

"No, but you were the breadwinner and this is what breadwinners do," Pearl said. She paused for a moment and Grace sat upright in the armchair. She hadn't been expecting any of this. "Being away, having some space – it gave me a bit of perspective, shall we say?"

"What do you mean?" Grace asked as Pearl shivered. "Here," Grace got up and put her own blanket on her.

"Don't be kind. I don't deserve it." A tear slid down Pearl's cheek.

"What? Don't be ridiculous." Grace pulled out a tissue tucked in her sleeve and handed it to Pearl. Then she sat back down on the armchair to give her daughter space. If she'd learned anything since she'd arrived in Strawberry Village, it was the importance of space.

"I'm sorry," Pearl said.

"For what? I'm a puffed-up wreck. You've got a long way to go before you meet my disgusting standards."

"Nobody could ever describe you as disgusting, Mum," Pearl laughed through her tears. Grace wanted to tell her daughter everything was going to be okay, but for the first time in both their lives, she couldn't. She didn't know it was going to be okay.

Pearl took a deep breath.

"I've suspected something for a while now."

"What do you mean?" Grace asked.

"Dad. Polly. I thought there was something not right."

"You did? Why didn't you say anything?"

"Mum. Please. You've got every right to be angry, but can I just explain?"

"Yes, I'm sorry." Grace took a rolled blanket from a basket next to her feet, and wrapped it around herself.

"I couldn't quite put my finger on it. I thought it was me. I promise you, if I'd actually seen anything, I would have said something. I swear. It was more of a…well, a feeling. Like when I spoke to each of them, they knew too much about the other one. It was almost as if…"

"Go on."

"Sometimes it felt like they were the parents. Dad would say, have you told Polly about this? Have you spoken to Polly? Polly would say, your father needs you to call him; your father is worried about you. I can see now, it wasn't right."

"No, it wasn't. And I was too busy, too caught up in my own world to have any idea."

Pearl didn't reply to this. "I asked him outright, a few weeks ago. I said, are you and Polly having an affair?"

"And?" Grace tried to ignore the rising nausea, her insides knotted, the pain almost unbearable. "I'm guessing he denied it?"

"He laughed, said I had a vivid imagination, and I ended up feeling ridiculous."

"A common feeling, when it comes to your father," Grace agreed, then paused. "I've been seeing a therapist."

Pearl choked a little on her champagne. "You what?"

"Well, more by accident. I met someone here who

recognised me. He was an intern years ago at work; he's now a therapist. I was walking past his rooms and I ended up speaking to him."

"You were just walking past?" Pearl raised her eyebrows.

"Fine, I did know he was free at the time I walked past. But the point is he was here, just before you arrived. He suggested that…" Grace couldn't bring herself to say it.

"Suggested what?" Pearl sat forward.

"He suggested that your father has been emotionally abusing me."

Grace waited for the onslaught of outrage and disbelief – everything she'd felt an hour earlier, but instead Pearl didn't speak.

"What? You're not surprised?"

Pearl shook her head. Grace saw the tears fill her daughter's eyes. "Actually, it comes as a relief."

"It does?"

"Since I've been away, I've had some space and some questions. It's funny – this is the best part of travelling: you meet different people with different views. I met people who are healers, or even just people travelling like me, and we'd end up talking about things I'd never talk about with anyone at home. As I said certain things out loud, it all started to make sense."

"Like what?"

"Like how it was always about Dad. It was always, always about him. We live in a house he picked. Everything is to *his* taste. If you were at work late, it was about *him* being cross. But at the same time, I heard your rows, and you offered to stop working so many times – I heard you say it. But then he accused you of giving up on your family. We ate at the restaurants *he* wanted. We went on the holidays *he* wanted. We walked on eggshells around *him* and his moods. *He* was the one threatened by everyone, but even his own insecurity was never his fault. When he came to school, he'd spend the whole time making it all about *him*: he told me to take that subject –wasn't I grateful? The school fees? It's all thanks to the sacrifices *he'd* made, even though he hadn't earned a penny. He'd tell me I took after him, that he was the one who'd made sure I did my homework, thank goodness I had him when you were always at work. It was always about him. Even my name. I've always been Pearl Matthews. Why wasn't I ever Pearl Matthews-Leven?"

"Your father hated that I didn't take his name, but I always wanted to hold on to something from my own past."

"You see, it was always about him."

Grace sat back. All these years, she'd felt an outsider. She'd felt like she didn't belong in her own home, or in her own little family. She'd felt she didn't belong in her own life.

"I had no idea."

"Nor did I. I idealised him. He's my dad, I suppose. I had no idea it could be any different, I had no idea there was anything wrong. It was when I started to talk about when I was away, it gave me a different perspective. They asked me about you," Pearl's eyes filled with tears. "Mum, I'm so, so sorry."

"Pearl, this is not your fault. Your father and I should have worked out our problems."

"Mum," Pearl's voice was raised. "You just caught him shagging your best friend. That's his problem, not yours."

Grace flinched at Pearl's words, which were so similar to Greg's.

"Sorry," Pearl said again.

"But you're right. Why am I not blaming him? I suppose

it's easier to blame ourselves than admit what an utter shit he's been."

Pearl wiped her nose, then took the bottle from the ice bucket and filled their glasses.

"Oh Pearl. I'm sorry. This is all such a bloody mess." Grace put her head in her hands.

"Yes, it is. But Mum…"

Grace looked up.

"My mother may be many things – stubborn, yes – but I do know she's a fighter. Didn't you once tell me resilience is a superpower?"

Grace squeezed her daughter's foot.

"But why have you come back? This is your time for adventure, Pearl. You shouldn't be here consoling me."

"I was so angry and cross when I left. I blamed you for everything, because it was easier I suppose. I didn't want to face the truth – and then when you kept calling, I ignored you. I am so, so sorry for ignoring you. I thought I needed to get away, but then it was as though I couldn't get away. I was still so angry and none of it made sense. When you lost your job, Dad told me you'd try to make me come back – that it was better I didn't speak with you."

"He told you to ignore me?"

Pearl nodded. "He did. I'm sorry I listened to him."

Grace shook her head. "Don't be sorry. In that case, he was right. I needed to work this out on my own, and you had every right to be on the other side of the world enjoying your gap year. I'm sorry I bombarded you."

"I feel terrible now."

"I tell you what," Grace said as she leant forward, "I've got no idea what will happen next, and I've no idea what I'm going to do. But what I do know is how great it is to have my beautiful daughter here in front of me. What about if we both make a deal to stop feeling terrible, and from now on we'll order honest conversations all round?"

Pearl nodded and held out her hand. "Deal," she said through her tears, as her mother held on to her hand.

"When did you grow into this fine young woman? You were my baby five minutes ago."

"You were too busy at work," Pearl smiled, then shook her head. "Sorry – too soon."

"No. It's not." Grace kissed her daughter's hand. "You and I are going to be open and honest, and the one thing your father can't take from me is my unconditional love for you. Besides, it may have escaped your notice, but I'm not working now. I'm officially a lady of leisure."

"I don't know which is more terrifying: Grace Leven, the CEO, or Grace Leven, the lady of leisure."

Grace laughed. "Me neither, but I'm suspecting it's the second. Well, according to Greg, anyway, but that's for another time."

"Who's Greg?"

"Greg is my accidental therapist."

"Your accidental therapist? That sounds like the title of a book."

"I haven't even told you about my column yet."

"A column? Mum – that's brilliant."

"I suppose it is," Grace nodded, then she put down her glass. "I tell you what, it's high-time I had a shower and dragged myself out of this cottage. I want to hear every single detail of your trip so far. What about we go to the bar, order more champagne, and for once we'll eat dinner in the restaurant and I won't be the complete saddo, eating and hiding in my room?"

"Sounds like a plan to me.

Grace stood up and kissed her daughter on the head,

breathing in the apple-like smell. More tears stung at the back of her eyes. Her heart ached; she'd missed Pearl so much. "I'm already on my way."

"I can't believe you still sniff my hair, Mum."

"It's a mother's job, my darling. It's called a blanket of love – just wrap yourself in it," Grace said, leaning over the banister before heading up the stairs.

Chapter Twenty-Two

Eric: Grace, after all I've done for you – call me x
Polly: Grace you're my best friend. I need you x

Grace hadn't felt so energised in weeks, even though she really wasn't sure why. Perhaps it was having Pearl there, perhaps it was talking with her until the early hours of the morning, perhaps it was a feeling that she wasn't going crazy after all…

But as she returned from her run, she stopped for a moment in the front garden of Strawberry House and let the spring sunshine beam down onto her face.

Her phone rang, threatening to ruin her better mood, but then she saw it was Iris.

"I've got some news. It's not major but it's something."

"Okay?" Grace braced herself and sat down on the wall. Her insides began to knot again – she should have known better than to allow herself to relax.

"I've got the names of a couple of the people who

claimed you'd been bullying them. I was out with the sales team and they volunteered it."

"They did?"

"I didn't push them, I promise."

"It's okay, Iris. I believe you. So, who are they?"

"Natalie Jacobs and Gabrielle Bancroft."

"Who?"

"That's what I thought."

"Sorry, Iris – I'm not following."

"Do you remember having any dealings with them at all?"

Grace thought. She dealt with so many people every day. "No. I don't. My god, is this why I'm so bad? I can't even remember the people I've bullied?"

"No, it's not that. There's something really strange about it."

Grace leant forward as she sat on the wall. "What do you mean?"

"It was as if they weren't saying everything. They kept looking at each other, then looking down. It was as if something was really off."

"What do you mean 'off'?"

"Then they just blurted it out. They told me they knew I was a journalist at the company doing a piece on Polly and they told me off the record that they were two of the people who'd complained. But they said you were really great – they actually admired you and I shouldn't write anything bad about you."

"They did? This is odd."

'Leave it with me. I'm going to keep going with this."

"I'll tell Leonard."

"He won't say anything, will he? I don't want my cover blown."

"I've known Leonard all my life." He wouldn't betray her, would he? She didn't know anything any more. The sense of unease settled in her.

"Iris, thank you. You do know how much I appreciate this, don't you?"

"It's an honour. There's something going on here, Grace, and we're getting closer. I can feel it."

An hour and a half later Grace had showered, left Pearl reading a book in the lounge and, at precisely ten fifty-nine am, she was standing outside Greg's practice rooms.

She had to stop doing this.

The door opened, exactly on cue.

"Grace?"

"Greg, I'm so sorry. Not just for last night but also for turning up again like this. I'm sorry for swearing at you, for being rude, for interrupting your morning coffee. I'm sorry for everything."

"There's no need to apologise."

"I wondered if you'd let me buy you a coffee?" She felt small and sheepish as she stood in the little street.

But then Greg's face broke out into a smile. "It would be my pleasure," he laughed as he closed the door behind him.

"I'm so sorry I told you to…you know…"

Greg shook his head. "I promise, you're not the first and you won't be the last. It's not pleasant to be faced with something like that. Also, there's nothing to say that I'm right."

"But that's the thing. I think you are."

She told him about Pearl arriving and their conversation as they walked to Dave's. Dave took their order and Grace then told him about her conversation with Iris. Then they sat in silence.

"I'm getting used to these – these moments of silence with you."

"Have you thought the two might be linked?"

"The moments of silence?"

But the unease was rising in her, the same unease she'd been feeling since she'd finished the call with Iris.

"Do you think it too? I feel like I'm going mad. I don't know what to think and who to trust."

"This is what happens, Grace. This is what they intend."

"But seriously, are we really suggesting this is all part of a masterplan to get me out the way? Polly would never do this. Polly is…"

"Your best friend? Who's been sleeping with your husband?"

Grace began to feel sick again.

The words stung. Even if they were true, they stung.

Dave brought out the coffees and Greg's breakfast bap. He chatted to Greg but Grace's head was spinning. This couldn't be right, could it? She had no idea if Polly was behind the allegations, but she also had no idea who else might be behind them. The familiar cold, white pain was there again, her heartbeat was rising and she felt like she was going to explode.

"I think I'm going mad, Greg." She rubbed each side of her head as Dave went back inside.

"It's okay, Grace. I'm here with you."

"But what if you're in on it? What if everyone's in on it?"

"Grace, you've got to listen to me; this is how it works. You've been so undermined and invalidated, you start to believe you don't know anything any more. You think everything is your fault and you think it's all because of you. This is part of the abuse."

"I still can't believe it." She had to get some sort of a grip. "They've stolen my life." She looked at Greg. His eyes were warm and sympathetic – she could trust him, couldn't she? "They've stolen my life and I need to get it back."

"But think about it, Grace. Do you really want to return to your old life?"

"Of course, I do." She looked at Greg. "What?"

Greg shook his head and sipped his coffee. "I'm not saying anything."

"But you not saying anything, is making me even more crazy." She rubbed her head again. "This therapy is actually making my head worse."

"But we're not in a session – we're having coffee here at Dave's."

It was like a bad nightmare, one thing after another. It had to stop.

"You are the only one who can listen to that inner knowing of yours."

Grace laughed a hollow laugh. As awful as she felt, she felt better being here on this little pavement with Greg and Dave, knowing Pearl was nearby. She sipped her coffee.

"What if I can't hear the sound of my own voice because of the chaos in my head?"

"Then perhaps it's time to get that chaos to quieten down."

"And how do I do that?"

"Look, we love having you here in Strawberry Village, but maybe you need to go somewhere where are alone – completely alone."

"But why would I do that? Pearl's just arrived."

"From what you just said, she's not going anywhere for a

while. It's important you work out what's right for you, Grace."

"But I've never been completely alone. Even when I've travelled alone for work, I was always going somewhere to meet someone."

"And what does it feel like – the idea of being completely alone?"

The truth was, it made her feel edgy and unnerved.

"I don't know. This is the point – I don't know anything any more."

"Well then, Grace Leven," Greg said as he sipped his coffee. "Perhaps it's time you looked inside that chaos.

Midlife Murders & The Lost Path

1

Hello dear reader

I'd like to start this column with a question and I'd appreciate your thoughts.

Is it a crime that at fifty-three I've never been truly alone? It sounds absurd as I write this. But when I think about it, it's true.

First, I had my parents; they were just always there. When I went out, they were still there. When they went out – they came home.

Until one day they didn't.

My life changed forever that day but even then, in the most awful of times, I had a boyfriend who became my husband, so I was never alone. If I travelled for work, there'd be someone to greet me. Wherever I went I had someone to meet.

The first time I travelled alone where nobody was expecting me, I went to Strawberry House. It sits nestled in Strawberry Village, waiting to welcome you. I didn't know it when I arrived, but I've since discovered it's impossible to be at Strawberry House and ever feel alone.

Someone asked me recently what I like, and do you know? I have no idea. Is this a crime at fifty-three, too?

I know what I think I should like, I know what I ought to like, but what do I really like? I haven't a clue. I eat food I think is good for me, I drink wine that has become a habit. The clothes I wear are a uniform and I don't even really know how I'd like to decorate a home. At this precise moment, I don't even really have a home.

So, it seems at fifty-three I'm lost.

It turns out the whole time I was convinced I knew where I was heading, I was really on The Lost Path. I'd even managed to make the outside world believe I had it all figured out – I was that good at pretending. So let this be a lesson to you. The ones who look like they really do have it all figured out are very likely on The Lost Path too.

The way off this path is, I know, inside me, but it's been so long since I've listened, I began to wonder if the voice is even still there. But every now and then I do hear tiny whispers – have they been there all along? Is it by not listening to them that I've arrived where I am today – a great big midlife mess with nothing worked out at all?

If I am to move forward, I need to hear. What are the whispers trying to tell me? The more I try to listen, the more I'll find the path that will set me free. But my fear is it's quiet and lonely in the dark, and I really don't like being here at all.

That's why I'm grateful to have you here too.

Chapter Twenty-Three

Eric: Grace, stop ignoring me. It doesn't become you.
Pearl: You'll have to speak to me one day, we're like family Grace x

"I know exactly where you need to go." Lulu clapped her hands.

"And where, please tell, is that?" Grace asked.

"Lemon Cove. You need to meet Beatrice. Everyone needs to meet Beatrice."

"But if I go to meet this Beatrice, then I'm not alone. It's cheating."

"I don't think it's cheating," Pearl said.

The three of them sat at the bar in Strawberry House. Since she'd introduced Pearl to Lulu, they'd talked non-stop. Lulu had loved hearing about Pearl's travels and Pearl was learning everything she could about *The Strawberry Times* and what it was like to run your own business.

"Difficult, tough, impossible, and I'm completely out of my depth," Lulu had told her. "But I have your mum – at least for now – and she's my knight in shining Prada."

Grace had blushed at the compliment – more at the look of pride on Pearl's face. She felt childish and ridiculous and had told herself to get a grip.

For now, Grace was enjoying watching her daughter's face light up with excitement. She was bright, engaged and with a look of passion in her eye. The irony wasn't lost on Grace that she was now the one who was lost.

"Here, look at this."

Lulu handed Grace her phone. "This is Jack's place in Antigua – Antigua House. The hotel is not on Lemon Cove – only very special people ever get to go to Lemon Cove. But I would suggest you qualify."

"You flatter me. Thank you." Grace looked at the phone. The blue skies, the white sand, the never-ending beach looked inviting.

"And which special person are we discussing today?" a voice interrupted them.

"Harvey. Lovely to see you. This is my daughter, Pearl."

Harvey held out his hand as Pearl stood up.

"No need to stand for me. It's lovely to meet you." Harvey shook her hand.

"You too, Harvey," Pearl nodded. "Would you like to join us for a drink?"

"Harvey might be busy," Grace said. She could feel herself getting hot again under her dress – she really needed to think about getting some new clothes – some that didn't make her feel like she was a CEO out of work – which she was.

"I'd love to. Another round for all?" Harvey sat on the bar stool next to Grace and nodded at Ollie the barman.

"I was just telling Grace about Lemon Cove," Lulu said.

"Ah, the wonderful Lemon Cove. Everybody should experience Lemon Cove at least once in their life."

"This is what I'm hearing," Grace said.

"Beatrice and her magic hands, and Claudia and her lemonade." Harvey held his hands up in the air. "I've never known anything like it."

"You see Mum, this is the perfect place for you to go," Pearl told her.

"Are you thinking of leaving?" Harvey turned to her.

Grace shook her head. "I don't know. I keep being told I need to learn more about myself, but it feels like I'm cheating if I go somewhere where I know someone."

"Believe me, if you need to be alone, you'll find your space there."

"I still think it's cheating if I know someone there."

"That's what Iris said," Lulu said. "She went there too, when everything went wrong with Jack when she was writing the article. She'd always promised to go travelling, but felt going to his hotel was cheating. But she went – and came back a completely different person."

"I like the idea of being a different person."

"I like you how you are," Harvey said, and Pearl raised her eyebrows at Grace.

"What?" Grace asked.

Pearl shook her head and sipped her drink. "I know how going somewhere far away gave me a different perspective. This is what you need – plus, you are owed many holidays after all these years. You always worked on the ones you actually took.

"I sound quite the barrel of laughs." Grace rolled her eyes, and they met Harvey's.

"Children. They think they know it all," Harvey said. "The trouble is – they do."

What Really Happened To Me?

Grace laughed. She was definitely curious. She'd spoken to Leonard earlier and he'd told her she needed to keep on keeping her distance and let the process take its course. He'd reminded her of her bonus money.

"All those years of working – is it so bad to take something for you?" Leonard had asked.

"I'm heading away too, for a couple of weeks," Harvey interrupted her thoughts.

"You are?" Grace heard the disappointment in her voice, as Pearl raised her eyebrows again.

"I'm going on a bit of tour – checking the hotels. I do it for Jack every year."

"But I've got my cottage here – it all feels very indulgent."

"Mum, you've worked all hours for decades. Most of our holidays were business trips combined – and let's face it, you've had a really shitty time. Besides, I can guard the cottage."

"You can, can you?"

Pearl squeezed her mother's hand and Grace felt the tears sting at the back of her eyes. She looked at her daughter, so bright and strong and so different to the teenager who'd traipsed to and from her expensive school – the one Eric had insisted she'd gone to.

How had she become quite so pathetic?

"I'll think about it," she said.

"I have an idea," Lulu gasped, and all eyes turned to her.

"What about if we treat it as an assignment, make it part of the Midlife Murders column? You go off and post each day about what you're learning – your very own soul-searching mission. Think of it as *The Strawberry Times* version of *Eat, Pray Love*." Lulu clapped her hands. "Only this is *Midlife Murders* and finding our way back from the Lost Path." She paused. "We might need to work on the title."

"Just think, Mum, Julia Roberts could play you in a film," Pearl said.

"I don't think that would happen any time soon." Grace felt the warmth in her cheeks as Harvey looked at her.

"I think she'd be honoured to play Grace Leven," he smiled, and Pearl raised her eyebrows yet again.

Grace would really have to speak to Pearl about that.

"The point is, you'd have a mission – almost like a work mission, and you know how you love a mission."

Grace didn't hate the idea.

"I'll think about it," she conceded, but Pearl shook her head.

"Mum – you're going to do more than think about it. You're going to book the flight."

Chapter Twenty-Four

Eric: Grace we really need to talk. After all I've done for you, you can't leave it like this. x
Polly: Grace please. I need to talk to you. x

Grace Leven left the duty-free shop with three fiction books.

She'd also picked up four magazines about fashion and interiors. She'd hovered over celebrity magazines but she knew this would lead her thoughts back to the gossip around Hi-TV. She needed something different. The only books she'd read since she'd been CEO had been non-fiction – about either brands, leadership or money.

She'd decided to go for a mixture of genres, swallowing down the shame that she had no idea which one she actually liked. A romance, a domestic noire and a thriller. Still, she told herself, this was all material for her column.

Half an hour later, she sat in the first-class lounge, feeling awkward and out of place. When her company had been paying for her, she hadn't taken any notice of her surroundings – her head was always too deep in work. Now it felt horribly indulgent as she looked around. There were men and women with their eyes glued to laptops, just as hers had been. Older couples read their newspapers and books in silence; a younger couple sat holding hands, excited about their coming trip.

Then there was Grace – neither one nor the other.

She pulled out the romance book, *To Love You and Back*. It had recently been turned into a film and she'd been invited to the premier. She hadn't even told Eric about it as she knew he would have wanted to go and she didn't.

You see, she wanted to tell Greg, I did have a mind of my own.

"Drink, madam?"

The voice startled her.

"Yes please – a champagne."

She was about to thank the young man but he was gone – none of the warmth of Strawberry House in the airport lounge.

She looked back down at the book – a man and a woman were drawn on the front, their backs to her as they held hands.

Who was she kidding, she thought as she looked at them. They weren't hiding from each other like she'd had to with Eric. She looked up at the couple in front of her and saw them still laughing and still holding hands.

The sickening feeling rose in her and she started to feel even more alone. Had she been right about anything?

The warm air wrapped around her as she got off the plane, and her mind went back to Elizabeth, placing the blanket over her as they had sat in chilly Somerset. A blanket of love, she'd told her. Well, Grace thought, as she took a deep breath, the warmth felt like a blanket of love around her now.

The whole landing had lifted her spirits. As she'd looked down on the island, the view beneath the plane took her breath away. When she travelled for work, she hardly ever looked at views; she was too busy writing reports or reading them. But throughout the flight, she'd been unable to concentrate on the films or her new books, so as they'd landed, instead, she'd looked down at the tiny island beneath them. The multi-coloured buildings were stunning against the immense clear blue sky and sea. The white sands alongside the greenery jolted her from her gloom, and she was reminded she was taking a trip to actual paradise.

She looked down at the colourful buildings as they became closer. They were beautiful shades of pink and orange. When the wheels touched the ground, she felt a flash of something. She wasn't sure what it was.

"Everyone's excited when they land in Antigua," the stewardess told her as she'd walked by.

As she stood on the tarmac, she thought of the last time she'd been in the Caribbean. They'd been to Barbados with Pearl as a sulky teenager. She'd spent most days inside their smart air-conditioned all-inclusive suite, working all alone.

"I was so ungrateful," Pearl had said, as they'd shopped for new clothes the day before.

"You were a teenager who wanted your mother's attention."

"I thought we'd agreed we weren't going to keep dwelling on the past," Pearl said, and then turned Grace's attention to the flowing dress she thought her mother should buy.

Grace shook her head and brought herself back to the moment – just as Greg had instructed.

"Just be in the moment, Grace," he'd told her. "Look at it as part of the assignment."

Grace had spent time on the flight planning her Lost Path column. But as she walked through customs, the feeling of dread returned again. She was surrounded by people on holiday and there she was, all alone.

"Ms Leven," a voice called. "I'm Lionel and I'm here to take you to the hotel."

Grace held up her hand, grateful.

"Welcome to Antigua." His smile was wide and warm.

"Hello Lionel," Grace said, then burst into tears. "Oh Christ. I'm sorry." She looked in her bag for a tissue, but Lionel handed her one.

"Nothing to apologise for, Miss. Don't you worry. Believe me when I say this happens all the time."

As they drove towards the hotel, Grace looked up. She'd been so lost in the fog of her thoughts, she hadn't taken much notice of anything on the drive there.

Lionel had been quiet, which she'd appreciated, but her mind wouldn't stop going over and over the same thoughts. How could this have happened? How could she be here alone?

She tried to admire the flowers which lined the path of the long drive.

Be present; if nothing else, do that.

Easy for Greg to say she thought, as she begged her thoughts to stop.

When they pulled up at the open-air reception, a man

stood waiting for them. She hoped she wouldn't burst into tears again as she got ready to get out.

"Welcome, Ms Leven. I'm Bernard and I'm the manager of this hotel," he said as he opened the car door.

"Thank you, Bernard," Grace said as her eyes began to sting.

"Please come; you've had a long flight. Welcome to our corner of paradise."

Grace nodded and clutched her handbag as one small tear slipped down her cheek behind her sunglasses.

All she wanted to do was to get to her room.

Operation Lost Path, as Lulu had called it, could begin the next day. She felt exhausted and her body ached. She looked at her watch. It was four in the afternoon local time and she knew she shouldn't sleep. But she just wanted to crawl into bed.

"Ms Leven, if you would like to take a seat in the bar area, someone will be right with you."

"If it's okay, I'd rather go straight to my room."

"It will only take a few moments," a woman whose name badge identified her as Dominique replied in a firm voice.

Grace was too tired to argue so she nodded and walked through the open-air foyer. It was filled with sofas with pastel cushions scattered on them. Large blooms in vases sat on tables dotted around and a woman played a saxophone, while another sang. The seats were filled with people wrapped in sarongs. Some were sipping tea, others were enjoying a cocktail. She felt even more out of place.

"Can I offer you a welcome cocktail, Ms Leven?" Dominique asked.

"No, thank you. Can I just go to my room?"

"Of course. We just need to go through a few things, which won't take very long. Herman will be with you shortly."

"Herman?"

"Our Head of Wellbeing."

Grace could feel the irritation rising in her. She didn't need a head of wellbeing; she needed her room.

"Can I get you anything else?"

"No," she snapped, then stopped. "I'm sorry – a sparkling water, please."

Dominique smiled and Grace felt even worse.

A few moments later a man sat down next to her.

"Welcome, Ms Grace Leven."

"Herman?"

"The one and only," he beamed. His smile was wide, and several people sitting near them turned and waved at him.

"I just need to go through your stay."

"Why do you need to go through my stay?'

"So, I can design a programme for you."

"I don't want a programme."

"Everyone has a programme, Ms Leven."

"Did Lulu put you up to this, or Jack?"

"I'm sorry?"

"I'm tired. I'd like to go to my room."

"Of course, Ms Leven. But first," he held up a finger. "Let me just ask one tiny question. What would you like to get out of your stay here? Rest? Relaxation? Or would you like to feel re-energised?"

Grace rubbed her head, which was starting to ache. "I don't know."

"You don't know?" Herman looked at her.

"What? Is there something wrong?"

His eyes stayed on her. "Of course not. There's nothing wrong with that."

Grace could feel her own eyes stinging with tears again behind her sunglasses.

"I've had a…well, busy time, shall we say? I'm exhausted. I needed some space."

"Then we shall give you space."

Grace nodded.

"What do you enjoy?"

"But that's just it. That's just bloody it. I have no idea. I'm lost, Herman. I'm fifty-three years old and I'm lost, and this was not supposed to happen to me."

She could feel other eyes on her but she was starting not to care.

"Ms Leven," Herman's voice softened. "This is absolutely fine."

"Really? Is it really, Herman?"

Grace picked up her water and noticed her hand was shaking. There was no blanket of love – more one of awkwardness which was settling around them.

"Sleep," she said. "I like to sleep."

Herman smiled his big smile. "Well, there you are. There's one thing you like doing at least."

Grace smiled a small smile too. She sat back and tried to breathe out. She knew she wasn't helping anyone, acting like this.

"Would you mind if I offered you some advice, Ms Leven?"

"If you must."

"Just listen to you. You know your knowing." He touched his chest.

She couldn't take any more.

"Not bloody you too. Why does everyone keep going on about inner bloody knowing? Why didn't anyone tell me this before? All I know is mine is wrong, completely bloody wrong. It's left me with a cheating husband who had an affair with my supposed best friend. I've got no job – I think I've been stitched up – and I don't even have a home any more. I'm here on this island, I suspect having some sort of breakdown, but at the same time writing a column about me being on a Lost Path, which no one will read and is a feeble attempt to give me some sort of bloody purpose. But how the bloody hell am I supposed to have any knowing when I have no idea who I am?"

More heads turned, but she was starting to care even less.

"Well, there you are." Herman sat back, put his hands together and smiled.

"What do you mean?" She was starting to dislike Herman.

"You have your starting point. You know where you are."

"No, I don't. I'm lost Herman. Bloody lost."

"And that's where you are. Your starting point."

Grace put her head in her hands – she didn't care who was watching her, she just needed this all to stop.

Herman leant forward. "I appreciate we've just met, Ms Leven, but if I may be so bold, I'd like to suggest that you know exactly where you are."

"In some sort of hell – that's where I am," Grace hissed.

"Your voice. It's telling you, loud and clear. It's telling you that you feel lost, therefore it's telling you exactly where you are. You're just choosing not to listen."

"The lost bloody path," she muttered, then looked up. "I'm sorry. I'm being a bitch."

"You're not. Many of our guests arrive in the same place. Tired, overwhelmed and lost." He smiled his big smile again. "We all find ourselves there at some time, and it's a wonderful place to be."

"It is?"

"Yes it is, and you must look at it as a gift." He leant forward, his elbows on his knees. "There's one much more dangerous path you never want to be on."

"And that is?"

"The path where you're so truly lost, you don't even know that you are."

Herman nodded at a member of staff who arrived with glass of champagne.

"At least toast your arrival," Herman said, and Grace took the glass. She'd promised herself she'd keep away from alcohol, but one wouldn't hurt.

"So, what actually happens at Antigua House?" Grace sat back.

"Everyone has a different experience here; it's unique to all our guests. But we have helpers, shall we say – chefs, masseurs, trainers, artists – who are all here to help you discover what you need. But," he lifted his hand, "as you will tell me you don't know what you need, we will start you with some basics combined with some space."

"I see." Grace nodded. She liked the idea of some space. "Okay," she nodded again.

"But first we must get you to slow down. Until you slow down, you'll never see what's in front of you."

Grace picked up her champagne. Slowing down was the very last thing she needed to do. She gulped the cool liquid and wondered once more, if she'd made a terrible mistake.

Chapter Twenty-Five

Eric: Grace. This is childish. Where are you?
Polly: Please Grace. We need to talk.
Pearl: You've got this mum x

When Grace opened her eyes, she couldn't remember where she was. Was she in the cottage at Strawberry House or was she back at home?

But no, she was somewhere different again. The room was large and cool, with a white wooden floor. Through the billowing curtains, she could see a wide balcony which wrapped around the room, overlooking the sea. When she got up and went into the bathroom, she saw it was large and well-designed. A roll-top bath sat in the middle of the room – a walkthrough rainfall shower covered another side. Two sinks sat on a large pale-pink unit with a mirror edged with bulbs above.

She went back into the room, and sat down on the armchair. It was pink, just like the ones at Strawberry House, but this one was covered with tiny lemons. It made her smile. She looked around the room and she had to hand it to Jack. He knew what he was doing when it came to creating welcoming hotels.

She looked at her watch. It was five twenty-seven am. She'd slept for ten hours. She'd finished her glass of champagne with Herman, and by the time she'd arrived at her room she hadn't cared about jetlag or food – she'd just wanted to sleep.

She walked over to the coffee machine on the large white marble table and put in a pod. Even though she was thousands of miles away, there were touches which told her it was still the same family as Strawberry House. The coffee machines, the glasses, the basket of cookies, the fridge she opened to see it was filled with drinks. She'd only known Jack for a short time but there was something comforting about being in one of his hotels. It made her feel safe.

She walked over to the French doors and opened them. She was hit by the thick, warm air. She sat down on one of the large, soft white chairs and put her feet up on the footstool.

She smelt the jasmine in the air, heard the crickets, and a warm breeze touched her skin. It was dark still, but the sky was starting to glow. She sat back and sipped the hot, strong coffee.

What on earth was she going to do?

Operation Lost Path was so far not going well. She'd been rude to Herman and hadn't gone back for dinner like she'd said she would.

Grace looked back towards the room and felt thoroughly ashamed. She was better than this, wasn't she?

Or was this why everything had fallen apart?

Just as the shame began to crawl up inside her she spotted through the doors a white envelope which had been pushed through her door. She walked back into the coolness of the room and picked it up.

A full body therapeutic massage has been booked for you with Beatrice at our spa at 10.00am
Operation Lost Path begins
I hope you slept well.
Herman, Head of Wellbeing

She looked around the room and then at her watch. Five forty-two am. Four hours and eighteen minutes. What was she going to do?

Midlife Murders & The Lost Path
2

Hello dear reader

So here we are. Forgive me if I sound like a complete spoiled brat, but here I am in actual paradise.

Yesterday I was told that knowing we are lost means we know where we are.

Are you confused? Because I certainly am.

If I am indeed lost, how did this happen?

I thought that by the age of fifty-three, I would have gained all I needed to know to be where I want to be. Shouldn't I just be enjoying life with ease – with the hard part done, the ladder climbed, the daughter raised? Isn't it time I should be enjoying the so-called 'fruits' as it were? But nobody ever told me about the ache. The gnawing, nagging constant ache. I could say it was brought about by my cheating husband and losing my job, but if I'm really truthful it was there long before I discovered all that.

So, what now?

All this talk of inner knowing and paths might be fine in this world where I can spend days searching my soul, but back in the real world (where I hope to be again soon), is there really a place for this? There are meetings, lists and routines I must maintain. I must do my best, be well put together and at least give the impression I know where I am. Isn't that what we all do, whatever our job?

What I don't understand is why my knowing wasn't enough. It took me to CEO – a job so many wanted, but I was the one who got the prize. So then why do I feel so lost, at the top of a mountain I found so hard to climb? Where is the reward of peace and contentment?

I've been trying to think back to when I started to feel the ache. Even as a child I think it was there, at times. But on other days I do remember feeling free and as though everything was right in the world. I loved being with my dad as he pottered in his shed. I loved it when my mum came in and said, 'enough is enough, you two, it's getting dark'. She'd tell us dinner was ready and that we should wash our hands. We'd pretend to be annoyed and roll our eyes, then cross our fingers, praying silently that it wouldn't be lamb chops.

Now I feel like there's some sort of wall between me and this part and I don't know how I can ever knock it down. It's solid, hard and feels like a numbness I can't stand. I've pretended for so long it's not there but I've got nothing left to distract me now. It's there and it's all I can feel. It's blocking me from my freedom but I've got no idea how to break through it. I don't know when it arrived but I hate it. It exhausts me and nothing seems to make it go away.

So, as I sit here on this Lost Path, I wonder: if I can't push past the wall, what will I do?

I may be sitting on a beautiful balcony in paradise, with its warm breeze and endless view of the sea. I should feel peaceful, happy and excited about life, but all I'm doing is wishing that wall inside would go away.

What Really Happened To Me?

"Good morning, Ms Leven."

Grace felt her spirits lift immediately. Beatrice was tiny. She had a smile as wide as Herman's and she threw her head back and laughed a bellowing laugh you wouldn't imagine could come out of someone as small as Beatrice.

"It's a pleasure to meet you, Beatrice. I've heard a lot about you."

"Come, come." Beatrice ushered her into the spa. "Let's get you cooled down."

"Thank you," Grace said, and once again found herself trying not to cry. She was being ridiculous – she couldn't cry every time someone was kind to her.

But she was so hot.

She'd decided to run along the beach, and even though the sun was only just coming up, the heat was searing. She'd had a cold shower, eaten the breakfast she'd ordered in her room but, despite the air conditioning, she hadn't been able to cool down.

Inside the cool spa, Beatrice led her to a room towards the back and closed the door behind them.

"Here." She poured some iced water for Grace. "Sip this."

Grace took it, wiped her cheek and hoped Beatrice hadn't noticed.

"Please sit down." Beatrice nodded to a small white armchair in the room. "Now, tell me," she said, pulling another small chair in front of Grace and sitting in it. "How are you feeling this morning?"

She wanted to say she was great, but the words didn't come. "I don't know," she said instead.

"You don't know?" Beatrice clapped her hands. "Well, this is the most wonderful start."

"Are you going to tell me I need to find my inner knowing too?"

Beatrice threw back her head and laughed her deep laugh. "Don't be so ridiculous. How are you supposed to know anything with a body as rigid as yours?"

Grace didn't know if she should feel offended. She tried to slouch a little in the chair.

"Are you not going to tell me that I need to know where I am, what I like, who I am?"

Beatrice stood up and walked behind the small white desk in the corner of the room. She opened a drawer and pulled out a white notebook.

"Saying you don't know is a great first step. Believe me, the number of guests in here who tell me they're great – that's when I know I've got my work cut out."

Grace sipped her water.

"I don't feel great."

"No, I suspect you don't. But that's okay. This is why you're here."

Beatrice looked at her and wrote something in the little white book.

Grace looked around the room. There was a beautiful orchid. The sun shone in through the window and the tiles were a soothing aqua blue. But still a restless feeling came over her. She wasn't used to this. Sitting. Doing nothing. Couldn't they just get on with it all?

"Okay." Beatrice stood up again. "I'm going to ask you to put on this robe."

"Aren't you going to ask me any more questions?"

"No, my dear, there's no point. Not while you've got shoulders like yours."

What Really Happened To Me?

Grace waited for Beatrice to return to the room. She hadn't had many massages in her life. She'd never really seen the point. Lying down, with someone's hands touching her body? There was always something better to do.

"How long have you been doing this?" Grace asked as she heard Beatrice return to the room.

"My dear, I need you to be quiet, and I need you to be as still as you can. I know this is hard and uncomfortable, but that's okay – it's just the beginning. We'll take one small step at a time."

It all sounded very serious to Grace for what was supposed to be a relaxing massage. She put her head through the hole in the massage table and looked at the white wooden floor underneath. She tried to settle and she told herself to relax, but she could feel the heat in her rising.

She heard Beatrice open a bottle of oil and then rub it on her hands. Then she felt them, cool on her back.

"Nice and quiet," Beatrice said as her hands began to move.

If Grace was expecting anything, it would be that Beatrice would be soft and gentle. She was tiny with such a kind look in her eyes, it was hard to imagine anything else. But as soon as Beatrice's fingers touched her skin, she noticed how hard and strong they were – and they were soon digging into her shoulders.

This was more like it, Grace thought. When she had had a massage in the past she'd found it frustrating and weak. This was better, much better.

But Beatrice began to dig deeper and deeper and Grace began to feel a dense, sickening pain.

"That's too hard," she said, or did she? She didn't hear any words.

All she could see was her back garden when she was a

child. She was pottering now with her dad in the shed. Where was the white wooden floor beneath her? It had disappeared.

Instead, she could see herself. She knew she was nine years old because she was wearing a badge saying 'I'm nine'. She'd forgotten all about that badge her mother had made for her, like she had most years. She was waiting in the shed with her dad, while her mother was in the house getting her birthday tea ready. She knew there'd be a birthday cake with nine candles and she knew it would be chocolate.

The smell of the shed filled the air now. It was dusty and smelt of oak, just like her dad. He was next to her, sawing a small piece on his work table. He chattered – she couldn't hear about what – and he pottered. Then he sipped his tea.

The heat had stopped rising in her; it was more of a familiar warmth now – one she hadn't felt for a long time. She was excited too, not just about the chocolate cake. That night they'd go to their favourite restaurant. They rarely went out – only on special occasions – but there was a Bernie restaurant nearby which served ice cream in tall glasses with biscuit bits at the bottom. That night, she'd had chocolate sauce on top too.

But first there was the cake, and some more presents. She didn't even care what they'd be – she'd seen them earlier, waiting for her on the sofa, wrapped in yellow paper with white spots. She would open them and love them, as her mother always knew what she loved. Then she'd change into her favourite dress. It was dark red and made of velvet and her mother would plait her hair.

"Grace," she heard her mother calling. "Grace."

Just hearing her mother's voice filled her with more warmth. Oh, how she'd forgotten her mother's magical voice. She was happy there and she felt safe. She was calm and at peace – there was no feeling of striving and clinging, no low-level hum of needing to feel afraid. There was nothing to be afraid of. Everything was just as it was. They were all together in this little corner of their world and she didn't want to be anywhere else at all.

"Grace, Grace."

Grace hopped down from her stool. She opened the shed door and walked down the path towards their little cottage.

"Grace, Grace."

"Come on, Dad." She called behind to her father, but when she looked around, he wasn't there.

"Dad?" She called out, or did she? She couldn't hear.

"Grace."

She looked back towards the house. The lights were all out now. Hadn't the lamps been on a few moments before?

"Grace."

She looked behind her again. Where was her dad? Perhaps he was still in the shed? He did that sometimes – he got carried away with his sawing. But now, when she pushed open the rickety door and looked inside, he wasn't there. That's strange, she thought as she walked down the path.

"Dad," she tried to call but couldn't hear. Perhaps he'd gone ahead to the house? She walked along the path towards the cottage, turning back just to double-check he wasn't getting some wood from behind the shed. But when she looked back now, the shed was gone.

Why wasn't it there? Where was the shed?

"Grace."

She opened the back door of the cottage, but it didn't feel like home. The house was cold and dark. The kitchen was the same – small, neat and tidy. Her mother's red-and-white spotted oven gloves were on the counter, but the kitchen was empty and there was no smell of cake. She walked out of the kitchen and into the small hall towards the lounge. The unease was back now, that familiar feeling she was more used to. Where were they? Where were her mum and dad?

"Mum, Dad?" She wanted to call but no words would come out.

She turned back towards the hall, but everything was changing and it wasn't how she remembered at all. Where was she? Where were they? Who was she? She was tiny and afraid. The door had gone to the lounge and she could see the sofa with the swirly pink flowers, but it was all grubby and dirty. Her mother never let it get like that. She saw her red velvet dress – the one she'd been planning to wear that night – all crumpled on the floor. She looked up and she could see the house disappearing. The lounge had gone, now the kitchen. Where were her mother's oven gloves? They'd disappeared too. Everything was going, everything was disappearing into the dark. Everything she loved – the warmth, the cake, the dress, the gloves, her whole world was melting away.

Stop! she wanted to cry. Stop! Where are you? She tried to shout but couldn't.

She needed to get out. She needed to find someone she knew – perhaps Timothy the neighbour next door could help?

Timothy, she called. Someone, help me please. I need help, she called, and then she shouted the same. She pushed and she pulled and at last she opened her eyes.

She was back in the white tiled room and she was all alone.

What Really Happened To Me?

"What just happened?"

She'd found Beatrice in the reception of the spa, laughing with the receptionist. When she saw Grace, she'd greeted her. "Ah, there she is. Come, have some water," and she'd ushered Grace back into the room.

Grace sat now on the white sofa in the treatment room, wrapped in a soft, white towelling gown. She sipped the iced water, her hands still shaking.

Beatrice sat down next to her.

"Take your time, Ms Leven. You need to take your time, and you have plenty here."

Grace couldn't describe how she was feeling. She felt shaken and light-headed, as if she was in some sort of fog. She was sitting there in Antigua – the palm trees were swaying outside the window – and she was with a woman she'd only just met. But she could feel her little cottage all around her.

"It was so strange. It was as though I was a nine-year-old girl again. I was with my dad and it was my birthday. He was pottering in his shed and my mum was finishing my birthday cake, but when I went into the house, they'd disappeared. Everything had disappeared, Beatrice." Grace looked up at Beatrice. "It was awful."

"I'm sorry, Ms Leven."

Grace sipped her water.

"Did something happen to you when you were nine?"

Grace shook her head. "No. I remember that day; it was a happy day. I remember turning nine and going out for dinner in the evening. I was with my mum and dad and I remember feeling so happy – the kind of happiness which, when you feel it, makes you think you're going to burst."

"How wonderful." Beatrice smiled.

"My parents were killed in a car crash when I was eighteen. I'd just started university."

The smile slowly left Beatrice's face. "Ms Leven, I'm so sorry." Beatrice touched Grace's hand and Grace noticed how soft her hand felt, so different to the hand she'd felt on her shoulders earlier. It felt strange still, to have her hand held. When was the last time she'd held hands with anyone? She hadn't – with anyone, for so long.

The two sat in silence.

"Sometimes, we need two parts of ourselves to meet to be able to live again," Beatrice continued to hold her hand.

"I don't understand."

"Well," Beatrice leant forward. "Your body stores everything – all the trauma, the fears, those moments of pure joy – it's all here." Beatrice touched Grace's shoulder with her other hand. "The body keeps a sample of everything that doesn't fully pass through. It clings on tight. But this can fracture us and we lose the feeling of ever feeling whole." She squeezed Grace's hand. "When we do this deep massage, it can disturb these parts. Parts that have sat, hidden for years. Think of it like one of those old trees that lives deep in a dark forest for a long time. If you start to move it, old moths which haven't been disturbed in years can fly out."

Grace still wasn't sure she understood. When had she ever even felt whole?

"I think you should take your time. You need to sit with this."

"But I don't like it."

"Why ever not?" Beatrice asked.

"It's painful."

"But that's wonderful." Beatrice smiled. She leaned close to Grace and nudged her. "Not all feelings feel good, my dear, and pain is a sign of love. But what you must do is feel it, feel it deeply, because only then can you set it free."

Grace was still thinking of Beatrice's words as she sat on a beach bed in the shade an hour later. Instead of feeling relaxed, as she'd hoped, she felt hot and agitated. She watched the people around her. Couples and families laughing and enjoying the sea. They were capturing memories they'd keep forever. She, meanwhile, felt out of place.

She picked up a book she'd taken from reception and tried to read.

"Ms Leven," a voice interrupted her. It was Herman.

"Well, if you are Head of Wellbeing, I'm far from feeling well. I feel dreadful, Herman."

Herman beamed a big smile. "Ah, you've had your massage? Would you mind if I joined you?" He nodded at the empty bed next to her.

"Please." She didn't want to tell him she was delighted not to be alone. She braced herself for more wisdoms, not sure how much more she could take. But instead, Herman was quiet. He looked out at the blue sea – and took a deep breath.

"I never tire of this view."

She looked out at it too. She hadn't really taken it in since she had arrived; she'd been too busy lost in her thoughts. "It's wonderful."

"And just answer me one question." He looked at her. "Have you really been looking at the view, or have you been lost in your thoughts?"

Grace smiled and shook her head. "My thoughts never stop."

"Tell me about them."

"My thoughts?"

"Yes."

"I'd rather not."

"Of course."

Grace tried to look at the view again, but her mind was still racing. She was being rude, but she didn't want to talk. Who were all these people invading her life and privacy? Now she was being rude and she couldn't stop it. She didn't like feeling like this. She wanted to feel in control and back where she belonged. How was she supposed to stop the thoughts? Stop, she told them, stop. But it was as if they were getting louder and louder, knocking on a door she'd tried to close.

"It never stops." She sat back on the lounger. "The constant looping. From one thought to another. It's bloody exhausting, Herman."

"And are the thoughts kind or unkind?"

"I don't know. They're just thoughts."

"If you were to say them out loud, what would they sound like?"

"Is this a way of getting me to tell you my thoughts?"

Herman laughed. "I promise it's not. Just think of one; don't say it out loud."

Everything is my fault.

"Is it a kind thought?"

"It's a true thought."

"How do you know it's true? Do you have evidence? For example," he looked back out at the sea. "That sea I think we would all agree is a beautiful, glistening blue."

"Yes, it is."

"If I asked that gentleman over there in the sea, or that

woman, what colour they would describe the sea as, they would undoubtedly say some shade of blue."

"Well, yes." She was starting to feel exhausted again.

"The thought you just had – is it absolutely one hundred per cent true?"

"That all my problems are my fault?" Damn, she'd said it out loud. "You're worse than Greg."

"Greg?"

"My therapist. Well, former colleague, back at home, although it's not my home."

She was so hot and confused.

"I am not a therapist, Ms Leven. But I will ask you this. What is the evidence that all your problems are caused by you? Don't answer, please." He smiled his big smile.

Grace paused for a moment. Was she really responsible for Eric sleeping with Polly? And why, deep, deep down, did it feel easier somehow to think this?

"I think they're not particularly kind."

Herman nodded. "This comes as no surprise."

"So, what am I supposed to do?"

"Well, first I am going to teach you how to breathe."

Grace laughed. "Herman, please. The one thing I can do is breathe. I'm alive. I just need my job back. I need my life back."

"And why do you need your job? Why isn't Antigua enough for you?"

"Antigua is wonderful, but it's not real life."

"Isn't taking time for you real life?"

"No, well…yes? I don't know what I'm supposed to say."

"Don't say anything. You told me last night you feel lost. The best place to start is to be kind to yourself. Those thoughts in there – it's like a human punchbag. Would you treat your daughter like that? Would you tell her all her problems are caused by her?"

"No, of course not. I'd tell her they were caused by…" She stopped.

Herman smiled. "That's right, because her mother causes all her problems. You have the power to do this."

Grace looked at him. "It does sound a bit egocentric." She thought of the conversations she'd had over the years with numerous celebrities and their entourages. They all thought they were the centre of the world – so much so that there was no room for anyone else. Then they wondered why their marriages broke down, and their careers. Grace had seen most of them come and then go. The bigger the ego, the shorter the reign.

"So, why can't you be so kind to yourself?"

Grace shrugged.

"I don't know. I think I've always been like this, even before I lost everything. Isn't it just how I'm wired? It all sounds so…well, self-indulgent."

Grace felt a swell within her. A rise of something she didn't recognise.

"Have you, though?" Herman nodded towards the sea again. "Have you really lost everything? Look at this. You're here, you're in paradise, and you can breathe. If you can breathe, you're in a wonderful place."

"I can't do it, Herman," she whispered. "I can't keep living like this."

"Then follow me." He put his hand on his chest. "I want you to place your hand on your heart, and now breathe."

3

Hello dear reader

Today I was taught how to breathe.

I've overseen eye-watering budgets, I've headed staff of hundreds, I can make a decision in my job in three seconds if need be. I graduated from Cambridge University with a first.

Yet, here I am learning to breathe.

There are, it seems, many different ways. The square method – in for four, hold for four, out for four, hold for four – is just one of them. Who knew there were so many different ways to breathe?

Yet why am I the only one who feels like there is no time to breathe? Even here. Is it really just me?

Back in London, at no point in my schedule do I see "breathe". The days are filled with never-ending meetings, a work breakfast, a work dinner and we mustn't forget the work lunch in-between. Yes, there are moments, but my mind is always so occupied by the never-ending list of responsibilities – overnight figures, the latest advertising deal, the looming end-of-year results.

Please can someone tell me: when do I have a chance to breathe?

I know here I do have time – but my mind feels unable to stop. The constant whir of trying to make sense of everything is making my head spin too much to breathe. A schedule is easier; it gives me a little control. Give me a decision about a budget cut any day over this.

I'm lonely.

As I sit here, it's as though it's buzzing in my ears. I feel it everywhere: in my bones, in my soul. It aches a slow, throbbing, dreadful ache.

I try now to remember a time when I didn't feel this way – and there was a time. It was my birthday. I was going out to celebrate and I was nine years old.

Chapter Twenty-Six

Eric: Grace So, you're going to carry on like this? Rather childish don't you think?
Polly: Grace, please stop ignoring me. We need to talk. x

Grace sat back and looked at her page.

"Ms Leven," a voice called. Grace saw Beatrice waving at her as she walked across the terrace. She was wearing dark sunglasses and her small hands were in the air.

"Beatrice," Grace smiled, grateful to see a friendly face.

"Do you mind if I sit down?"

"Of course not. How are those hands of yours? Are they exhausted after a day of healing?"

Beatrice threw her head back and laughed. "No, no. It energises me Ms Leven. I love my work."

Grace nodded.

"The reason I want to speak with you," Beatrice looked around, then peered over her sunglasses, "and this is strictly confidential, but I, or rather we, were wondering if you'd care to join us at Lemon Cove?"

"Lemon Cove?"

Beatrice shook her head. "Lemon Cove is where I live." She looked behind her. "It's not something we always do."

"I see." Grace looked around, and tried not to smile. The guests were too busy enjoying themselves to take any notice of their conversation.

"So, would you like to? If you don't have any plans?"

Did she?

"Yes, I think I would. When were you thinking?"

"Now."

"Now?"

"Yes, now. Claudia is waiting out the front."

"Claudia?"

"Ms Leven, you ask a lot of questions." Beatrice stood up and looked around again. "This is neither the time, nor the place. "So let's go."

Grace had never been spontaneous. She heard Eric's voice, complaining that she scheduled even her teeth-brushing.

Grace stood up. "Should I change?"

Beatrice shook her head. "You're perfect."

They started to walk.

"Beatrice?"

"Yes, Ms Leven." Beatrice looked around again.

"You and Herman are being awfully attentive. Does everyone get looked after like this?"

"Of course, Ms Leven. We look after all our guests." Beatrice looked behind her again, "but every now and again, we have a someone who just needs a visit to Lemon Cove."

The journey to Lemon Cove took around twenty minutes. Grace sat in the back of the small open-air jeep, which was driven by the woman called Claudia. Claudia, who was taller than Beatrice, greeted Grace with the same warmth and smile.

"Ms Leven, it's my pleasure to meet you. Now, jump in. Let's go."

The journey passed mainly in silence. She noticed Beatrice and Claudia shared the occasional glance, and she hated feeling out of control. She thought about texting Pearl so at least someone knew where she was going. But when she reached for her bag, the pair of them looked around with such a fierce glare, she put it back down.

They pulled up in what looked like a layby. "We're here."

Grace looked around at the road. "Here?"

The two of them threw their heads back and laughed again. Claudia towered over Beatrice as she put her arm on her shoulder, and Beatrice put her arm around her back. Grace wondered if they were sisters? She was about to ask but she was ushered on.

She followed them along a sandy path, and then they started to climb.

It was hot, and she didn't like it. She felt itchy and uncomfortable and she didn't want to be there at all. What was she doing? She was walking around an island she didn't know with two strangers.

Her life was a mess and she just wanted to lie down. All she wanted to do was to lie down.

"Please, Ms Leven. Give us your trust," Claudia said.

Grace took another step – one step at a time. The irony hit her. "I'm writing about being on the Lost Path and here I am," she said, but the two of them swung around.

What Really Happened To Me?

"Please, you must be quiet Ms Leven, you need to take this moment in." Claudia's face was stern and then transformed into another enormous smile.

As Grace climbed, with every step she felt more rage. More anger and rage that this is what her life had become. She was so lost and pathetic, with no way home. She was supposed to be strong. She wasn't supposed to be like this – lost, broken and ungrateful.

She followed them because she was too pathetic to tell them she couldn't continue. Perhaps she could just turn back? Perhaps she could just leave. She could run, she would find someone – anyone – who would help her find her way.

"It's okay, Ms Leven. You can relax now. We're here."

Grace had never been anywhere quite like Lemon Cove. It wasn't just the view or the never- ending sparkling sea. It wasn't the way the trees swayed in the breeze. It was something else which she couldn't quite put her finger on.

There were small, colourful houses dotted around the bay. Children ran along the beach playing football. They laughed and cheered, while men and women of all ages sat on their porches, reading, peeling vegetables and chatting. It was like a small piece of paradise you hoped existed somewhere but deep-down never believed it really did.

Grace sat in a large chair under a large shady tree. Beatrice and Claudia had told her not to move, and had disappeared. Now Claudia was walking towards her carrying a tray.

"Here, Ms Leven, have some lemonade." Claudia handed her a glass.

"Thank you. This is wonderful, I've never been anywhere quite like this."

'We're very blessed,' Claudia smiled as she took a seat by her side.

"Mama," one of the boys called out from the beach, and waved.

Grace thought of Pearl, growing up in London, walking to and from her expensive private school. The discipline and the rigidity had always grated on her. Did it really have to be that way? It hadn't been like that when she was a child. She'd tried, but Eric had always sighed and told her to stop living in the past. But this wasn't the past; this was very much the present, and the children in front of her looked healthy and happy – they looked free.

"Welcome to Lemon Cove." Beatrice sat down on the other side of her and took a glass of lemonade.

Grace sipped her drink through the straw. It was cool, tasted of lemons and had a strong kick.

"Is there alcohol in this?"

Claudia laughed. "Just a little. We checked on your notes – that you participate. This is the speciality drink of Lemon Cove. So, tell me Ms Leven, how are you enjoying Antigua House?"

Grace sat back into the chair. The cool liquid was refreshing in her dry mouth.

"It's a beautiful place."

"But…" Claudia added.

"She had her first massage, this morning."

"I see," Claudia nodded.

"I see what?" Grace asked, and sipped more of the lemonade.

"You are no doubt feeling a little…"

"Disorientated," Beatrice filled in.

"Yes." Grace looked at Beatrice, who smiled one of her great big smiles. She raised her glass. "Exactly that. How did you know?"

Beatrice clinked her glass with Grace's.

"This is what happens. It's nothing to worry about."

Isn't it? Grace thought as she sat in this pocket of paradise. "Then why do I feel so dreadful?"

"Is it really so dreadful?" Claudia asked.

"Tell us, who says you shouldn't feel like this from time to time?" Beatrice asked.

Grace thought for a moment. "I don't know. The world?"

"Well honey, not this part of the world. We embrace all the feels – the good and the bad."

"I can't imagine you ever feel anything bad here."

"Oh, we have our ups and downs – it's called being a human being. When they don't score their goals and someone else does," she nodded at the children, 'when the fish don't come, and they think they've failed," she nodded at the fishermen in their boats. "We all have our storms, just like everyone else. Everyone has their storms, no matter who they are."

"Agreed," Beatrice nodded.

"And what happens then?"

"Like all our storms, we let them come, we don't fight and we ride them out. We let them do what they have to do, then they pass and everything is okay."

Grace looked out at the sea. It was calm and pond-like – so hard to imagine it ever in the midst of a storm. The sky was clear blue, even late in the afternoon. How could a storm ever reach such a place?

"We all have our storms, Ms Leven," Claudia said again.

"Please call me Grace."

"The problem comes," Beatrice continued, "when we try to stop the storms from coming. When we resist them, they build up and up. We think they've gone away but they haven't gone anywhere. They sit inside, and we carry them and then everything we do is affected by that built-up storm we carry inside. One day it comes out, but sometimes it doesn't, and this is even worse, because then we're too disconnected from who we really are." Beatrice turned to her. "But your storm is coming out and this is a wonderful thing."

"It doesn't feel like that at all. Beatrice, am I having a breakdown?"

"Well, I'm no doctor, but what it looks like to me is you're having a release. I see it all the time, and as it comes out, it's not going to be sunshine and calm waters.

There's going to be anger and rage and resentment, which is fine. These are all your friends telling you something.

Even the numbness and disconnection are ways our minds and bodies protect us from the pain. However, if we don't let ourselves feel the pain, we carry it around with us forever. And this, my dear – it's not good."

Claudia shook her head. "It's not good at all."

"But here's the thing." Beatrice leant forward.

"Yes?" Grace leant forward too.

"We can get too attached to our pain. We're defined by it and we don't know how we will exist without it. We can be so attached, we can't even let it go."

"But how can I let something go when it's ruined my life?"

"Can you change what happened?"

"No."

"So what if you just let it be?"

"But I don't want to – it's ruined my life."

"What if it hasn't ruined your life? What if it's taking you on a different path?"

"What if I don't want to go on that bloody path? What's with all these bloody paths?"

Beatrice clapped her hands. "I love it when we have a fighter."

Claudia laughed too. "The fighters are the best. We love a challenge."

"I'm not a fighter." Grace sat back. She was sulking like a child, with a big glass of lemonade.

"My dear," Beatrice turned to Grace. "These are mere thoughts your mind is creating. The ego loves to feed on negativity and pain, so it tells you that everything in life is your fault, to create more of that same pain."

"Well, isn't it?"

Claudia touched her hand.

"Look around you. Henry over there – he's just fallen over."

Grace looked at the boy who was on the sand. He was laughing as he dusted himself off and started running again.

"Are you going to tell me that's your fault too?"

"Of course not."

"Then why is everything your fault?"

"My husband, my best friend, my employees – I've done something to lose them all."

"Really?" Claudia and Beatrice looked at her. "Can you tell us that you are responsible for your husband's behaviour?"

"I pushed him away."

Beatrice touched her other hand. "We are never responsible for anyone else's behaviour. Just

as we are always responsible for our own."

"This is what I'm saying. My behaviour pushed him away."

Beatrice and Claudia each squeezed one of her hands tight.

"Have you been disloyal?"

"I've been angry. Really bloody angry."

"But isn't that a natural reaction? Wouldn't you tell this to a friend?"

Grace thought for a moment. Yes, she bloody would.

"The point is when we slow down and observe our feelings, give ourselves some space between us and them, we can see they are protecting us. But it doesn't mean we have to react and make it all worse. Give those feelings space and love, they are only doing their job, keeping you safe." Beatrice said.

"Your husband's betrayal belongs to him," Claudia said.

Grace looked up. "How did you know my husband betrayed me?"

"We can see it in your eyes. That pain tells us a million stories. But you have nothing to fear here with us. Here you are safe, and this is why we brought you to Lemon Cove."

Chapter Twenty-Seven

Eric: Grace, where are you?
Eric: Grace, when are you coming home?
Eric: Grace, we need to talk?
Eric Grace, you can't keep on treating me like this. After everything I've done for you.

The next morning Grace woke just after six am.

She'd slept solidly and when she opened her eyes, for a moment she wondered if she'd dreamt about her night in Lemon Cove.

She'd stayed with Beatrice and Claudia for several hours. She'd had dinner with them. They'd eaten mahi-mahi, squash and greens. It was simple, fresh and delicious. They'd drunk more of Claudia's lemonade and then they'd played Black Jack. She couldn't remember the last time she'd played cards.

The driver from the hotel, Lionel, had come to collect her and take her back. Beatrice and Claudia had walked back along the path to escort her to the car.

"Thank you," she told them as they put their arms around her. "I'll never forget Lemon Cove."

"You're always welcome here." They squeezed her hands. "And remember," Beatrice had said, "every time that mind wanders away, bring it back to here," Beatrice touched her chest, "or at least just look at our wonderful sea."

"What is in that lemonade?" Grace asked again as she got into the cool, air-conditioned car. She felt relaxed and mellow in a way she never did with alcohol.

"Darling, that secret is locked up tight. None of us have ever known and I've known Claudia all my life," Beatrice said.

Claudia nodded a small nod and closed the car door.

Grace decided she'd go for a run before the sun became too hot. She ran along the beach and every time she felt her mind begin to fill with thoughts she looked back out at the sea. It surprised her how much better she felt. She showered, dressed and decided that day would be the day she'd have breakfast in the restaurant.

She'd just sat down when Herman walked towards her, waving at the people on various other tables.

The restaurant was open-air, shady and beautiful, like the rest of the hotel. A waitress came to pour her coffee.

"Can we interest you in anything from our menu, madam?" she asked.

"Just fruit would be great. Thanks."

"Just fruit?" Herman raised his eyebrows. He looked at the waitress. "Doris, bring her some of the chef's best pancakes with some fruit on the side."

"Really, there's no need."

What Really Happened To Me?

Herman shushed Doris away. "Do as I say. She'll need it where she is going today."

"I'm sorry?" Grace put down her coffee.

"Would you mind if I join you?" Herman was already sitting opposite her.

"It appears you already have."

"Now, that's the spirit. I see Lemon Cove worked a little magic."

"What do you mean?" Grace felt the familiar irritation.

"Those dark eyes" – he drew circles around his own – "they're not quite so offensive."

"I think you're being offensive."

Herman paused and peered at her, then slapped the table. "I love this. The spirit is coming through."

"You haven't answered my question. What do you think I'm doing today? I hadn't planned on doing very much."

"The Lost Path," Herman said. "You're going to walk along it and find out where you are."

"I am?"

"Yes, you are. So, eat your pancakes." He stood up and leant towards her, his hands on the white linen cloth. "Then I'll meet you in reception in one hour's time."

"But…" Grace tried, but he was already walking away.

"One hour," he called over his shoulder. "And don't be late."

An hour later she was sitting next to Herman in his jeep. Although she was irritated by being commandeered in such a way, at least there wasn't anyone else in the car. The idea of making small talk made her want to hide.

"I thought there'd be others."

"Why? Your Lost Path is your Lost Path."

"Do all your guests get taken on a random path?"

"Ms Leven, I'd kindly ask you to just take in where you are."

They drove along the winding road, the palm trees swaying at the side. The air was warm and wrapped around Grace. Around every corner was another view of the magnificent sea. Every time a negative thought came in, Claudia and Beatrice's words reminded her to stay focused on the sea.

Half an hour later, when they arrived at their stop, her irritation had melted away.

"Okay." Herman jumped down and held out his hand for her. "You're here."

"Where?"

"On the Lost Path."

"But how can I be lost, if you know where I am?"

"Because I'm not coming. I want you to follow the path."

"What? Do you mean you're not coming?"

"Ms Leven. You told me this trip was to help you find your way."

"I did. But walking alone in the jungle isn't the way for me to do this."

"Then what is? You're on a Lost Path."

"You're not making any sense."

Herman laughed and leant into his jeep.

"So, you're just going to abandon me?"

"You have everything you need." He handed her a map and a flask of water. "There. Now it's time for you to find your way."

"But where will I meet you? And when?"

"I'll meet you when you're ready."

What Really Happened To Me?

"But, how—"

"Enough of the questions Ms Leven. Enjoy. Now go." Then Herman jumped in the jeep and drove away, and Grace Leven found herself standing all alone.

She started to walk along the dusty path in front of her. All the irritation she'd felt earlier had returned. What was it with the people out here, taking her to places she hadn't asked to go to? She walked along the track, which was leading her through a cluster of trees. She considered turning back and calling the hotel to pick her up.

But then she thought of what Herman had said.

"This trip is to help you find your way."

She could hardly write her column saying she'd turned back and called the hotel. She sipped her water and carried on. The truth was, what was she going to do back at the hotel anyway?

A cool breeze wafted across her and the trees provided welcome shade from the belting heat. She could smell an inviting smell – a mixture of wood and lemon which was oddly comforting. She felt her nerves settle slightly. Herman wouldn't leave her anywhere dangerous, would he?

She wished she wasn't alone.

She walked forwards through the trees and saw the path rise steeply in front of her. She began to climb, the green trees had now been replaced by tropical trees with orange roots, and they lined either side of the track. She heard rustling and she felt a wave of fear. Then a bird flew up from a branch.

When had she become this afraid?

Why had she never seen it?

Eric didn't love her; he controlled her. Are control and love the same thing? No, they're not. She knew that deep-down she just hadn't wanted to listen to herself. She'd done everything to please him, and she'd allowed it all. His invalidation, his need to be superior, his need to control. There was always a problem, and it was never his fault. As long as she kept fixing and sorting, he'd be back to old Eric one day.

How could she have been so stupid as to let this happen to her?

She carried on climbing. Something scratched her ankle but she didn't care.

She was hot, flustered, agitated and alone. This was her now – this was Grace Leven – and she didn't like herself at all.

She walked through to a clearing and out into the sun. It was even hotter now. She was wearing her hat but she could feel the heat pounding down on her. It felt different and somehow it felt good. It felt good to feel something other than numbness. Her anger was fuelling her; it was making her charge on.

As she walked further through the clearing and back into the forest, she allowed more questions into her mind – the ones that had been lingering and festering, the ones she needed to set free.

Did she actually like her job?
Did she like where she lived?
Did she even want to go back to London again?

"No, I bloody don't," she said out loud. She looked around, worried that someone was nearby and would think she was mad. But of course, there was no one. There were just trees, shade and quiet. Beautiful quiet.

"I never want to go back," she dared to whisper. It felt

good – really good. "I never want to go back," she said, this time a little louder.

She kept walking, her pace getting quicker. The itchy, painful agitation which had filled her for so long was stronger than ever, but she was walking through it and feeling it. She didn't feel so scared.

Whatever was ahead of her, she had power. She could do this.

She kept walking and following the path. She'd find her way, she knew, and she knew Herman would never have left her somewhere unsafe. But for now, she was just herself, free to walk and discover. She started to take in more of the trees, the birds. The questions kept coming in, and the answers flying out.

How could this have happened to me?
Because you never stopped to see.

She stopped at the top of the path.

The trees had cleared and she looked out at the endless blue sea.

The sky was a matching colour, the sun blazed from the sky and the warm breeze touched her shoulders. Yellow grass surrounded her and she felt she'd reached the top of the world. She stood with her shoulders back and breathed in the air.

Even if she didn't know the answers, she didn't care.

A voice startled her.

She turned around to see a group of people emerging from a different part of the clustered trees – this group was led by a guide.

Ha, she thought, triumphantly. I'm here by myself. Small steps, she told herself as she turned around.

"Hello," she waved to the guide, who returned her smile. "It's a beautiful day."

"Yes, it is, miss," the guide nodded and continued to walk along the coastal path.

"Grace? Grace Leven."

Her heart stopped and she swung around.

"Fancy seeing you here."

Grace couldn't believe what she was seeing. She blinked again – she must be mistaken.

"Christopher?"

Christopher Wakefield. Her nemesis. The disgusting man who'd kept his job, whose smirk filled television screens and whom the fellow members of her board described as talent.

Bullshit it was talent.

Her anger was back, but this time Beatrice's words rang in her head.

Space. Give the anger space.

"What on earth are you doing here?"

She prepared herself for his smarmy spiel and she could feel herself about to lash out. How dare he act the innocent. But she caught herself before the rage exploded. She caught herself in time, just like Herman had told her, and she breathed a deep breath instead.

She felt her control return and she watched the smile on his face falter as she looked behind him.

"Anne."

Grace had met his wife on several occasions over the years, but she hadn't seen her since the scandal. The scandal Grace had pulled many strings to keep out of the press. A sickness churned in the pit of her stomach. *What had she been thinking?*

"Grace," Anne said, unable to quite meet her eyes. There was an awkward pause between all of them. Then Anne spoke. "Jacob, Benjamin, this is Grace Leven, your father's…boss."

The pause before the word boss punctuated the air. The whole meeting was oozing a dreadful energy into this beautiful space.

"Hello boys," Grace smiled at them. "You're all grown-up."

"Teens – they eat everything," Anne said, and Grace felt even more guilt that it was Anne who had had the decency to fill the uncomfortable air. Anne, the woman who'd supported her husband, who'd given up her own career as a television production manager, who'd raised two beautiful boys, who was repaid by her husband's love for prostitutes. That and his love for the intern whom he had prayed upon then discarded with equal speed.

And she'd played her own part in it by turning a blind eye.

She forced herself to look at him. The man she'd help keep in his enormous job. He looked smaller somehow, less smug, without his entourage behind him. Was she imagining it or could his sons not look at him either?

"So," he coughed a small cough. "What brings you here?"

"Well, as you know Christopher, I've been suspended." She stared into his eyes with a directness he couldn't maintain. His gaze shifted and he looked at his sons, who didn't look at him. He looked at his wife, who didn't look at him. She watched his continuous wandering gaze and the more she watched him the more she could see the panic in his eyes.

You sad, sad little man.

Say something, she thought, you brazen arsehole. You'd been full of it in the meetings where you told us Hi-TV couldn't exist without you.

She didn't fill in the silence and neither did Anne.

Grace allowed the discomfort to fill the air before she spoke.

"However, I must say I'd love to thank whoever it was who stitched me up. It's the best thing that ever happened to me. I'm just so cross with myself that it took me this long to really see what was in front of my eyes." She looked back at Wakefield, who again looked away. He really was a coward.

"So." She didn't move her eyes off him. "What about you?"

"Just a bit of time with the family." He shuffled, looking even more pathetic.

She was used to seeing him in expensive suits, or more casual shirts and trousers – not in shorts and t-shirt. He had sweat pouring from his head, and Grace knew it wasn't just the heat. The other people in the group had no idea who he was. He looked completely lost without the admiration he usually commanded around him.

"Yes, it's so wonderful to get a different perspective." Grace glared at him one more time, before turning away. "Anne, Benjamin, Jacob, have a wonderful rest of your stay." She turned and started walking.

"Are you alone?" Christopher asked. There was a flicker of that smug smile again. Was he trying to humiliate her?

Another deep breath was enough for her to keep her cool.

"Yes, and I'm having a fabulous time." She was about to start walking again but then turned. "You know, Anne, if you ever fancy a chat and a different perspective, I'd love to catch up."

"That would be great, wouldn't it, Mum?" one of the boys – Jacob – said.

"Yes, thank you." Anne nodded a small nod, her cheeks flushing red.

"Enjoy the walk and the wonderful view. It's incredible how different everything looks from here." Grace waved goodbye, and began to march, her anger fuelling her strides, making her feel even more powerful than before.

"Well, look who it is. You're early." Herman stood with his arms crossed, leaning on his Jeep. She'd followed the path all the way back down the other side of the cliff to find him waiting for her in a layby.

"I'm disappointed. I was just getting going."

Herman clapped his hands. "That's more like it. I told Beatrice and Claudette you could have done the tough route."

"Next time, I'm all in."

"And this too is wonderful news. There's a next time." Herman handed her a cold bottle of water. She gulped it down and put the bottle on the back of her neck.

She leant next to Herman on the Jeep. "Thank you. That was quite the adventure." She nudged him on the shoulder and he nudged back.

"Well, spare the thanks, there's more to go."

"There is?"

"Unless you want to go back to the hotel."

Grace shook her head as she gulped the rest of the

water. "Of course not. You're mistaking me with someone else."

Herman laughed and took the empty bottle from her. "That's my girl. I knew she was in there all along."

By the time Herman pulled into the turning circle of Antigua House, Grace felt more elated than she could remember feeling, for, well, decades. They'd swum at a different beach, they'd taken another hike, they'd sat at a roadside cafe and played cards, she'd chatted with locals and drunk two beers. Nobody asked her what she did. Nobody asked her who she was or why she was there. They just welcomed her to their island, and she'd learned the rules of their games.

"Welcome Ms Leven." Beatrice and Claudette stood at the foyer with their arms wide open.

Grace felt the waft of cool air come from reception, and breathed in the vanilla fragrance of the hotel. Her cheeks flushed bright red at the sight of the two women standing there, and she felt ridiculous. What was she – a child again?

But she hugged them both. "Please. I told you to call me Grace."

"You've had a good day?"

"Yes, I've had a wonderful day, the best day. It's been, well…"

"Wonderful?"

"Wonderful – and interesting."

"We're so pleased."

Beatrice and Claudia began chatting with Herman, and Grace looked around the foyer. She would tell them everything when they had time. She reminded herself she wasn't their only guest. She looked at the families on holiday, sitting for an early-evening cocktail, dressed in their swimming costumes – and this time she didn't feel the need to run away.

She turned back towards Herman, but then for the second time that day, someone caught her eye. A person she recognised. It couldn't be, could it? He was leaning on the reception desk, and looking down at a large white sheet, deep in conversation with the staff.

"Harvey?"

He turned around.

"Grace Leven. Well, fancy seeing you here."

Chapter Twenty-Eight

Eric: Grace, you can't just abandon me like this. You owe me. I made you what you are.
Polly: Why are you doing this Grace?

"I'm sorry – I didn't know if this was a good idea or not."

"Don't be sorry. It's lovely to see you." It really was – so much so she felt her eyes well up with tears. She looked away. She really must get some sort of a grip.

"I was travelling around the hotels, as you know, and I was due a visit here."

"Well, how could I stop you from doing your work?"

"Have you time for a drink?"

"Yes," she nodded. "Yes I do."

She walked over to the bar and sat on a stool. Harvey sat next to her.

"You look really great," he said.

She nodded, but the tears filled her eyes even more, and she felt one slip down her cheek. She kept her sunglasses on as she wiped the tear away. She felt even more ridiculous.

"Are you sure you're okay?"

She nodded. "Yes. It's just it's…well, good to see someone who is so lovely."

"Ha," Harvey nodded at the barman. "We aim to please, don't we Marvin?"

The barman punched his fist. "Good to see you, Harvey. The usual?"

"Please. And for you?"

"I'll have a beer too."

"A beer?" Harvey raised his eyebrows. "They're starting to rub off on you I see."

Grace nodded. "They call you Harvey, but me Ms Leven."

Harvey laughed. "They like their rules. You are a guest. I'm a worker." He sat back on his stool and ruffled his hair.

"So, you're enjoying Antigua House?"

She nodded again. "Jack really knows how to do it."

"That he does," Harvey agreed and thanked Marvin for the two beers he placed in front of them.

"And you're the one who builds them."

"Hardly." He shook his head. "I simply follow instructions."

For a moment Grace couldn't take her eyes off Harvey. He was so humble and appreciative, yet at the same time knew exactly who he was. She hadn't known him for long, but he oozed an energy which meant he didn't need anyone else to tell him how great he was. He was completely confident in himself and was everything she wasn't used to in the men she'd been surrounded by. Her cheeks flushed pink and she made herself look away.

"Are all his hotels like this?" She shook her head. The heat must be affecting her.

"Pretty much. Well, they're all different but similar at the same time, if you get what I mean."

"I do," Grace agreed.

"So, have you had one of Beatrice's famous massages yet?"

Grace laughed. "Is it that obvious? I don't think I'll ever be the same again."

"That's the one. I've had a few myself." He turned to face her. "After my wife died."

"And did they help?"

He sipped his beer. "It's strange because it's like your body wants to cling on to all that pain, as if it keeps you safe somehow. You spend more energy clinging on to it, and all you're doing is spreading the agony. It was as though, in some way, by holding on, I was keeping Alice here. But she wouldn't have wanted that. I didn't want it even, but it's strange what we do without even realising it."

Grace swallowed. She was taken aback by his openness.

"Oh Harvey, I've been clinging on for so long. I've been clinging on to a world that doesn't even exist – one I don't even want – and one that clearly doesn't want me. I've had this belief that if I just work harder, or be a bit better, then everything will be okay. It'll all be okay. But the truth is, it won't."

Harvey nodded. "So, if you don't mind me asking, what is right for you? Have you worked that part out yet?"

"That, Harvey, is work in progress but I do know being here, and finding Strawberry Village, has shown me there is another way. It doesn't have to be a world where people are all out for themselves. I thought I had a big job and a big life, but I had no idea I was living in such a small world. A world filled with egos and selfishness where I wasn't enjoying my life at all."

Grace waited for Harvey to say something, but he just nodded instead. It surprised her – he was just listening. No glazed look in his eye, no irritation about what she'd just said, no turning everything she said back to himself.

"Thank you, Harvey."

"For what?"

"For listening."

"It's lovely to listen to you."

Grace felt her cheeks flush a brighter pink.

"I'm sorry, I don't want to embarrass you."

She shook her head. "It's just the sun." She knew he didn't believe her.

"So, look, I don't want you to think I'm going to intrude on this wonderful time you're having. I know you came out here to research your lost path. I don't even have to stay here at the hotel, in fact…"

"It's okay. You're not intruding in the slightest, and you'll never believe this, but you're not the first person I bumped into today."

"I'm not?"

A wave of boldness rushed through her. "Do you have plans for dinner tonight?'

"None at all."

"Would you like to join me? – and I'll tell you all about it, as long as you promise not to tell a soul."

"My lips are sealed, Grace Leven," he drew a line across his face. "And I'd love to. Thank you very much."

Midlife Murders & The Lost Path

4

So my question is, if our true self disappears, where exactly does it go? Is it left somewhere behind, in between the promotion-chasing or the clinging to lives and people not meant for us? Or is it living in us all along, hidden and restless, simply waiting to be seen?

I suspect it's the latter and that explains a lot. For so long I've thought there must be something wrong with me. No matter which boardroom I sat in or who I was with, I always had this internal 'ache.' It would move around to different parts of my body. Sometimes in my shoulder, sometimes in the chest, at the bottom of my diaphragm, or at the back of my throat.

It came with a continual sense of restlessness that I've felt for so long but have chosen to ignore. I always thought it was because I was ungrateful or unable to appreciate what was in front of me. I always thought I was flawed.

But perhaps I wasn't, or rather, perhaps I'm not. Perhaps – curled tightly in a ball because it's been ignored for so long – was my true self all along. Perhaps it was so pushed down and suppressed it hardly knew it was still alive, because, let's face it, I'd forgotten it was there.

Perhaps the restlessness was it moving around, trying to break free, or at least letting me know it was still there. It came with a sense of dread and fear, as if something was about to go wrong – and perhaps it was. I was too busy looking outside to ever give it the attention it needs.

So here's a thought. Perhaps I'm not flawed after all, and perhaps neither are you? Perhaps it's simply our true selves warning us something is wrong. I'm not a psychologist so I don't know for sure. But today I think I felt something I haven't felt for so long.

I met a man who's been in my life for a long time – yes, a business acquaintance, but still one who has dominated my days. I was walking on my Lost Path and out of the blue, he was there – a coincidence perhaps? Or perhaps it was a lesson. All of a sudden, I remembered. The feeling of walking on eggshells returned, and it was as though I was no longer relevant any more.

Then, later, I met another man I know and the lesson repeated itself, but this time I was ready to listen. He was a person who is so complete in himself, he also gives space for me. I in turn felt seen and appreciated – so why have I been living like this so long? Ignoring my soul and surrounded by people who make no space for me? I've found a place called Strawberry Village, which is teaching me I don't have to live like that at all.

I suspect the ache in my soul is its way of telling me it's tired of walking on eggshells. Someone said to me a broken world offers many beginnings, so what if this is my chance to no longer have to live like this?

Chapter Twenty-Nine

Eric: Grace, you can't just fob me off like this. Who do you think you are? I gave up everything for you.
Polly: Grace, please. I need you. x

Grace stepped out of the shower and wrapped the large white towel around her. She walked across the bathroom to the mirror and forced herself to look at the reflection.

She wasn't really sure who it was looking back.

Her skin was less pale, the circles under her eyes less dark. Her hair was wet and full of its curls and now she was going to meet a man for dinner who wasn't her husband. He was a friend, just a friend. But what was she? She was married, but was she separated? She and Eric may not have had an official conversation, but surely the sight of him in bed with your once-upon-a-time best friend is a status update?

As she put mascara on her lashes, she tried to remember the last time she'd had dinner with a man who was a friend. Not a business acquaintance, or Eric. Just a friend.

"Who are you kidding, Grace? You don't have any friends," she told her reflection through the steam. She could feel herself begin to wallow, so again she took a deep breath.

She thought again of Claudia's words.

Your broken world offers many beginnings.

She smiled as she put on her lipstick.

"Well, look at you. You look wonderful. We're both in the pink."

Harvey stood up and Grace laughed. He looked as nervous as she was. She had picked a pink sundress which tied around the back of her neck. She'd bought it on her shopping trip with Pearl and it was a million miles away from her black Prada uniform. She too felt a million miles away from the Prada-wearing Grace.

"You look great too."

And he did. He wore a loose pink shirt with white trousers, and he looked a million miles away from the odd-job man she'd bumped into at Strawberry House. His hair was still wet from the shower, and he looked at ease. A vision of Eric flashed before her. Whatever he wore he never looked at ease, and he'd never, ever wear sandals.

"I like your shoes."

"Thank you. I like yours."

She looked down at her jewelled flat sandals, which were comfortable and didn't make her wince as she walked. They stood for a moment, both looking at their shoes.

"Harvey, I'm going to be honest. I've never had dinner with a man who isn't my husband or a business colleague in my whole life – and I'm fifty-three."

Harvey looked at her, and for a moment he didn't say anything as he studied her face. "Well, Grace Leven, I must say, you never cease to surprise me."

Grace felt her cheeks go a deeper shade of red.

Then he smiled his great big smile. "What a privilege this is for me. Shall we?" He held out his arm and she took it as they walked across the terrace.

They sat at a table at the side of the open-air restaurant. A live band was playing on the terrace outside and Grace could hear the sea gently lapping on the shore.

It was cooler now, and the air was filled with the sound of clinking glasses and laughter.

They laughed, they talked and they ate delicious food. She chose tomato salad and red snapper; Harvey ate scallops and steak. She thought back to the days of sitting opposite Eric. Uptight, not eating, wondering what to say next.

She sipped her wine.

"What is it?" Harvey asked. "You look very serious."

"Can I ask you a question?"

He sat back. "Anything."

"Do you ever wonder how you could get something so wrong?"

"All the time," he said without a beat.

This was something else she liked about Harvey. He never made her feel bad. In the short time she'd known him, she felt as though she could say anything to him and she wouldn't feel embarrassed. She could be herself.

You like Harvey, a voice whispered in her mind – which quickly she pushed away.

"Like what, if you don't mind me asking?"

"Like I said, Grace Leven – you can ask me anything." He leant forward. "I get a lot wrong all the time. I get people wrong. I get ideas wrong. I feel absolutely certain something needs to be done on a project, then I realise I've got that wrong. I get another idea and I think this is so much better, then that's wrong. In short, I'm the king of getting it wrong."

Grace laughed. "Well, this makes me feel better. So how do you handle it?"

He sipped his wine and thought for a moment. "A while ago, I made peace with it – that I get life wrong. Life became so much easier once I just accepted this. I don't have to be right all the time. I'm human just like everyone else and it's human nature to get it wrong."

"And it's as simple as that?"

"Well, not quite. It was a long winding road to get to this point, and it's a still a practice every day. Even today, I knew you were out when I came to the hotel, and I thought, should I stay and say hello? Or should I make myself scarce?"

"Well, I can confirm you got that right." Their eyes met, and she felt more heat filling her cheeks. She had to stop acting like a teenager with a crush.

Grace Leven, do you have a crush?

"But as long as I don't get stuck clinging onto the need to be right, then it keeps me moving through life, rather than holding on in the past and keeping me stuck. All I can do is listen to my instincts, and even if they're wrong the first time, they normally help me get there in the end."

For a moment they were quiet and Grace noticed how comfortable it felt, just to sit there with him.

"So," he leant forward. "Do you mind me asking what you think you've got wrong? If it's not too big a question?"

"I don't mind at all, as long as you don't mind the answer."

"I've got no other plans," he smiled, and she watched as his smile met his eyes. She loved that he smiled proper genuine smiles that met his eyes.

She sat back in her chair and played with the stem of her wine glass. "I think I've got everything wrong. My marriage, my career, my life. Everything except Pearl. Today, on my hike, I bumped into a man who was a colleague." She held her hands up. "I know: it was a coincidence, or it was spooky."

Harvey laughed. "Believe me, it happens all the time here, especially after one of Beatrice's massages."

"I've spent years and years dealing with people like him. Their egos are so big they can barely fit through the door, and I suppose, even though I was the boss essentially, deep-down I felt powerless around them. There's almost an acceptance that people like him are just the way they are and we have to accept that. There's no room for anyone else – just them and their egos."

She thought back to Wakefield earlier that day. With the sweat pouring down his head, he looked like a little, pathetic man.

"Today, though, he looked so uncomfortable. Away from the studio and all the lights, I could see him so clearly for who he is. He is a man who's betrayed his lovely family, who's treated people around him appallingly, and whom I did everything in my power to protect. I suppose there was a part of me that had been in awe of him. He was – or rather is – a celebrity, and at Hi-TV you think this is everything. But all along we've been backing a pathetic man with no values. How could I have been so stupid?"

"You were doing what you thought was right at the time," Harvey said.

"But was I?" Grace leant forward. "I don't think it ever felt right. Nothing felt right, and deep down I knew this with my husband also. My husband was – or rather is – not the person I wished he was, and my best friend was never really a best friend. I've never even felt at home in the house I call my home. Everything, Harvey – I got everything wrong."

She felt a wave of shame wash over her. She expected Harvey to look awkward, but he didn't. Instead, he simply sat back and looked at her. "So, isn't it wonderful, then, that you've realised this now? Think of all the people who don't, and they go through their entire life in the wrong place. But look at you. Here," he nodded at the terrace, "in this wonderful place at this moment in time. Just by knowing this, you've set yourself free. You've been brave enough to do this, so I don't think there's anything wrong with you at all."

Grace's eyes stung with hot tears. "Oh Harvey, thank you."

"Now, at the risk of getting this wrong," he stood up and held out his hand. 'Would you like to dance?"

Grace nodded as she wiped her tear away. "Yes please, I think I would."

For the next few hours, they danced, talked, laughed and drank more wine. They chatted to other guests who sat nearby and then they danced some more. Grace Leven couldn't remember the last time she'd danced.

"You're a lovely couple," one elderly woman said as she walked away with her husband.

"Oh, we're not a couple," Grace said for the second time since she'd met Harvey, and the woman raised her eyebrows, just as Elizabeth had a few weeks before.

It was past one in the morning when they finally decided it was time to leave, but Grace didn't really want to go. She wanted to stay there with Harvey all night.

They walked along the path, which was lit with tiny lights. The air was warm and filled with the smell of vanilla. They walked in a comfortable silence, until Harvey stopped walking.

"At the risk of getting this wrong…" he said.

"Yes?" Grace's heart began to race.

"Do you have plans tomorrow?"

Grace laughed and she breathed out. "Well, let me think about my jam-packed schedule. No, no I don't think there are any plans in there at all."

Harvey stood in front of her. "Then would you like the Harvey private tour of the island? I promise not to leave you on a path to find your way, and while Herman might live here, I can show you parts of the island even he doesn't know." He held his hands up. "If I'm not interrupting your time to be alone? I always schedule a day off when I come here, but if you'd rather not…" He looked a little flustered.

"Harvey, I'd love to."

"You would?"

"I absolutely would. That was not something you got wrong."

"Well, there's a relief."

They stood again in silence.

"My room's here." She nodded behind her.

"Yes. Right. Okay," Harvey said.

"Thank you for a lovely evening."

"I hope it wasn't too bad for the first time you had a

dinner with a man who wasn't a business acquaintance, or your husband."

"It was the best – and I hope there'll be many more," Grace added. She'd drunk too much wine.

"I hope so too. See you tomorrow? In the foyer? Ten am."

"That's perfect for me."

"Goodnight Harvey."

"Goodnight Grace.

They stood not moving.

"I'll see you tomorrow."

"I'll see you tomorrow."

He turned and she turned and put her hand on her door.

"Great dancing, by the way," he called out.

"You too," she laughed as she opened her door.

She closed it and leant back against it as she felt the cool air-conditioned air. She took a deep breath and allowed herself to feel the feeling she hadn't felt in a very long time. She didn't recognise it straight away, but after she took another deep breath, she realised the feeling she was feeling.

The feeling was joy.

Chapter Thirty

Eric: I can't believe you're just abandoning me like this – after everything I've done.
Polly: Just one phone call, that's all I want. Why can't you do this Grace?

Grace stood in the foyer of Antigua House at nine-fifty-nine am. She looked around as guests wrapped in sarongs milled around her. There was a buzz in the air and it was filled with excitement. Some were ready for the day in this wonderful hotel, others were about to explore the island. Grace, on the other hand, felt nervous, which she tried not to think about.

"There she is."

As soon as she heard Harvey's voice, she relaxed. She looked over to see him walking towards her with Herman, who smiled his big smile at her.

"I hear he's going to try to convince you he knows this island better than I do," Herman nudged Harvey.

"And he says he's not going to abandon me on a path," Grace laughed.

"That was research." Herman raised his eyebrows at her. Why did everyone keep doing that?

"And here we are." Claudia appeared out of nowhere, carrying a large picnic hamper. "I can't have you going hungry now, can I?" She passed the hamper to Harvey. "And there's some fine lemonade in there." She gave him a knowing wink. "If you know what I mean?"

"I don't, but thank you Claudia, you spoil us." Harvey took the hamper, now looking as flustered as Grace felt. "Are you ready Ms Leven?" He held his arm out.

Grace nodded. "Yes I am." She took his arm.

Grace blushed, and she was sure she saw Harvey blush too. But they kept walking across the foyer and then both of them turned. Herman and Claudia stood watching, arms crossed and smiling.

"Bye then," they both called.

"Bye," Grace and Harvey waved back.

"Why do I feel like I'm fifteen again?" Grace whispered.

"I was just thinking exactly the same."

As they wove around the island in the open-air jeep, Grace tried not to glance over at Harvey. It felt odd and natural, all at the same time. She was the same person she'd always been, but at the same time she felt like a different woman in a different world.

A text arrived on her phone. She almost didn't look at it, in case it was another one from Eric, but it was Pearl.

Don't overthink it mum. Just enjoy x

Grace smiled.

"Is everything okay?"

"Yes. It is." Grace breathed out and stretched her legs. "So, where are we going?"

"Well, I thought we'd start off with another hike. This one takes us to a great little beach bar and only the locals know it's there."

"Sounds good to me." Grace felt the warm breeze on her face. She'd wrapped a scarf around her head. She hadn't worn one for a long time – not since Eric had mocked her, telling her she looked ridiculous.

"You look great, by the way," Harvey said, as if reading her mind.

"Thank you."

She tried not to look at him, but when she did, she found she couldn't look away. He smelt fresh – his aftershave was lemony. He wore sunglasses and a pale pink shirt. He looked as at home in Antigua as he did back in Strawberry Village – but Grace got the sense Harvey felt at home wherever he was.

"So, you're doing okay?"

"What do you mean?" She looked away quickly and stared at the other side of the road.

"Not only a dinner with a man who wasn't a business acquaintance or a husband, but now a whole day out too."

She laughed and breathed out. "This really is advanced territory."

He laughed too.

"Harvey, do you mind if I ask you a question?"

"We agreed. Anything you like. Go on, hit me with your best."

"Have you been out with many women since your wife died?"

When he didn't answer, she regretted the question.

"I'm sorry. I've embarrassed you."

"No, you haven't at all. I was just thinking should I tell you the truth or the real truth?"

"Er, the real truth please."

"Well, I've been out with women. Not many. All of them pretty much set up by my son Josh or Jack. Lulu put in her tuppence too. They think I don't know, but I do, and now Iris has joined their gang too.

"The Harvey Dating Committee."

"Exactly." He laughed.

"And?"

"I've met some really great women."

"Harvey," Grace peered over her sunglasses. "You can be honest with me."

"They were dreadful. I don't know what they were thinking. One was rude to the waiters, another showed me endless photos of her cat."

"Was it a nice cat?"

"I don't know. I don't really like cats."

Grace laughed again. "Did you tell your dating committee?"

"Christ, no. It would have broken their hearts."

"You're very kind, Harvey."

"Or picky." Their eyes met, and Grace felt her cheeks go an even brighter red.

They drove along in silence for a moment.

"So, was there anyone you liked?"

"There was one. Sylvia. She was lovely. Smart, sophisticated – and kind, too."

Grace ignored how much she didn't like him using the word lovely.

"And?"

He shook his head. "It just wasn't right. I saw her a few times – and I had a nice time, which in some ways made it worse. With the others, it was so bad it was funny, and I could at least laugh. But with Sylvia, it should have been great. On paper it was, and it almost was in real-life. But somehow it made me feel lonelier, and it made me miss Alice even more. Do you think I sound like a weirdo?"

Grace shook her head. "I don't think you sound like a weirdo at all."

Grace ignored the relief she felt that it hadn't worked out. She shook her head. She was being ridiculous. She didn't have a crush.

Oh yes you do.

"So, what about you? Did you go out with lots of men before you met your husband?"

Grace shook her head. "Not one. Eric was my first boyfriend. I met him at university and we've been together ever since."

"Once again, you never cease to surprise me, Grace Leven."

Grace laughed. "I don't see what's surprising about that."

"I do – when you see you how I see you." Harvey looked across at her and their eyes met for the briefest of moments before his returned to the road ahead.

This path was different to the one Herman had taken her on the day before. It was less rugged and took them along a different part of the coastline. One side was filled with trees; the other side with the vast blue sea and sky. The sunshine sparkled on the water and the breeze kept them cool.

"I feel like I'm in actual heaven."

"It's great, isn't it?"

They walked and talked. They talked about everything. Politics, housing, television, favourite foods. Grace couldn't remember the last time she'd talked with someone like this. There was always an agenda at work, or a tension with Eric.

They discussed the places they'd been to. As Grace talked about where she'd visited, she noticed it was mainly because of her work. But Harvey had been travelling since he was a teenager. He and his wife had met while backpacking, and this love of adventure had carried on. At the same time he'd always loved to return home and build something. A sign of a good holiday was a set of new shelves, he'd laughed.

They talked about how he'd grown his business and how he wasn't sure he wanted to grow it any more. He asked her more about her work – what it was like, where she'd grown up. She only stumbled when he asked about what she liked to do. When it came to films, hobbies or music, she didn't know.

"Harvey, how can I be fifty-three and not know this?"

"Well, do you like this?" He stopped and waved around him.

"I love it."

"So, there you are. Grace Leven likes this – and this is a great place to start."

Grace felt a wave of shame wash over her. Was she really this pathetic?

She shook her head. She wasn't going to let anything spoil her mood.

"Thank you, Harvey."

"Nothing to thank me for. Now come on, we're nearly there."

When Harvey had said 'there' he meant a small beach, which felt so magical as Grace stepped onto it that she had to catch her breath. The tiny cove, was tucked away under the trees and hills. The clear water glistened, a small beach bar made out of wood sat in the corner, and a handful of people sat on the beach or swam in the sea. It was almost as though the magic crackled in her ears. It was perfect.

"Harvey?" a voice called and Grace turned to see a man in a tropical shirt, waving from the beach bar at them. "It's been a while."

He walked over to them, a white cloth thrown over one of his shoulders and he shook Harvey's hand and clapped him on the back.

"Grace, this is Charles," Harvey introduced him.

Grace shook his hand. "I'm pleased to meet you, Charles."

"The pleasure is all mine. Come inside, you look hot and thirsty. Did he drag you up that hill?"

"Not dragged exactly. But it was worth it. This is wonderful."

"Welcome to Paradise." Charles nodded as he led them to a table. Grace sat down underneath a fan, although the sides of the bar were open and they could look out on the water.

"So, how well do you know it here?"

"I've been a few times." Harvey sat forward. "I didn't really drag you, did I?"

"Not at all."

Charles came over with a tray carrying two large glasses of juice filled with ice – and two large glasses of iced water. "Our specialty. Mango juice."

Grace drank the water and then the juice. It was delicious, sweet, fresh and tasted like heaven. It was wonderful. She breathed one of Herman's deep breaths. Just for a moment, everything felt wonderful.

"So, this is a hidden gem?" She looked out at the cove.

"You could say that. Fewer tourists, more locals. I discovered it after Alice died. I would come here often and it somehow made me feel a little better."

Grace looked around her. The sea was calm and it felt peaceful. "I can see why."

"When Alice died, I was a mess, only I wouldn't allow myself to admit it, most of all to myself. I didn't stop working, I told everyone I was okay. All I really cared about was Josh, and that he was okay. I didn't really see any point to me being okay; it didn't seem to matter any more. What was the point for me? But Josh? He had his whole life in front of him."

"Oh, Harvey."

"Inside, it was as though this wall was building – a big concrete brick wall. It was as if on one side was life and everything it had to offer and on the other side was me. I didn't want to be anywhere else – I thought anything would be disloyal to Alice. I had no right to enjoy life when she was gone."

Grace nodded. "I get it."

"I didn't even think it was a breakdown. I thought if I looked okay, I must be okay. I didn't break down into tears. I got out of bed. But the numbness was eating me alive. It wouldn't even let me feel the grief – all I could do was survive."

"Oh, Harvey," Grace said again.

"I went on for a long time like this. People said, 'You're taking it so well, Harvey. You're so strong,' and I thought I was. But here's the thing, Grace, nobody is that strong. Ignoring feelings, striving, going around from one thing to the next – that's not living."

Grace sipped her juice. She looked at Harvey, his sandy-brown hair, the twinkle in his eyes – it was hard to imagine him not like this.

"What happened?"

"Josh and Jack – they did one of those interventions or whatever they're called. The irony was, there I was thinking I was keeping myself strong for my son, but all I was doing was making him more and more worried about me. I may not have been wallowing but I was getting angrier and more resentful by the day. Josh would tell me something and I'd have no empathy; I was just numb. All I cared about was surviving with this great big iceberg of numbness I was lugging around with me. It was exhausting. So, when they came to see me for this intervention, I snapped."

"You did? I can't imagine you losing your temper."

"Believe me I did, and it was really ugly."

"So, what happened?"

"Jack suggested I come out here. I'd been out here when we were building the place, but I'd never really taken time to look around the island. I didn't think coming on my own to a place like this would suit me. In the past I'd hop from island to island, not stay in one place. I told him no, then do you know what Jack did?"

"What?"

"He suspended me. Can you believe it? He told me he wouldn't employ my services any more unless I did this.

That in his mind I was unfit for work. If I didn't come here for one month, I'd be off the job for good. Bloody cheek."

Grace smiled. "So young yet so wise."

"Bloody patronising, I thought. But the look in their eyes... I could see their pain and then I felt something for the first time: I felt for them. I know what fear and helplessness looks like, and all the pain and anger that comes with it. I'd been the same watching Alice suffer like she had. I didn't really think it would help me, but I knew just trying would. So, I came here." Harvey picked up his juice and sipped it.

"For a month?"

"For one long, wonderful month." He leant forward. "And I had the works. The Beatrice massage, Claudia and her lemonade, the Herman hikes. I was taken to Lemon Cove, I fished, I sat – and I was taught to breathe. I hired a car and wandered around. I never knew where I was going really, I just always wanted to be somewhere else, and this is how I discovered Charles and here. But when I got here, I found myself wanting to return the next day, and it was the first time I actually wanted to be somewhere rather than just going through the motions."

Grace looked around again at the bay. The trees were full of vibrant colours – orange and red – it was as though nature had provided a place where they could hide.

"So, I came back the next day, and the next. Each time I felt a little softer, as though the wall was coming down. I'd have the massages too, and the lemonade, so I never really knew what it was. But something was helping. The darkness was there, but when I was alone I'd cry, which was something I hadn't been able to do. It was as though the iceberg was melting." Harvey sat back and laughed. "Look at me, becoming all poetic."

"I think you're describing it perfectly."

Their eyes met again. His face was happy and relaxed and it was hard to imagine him ever in the dark state he was describing.

"What I'm trying to say is, we want to control everything, but we just can't. Nobody can. We think one day everything will be okay again and we won't hurt. But hurting is part of living. Pain is part of living. If we don't feel that part, we don't allow the other parts either. I can't switch off one without the other; no one can. All you can do is give yourself a bit of time and space. You need to listen to you really carefully, to hear what you need."

Grace leant forward now, and this time she touched his hand. "I'm sorry Harvey. I'm so sorry you lost your lovely wife. And I'm sorry now you're sat here with me, moping, carrying my own iceberg."

"Believe me when I say, it's my pleasure. Grief is grief, and you were betrayed too; it makes it complicated. It's going to take some time."

Grace nodded as a hot tear slid down her cheek.

"For the record, anyone who treats you like that…well, let's just say I'd lose my temper big time again."

Grace laughed and wiped the tear away.

"Thank you, Harvey." She let go of his hand, but he now held hers. "You were suspended, for very different reasons," she added, "and I was too. Thank you for sharing your suspension place."

"No, thank you, Grace Leven. It's lovely spending time with you." He let go of her hand now as he sat back. "There are very few people who get the Herman Hike and the Lemon Cove lemonade; that's all I'll say."

"Well, I feel very honoured." She smiled and looked out to sea. Then she looked back at him. "Harvey, what is in that lemonade?"

What Really Happened To Me?

"That, Grace Leven, is one of the greatest mysteries of all time."

Grace started to laugh, and this time she laughed longer than she had in a very long time.

They spent the rest of the day swimming, talking and swimming some more. They ate crab at the beach bar and as they sat back on their towels, they drank some of Claudia's lemonade. They snorkelled and looked at the endless collections of coloured fish swimming underneath them. Grace picked up a book in the back of the beach bar and began to read. It was a tattered romance about two people who met and were desperately trying not to fall in love. For a short while it engrossed her so much, she forgot where she was.

Harvey pulled out his own book from his backpack – a book about restoring old houses – and they lay next to one another and read. It felt odd and not odd, all at the same time. Every time a thought of Eric came into her mind, she let it float by. It felt liberating and magical.

Harvey sat up as the sun started to slip away.

"So, Grace Leven, may I be so bold as to ask if you have any plans for dinner tonight?"

"Well, Harvey Millar, let me check that schedule again. Nope, I think I'm wide open."

"Well, would you care for a cocktail with Charles? Friday is his big night, and when I mean big, I mean big."

Grace laughed. "Are they going to play darts, like in the Strawberry Arms?"

"Oh, believe me, it's much bigger than that."

"More than that? Well count me in."

She slipped her dress back on, trying not to feel too awkward as she did, and then they both climbed on to two stools back at the bar. There were more people in there now – drinking pina coladas and rum punches.

"Well you two look like you've had a good afternoon at the beach," Charles said as he wiped down the bar in front of them. "What can I get you?"

Grace was about to order a rum punch because she thought she should join in.

"Would you care for a glass of champagne?" Charles asked her, and smiled his large wide smile. "Don't think you have to have the punch like everyone else."

"Is that okay?" Grace didn't want to offend anyone.

"It would be my absolute pleasure – I have a wonderful bottle on ice."

"And I'll have a beer," Harvey said. He turned to Grace on his stool. "You see, it's okay – you can have exactly what you want and the world doesn't fall apart. Perhaps you need to do a little more of this." He nudged her.

Grace felt a shift of the heaviness move in her, and it felt good – really good. "Do you know, Harvey? I think you could be right."

Half an hour later, a small all-female band was playing. A singer and a saxophonist were filling the now-packed bar with music as Harvey ordered another round.

"I'll leave my car here. In fact, our lift has just arrived."

Grace turned to see Herman, Beatrice and Claudia dancing through the crowds. Harvey leaned into her as he said, "I told you Friday night was a big night."

Grace laughed as she got down from her stool and Beatrice and Claudia put their arms around her. "Look at you! Our girl looks good." Beatrice peered at her. "Look Claud, the frown is going. Herman, quick, come and look at this."

Herman left the person he was talking to and peered at her too. "Good god, woman, the frown has almost gone." He slapped Harvey on the arm. "You've done good work, my man."

"Excuse me – am I some kind of project?"

Claudia clapped her hands. "We're all projects, Ms Leven. This is the joy of life."

"I told you, please call me Grace."

But Claudia and Beatrice weren't listening as they were greeted by more people in the bar.

"Do they know everyone?"

Harvey nodded. "They know everyone everywhere they go."

"This truly is a magical place." Grace sat back on her stool.

"Yes, it is." Harvey's eyes met hers. "And you are a magical person, Grace Leven. I'm just sorry this has escaped you for so long."

"So, who's ready to sing?" The singer of the band asked, and everyone clapped and cheered. "It's karaoke time."

Grace watched, mesmerised. A woman jumped up and started to sing as more and more people filled the dance floor. There was no awkwardness or hesitation. Two men followed, and another woman after that. It wasn't even that they had incredible voices, but their energy was electrifying. Grace loved it all. The fairy lights were starting to twinkle as the sky turned dark. Everyone was dressed in shorts and t-shirts, their hair was messy and ungroomed. There was no judgement, no edge – just people loving life and having fun. It was a million miles away from the stuck-up places she'd spent the last thirty years in.

"Didn't you tell me you like to sing?" Herman stood at her side.

Grace looked at him. "No, I didn't Herman."

"And why not, please tell?"

"I haven't sung since…well, a long time ago. I'm not very good."

"Who says you're not good? Besides, good is not necessary here." He took her hand. "I have someone." He raised it in the air. "Her name is Grace Leven."

"Herman, no!" Grace hissed.

The lead singer opened her arms. "Welcome, Grace Leven. Come join us and let's sing."

Grace felt the heat rise in her cheeks. "I can't do this."

Beatrice whispered in her ear. "Tell me, what are you afraid of?"

Grace looked down at the tiny, friendly woman. What was she afraid of? Nobody was unkind here – nobody would sneer.

"Let the love in," Beatrice whispered again and squeezed her hand.

"Here, drink some lemonade." Claudia held a glass in front of her.

Grace took a large gulp, a deep breath, and then ran up to the stage. The singer showed her a list of songs and she picked one.

She looked down at her feet, closed her eyes and the music began to play. Then she took one more deep breath, dared herself to feel the love…and started to sing.

What Really Happened To Me?

There was a moment of silence when she finished the song, before the whole bar began to clap and cheer again. Grace couldn't remember a time when she'd ever felt quite so alive and free. For a moment, she'd forgotten herself as she'd lost herself in the song. But now she was back in the bar, and there was so much love and celebration that tears stung at the back of her eyes. She handed the microphone back to the singer.

"Thank you."

"You were incredible; you have to come back soon." She kissed her on both cheeks. "You're welcome here any time."

She made her way back to the bar, where Harvey stood with his arms folded.

"Well, who knew? Grace Leven can sing."

Grace blushed and laughed. "I need a drink."

"Coming right up." He turned – but as he did, their eyes met again. She felt a rush of heat run through her, and excitement too. Did she have butterflies in her stomach? She must be a bit drunk.

But then their eyes met again, and this time they held the look – and then she realised she wasn't being ridiculous at all.

When Herman dropped them back at the hotel, Grace was having such a wonderful time, she didn't want the evening to end.

When she leant forward and thanked Herman for the lift, he said in a quiet voice, "Don't overthink." Then they both watched him drive away.

"Is it too late to go for a walk?" she asked Harvey.

"Not at all. I was going to say exactly the same."

They walked through the hotel, where a few people were still sitting at the bar. The barman waved at them both as they walked past.

They walked down the path onto the beach. The breeze was cool and the sky was lit up by stars.

"Thank you, Harvey. I've had such a wonderful day."

"Thank you, Grace Leven. I've had a wonderful day too."

She could feel his presence and she couldn't deny it any more. She'd felt it all day. Who was she kidding? She'd felt it since the moment she'd met him. Thoughts telling her to stop it spun around her head, but then the words of Herman came back.

Don't overthink.

They carried on walking and she could feel her heart racing. She didn't want to reach the end of the beach because she didn't want the moment to end. She didn't want her time with Harvey to end. She didn't want the whole trip to end. She wanted to be in the moment, where she was.

Her heart raced against her chest – making her feel she was going to explode.

"Harvey." She looked up at him, and the same look was in his eyes. Before she could say anything else, he was leaning down towards her. The look in his eyes matched the feeling in her insides. She didn't say another word as his lips met hers.

Her mind buzzed. His mouth, his lips, his smell. She hadn't kissed a man who wasn't Eric since she was eighteen years old. Everything felt so different, but so right too. Her body was waking up as though it was coming alive.

He pulled back.

"Grace, I'm sorry."

"Why are you sorry?"

He looked flustered. "You're here. You're on a trip. I arrived. I hadn't meant for this to happen. I can see how it might look."

"Harvey, it's okay. I know. I feel it too."

"You do?" He looked down at her. He was so strong, so open, so warm. It should feel so wrong but it felt so, so right. She could feel it all over her body. She'd never felt that way before. She didn't know if it was being in Antigua, if it was the champagne, the lemonade, the singing, or if it was because her life had fallen apart. But in that moment, it all felt so right – as if there was nowhere else she'd rather be.

He stepped towards her again. He was strong and confident and she felt strong and confident. She didn't feel like he was doing her a favour – as it so often had felt before. She didn't feel as though she was some sort of chore. She didn't feel small, or any need to feel grateful. She felt as if she was in the right place, with the right person, and everything was how it was supposed to be.

"Grace Leven, you're truly beautiful."

And in that moment, she felt it. She couldn't ever remember feeling safe in her own skin – not without the uniform of a CEO, or the job title which convinced her deep insecurity she was someone. She felt someone with him. More than that, she felt herself. He was kinder and more caring than anyone she'd ever known. She'd been lying to herself for so many years that what she was living was life, that it was how life is. But this was life too, and she had had no idea a world like this could exist for her.

Don't overthink it. Trust your inner knowing.

She stepped forward and his lips touched hers again. She knew as she did that she was crossing a line, and she also knew she never wanted to return.

"I never knew I could feel like this." She looked at Harvey.

He laughed. "It does feel good."

He was naked in her bed, the white sheets across him. They'd made love, had sex – however she should describe it. She'd stopped reading romance books years ago. She'd stopped thinking about romance years ago. She'd become the classic cynic who believed that romance only existed in fiction and in the shows she sometimes agreed to commission. But whatever it was they'd just experienced, it was what she used to read about – what she never thought could happen in real life.

She felt like she'd lost her mind and all her thoughts had left.

"Grace Leven." He leant over to her. "Are you overthinking this?"

"No. Maybe."

He kissed her again. She couldn't believe that there was no awkwardness either. She was expecting him to be different now, and for something to change. But nothing did. He was just the same Harvey, looking at her with the same twinkle in his eye. He wasn't running away. He wasn't checking his phone. He was still there.

He wrapped his arms around her.

"You know we've still got a bottle of Claudia's lemonade."

She laughed. "Do you think we can work out what's in it?"

"I think if anyone can, you can, Grace Leven." He leant across her and kissed her again. "You're capable of making me feel things I didn't think I could," he told her.

"Well, I'm very happy to hear that." Grace met his mouth with her own and once again she found him and he found her in a way she had never believed could be real.

Chapter Thirty-One

Eric: What are you doing Grace? Why are you ignoring me? I've put my whole life on hold for you. I did everything you wanted me to.
Polly: Grace, please. Just one phone call. I've left you so many messages.

When she woke up a few hours later, it was raining. Something was wrong and she didn't like it. She turned to see the bed empty and her feelings were confirmed. The magic of the night was over. What had she been thinking? The sunrise had brought with it the same old feeling of shame and the feeling of heaviness settled again.

She began to rehearse it in her mind. She could get an early flight. She'd had a holiday fling. It happened all the time. Even if it was one that she'd never forget.

She didn't live in a world of romance, and it was safer that she didn't. It was better this way: edgy and on guard. She had a strength back now.

There was a knock at the door.

She couldn't face anyone, not even Beatrice and Claudia. What was the point? This was not real life. This was a beautiful island where people came to holiday. In her world, people hurt people and disappointed them. The rest of the world was a different place to Antigua and Lemon Cove.

There was the knock again.

She wrapped a gown around her. She opened the door and got ready to tell whoever it was to go away.

But there was Harvey, dressed in shorts and a tropical shirt, carrying a tray with coffee and flowers.

"Breakfast, my lady." He held it in front of her and she burst into tears.

Everything felt odd. Her insides were twisting and her face was blotchy and red. She was a mess and she hated it.

They sat outside on her balcony. It was late morning and people were milling around. They sat under the large umbrella and Grace sipped her coffee. She'd cried like she'd never cried in front of anyone before. She felt a thick, grey, sticky shame.

What had she done?

"I'm sorry, Harvey."

"Why? What you're feeling is normal, you know," Harvey said.

"How do you know what I'm feeling?" She could hear the edge in her voice.

"I remember the first time I slept with a woman after Alice. I was a mess. I felt ashamed, guilty and disloyal. I was morbid and morose and a total mess."

He touched her leg and she couldn't deny she liked it. "I'm also well aware your situation is different to mine.

You're still married and your husband is still very much alive."

"You're very good at mindreading."

"I've just trodden the path before."

Grace breathed out. She felt safe there on the terrace with Harvey, with his honesty. She breathed in the lemony fragrance of the flowers and took comfort in the humidity. It was a warmth she needed. She sipped more coffee.

"I don't think I've ever had a proper marriage."

Harvey sipped his own coffee.

Grace looked out at the view of the endless sea. "It's easy here, isn't it? Here, it all makes sense. I can see how I kept clinging on because I was too scared to let go. But then I lost it anyway. I am starting to understand it wasn't meant for me."

"Perhaps it wasn't."

Grace breathed out.

"So why do I feel so battered and bruised?"

"Why would you expect to feel anything other than the way you do?"

"I've never felt like this before because I've always just kept going. I've always been able to shake it off and just keep on keeping on."

"Well, that's not always healthy."

"But it's life, isn't it?"

"Life is hard – or it can be. Keeping on keeping on isn't the only way."

"But it's the only way I know."

"Perhaps it's time to try something different. Besides, you've had one of Beatrice's massages. It derails the best of us."

Grace smiled. "That reminds me; I have another one this morning."

"Hold on tight."

She looked at Harvey. He looked so calm and peaceful.

"I can't imagine you ever derailed."

"Believe me, I was.

"So, how did you become un-derailed?"

Harvey shrugged. "I let myself feel it all. All of those horrible feelings – and it was absolutely dreadful. I let them come to me and belong to me, rather than pushing them out and blaming everything and everyone else."

Grace looked at him. "And now you're going to tell me it was all worth it."

"Yes I am." He laughed. "It's so hard holding onto the anger. Slowly it turns into resentment and no matter who or what made you angry, you're the one carrying around this bitterness with you wherever you go. The whole world turns grey and you can't find a way out. I just didn't realise the only way through it was looking at what was inside me. It didn't take away the grief of the sadness, but by looking at what I was feeling rather than ignoring it, it slowly started to dissolve the nasty rigid stuff and become more manageable. It's exhausting walking around pretending you're something when you're not."

She looked into his sparkly blue eyes. He looked so assured, so confident – everything she had pretended she was at Hi-TV, but didn't feel. He was right: pretending to be something else was exhausting.

"You are the first person in my whole life, other than a Greg or Beatrice, that I've ever been able to speak to like this. Well, apart from my parents."

"You haven't told me much about your parents."

She paused as she got ready for the inevitable.

"They died, both of them. In a car crash. It was just

after I started at Cambridge. They were driving back after a visit with me. I was eighteen."

Harvey sat forward. "Grace, I'm so sorry. That's dreadful."

She held her hand up. There really was no need for another head tilt. "It was a long time ago."

"So?"

"So what?"

"It doesn't take away how dreadful that was."

Her insides twisted again.

"I'm sorry Grace, I'm prying."

"No, it's not that. It's just…"

"What? Tell me."

"I just…" But she couldn't find the words, she couldn't get past the wall. She needed to change the subject. "How am I ever going to move on, Harvey?"

She watched him think for a moment.

"When Alice died, I thought life was out to get me. I was angry all the time, and I kept thinking, why me? Why her? Why us? All these dreadful people were walking around still able to enjoy their lives – why not them? It made no sense. Everyone around me looked like they were living their life, but I was just existing. Anything else felt terrible. And the guilt… Don't even get me started on the guilt. I was still here and she wasn't. But gradually, after all the raging and the feeling it at full force, I started to have a different perspective. I'd had twenty-three wonderful years with her. I'd had more happiness in those years than many people have in a lifetime. I had a wonderful son who was still here. Yes, I was still devastated and full of grief, but the bitterness and the resentment began to melt away."

"It makes sense." But why did she have a nagging feeling?

"It's early days, Grace, and you came here for space. I can leave; it's no problem at all. Don't think I'm expecting some big heavy relationship – I never meant for anything to happen."

She shook her head. "I've enjoyed myself here more than I ever have enjoyed myself anywhere, and that includes my time with you." It was true: she had. She looked at him and noticed she felt safe next to him, after feeling so out of place for so many years.

But what was she doing? She decided to ignore the thought.

"I think it also might just be one of the most irresponsible things I've ever done in all my life." She leant towards him.

"I'm very happy to be irresponsible." Harvey's lips were near hers.

"I'm happy, you're happy."

Her lips met hers and as his arms wrapped around her, she thought to herself how wonderful being irresponsible felt.

Midlife Murder & The Lost Path
5

There has been much talk here about paths, inner knowing and having the courage to listen to ourselves again. I've listened, learned and taken the knowledge of people further along the path than me.

But even though I know my location – on the Lost Path – for some reason, I can't move on.

There's a great, big giant wall in front of me and it won't budge. I am, it appears, stuck. It's a dreadful feeling and I don't like it at all. It's different from feeling out of control, but it's equally distressing, nonetheless. All the knowledge and talk doesn't seem to move the wall.

I've talked, walked and I've told myself to let go. But still there is a great big wall.

No matter how much I want to move forward I just can't. Is it fear? Perhaps.

I've even had a taste of a world which I'd forgotten was there. A love for life, each other and, most of all, oneself. No edge and no ego; just kindness instead. In recent weeks I've discovered places and people who are all of these things, and it's made me happier than I've felt in so many years.

But still, there's this wall.

I think I want to move forward into a Next Chapter but I stay here anyway. Somehow it feels right in the dark and grey.

So, is this where I'm meant to be? Should I just accept this is my destiny? Have I gone as far as I can? Should I ignore the wall and hope for the best? Or should I turn around and live where I'm meant to live – in the shadows with the sticky air?

I write this, not to take away hope but to share the reality of what is. We can read, talk, think and try but if we can't go any further, is it time to accept this as our path instead? Is everyone's path meant to take them somewhere else, or is it the reality of human life that we can only go so far?

Chapter Thirty-Two

Eric: Grace, this is abuse. Ignoring me like this is abuse. I made you. I made everything you are.
Polly: What I did was wrong but I deserve to be heard. Why won't you talk to me Grace?

"What is it?"

"What's what?" Grace touched her hair.

Beatrice sat down next to her and peered at her. "I can see, there's something. What's happened?"

"Nothing's happened." Grace blushed. This was a lie. Everything had happened. She was just pretending to be the same.

"Yesterday when I saw you sing, you looked so free. But now?" Beatrice stopped.

"Now what?"

"Something has changed."

Grace was about to protest, but then stopped. There was no point and besides, she was suddenly exhausted. The exhilaration she'd felt from the previous day and night had been replaced by a heavy dread.

"I feel like there's a wall, Beatrice. Does that sound strange?"

Beatrice shook her head and took her hand.

"My darling, it doesn't sound strange at all. It sounds absolutely normal and believe me when I say I've heard it said many times before."

Grace nodded, grateful at least for this. "So, what do I do?"

Beatrice paused, looked down and then looked up. "Would you like the truth?"

"Of course."

"Sometimes the truth isn't what we want to hear."

"Please. I've heard so much I don't want to hear recently. I can take it."

Beatrice smiled. "We can talk to therapists, friends; we can read and learn, I can work these hands and help you as much as I can. But this will only take you so far. To get to the place where the magic really happens, you have to do that part alone. You have to find your home, here." Beatrice touched her chest.

"But I don't feel at home anywhere."

"You know anyone can build a house and decorate it, but it takes a person filled with love to create a home."

"I don't understand." Grace felt her old irritability rise again.

"My darling," Beatrice smiled her big wide smile. "You have all the answers, inside that beautiful soul of yours." She squeezed Grace's hands again before letting go. "Now, come on, it's massage time."

Grace nodded and Beatrice turned to her.

"It might help if you work out what you're afraid of.

Sometimes that wall you describe, that's blocking you, is just a little bit of fear."

Grace lay on the massage bed, her head looking down through the hole. This time she was going to stay awake. She was going to be completely conscious throughout the massage, so there would be no bad dreams.

She felt Beatrice's hands and breathed out. Besides, she was Grace Leven. She wasn't afraid.

"How long have you been doing these massages anyway?" she asked. But Beatrice didn't answer. The massage had stopped.

"Beatrice?"

Grace was going to sit up, but then felt tired. Her shoulders ached and her body felt heavy. Beatrice must have popped out.

"Grace Leven?"

This time it was a man's voice. That was strange. Where was Beatrice?

"Grace Leven?" the man repeated. Funny: it sounded familiar but she couldn't work out for a moment who it was.

"I hope I'm not interrupting."

Grace opened her eyes and the sight startled her. It was the Dean from her university college. What was he doing there?

A feeling of panic began to rise in her. How had he found her?

"I'm afraid I have some bad news, and I'm going to need you to be brave."

Why did he have to come back? Wasn't the first time enough?

"There's been an accident."

"Right." Grace tried to stay calm. Why was he spoiling her fun? It was just like the last time. She'd finished her lectures and was getting ready for a party; that's what you're supposed to do, isn't it, when you're at university? Study and party. Study and party. Not study and party, then have life-shattering news. That was supposed to be much later in life.

"Is it Pearl?"

But he wasn't listening. He was talking with a kind look in his eye – a kind look she didn't like. That kind of look accompanied grief and pity. Something terrible had happened. You see, she wanted to say, I knew this would happen.

"We're not sure of the details, but the police are here. I said I'd come in first, but I'm afraid there has been an accident involving your parents."

"My parents? But they're dead," she tried to say, but the words didn't come out. She couldn't say anything. She hadn't been able to speak then and again she couldn't now. But she was grown-up now – why couldn't she say anything? What was wrong with her? She stood frozen and nodded. I already know this, she wanted to say.

He was telling her details of where and when it had happened. But she hadn't cared then and she didn't care now. All she could care about was that he was ruining her massage, just as he'd ruined her life back then.

"It was a dreadful accident."

No, it wasn't, she wanted to say. She'd caused it. If they hadn't been visiting her at university, they'd be alive now. If she hadn't chosen to go to Cambridge, they'd be alive too. If she'd gone anywhere else, they wouldn't have been on that road. This was all her fault. It's what she'd always known. Why was he going over it all again?

What Really Happened To Me?

She stayed stuck in the pain, back in her room in halls – the same one her mother had decorated and made feel like her home. All that excitement had disappeared forever. She would never allow herself to feel excited again. There was no point; it would just be snatched away. If she didn't feel it, she wouldn't make her self vulnerable.

"Grace?"

Go away. She didn't want to talk to him.

"Ms Leven?"

Not now.

"Ms Leven?"

But this time it was a woman's voice.

"We've come to an end."

Grace opened her eyes just in time to feel Beatrice pull a towel over her back and hear her close the door.

Grace switched off her phone as the plane readied for take-off. She was grateful there was a seat still on that day's flight, so she'd packed and left. No goodbyes or explanations; she'd just ordered a taxi and left.

She pushed away the guilt as the plane moved along the runway. If she'd told Harvey or any of the staff she was going, they might have persuaded her to stay, and she couldn't. This was best for all of them.

She looked down at the island as it slowly disappeared. This was the way she had to live her life, and now there was no going back.

Chapter Thirty-Three

Eric: Grace I love you, we're meant to be together. You and I are soulmates.
Polly: Grace you're my best friend. We've been through so much - we just need to talk. x

"I'm really sorry to tell you this."

"Please Iris, just say it."

Grace was in a car returning to Strawberry Village. She would collect her things, then go somewhere – anywhere else where she didn't know anyone. No more drama. She couldn't face any more drama or talks about feelings and paths. It was making her crazy. She wanted to move on, not go over and over the past. This was not the life for her and she needed to be alone. Away from everyone, including Harvey – especially Harvey. She wasn't meant for a life going over and over feelings and walking along paths. She didn't need to unravel, she needed to work.

"I think Polly helped set you up."

"I see." Grace looked ahead.

"I'm so sorry, Grace."

"It's not your fault, Iris." Grace was aware her tone was sharp. "I'm sorry too. I'm also not shocked in the slightest."

"Look, I'd better go, but I'm going to come back so I can tell you everything. I know you'll be tired but shall we meet later? You're not alone in this, you know, you have all of us now – and you need to tell us everything about Antigua.

No, she didn't. She would meet with Iris and then leave. This was the closure she needed.

She looked at her phone expecting to see a message from Harvey, but there wasn't one.

She shook her head – it was for the best. She looked out of the window at the M4 and watched the trees on the side slip away.

At seven-thirty that night, Grace saw the four of them sitting around a table, worried looks in their eyes. She pushed away more feelings of guilt. She waved at Lulu, Iris, Jack and Pearl. She wondered if Jack would be angry at her for leaving Harvey, but he smiled at her along with the others.

"You look amazing," Lulu said.

"She does, doesn't she?"

Grace had already had tea with Pearl in the afternoon. She'd wanted to know all about Harvey arriving in Antigua but Grace hadn't told her much. It wasn't fair to put Pearl in an even more awkward position with her father.

"Beatrice and her magic hands." Iris nodded.

"You do have a wonderful taste in hotels and staff," Grace said to Jack as she sat down.

"Thank you," Jack said, and a silence lingered around them.

"There's no need to feel awkward. I'm a grown-up. Just tell me as it is." Grace ordered a glass of sparkling water. She needed to keep a clear head.

Iris took a deep breath. "I've had three confessions now from people who told me that Polly bullied them into making a complaint about you. She line-managed all of them, and she said any progression in the company would be jeopardised if they didn't, or if they breathed a word of what she'd said. She told them there had been other complaints but they didn't have enough to make an impact. But you'd made the lives of some young women miserable and you needed to be dealt with."

"I see." Grace felt the familiar numbness.

"I'm sorry," Iris said.

"Please." Grace smiled. "There's no need to be sorry. What next?"

"We get these people to go on record," Lulu said.

Grace shook her head. "I'm not going to do that."

"But you have to," Iris said.

"I'm not going to manipulate them any more. What we're going to do is get Polly to confess."

"We are?"

Grace nodded as she watched what she'd said sink in.

"I'll do it," Pearl said, her eyes bright.

"Darling, I don't think so."

But Pearl held up her hand. "Please Mum, it's the least I can do. I want to – it's my way of saying sorry, and dealing with my anger."

Grace had no idea how she'd raised such an emotionally intelligent daughter, when she was such a mess.

"Okay," she nodded. There was no point in arguing with her daughter. "How do we do this?"

"I'll accidentally bump into her and be so happy to see her. I'll suggest we go for drinks. She's been trying to get hold of me, but I've been ignoring her and she doesn't know I'm here."

"Okay," Grace nodded, although she wasn't certain that Polly would admit her actions to Pearl.

"I'll get her drunk, I'll pretend to be drunk and I'll get her to confess. I'll record it."

"I can give you one of the hidden cameras we use," Iris nodded.

"She thinks of everything." Jack smiled at Iris.

"Plus, I'll know where she'll be, so you can accidentally bump into her," Iris added.

Pearl clapped her hands. "It's the perfect plan."

"I'm not sure." Grace didn't like this at all. Was she putting them at risk?

The three of them looked at her. "We're not going to publish anything," Lulu said. "All we need is the evidence, and then you can take it to the board. Then wham, bam, you'll be back at your desk."

"You make it sound easy," Grace said. Did she even want the job back? All this effort and she wasn't sure.

"This is about justice, Mum," Pearl said. "We need to do this to stop women like Polly doing it again to someone else."

"Women can't do this to other women, or anyone," Jack agreed. "It's not on. If there's a way of getting the truth out then it's worth a go."

She couldn't argue with that.

"The truth." They raised their glasses.

"The truth." She raised her glass to them, but she put it back down quickly so she could hide her shaking hands.

Chapter Thirty-Four

Eric: At least tell me where you are, I have a right to know. I appreciate you need to make your point, but this really is abuse you know. I deserve better.
Polly: I've got so much to tell you Grace. You wouldn't believe what's going on. Please, just one meet.

The next morning Grace felt edgy and unnerved. She kept checking her phone for a message from Harvey. But what did she expect? She'd left without saying goodbye.

Besides, it was better this way. This way she could get on with her life.

"Grace."

Grace smiled at Jack behind the reception desk as she walked past.

"Do you have a minute?"

"Of course." She pushed away the hope that he had a message for her from Harvey.

Stop. You are being ridiculous.

"We were just checking on the cottage. There's been a lot of interest in it," Jack leant forward, "but please, it's yours for as long as you want."

Grace nodded. "Yes, of course. I understand." She had planned to leave, but the truth was she had nowhere to go – and the night before, they'd all agreed to discovering the truth. Even she couldn't run out on them all now.

"I can see you have a lot on your mind. How about we book it for another month and we take it from there?"

"Another month?"

"Are you okay, Grace?"

"Yes. I'm fine."

Jack leant forward. "I know you left Antigua earlier than you'd planned. Is everything okay?"

"Yes," Grace nodded. "I just wanted to get to the bottom of everything here."

Jack nodded too now. "I understand. If I'd been accused of what you have, I'd be going crazy. If anyone can get to the truth, it's Iris."

Grace smiled a small smile. "Thank you – and thank you for being so understanding about everything." She paused. "Have you spoken with Harvey?"

"Harvey? No, he's on his way back. He should be back soon. Why?"

"No reason." Grace shook her head and turned around. She looked in her bag for her phone. Perhaps she should at least message him.

But then something happened. She felt something – a sensation in the pit of her stomach she'd forgotten.

Her skin prickled and her insides twisted tight. She could feel him before she saw him and turned around; it all made sense.

"Grace." His voice cut through the warmth of the foyer, and everything stood still.

"Eric."

There he stood, smile wide as if it was the most natural occurrence in the world.

He walked towards her and put his arms around her. "I've been so worried about you. Thank god you're okay."

She stood, frozen. She didn't know what to say or what to do. The white-hot feeling surged through her and everything she'd planned to say to him disappeared.

"You look great – really great." He held her back to look at her. "Your hair; it's all curly." He leant forward. "It's wonderful to see my wife." He leant forward and kissed her on the lips.

She looked at him, frozen.

He looked around. "Can we go somewhere?"

She looked towards the bar – the one she'd spent so many happy times in over the past few weeks. His poison was filling the air.

She nodded towards the bar.

"I was thinking somewhere more private." He held her arms.

"They're cleaning my room," she managed.

He pulled a sad face and her insides churned.

They walked towards the bar and sat down. Samuel, the barman, came over.

"Ms Leven, welcome back."

"Two Americanos," Eric told him. She'd forgotten how cold and rude he was. Had she ever even noticed this? She'd also forgotten how he'd order for her.

"'Welcome back'? 'Ms Leven'? Where've you been and how do they know your name?"

"How did you know I was here?"

"Pearl, of course. Pearl tells me everything, but you know that. Darling, you don't expect her to lie to me, do you?"

The feeling of powerlessness swept through her.

"What do you want, Eric?"

"Oh Gracie, don't be like that." He leant forward and took her hand. "I'm so happy to see you. You look different." He sat back again, looking at her. "I see you're wearing colour now – and your hair; it's different."

'What do you want, Eric?"

"What do I want? You're the one who just took off. I've been going out of my mind. You didn't reply to any of my messages. I've had no idea where you were. What were you thinking to just run off like that?"

The disbelief rang like a bell in her ears.

"*I* ran off?"

Samuel returned with the coffees. Grace took another deep breath, but it wasn't working; the rage was rising in her and it was out of control.

"Yes, you did. You ran off and clearly have been having a little holiday for one here. How much have you been knocking it back…Ms Leven?" He nodded at the bar, smiling.

"I caught you shagging Polly."

He didn't even pause. "Oh please, that was just a bit of fun that got out of hand."

"Fun?" Her voice screeched. She told herself to breathe; she needed to breathe. "You left me the day I was suspended."

He laughed again. "What's wrong with that? We all

need a bit of space at times. You were becoming too much, with all your aggression."

This time she was able to catch her breath and she lowered her voice.

"You slept with Polly."

"Now, about that," he picked up his coffee. "I really think you should think about the kind of friends you have."

"I'm sorry?"

"Seriously Grace, it was really quite embarrassing. She never stopped coming on to me. Of course, I always told her no, I'm a faithful husband to Grace. But then, when you disappeared like you did, I was lonely. I didn't even know if we were married any more. I didn't know where you were or what you were doing. I thought we were over. I was devastated – absolutely bloody devastated. She took pity on me. We went out for drinks and one thing led to another. She can be very persuasive when she wants to be. I mean, you know that; she's your best friend. You know what she's like."

"I caught you. In bed." The words choked out of her throat. "In *my* bed."

"It was a mistake; I'm sorry. We all make mistakes. We'd had a bit to drink. It meant nothing. Come on Gracie, look at all the mistakes you've made over the years. We've got the photos and videos to prove it. We all know that temper of yours gets the better of you. Let's just move on, shall we? Let's just put it all behind us."

Grace's insides twisted tighter. The white-hot searing pain ran through her and it felt like her insides were on fire. But still she sat, frozen yet on fire.

He leant forward.

"Gracie. We've been through so much; we've known

each other since we were kids. You and I are supposed to be together."

He touched her leg and she flinched.

"You know you can't live without me, Gracie."

"Don't call me that."

"Call you what?"

"Gracie."

"Okay." He raised his eyebrows at her. "Right." He looked around. "You're not going to cause one of your scenes, are you darling?"

"How dare you!"

"Oh Grace, I don't quite know why you're getting on your high horse like this."

"What do you mean?"

"You've lost your whole career because of it."

"Because of what?" The buzzing in her ears was getting louder.

He smiled at her. A smirking, knowing smile.

"Well, your manner, Gracie. You really do have a problem."

"A problem?"

He leant forward. "You don't need me to spell it out for you, do you?" He looked around him. "I'd have thought you'd want to put it all behind you."

"Please Eric. Spell it out."

"Well, let's just say your workplace has at last spoken up about the behaviour I've been dealing with for all these years."

"*My* behaviour?" Her voice was louder now – louder than she wished, but she didn't care. Her heart was pounding; she could barely breathe. How dare he? This was how she'd lived her life being married to him, this awful dreadful feeling – that she always thought was her fault. She always thought there was something wrong with her or that she'd done something wrong. The endless walking on eggshells, the trying to please. But it was never enough. She thought of Claudia and Beatrice:

Step back from your thoughts. Take a deep breath and step back.

She breathed a big deep breath. She could to do this. She had to do this. It was time.

"A lot of people have come forward, Gracie."

"And please tell me, how do you know this?"

"I'm sorry?"

Her sudden calm surprised him, she could tell.

"You left when I arrived home that day and we haven't spoken since. What do you know about people coming forward?"

For a moment he looked flustered. She'd dared to question him.

"It must have been Pearl."

"Pearl? But how would Pearl know?"

He looked around. Eyes were on them. Jack was also standing by the bar.

"Are you going to get angry? Are you going to show everyone here now the true colours of Grace Leven?"

"Fuck off," Grace said in the calmest of voices.

"I'm sorry?"

"I told you to fuck off."

"Here we go again." He looked around.

Jack walked over to her now. "Is everything okay, Grace?"

"She's getting angry – just like she always does. The real Grace Leven is out now, for the world to see."

"Grace Leven has been one of our favourite customers these last few weeks; we've got to know her very well. My staff and I don't like to see her this distressed now."

Eric looked at Jack, and at Samuel, who was now standing next to Jack. Grace saw the anger flash in Eric's eyes – then he laughed. "She's been throwing the cash around has she? Paying everyone off?"

"Not at all, sir. Now, if that's all, I would suggest you might think about leaving. Can I call you a cab?"

Jack towered over Eric, and Grace saw the child he was. For a dreadful moment she felt sorry for him, and fought the urge to make him feel better.

"She's my wife; she'll come with me." The smile managed to stay on Eric's face but his eyes told a different story.

"Not any more," Grace said, her voice still sounding calm. "We're separated, and we're getting a divorce."

"Yeah, right." He laughed again. "I can only apologise – my wife has these funny moments."

"Ah yes sir, believe me, I know about funny moments and the reality being distorted. It's a very painful experience."

Eric looked at Jack, a hint of recognition in his eye. "Are you the…"

"Miserable millionaire. Or rather I was, but not any more."

Grace's heart was pounding, the white-hot rod of cold pain throbbing in her insides, but a sense of clarity settled, as if she could see Eric for the first time. Jack's calmness flustered him. She could see Eric's mind registering that Jack was the hotel owner and a millionaire, not some barman he could feel superior to.

"Grace, please." Eric turned back to her, a pleading look now in his eye. "After all I've done for you."

Grace heard Jack take a sharp intake of breath, but she stayed calm.

"You never asked me."

"Asked you what?"

"When my parents were killed, you never once asked if I was okay."

"What are you going on about?" His face scrunched with the smirk he used to make her think she was mad. "You see, this is what I'm talking about." He looked at Samuel now, not Jack.

"I was never okay," she continued. "I've lived our whole marriage not being okay, doing everything you told me to."

"Darling, this is hardly the place. You're just embarrassing yourself now."

"It's over, Eric. All these years you've blamed me for everything. It's over. You're on your own now."

"Don't be ridiculous." He attempted to laugh.

"You can have the house; I don't want it. I never want to set foot in there again, but you will not get another penny from me."

She saw the flicker in his eyes. It was fear.

"All these years you've blamed me for not having your own career – well here's your chance. Go out in the world and earn your own money, Eric. Show the world what you've got. You're totally free now. I won't be holding you back, as you say."

"You're being ridiculous. I have rights."

"Am I? Is it so ridiculous that you have to fend for yourself?"

"I've sacrificed everything for you, Gracie."

"No, you haven't. You haven't sacrificed anything. You never liked going to work. You can't cope with anyone being better than you, you can't cope with anyone who is better than you at anything. When someone does do better you have to pull them down, just how you did with me. You've been living the exact life you want, just as you like it, while I made the sacrifices. I've had enough. Your ridiculous insecurity is no longer my problem. It ends now."

"I'll fight you. I'll have a lawyer."

"Why would you fight me? This is your moment, the moment you've been saying for years you had to give up. Well, you're free now. All your talents, everything you want to offer to the world, go and do it, Eric. You don't have me to blame any more. Let's see what you've got."

"I don't know why you're getting so uptight about this now."

"Don't you? Well I do. All these years you've blamed me, I've been carrying your blame, your shame, your lack of being able to do anything that makes you feel remotely uncomfortable. I've had to do it, Jack here has had to do it, Sam here does it. Every day we work and we have to face something which we don't like. But not you, Eric. You think you're immune. You think you shouldn't ever have to feel uncomfortable, which is why you blame me for everything. All your insecurity, all your laziness, your need to be the most important person in the room – but at the same time you feel so entitled to all the good stuff that comes with hard work and discomfort."

Grace took another deep breath. She knew she should stop, but she couldn't. Not now.

"The thing is, Eric, I like the truth. That's what I've discovered here. The truth is our friend. You feel it in your soul. The only thing wrong with me is that I've been living your lie for all these years. Well, I'm handing it back. All your shame, all your blame – you can have it. Think what you want about me, I don't care. So, off you go. Let's see it: everything I've been holding you back from, everything you've blamed me for. You're free now, to show the world what you are made of. You don't need my money, you can make your own, can't you?"

Eric's lip was quivering, his eyes were wild. She'd never seen him like this before.

"My lawyers will be in touch."

"Leonard will look forward to dealing with them."

He stepped forward. "Grace." Jack touched Eric's arm and he pushed it off. "Fuck off. Don't you dare touch me."

Jack stepped back, without the slightest flinch.

Grace took one last deep breath.

"You know, a wise person told me the weakest person has to be the most dominant. You're weak, Eric. A weak little bully. Please let's be clear: you don't scare me at all."

"Gracie, please."

"I told you, don't call me Gracie. Leave, Eric. Go."

"I'll book in. We can sort this out."

"I'm afraid we're fully booked for many weeks now, sir," Jack said.

Eric looked into her eyes. She saw the same look she'd always seen – the one she believed was his longing for her. But she could see it now for what it was: he was manipulating her.

"I shall walk with you to the door; otherwise we'll call security. There's a taxi outside," Jack said.

Eric looked around as she watched him realise the whole bar was staring at him.

"No need." His voice was curt. He walked towards Grace. "You're not getting away with this. I'll make everyone see what you did to me."

"Goodbye Eric," Grace said.

He turned and then turned back.

"Please Gracie, don't end it this way."

"It's over, Eric. Goodbye."

"I'll always love you," he tried for the final time.

"No, you won't, because you never have."

Grace stayed standing. She tried to move but she couldn't. Her head and heart were pounding but all she could do was stand, frozen.

"Why don't you come with me?" a voice said next to her. It was a woman she vaguely recognised from the darts evening.

"Penelope Fanshaw," she said in her ear. "I was rather rude to you when we met at darts a few weeks ago."

Grace wanted to say no.

"I saw what just happened, so please don't think I'm being rude. You've had a shock and you need some tea. Here, come with me."

Grace didn't know what to say. Everything in this room had been changed by his grey poison. All its warmth and colour had gone. It was just like everything else. Everything he touched he ruined.

"Here, let's go and sit outside."

Penelope led her through the patio doors and out into the open air. Grace had never before been out into the patio garden, and it felt cooling and refreshing.

She sat down on a white iron chair, but then stood up again. She was too restless.

"Just take a deep breath," Penelope told her.

Even though it was June, there was still a chill in the air and she was grateful for it. At least she felt something, even if it was cold.

Penelope disappeared inside, then returned. She sat

down and Grace did the same. Grace tried to take several deep breaths.

"Well, pardon me for being rude, but what a pig of a man."

Grace's first instinct was to defend Eric.

"I'm sorry, I know this is absolutely not the right thing to say." Penelope held up her hands. "But I had to get it off my chest."

Grace didn't know what to say. The buzzing inside her was still too much. It was as though she was somehow outside of her body.

A waiter she didn't recognise brought the tea over. She looked around the garden – she didn't recognise any of it.

"I think what you just did was incredibly brave."

Grace looked at Penelope. "I'm sorry?"

"I saw what he was doing, and I can see what he's done."

Grace was finding it all hard to take in.

Penelope poured her some tea and put some sugar in it. "Please, sip this. Your system needs it."

Grace didn't know what she needed. The buzzing was too much.

She sipped the tea and the hot sweet liquid slid down the back of her throat. She took another sip and then she placed the cup back down. Her hands were still shaking.

"I've seen it all before, my dear. I've been there," Penelope said.

Grace's mind tried to catch up. Why was this woman talking to her?

"I was married a long time ago. Very few people know this here, but it was the most awful of times. I was young, thought marriage was forever, and I thought my husband was the bees-knees. Until he left me for his secretary."

"I'm sorry," Grace managed.

"Please." Penelope shook her head. "I'm not trying to make this all about me; it was the best thing that could have happened – not that I knew it at the time. But it still lives with me, so I can see it when it's happening to someone else, like I've just seen in there. I've become very good at recognising the signs."

Grace wanted to keep up her Grace Leven persona; she wanted to be cool and in control. But she really wasn't, and the truth was, she never had been. She felt too exhausted to pretend any more.

"What I hadn't realised was, in our six-year marriage I'd completely lost sense of myself. I would say he eradicated it for me, but that would make me a victim and I wouldn't want to give him that pleasure – not even now. But the blaming, the manipulation, the controlling, the scapegoating – I didn't ever see what was happening. I just always thought it was me. He was charming, wonderful and so full of life that of course I thought everything he said was true. He could do no wrong in my eyes. If he was late, it would be my fault because I'd told him the wrong time. If he said a biting comment and I dared to defend myself, he told me I was being over-sensitive. Over time it stripped me to my core. I had no idea who I was any more. Other women were always a little more beautiful, while I should tidy myself up a bit more. When I found a small job in a shop I liked, he'd tell me I needed to be at home. Then when I gave that up, he'd remind me daily that I relied on him."

Penelope sipped her tea and Grace couldn't take her eyes off her.

"It was the constant hoop-jumping that chipped away, along with the walking on egg-shells. I was so busy navigating that, I lost any sight of who I was at all. I'd spend my whole time leaping from one problem to the next. I'd go over and over it in my mind. What had I done wrong today? How could I fix it? How could I make him happy again? What was going to go wrong today and how could I stop it? Because if I didn't, I'd be the one to blame."

Grace nodded. She couldn't take her eyes off Penelope.

"And do you know the very worst part of it all? The whole time I never once questioned it. I never stopped myself and asked – is this really my fault? I thought deep, deep down there was just something terribly wrong with me. He had seen it first and one day the rest of the world would cotton on too."

Grace looked at the woman in front of her – so poised and assured.

"When he left me, I thought I was actually going to die. It was as if my soul had been ripped out and he'd taken it with him. I saw no point in carrying on. I told myself I was being stupid, I told myself to pull myself together, but nothing worked. I was so far away from myself, so tied and attached to him, I didn't think I could ever find a way to live again. More to the point, even if I could, I didn't want to. Life seemed utterly pointless without him."

"I'm so sorry," Grace whispered.

"I thought about it, you know – ending it. I was trying in many ways, by drinking myself into a stupor every day. I lost any sense of self-pride and I'd call him, begging him to come back. He would only snigger and laugh and tell me I was pathetic. If I'd been a better woman he wouldn't have had to look elsewhere, he'd said. He was consistent, I'll give him that. So it just fuelled the fire. I never once questioned that he wasn't right. I was the one who was flawed and ugly, both inside and out."

Grace looked at the woman in front of her: her silver

bob; the black-and-white spotted blouse and white trousers she was wearing; a pink cashmere jumper loosely wrapped around her shoulders; a silver necklace and bracelets – all exactly where they should be.

"What happened?"

"I had a neighbour, or should I say, saviour? She noticed something wasn't right and had spotted I wasn't leaving the house for days. Back then I would think of her as a nosy neighbour, but she wasn't. She was kind. She'd call on me and I wouldn't answer, but then she'd persist until eventually I let her in. She started to come in every day. I'd open the door, she'd walk into my kitchen and make me a coffee. I didn't want to talk and she'd just come in anyway and sit with me. I didn't tell her anything that had happened, but she could see. Then one day she told me a story about a man whose trousers had fallen down in the local shop. Everyone had laughed including him; she'd laughed as she was telling me and somehow, I laughed too."

Penelope paused, and Grace could see the distant look in her eyes.

"She leant forward, touched my hand and said in a quiet voice: 'look at that; you're still in there'. She was so soft and gentle, but she said something which took me by surprise."

"What did she say?"

"She told me that it wasn't love. He was being a bastard. She said I am me and I am full of love; anything else belongs to him."

Grace watched Penelope as her eyes glimmered with tears. It was as though she was back in that moment for a few seconds, and then she shook her head and sat back in the chair. Penelope looked up at Grace.

"It was the kindest thing anyone had ever said to me. My parents didn't speak about their feelings; I hadn't even told them what had happened or that he'd left, I was so ashamed. I don't quite know how, but there must have been something still inside me, like a knowing I could just about cling on to. I cleaned myself up and went back to the shop again. I was able to get my job back and the women in there were kind and friendly too. In fact, the more I started to live again, the more I noticed how kind and friendly a lot of people were. Then I started to laugh a little more. I had my own routine, which kept me going through the difficult days, of which there were more than the better ones." She nodded towards Grace. "Then one day I realised I wasn't just surviving any more – I was living."

Grace looked at Penelope with her red lipstick and the glow in her cheeks. She was so well put together, it was hard for Grace to imagine her ever being broken.

"I still have it, you know. That broken part of me, deep in my insides. It whispers every now and again and tells me it was all my fault and he was right."

"And what do you do with it?"

"I thank it. I know it's keeping me safe because sometimes it's easier to blame ourselves – it gives us a sense of control. It stops us from feeling all the hurt and pain, and it stops us from facing the brutal reality we have to leave."

Penelope picked up her cup, and Grace noticed how her bangles jangled on her arm.

"It's a bloody shit though. I still have my prickle – as you saw when I met you at the darts. I'm sorry – I was a cow. It always pops up when insecurity takes hold."

Grace laughed. "I know all about the prickle, believe me. There's no need to apologise."

"I say it again though – what you did back there takes courage. You won't feel like it for a long time and it's a courage you wish you didn't need. But it would have been so easy to have slipped back and to let that part – the one that believes you don't deserve any better and that you should feel guilty and ashamed for someone else's behaviour – take over. I say to you, what my neighbour said to me: you're full of love; I promise."

Grace wished with all her heart Penelope and her neighbour were right.

"I've been loving the Midlife Murder columns by the way."

"You have? I suppose we are naïve to think you wouldn't guess who was writing them."

"Fear not. It's only me. But it didn't take long for me to put two and two together. If the Strawberry House committee all guess, they won't say a word. They're good like that."

A thought came to Grace. "What you said, about your neighbour – her kindness – that's how I feel about Strawberry Village."

"And I bet it's bloody terrifying?"

"Yes, it is."

"Does it feel a little small, unsettling, not dramatic enough, but at the same time just where you want to be?"

"It feels exactly like that."

"Well, just allow the fear, darling. Don't let it take you away from where you're meant to be."

"But that's just it – I don't know where I'm meant to be."

"Really, is that true? Because I'd say, with a heart and brain like yours, you can work it out."

Penelope nodded to the doors behind where they were sitting. Grace turned to see Pearl and Lulu, trying to open them.

"Mum, I'm so sorry." Pearl stepped outside. "We came

as quickly as we could. Is he still here? I didn't mean to tell him where we were, it just slipped out. I'm so, so sorry. Did he hurt you? What did he say, you know it's not true, don't you?"

Grace looked back at Penelope, who raised a perfectly groomed eyebrow. "You know it's a wonderful thing. When you put down their shame, you get to listen to your heart again and see the love that's been there all along."

Chapter Thirty-Five

Eric: You can't do this to me. You can't just drop me like you do everyone else in your life. We're soulmates.
Polly: One meeting Grace, please. x

"I've made a mistake. I've made a bloody horrendous, terrible mistake," Grace said out loud.

She'd gone back to her cottage, but all she could see was Harvey's work. The bookshelves, the cabinets; everything had been put together with such love. She'd walked along the corridor and seen the cabinet he'd been working on that still needed doors. The unease kept rising, the confusion and the despair. She'd walked and walked for miles.

She needed space. She needed to think. She needed to observe. She needed her own path to work it all out – and she'd found it. She'd walked over the bridge and through the Somerset countryside. These paths, it turned out, were everywhere around the world; she'd just been too busy to notice they were there.

She stopped walking when she couldn't walk any more.

"What the bloody hell have I done?" she said out loud to the endless rolling hills. She took a deep breath and took out her phone. She'd call Harvey, apologise and explain.

She let it ring, but then it went to voicemail.

"Harvey, it's me, Grace. Well, I suppose you know that. I just wanted to say, I'm sorry. I'm sorry to have left like that. I just needed to think. Anyway, I won't keep going on. Could you call me please?"

Grace put her phone back in her pocket. He'd call back; she knew he would, or at least she tried to convince herself he would as she walked back to the hotel.

Grace went to the front desk.

"Has anyone seen Harvey?" she asked.

"He was here and then left," one of the younger members said.

"How long ago?"

"About two hours ago."

Grace's heart began to pound again. There were no messages or texts on her phone. He must have seen her with Eric.

She ran out of the hotel and into the village. She ran along to Dave's Deli.

"Have you seen Harvey?"

"Grace. You look wonderful. Lemon Cove has worked its magic again."

She didn't want to be rude but the panic was rushing through her.

"I'm sorry Dave, I'm in a bit of rush. I really need to see Harvey."

"Of course. I saw him here briefly but there seemed to

be something going on with him too. He took a coffee and then left. Is everything okay?"

"I don't know. Do you have any idea where he went?"

"I don't. He said we'd catch up later and then was off. He could have gone home."

"I don't even have his address and he isn't answering his calls."

Dave took the pen from behind his ears and pulled out his pad. "Here. I know he won't mind. Here's his address."

"Thank you, Dave." Grace took the paper, and as she did, she hoped he really wouldn't mind.

Grace was so busy looking at the map on her phone that she walked directly into someone.

For a split second she hoped it was Harvey, but it was Jack.

"Grace."

"Jack, I'm so sorry. Have you seen Harvey?"

"Yes, I have," he replied, and his sharp tone surprised her.

"Is everything okay?"

"Are *you* okay? That was quite something earlier."

Grace nodded. Everything was blurring into one. All she knew was that she needed to see Harvey.

"Do you have a moment, Grace?"

"Not really," she started.

"I know what happened with Harvey. I know what you did, Grace."

"I see," Grace said. He knew.

She was close to the bridge and was about to cross it.

"Here, come and sit down." Jack nodded at a bench.

Grace followed him and they sat down. "This is a special bench." Jack nodded at the plaque on the back of it.

Grace read it out loud.

"For Peggy and Basil and all the magic moments they spent here."

"Peggy? The therapist?"

"The very one. This is where we met for the first time, but that's another story."

Grace nodded and she leant forward on her knees; took a deep breath.

"I see Claudia and Beatrice got you breathing then."

Grace smiled. "Yes, they did."

Jack leant forward too. "And is it helping?"

"Yes. No. Oh, I don't know." She looked at him. "I've mucked up big time, haven't I?"

"Yes, you have," Jack nodded. She smiled again. She admired his honesty.

"I've hurt him, haven't I?"

"Yes, you have," Jack said, his smile disappearing.

Grace ran her hands through her hair.

"What can I do?"

Jack shook his head. "I don't know."

A panic filled her. "There must be something."

Jack looked as though he was thinking what to say.

"Go on, you can say it."

"You've had a rough morning."

"I know, but I need to know what's happening."

Jack sat back, and thought for a moment, then he turned to her. "My mother," he said. "She is, shall we say, difficult? She's unkind towards me and has been my whole life. Nothing I've ever done is enough for her, and she's cruel, invalidating, and every time I see her, it's brutal."

"I'm sorry," Grace said.

"I knew as soon as I saw your husband, he was a difficult

person too – and please know, I understand what it does to you, when someone who is supposed to love you treats you in this way – whoever it is."

"I sense a but coming on."

"But I've also learned, no matter how badly someone treats us, it's never an excuse to treat other people badly too. I used to go around being so angry with the world because I could never find what I really needed. But this was still me acting like an idiot – I couldn't keep blaming my difficult mother for my bad behaviour."

"So what you're saying is, there's no excuse for leaving Harvey."

"I don't know what happened, but all I know is he's really, really angry and he's really, really hurt. He was so broken after he lost Alice. Josh and I were so worried about him; we thought he'd never get better – but then he did start to get better, and back on his feet. But now he's hurting all over again, and I hate seeing him like this."

"My leaving is not the same as his wife dying."

"You were the first person he really liked since Alice, and then you just left him in Antigua without saying goodbye. You can't treat someone like Harvey like that – you can't treat people like that."

She wanted to argue with him, but the sickness she was feeling in her stomach told her she knew he was right.

"I panicked and I ran," she said, as if it was some kind of an excuse. "Everything was getting overwhelming."

"That might be, but you still hurt him. Believe me, I know how easy it is to hurt someone – but we should know better than anyone. We know what it's like to be looked over and discarded – why would we ever want to do that to anyone else?"

What Really Happened To Me?

He was right, and this time she didn't even want to argue. They sat in silence for a few moments.

"What changed in your world?" she asked him.

"Iris." He smiled and his whole face softened. "Iris and her dad Bruce, actually. They showed me that even when you're hurting, you can still be kind."

Grace nodded. "I'm so pleased you found Iris."

"And I was pleased you'd found Harvey. Only…"

"He's not so sure he's pleased he's found me."

Jack laughed. "You took the words right out of my mouth."

"But that's it, Jack – you saw this morning. I'm not even divorced yet. This is hardly the right time to jump into another relationship."

Jack thought for a moment. "If Peggy was here now, she'd tell you about moments, the magic ones we have to collect. Like she and Basil used to do here on this bench – while they could."

Grace nodded, breathed in, and this time she did feel her insides relax.

"Just talk to him – that's all you can do. But I know special people when I meet them. I can't walk away completely from my mother, but you can leave your husband and you don't need to take that pain into something actually special – because that gives him a power he doesn't deserve."

Grace nodded as she took in his words.

"Thank you, Jack."

"For telling you off?"

"For bringing me back to the moment."

"Well, you have Peggy to thank for that."

"She sounds quite the woman."

Jack smiled and nodded. "She really was."

Chapter Thirty-Six

Eric: It's not over Grace, we belong together.
Polly: We need to talk. I need your advice about work x
Grace: Harvey, I'm so sorry. Please can I explain? G x

The next day she sat in the same spot she'd sat with Penelope Fanshaw the day before. She'd left three voicemail messages for Harvey and sent several texts but he still hadn't replied. She pushed the disappointment aside as she looked now into the faces of Iris, Lulu and Pearl.

"Are you ready for this?" Iris asked.

"Of course," Grace said, although when she looked at the worry in their eyes, she started to doubt herself.

"You know I was acting, okay?" Pearl said.

Grace touched her daughter's hand. "I know."

"And you know I didn't tell Dad you were here – I let it slip I was and he put two and two together. I'm so, so sorry."

Grace squeezed her daughter's hand. "It's okay. Really. I

needed to face him sooner or later. Come on, let's get this over with."

Iris handed her some headphones and then she pressed play.

Grace took a deep breath. She could hear Pearl talking, and then Polly.

Her heart began to race when she heard the voice of the woman she'd thought was her best friend – the woman who had been betraying her and lying to her all along.

"I should see my mother, but I can't bear to," Pearl said.

"Who can blame you, darling? She's clearly having some sort of a breakdown."

"Have you spoken to her?" Pearl asked.

"No." Grace noticed Polly was slurring.

"My dad's told me everything."

"He has?" Polly said.

"I always hoped you two would get together; you're so much better suited than Mum and Dad."

"Darling." Grace heard Polly squeal and clap her hands. "I'm so pleased you think that." Grace could picture Polly hugging her daughter. "There I was, so worried you'd be cross."

"Please. I could never be cross with you," Pearl said. Grace heard her daughter hesitate, then lower her voice. "He also told me about the company and the plan."

Grace's heart began to race, for her daughter as much as herself. She squeezed Pearl's hand again.

"He did?" Polly slurred, although Grace detected a hint of surprise.

"Don't be cross with him. I think it's a genius idea."
"You do?"

Was Polly suspicious? Surely, she wouldn't fall for this?

"I do," Pearl continued. "My mother has been a bully to my father for years. I can't believe she's never bullied anyone at work; it makes perfect sense. You've done the right thing."

"That's exactly how I see it. Sometimes I think you could be my very own daughter," Polly squealed again, and this time Grace felt sick.

"Did anyone actually tell you that she was a bully?" Pearl asked.

"Not exactly," Polly said. "Another round?"

"So, how did you get them to complain?"

"Let's just say, I used my ways. I told them what they needed to hear – that other people were complaining and if they didn't come forward it would look bad on them that they hadn't spoken up. They were doing it for the company; none of us wanted a toxic culture."

"And they took it?" Pearl asked.

"Of course. Plus I may have suggested I would remember their courage when I was in charge, which I'm likely to be."

"You want her job?" Pearl asked.

"It should be mine anyway. All the years I spent encouraging your mother, pushing her, telling her how brilliant she is. I have a first-class degree in making people believe in themselves. Nobody has to mollycoddle me."

Grace heard Pearl cough as if she were choking on her drink.

"There, there, darling. You don't have to worry about anything. I'm here for you now."

Grace heard Pearl gather herself. "But what about the video – in Soho, of her arguing with my dad?"

"Ah that was a stroke of genius, don't you think? Your father knew how to provoke her, and I waited outside. It was sickening, really, how easy it was to do. The board are so bloody gullible they'll believe anything their darling Head of Daytime tells them."

Grace took off the headphones. She'd heard enough.

"I'm sorry, Mum," Pearl said.

"Why are you sorry?" Grace asked, the same numbness she'd felt with Eric the previous day returning. She thought of Jack's words. He was right. This was her chance. She could leave Eric and Polly – and the part they brought out in her – behind.

"Well, that's just it. She couldn't have thought it was out of character for me to be like that. I'm sorry."

"Pearl, I acted badly; I can see that now, and there's no excuse. Someone recently reminded me that it's never okay to act badly, no matter what we're going through." She met eyes with Iris, who smiled a small smile. "I'm sorry that we can't go back and change time, but we can change what happens from now on in this magic moment." She touched her daughter's cheek and Pearl smiled back.

"You're starting to sound like our old friend Peggy," Iris told her, then she sat back in her chair. "So, what do you think?"

Grace rubbed the sides of her head. "It's so much to take in, but then again," she stopped and looked up, "it's not. It all makes perfect sense – all of it."

"She was trying to steal your life," Lulu said to her.

"I'm so please you found us," Iris told her.

"She's a complete and utter bitch," Lulu said, and Iris and Pearl nodded.

"But the question is, what do you do now?" Iris repeated.

"Well, there's only one thing I can do. I'm going to have to go to the board and tell them."

"Are you sure you can do this?" Pearl asked.

Grace nodded. She was certain she could. But whether she even wanted her job back? That was a whole different question – and she wasn't sure about the answer at all.

The train journey to London slipped by and before she knew it, she was pulling into Paddington. She hadn't even planned what she was going to say. She was meeting Leonard, who said he would come in with her, but other than that she didn't know what she was going to do.

She also didn't care. She knew she needed to set the record straight, and she also cared about all the time and effort Iris, Pearl and Lulu had taken. Jack had also called to wish her luck. But she felt so different to the person who'd been marched away from Hi-TV.

"Just tell it to them straight. That's all you need to do," Jack had advised.

As she took a taxi across the city, Grace felt uneasy. Everything was so familiar, but so different too. Nothing made sense there any more.

"Grace." Leonard was standing outside the Hi-TV buildings. He kissed her on both cheeks and then held her back to look at her. "Well, I must say, you look wonderful."

"Thank you," Grace said.

When she looked up at the Hi-TV building her first instinct was to revert back to Old Grace mode. She'd planned to wear her usual uniform of a black Prada dress, but when she'd gone to put it on that morning, she hadn't wanted to. It was as though she was stepping back to a time she had no desire to return to. So, she'd worn a light pink blouse with a straight black skirt, and kept her hair wavy.

She'd worn her Manolo heels though – New Grace still needed to feel some sort of power.

She walked with Leonard to a nearby coffee shop they had always met at to discuss tactics.

"I'll do the talking," he said when they sat down. "But what would you like me to get out of this?"

Grace stirred her black coffee.

"I have no idea. I can't believe I'm saying this. What's happened to me, Leonard? Does this make me a weak and dreadful person?"

Leonard looked slightly taken aback, as though he wasn't used to seeing this side of Grace.

He took off his glasses and rubbed his face.

"No, Grace, it doesn't, and I owe you an apology too."

"You thought there was some truth to it?" Grace asked.

"I wondered, for a brief moment. I'm sorry, and I feel very disloyal to say this."

"Leonard. Please. I may not be a bully, but I had an act which some would find off-putting, to say the least. If I were you, I would have wondered exactly the same."

"You're being very gracious."

"I didn't even like that version of me. Who would ever have believed this was all exactly what I needed? I've had some time and space, which I had been needing for so long. I just didn't know it. I had no idea how unhappy I was."

Leonard smiled.

"Well, wherever you've been and whatever you've been doing, it's done wonders. I hardly recognise you. But look, let me at least make it up to you. Let me get the best possible deal, and then you can decide. It might make it easier for you when it's laid out on the table."

"Okay," Grace agreed. It wouldn't do any harm. She

looked at Leonard, the family friend who'd been with her all her life and had never left her side.

"You always knew about Eric, didn't you?"

Leonard took off his glasses again, and sat back in his chair. "I had my suspicions," he told her. "I saw the signs. I promised your parents I'd always look out for you. I was your guardian, not just your lawyer. I'd known your dad since we were boys. But you were old enough to make your own decisions."

"Even if they were wrong."

"There's never a wrong decision, Grace. You weren't to know. You thought you were in love, and look at you now."

"Thank you for advising me about the money. You saved me."

"It's my job." He smiled and touched her hand. He looked at her again. "So, where have you been? I think I need to go there."

Grace laughed. The idea of Leonard with Beatrice and Claudia.

"Have you got any time off coming up, and have you booked anywhere? Because if you haven't, I know just the place – have you ever heard of somewhere called Lemon Cove?"

The room felt different; the atmosphere felt different; everything was different. The long table of men shuffled, coughed, smiled and fidgeted. Grace, on the other hand, remained unmoved.

Once they were all settled, Leonard played the recording.

She watched their faces as it sank in. They'd all been

well and truly conned by their darling Head of Daytime. The more they listened, the paler their faces became. When Polly sneered about the gullible board, she could see the rage in their faces, all of their egos prickled. Polly hadn't just undermined Grace, she'd insulted them all.

When it came to an end, Leonard pressed stop and they sat for a moment, the discomfort lingering in the air.

Trevor spoke first.

"How was this obtained?"

"Please," Leonard said. "We're not going to go down that route, are we? This is not for broadcast – but this is clear evidence of a campaign of bullying."

"But still there are laws," Jonathan tried.

"Yes, but there are also opinions – and if this was accidentally leaked, can you imagine the damage it would cause to Hi-TV, so soon after the Wakefield scandal? I'd suggest we don't get distracted from the point."

"You wouldn't," Jonathan said.

"Of course we wouldn't. But the recording is not our property. Who's to say what the owner could do with it?"

Godfrey, who was sitting in the middle of them all, sat back.

"What do you want?" He directed his question at Grace.

"Her job returned, double the salary and a lump sum compensation of the same annual amount."

Grace swallowed, but stayed still.

"It goes without saying, we have missed your presence." Godfrey continued to look at her.

Grace remained quiet, and the uncomfortable silence returned.

"We clearly need to have a discussion about it all."

"Indeed," Leonard said.

"Grace, you're very quiet. Is there anything you'd like to say?"

Grace looked at Leonard, who nodded a small nod.

"I do have one question."

"Yes?" Godfrey replied.

"I'd like to ask why you all fought so hard to protect Christopher Wakefield."

"I'm sorry?" Godfrey said.

"I said, I'd like to ask why you fought so hard to protect Christopher Wakefield."

"He's one of our biggest names," Jonathan replied.

"And so, because I'm not a household name, I don't deserve the same protection – despite all the years of loyalty I've shown the company?"

"We did have several complaints, Grace," Trevor said, his voice low.

"False complaints, yes, and I understand you needed to investigate. But you also have clear evidence of Wakefield with prostitutes, he was cheating on his wife, he was bullying the staff and he lies daily on our channel that he is a family-orientated man with strong values. Yet he's in his position thanks to all the effort and hours this board put in to protect him."

"But he's…" Trevor started then stopped.

"Go on, say it," Grace said.

There was more uncomfortable silence.

"He's *the* face of Hi-TV," Jonathan said.

"And that makes it okay, does it? Do you really think our audience would not watch us if he wasn't here? Is the success of this channel all down to him? Nothing to do with the work our staff do? Or even the work we all do?"

The silence hovered like a weight.

"Would it have been different if I'd been a man, I wonder?"

There was a barrage of 'nos' and 'of course nots'. Then, when they calmed down again, Grace spoke.

"Is that really true? *Really?*" she repeated, and then paused.

"I don't expect you to answer now, or to ever tell me the truth, but please – you ask me what I wanted and I ask you this. Tonight, when you all go to bed, I want you to lie there and answer this question honestly. You're the ones who have to live with this. Godfrey, you have daughters and granddaughters. Is this the world you *really* want for them? If you're absolutely telling the truth, then you'll sleep well. But if you're not? Are you really comfortable that you're playing a part in keeping the world going like this?"

There was more uncomfortable silence around the table. Grace met eyes with Leonard and they both stood up.

"We trust your Head of Daytime will be correctly dealt with too," Leonard added, and the silence returned. Leonard met eyes with Grace and signalled it was time to leave.

"We'll be in touch," Leonard said as they started to walk away.

"Grace?" Godfrey said.

She turned. "Yes?"

"We're sorry."

Grace nodded.

"Goodbye Godfrey," she said to him, then she turned and walked out of the door.

Chapter Thirty-Seven

Eric: You can't do this to me. Who do you think you are?
Polly: Grace. Please. I hear you're meeting the board. What's happening? Do you need me there for support? I can be there x

"And that was it? And then you left?"

Grace nodded. "Yes, I did. I suppose, looking back, it was quite the moment."

Grace breathed out. She felt safe in Greg's white room. It felt a million miles away from the large glass boardroom she'd been sitting in the day before.

As they'd left the offices, Leonard had walked with her to the taxi.

"You did well, Grace," he'd told her. "Exceptionally well."

She'd just arrived back in Strawberry House when Leonard called again. "They've agreed to everything," he told her.

"They have?" Grace said. "That was quick."

"I think you hit a nerve."

What Really Happened To Me?

Pearl had wanted her to go out and celebrate. "Go on Mum. I booked a table for us at a restaurant in the village. Iris and Lulu are coming too."

Grace had declined. She said she'd absolutely celebrate their wonderful work, but that they should go out without her that night. She'd called the restaurant and given them her card details and ordered the girls some champagne.

She hadn't really slept the previous night – she went for a run in the morning, and there she was again, back in Greg's office, just before eleven am. She'd brought them both coffee from Dave's and now they sat there, Greg looking slightly amused.

"What's so funny?"

"It's just great to see how far you've come since you arrived here."

"I'm not sure it feels like that."

"When you're breaking up with a life it feels like that."

"Is that what I'm doing? Breaking up with my life?"

"Is that what you want to do?"

She didn't answer the question.

"Penelope told me what happened with Eric. She said you were brave. Have you heard from him since?"

"Not today," Grace told him. "However, news travels fast and I suspect when he hears about my offer, I'll hear from him again."

"I suspect you may too." Greg sipped his coffee. "So, have you decided what you want to do about the job?"

"There's not an ounce of me that wants to go back."

"But?" Greg raised an eyebrow.

"I feel like I'm giving up. All those years of working and everything I've built – I feel like I'm just walking away."

"But are you?"

"What do you mean?"

"Everything you've learned and experienced hasn't gone anywhere – you'll be taking it with you wherever you go. Nobody can take that away from you, as long as you don't let them."

"I suppose I hadn't looked at it like that." Grace sat back in her chair. "But it's a lot, isn't it? The marriage, the job?"

"It's a new, fresh start – what's wrong with that?"

"But was my life really that wrong for so long that I need to walk away from it?"

Greg paused.

"Grace, when you arrived, you were broken. At the risk of being rude, you were a wreck. You were dazed, you didn't know who you were, and you were exhausted. A life that is meant for you, doesn't do that to you."

"But isn't that life? Isn't it supposed to be hard?"

"Who says?"

"I'm sorry?"

"Who says life has to be so hard?"

"Well, it is, isn't it? As someone who lost their parents as a teenager, I know." Grace's insides twisted their familiar turn.

"It was a tragedy and it was possibly the worst thing for you to go through. Nobody is saying life is a picnic – it is hard. Bad things happen to good people. But it doesn't have to always be so hard – it doesn't have to be full of so much suffering."

Grace felt tears sting at the back of her eyes. "I'm frightened."

"Of what?"

"Of being happy. When I had those massages when I was away, they made me remember how happy I was with my parents, and then in a second it was all snatched away. I was so frightened of it happening again. That's why I ran away from Harvey."

Greg was quiet for a moment.

"Do you ever think that perhaps you're punishing yourself? For being alive?"

"That's ridiculous. Of course not."

"Is it? We do so much subconsciously, and we can have no idea we're doing it. But is there a part of you somewhere that feels guilty about being happy?"

"No."

"Really?"

Grace shifted in her seat. "Perhaps. Maybe."

"And can I ask you about Harvey?"

"What about Harvey?"

"Have you spoken to him?"

"No. He's not answering my calls."

Greg took a deep breath.

"If you explain to him…"

"So, what you're saying is, I leave one marriage to go into the arms of another man. Whatever happened to be being happy on your own first? It makes no sense. If I'm going to do any of this, I have to do it on my own."

"Yes, you do. But who says you can't allow some joy along the way too? And Grace – I say this with respect – your marriage was not a marriage of love."

No, it wasn't. She could see that now.

"Look Grace," Greg sat forward. "I'm not telling you what to do – I have no right to do this. But aren't you keeping yourself locked in this suffering? There are no rules, really. Your life is your life to live. God knows, you've had your fair share of unhappiness. Deep down, if you are happy with Harvey when you're with him, then for God's sake, give yourself a break."

Grace smiled. Every time she thought of Harvey she smiled. But then she remembered what she had done.

"I've known Harvey for a long time – he understands more than most. This is the golden charm that comes from troublesome times."

"Was I really that unhappy in my life?"

"Only you know. But what you can do is take the bits that you did love. The parts from your work – why not think of those? Write them all down and make a list. Someone with your strength can see from that list what you need to do next. And if anyone can make it happen, you can, Grace Leven."

"Do you really think so?"

"Look at you. You're not just surviving, you're beginning to thrive; it just feels scary. The Grace I see before me now looks like a woman who is coming home to herself – that's something to be proud of."

"In some ways, it's funny how easy it feels. That sounds ridiculous, doesn't it? What a contradiction? The idea of divorcing Eric, now, after being here, doesn't feel nearly as intimidating as I thought it would."

"But when something is right, it feels right. That's why we live in so much suffering – because we're living in something that's wrong for us. It doesn't have to be that way."

"Thank you, Greg."

"I didn't do anything. You're the one who's making change, Grace, and it's a pleasure to watch you as you do."

Midlife Murder & The Lost Path

6

Dear Reader
So, it appears I'm faced with a dilemma.

What Really Happened To Me?

After all these months of searching, the chance has come for me to return to the old. A few weeks ago, if you'd asked me, I'd have jumped at the chance. I would even have said thank heavens for that.

These last months, however, have shown me so much – most of all, that there is another way.

But the question is, do I (and you) choose it?

The truth is, it's hard, isn't it? Bloody hard. To admit something is over and there's no going back. How much more grief do I need to wade through? I'm exhausted enough as it is. That said, a new life sounds wonderful, but there are no guarantees there either. At least I know the old one. But if I continue to wade through what's in front of me, how do I know I'll like it when I get to the other side?

I've spent weeks looking, pondering, wondering and worrying. But the truth is, this won't get me anywhere; only action will. All I've been doing is waiting for others. Somebody else to give me the answer I'm seeking – when all along the only person who can ever give me this is me.

The truth is, underneath all this pondering and procrastination lies a wonderful gem. The absolute, wonderful, unshakeable truth that all the power lies within us.

There are a million reasons to stay in comfort – and why wouldn't we? – it is comfortable after all. But ultimately, we are also making this choice. We can blame, excuse and wrap ourselves up in this comfort blanket, but it's still a decision we made.

This too is fine – it is after all our life, and if we are in control, then aren't we the ones who decide? But the question we must ask ourselves, even if we reply in the quietest of whispers – is: is this really what I want? Really? Is this the life I want to live for my short, precious years while I'm here?

If there's a falter, a whisper or even any hesitation at all, then the answer is no.

The only person I've been lying to is myself. There's nobody watching over me and I have nothing to prove. Time will wait for nobody and my answers are here – now I need to act. Simple when put like this, but we all know it's not.

But I thank you for being here with me – for listening as I find my path. Only action will change the circumstances which need to be changed now, and you have helped me decide what I need to do. While it may only be us who can make that change, to know someone who cares is by your side, well, darling, it makes this whole shit-show that little bit more worthwhile.

Chapter Thirty-Eight

Eric: Grace, I heard about the job – congratulations! We really need to talk x

"I didn't think you'd actually show up."

"Why not?"

"I did ruin your life."

Grace nodded and sat down next to Polly. Grace had chosen to meet in a park in Bristol. She hadn't wanted Polly to come to Strawberry House. She'd picked the park, with its view of the city spread out in front of them, because she'd hoped there'd be enough air for her to breathe there.

"Coffee?" Polly handed her a cup. "Just as you like."

Grace took it. She was surprised by how calm she felt as she sat down. She sipped the coffee and looked out at the view.

"It's lovely here."

"Why did you want to see me?"

Polly nodded. "I've always loved how direct you are."

"Please. Spare me the act. Why?"

Polly nodded again. "I get it. I'd be angry if I were you. But you're decent, Grace – you always have been."

Grace didn't reply.

"I just wanted to see you. It's been so long."

Still Grace didn't reply.

"They got rid of me. Sacked. I've got no job."

"I heard."

"And? Aren't you going to say anything?"

"What do you want me to say?"

Polly turned to her, and Grace saw her dark, haunted eyes. Her skin was pale and grey; she looked terrible. Nowhere near the confident woman Grace had known. She resisted the urge to tell her it was okay – because however awful her former friend looked, it wasn't.

"Come on then, say something. Be angry at least."

"So it'll make you feel better?"

Polly sat back. "Yes."

Grace took a few breaths. She knew what Polly was doing, just as she'd known what Eric was doing. Why hadn't she seen it before?

"And Eric?" She kept her voice calm.

Polly shrugged. "I guess I've lost my appeal to him now."

Grace took a deep breath. She sipped her coffee, letting the hot liquid be a distraction. But this black coffee tasted bitter and sickening. She put the lid back on the cup.

It was a sunny day. People around them were pushing babies in prams, children were swinging in the swings, workers were walking along with laptop bags, talking into their phones.

"It's different here," Grace said. "It looks the same in many ways, but it's different."

"You look different," Polly said. "You seem different too.

What are you going to do about the job? I hear they want you back."

Grace turned to Polly. "Really? You think you have the right to ask me this?"

"I'm sorry."

Grace took another deep breath. She'd promised Greg she wouldn't bite. She was to leave with her peace and dignity, no matter what Polly tried, however hard it was. She let the silence settle between them.

"Will you just say something, Grace? Please."

"Okay then." Grace turned to her. "Why?"

"Why what?"

"Why? Why did you do it? All of it? Eric, my job, my reputation? What was it all about?"

Polly shrugged.

"You can at least tell me why?"

"What do you want me to say?"

"Oh Polly. I've had enough." Grace stood up.

Polly grabbed her hand and Grace flinched.

"I wanted to be you, okay? I wanted your life. You had it all figured out, and I wanted it too."

"So you decided to take it from me?"

"It wasn't quite like that. Eric was part of it too."

"Oh please. Enough." Grace pulled her hand away. "All the pair of you ever do is blame. It's always everyone else's fault. Have you ever considered just stopping for a minute and looking at yourself?"

"Now you're just being cruel."

"Cruel? *I'm* being fucking cruel because I found *you* shagging my husband in my bed?"

Grace was aware of heads turning around her. She'd kept her cool with Eric; she could do this. Besides, she'd promised Greg.

Polly didn't answer and looked ahead.

"The worst part of it all was I really thought you were great. I thought you were talented and had everything you needed to rise all the way to the top of that company. I knew what I had done and I thought you could do it too. The late nights, the early mornings, the clear vision, dealing with people, the resilience. But I was wrong."

"You weren't wrong. Let's do it again."

"I'm sorry?" Grace looked at her former friend.

"You have power, Grace, I can't do it without you. You've got your job back; you can help me get re-instated and we can carry on with our plan – women helping women, women being on that board."

"You think we're going back?"

"You and I are a power-house. You said it all the time, the board needs women like us. Television needs women like us; the world needs women like us."

Grace took another deep breath.

"They'll listen to you. If you forgive me, they will too. We all make mistakes, Grace."

Grace swallowed down the fresh air.

The silence settled around them, Polly looked at her, with her eyes wide. "Please. We've known each other for so long."

Grace took another deep breath and sat down on the bench.

"Polly, I'm going to tell you, what I told Eric. Fuck off."

"Grace, now you're just being crazy again."

"And there you are." Grace nodded. She didn't need evidence, but she had it anyway. Everything clicked into place and she could see this person, the person she thought was her best friend, with clarity. "I'm not crazy," she said, her voice calm.

"Grace, you're just upset. In time you'll see."
"You're deluded, Polly."
"No, I'm not. I've made a mistake."
"You're not getting it, Polly. Hi-TV does need more women on the board; the media needs more women at higher positions. But it's not just about women and men, it's about values. Good people, kind people, caring people, strong people. The kind of people who don't look at everyone around them as some kind of stepping stone or a source. This is what we need, Polly – and you couldn't be further from it."

Grace stood up and Polly grabbed her hand.
"Please Grace, I've got nothing left. You're all I've got."
"You don't have me any more. It's over."
"But you're the only friend I have."
Grace took one last deep breath.
"Then you should have treated me better. But then again, our friendship was never a friendship to you, was it? I was a source – a simple source, from whom you took until there was nothing left to take. I've seen a different world – one with proper friends who care without taking anything."

Grace turned to walk away and then stopped.
"I will give you this, my last piece of advice. If you want a friend, a true proper friend who supports you and helps you like you expect – then perhaps you should look at yourself. You give when you think you'll get something in return. You're entitled, and just like Eric, you don't think you have to do the work to earn it like the rest of us. You take what you want and spit out the rest. The whole world doesn't revolve around you Polly, like it doesn't around Eric."

She took another deep breath.
"If you want to know why you're lonely and the world is turning its back on you, look at yourself. Look at how you

treat people. What do you really expect? I was wrong, I thought we had friendship. It wasn't proper friendship. Proper friendship doesn't make you feel grateful for the mere basics; proper friendship is two-way. It's unconditional. It's turning up when there's nothing to gain. It's not having to be in permanent competition, or having to walk on eggshells or feeling like there's something I'm doing wrong all the time. It's not the need for dominance; it's quiet and kind. I've seen what proper friendship is here, and the way you and I were living our lives was a million miles away from it."

"How dare you..." Polly started, but Grace was already walking away.

"Go and find yourself another source, Polly, because this one is done with you. Goodbye Polly. Don't message me again."

Grace turned and threw the coffee cup in a bin. She watched for a brief moment as the final bitter remnants of her old life slowly slipped away.

Chapter Thirty-Nine

Eric: We can begin a whole new life together now x

Grace pressed the buzzer outside the large Georgian house – a young woman smiled as she opened the door and showed her to a seat in the large foyer.

"He won't be long." The young woman smiled again.

Grace nodded and sat down. She looked at the young woman as she began to type – she thought of Matilda, her own assistant who'd greeted people on her behalf. She had a warm smile too, which Grace had loved when she'd met her. Grace looked around now at the different photos on the walls – of all the different hotels. Each and every one creating magic. Places which gave people what they needed when they needed it the most. Jack was creating miracles.

The door opened.

"Grace."

"Jack." She stood up. "Thank you for seeing me. I appreciate you sparing me the time."

"It's my pleasure."

Grace nodded to the large entrance hall. "This is really something here." She looked back at the photos. "You did this, Jack. You created all this."

She hid a smile when she saw the colour flush his cheeks, and she noticed the young woman smile too. "I'm helped by a lot of people," he said.

"You're being modest. You don't have to be in front of me. This is your creation, Jack – your vision – and you should be very proud.

"I am." He smiled back at her. "Thank you."

They walked up the stairs of the Georgian building. It was stunning. The floor was black and white marble, and large white walls were covered with more photographs of Jack's hotels. They captured moments of evenings, dancing and laughter. She recognised Antigua House; an older man and a woman were spinning each other around. She could feel herself back there for a moment, dancing in the warm air, the smell of the jasmine and the crackle of something special all around. She thought of Harvey there, the two of them dancing.

"Ah, so these are magic moments. Peggy?" Grace asked.

"You guess well – she made her mark." Jack laughed.

They carried on climbing – and she saw more pictures of his staff. Claudia and Beatrice were beaming and waving and she could feel their warmth from the photo. She smiled as she kept walking down the corridor into Jack's office.

"It's funny," she said as they walked into the spacious room. "All those years I worked for a big company, I've never quite imagined what it would look like to have something that is actually my own."

"I can highly recommend it." Jack beckoned Grace over to one of the large sofas. "Although it comes with its ups and downs. But at least I'm the one riding the rollercoaster, even though it often feels the other way round. Sometimes I wonder what it would be like to work for someone else and let them make all the decisions."

"You'd hate it," Grace laughed as she sat down.

"I would," he agreed. "Coffee?"

"Thank you," she nodded. "And you make your own coffee?"

"Of course. It's known around here as The Iris Effect. In other words, before she came into my life, I was a first-class arse."

"Seriously?"

"Seriously. There was even a headline describing me as one."

"I thought there was no such thing as bad publicity."

He brought the coffees over and sat in front of her.

"I'm guessing you know why I'm here."

"I suspect I know."

She saw the flicker in his eyes.

"It's not just you who is capable of being a first-class arse. I mucked up big time."

Jack sipped his coffee.

"I'm sorry," Grace said. "I'm really sorry, and I need to tell Harvey this."

"And you don't know where he is, he won't answer your calls and you want me to tell you."

Grace nodded. "I know I hurt him, and there's no excuse for my behaviour. I don't expect him to forgive me, but I need to tell him just to hear me out."

Jack sat back and thought for a moment. "Harvey has been like a dad to me in so many ways. I never really knew my dad. He hates it when I say that though – says it makes him feel old."

Grace laughed. "I bet he doesn't hate it really."

'When Alice died it was as though he just gave up. Josh didn't just lose his mum; I thought he'd lost his dad too."

"He told me a little about it."

"He wouldn't leave the house, then he would and he'd go missing and we'd think the worst. But he got through it. He went to Lemon Cove and they looked after him for a few weeks. It was what he needed. When he came back, he started to take part in life again. For a long time it still felt like he was existing, but then very slowly he started to enjoy life again."

Grace remembered everything Harvey had said – how he hadn't wanted to live but he knew this was selfish. He'd at least had the decency to recognise this.

And now I must accept how selfish I've been too.

"When he came back the other day, it frightened me. I saw a glimmer of that haunted look in his eye – the distance. I realised it must always be there. I suppose I'd just forgotten for a while, as he does such a good job living with it. It scared me, and it scared Josh too."

"Is he okay now?"

"Yes. It shocked him, you leaving him like that. It shocked him when Alice died, and you don't recover from that. Just when he started to trust something again, it disappeared. It's hard to trust it again."

Grace looked down at her hands. "I'm so sorry."

"I'm not saying this to make you feel bad; I'm telling you this to explain. We're all very protective of him here."

"I understand. I do."

Jack sat forward.

"Iris told me about the job. So, are you going back?"

Grace looked up at him and saw the worry in his eyes. "You think I'm going to leave and forget all about him?"

"It's none of my business," Jack said.

"It's okay. I understand. I don't have a good track record."

She looked around the office as she sat back.

"Where did you even begin, with all this?" she asked.

"I worked in a pub and I liked it. It gave me the feeling of a big family I'd never had in my own. I liked working hard too – cooking and creating – it was rewarding to see people come in and enjoy what we did. Eventually I saved enough money to start my own pub and it went from there. But it was only when I met Iris, and then Peggy, that everything fell into place."

"How?" Grace was intrigued.

"They made me see everything differently. I used to look at everything and think that it was somehow wrong and that it was all my fault. When I met them, I started to see everything in a different light. It had been inside me all along, but I was too busy trying to make everything on the outside a success. I didn't know what I was really all about."

"You were on your lost path too."

"Yes, I suppose I was." He smiled. He sipped his coffee and put his cup down.

"Grace, it's not your fault. I mean, leaving Harvey like you did – that's your fault," Jack looked at her, "but you're human, and you make mistakes. We all do that."

Grace sat forward.

"I've been with Eric since I was eighteen years old. It makes sense I have time on my own."

Jack nodded. "I get it. But I also know Harvey. He'll give you all the space you need; just don't mess him around. But something I learned is you can't control life, Grace. None of us know what tomorrow will bring."

He was right – she knew this.

"Harvey needs to live his life too."

"I know."

Jack paused. "Do you mind if I say something?"

"Not at all."

"I suspect it's because you're not used to it. You're used to being on edge, always guessing what you've done wrong. You go from trying to solve one problem to another but nothing is ever right. The guilt keeps you connected to them – because without the guilt, what do you have? It's too much to take in that deep down they don't love you in the way you want to be loved."

"You've just described my marriage."

"Think about when you arrived in Antigua. It feels great to land in the sunshine but it still feels a little strange – you feel wired and edgy and things don't feel right. You have to allow yourself to get used to it, and eventually you unwind and you feel lighter and better. You lived that way for so long – without even realising it – it's no wonder your whole body panicked and you ran away."

"You're being very understanding."

"I haven't told you where Harvey is yet."

"Will you?"

"That depends. Not if you're going to hurt him again. Running away like that was always going to hurt him. Pushing them away is only hurting them as well as you, and really what's the point of that?"

Their eyes met, and she knew he understood. Like a secret knowing, like it was with Penelope.

"Let go of the guilt, Grace. Thank it for keeping you safe, but you don't need it now. You'll feel strange at first but I promise you'll get used to it, and when you do, it's a wonderful way to live."

"It looks like it."

Jack sat back again.

"So, have you ever thought about going out on your own?"

"Me?"

"Why not? You seem to like the idea."

"I've never really thought about it, as if it's an option. What do I have to offer?"

"A CEO of a major broadcasting company – where do we begin? No more bosses, no more boards – I think you'd make an excellent entrepreneur."

"No more boards – now there's a thought!" Grace sat upright. "Jack Jones, you're making me think."

Chapter Forty

Eric: Please Grace, I'm begging you. One more chance. I promise to make it all up to you.

Her phone rang.

"That was quick."

"You are officially a free woman," Leonard said. "No more Hi-TV, and the compensation will be with you by the end of the day."

"I didn't expect them to agree so quickly."

"I think you hit a nerve. Have you seen the latest development at Hi-TV?"

Grace hadn't. She checked her phone.

"Christopher Wakefield has decided to leave Hi-TV to spend more time with his family," she read out. "Well I never. They got rid of him?"

"Yes, they did."

"So they did the right thing in the end?"

Grace leaned back on the wall at the front of the hotel.

"Yes, they did," Leonard said.

"So why doesn't it feel any better?"

She heard Leonard sigh on the other end of the phone. "Because it's all dreadful, Gracie. It's a total mess. They've lost sight of who they all are and what the company needs. It's not about the on-screen egos – it never was – it's about making decent television for their audience, with decent standards for their staff. But what do I know?"

"I think you know a lot," Grace smiled.

"So, what will you do now?"

"I don't know – is the answer. But for once I'm okay about this. When I really listened to myself, I got my answer about the job. I suppose I just need to keep listening."

"They'd be so proud of you, you know. Your mum and dad."

Grace's eyes stung.

"Now, off you go. I'm a professional lawyer, don't you know? I can't be all emotional for my next client."

"Leonard?"

"Yes Gracie?"

"Thank you."

"You're more than welcome."

"Will you come and visit me here?"

"I'd be delighted to."

Grace took another deep breath.

"Leonard, before you go, there is one last thing I need to ask."

"Fire away – you know I'll do anything for you."

Chapter Forty-One

Eric: I'll go to counselling, therapy, whatever it takes. Please Grace. Please.

The car pulled up outside the hospital. When Jack had told her Harvey was spending most of his days in a hospital in Somerset, she'd feared some awful news, but then Jack reassured her.

"It's okay – Elizabeth had a fall. She was climbing a ladder in the garden – and fell. Harvey found her, but she's going to be okay. Harvey has been staying at the house and working on it, then visiting her in the afternoons."

So that was where he'd been.

Grace found her way to the ward, where Elizabeth was sitting on a bed, her arm in a sling. Grace was pleased to see her cheeks were pink and she was chatting to the woman in the next bed, who looked thoroughly bored.

"Grace, how lovely to see you. Here, come and sit down." Elizabeth tapped the bed. "I suppose you're going to give me a bloody lecture like the rest of them."

"I wouldn't dream of it," Grace said as she sat down.

"I suspect it's not just me who you've come to see. He'll be back in a minute. He's just gone to get me a sandwich. I said I'd be happy with one from the Co-op, but you know what he's like. He's gone down to M&S, muttering something about the Eat Well range. I'm too bloody old to eat well now."

"That's not true."

Elizabeth tutted then took Grace's hand. It surprised her – to feel her cool touch, and she liked it.

"Well, you made a bloody mess of it all – didn't you?"

"I see you haven't lost your straight-talking." Grace glanced across at the woman in the next bed, who rolled her eyes.

"Life's too short to skip around the point. He told me all about it, and of course I gave him a piece of my mind. He came on too strong – what did he expect? Still, now it's your turn."

"I see." Grace took a deep breath.

Elizabeth tapped her hand. "I'm only joking – the look on your face! You two are both miserable enough; you don't need me putting my oar in."

"Is he…miserable?"

"Is he? He's supposed to be cheering me up, but he's been moping around like a wet lettuce."

Grace didn't know what to say.

"Good for you about the job though. You really socked it to them. And I never did like that Christopher Wakefield. There was always something in his eyes." Elizabeth leaned towards Grace. "I suspect he didn't really choose to leave for family reasons."

Grace leaned towards Elizabeth. "They never do, Elizabeth," she whispered in a low voice and Elizabeth clapped her hands in delight. "So, what are we going to do about your cruise?"

"Well, I've messed that up too, haven't I?"

"Oh Elizabeth, don't say you can't go."

"I was due to leave yesterday."

"That's awful."

"Yes – it bloody well is. So, let it be a lesson to you."

Grace was confused. "I don't know what you mean."

"I waited for years to book that cruise. I spent years arguing with my sister, trying to prove her wrong, she was trying to prove me wrong – and what was it really all about? We both missed out on so much because of all that fighting. I should have just walked away and gone on the cruise. I could have been on ten cruises if I'd sold the house to Jack earlier. I know he's not going to rip me off. I've just been so busy clinging on that I've missed out on life."

This time Grace squeezed Elizabeth's hand. "I'm not sure that's true."

Elizabeth sighed. "It bloody is. Now, I know you've been through a lot and believe it or not I do mind my own business, so I'm not going to pry, but let this be a lesson to all of us." Elizabeth nodded at her arm. "Do what we can when we can, and we'll all be better off."

Grace nodded. She knew what she wanted but would Harvey agree?

An idea came to her. "Has Jack ever told you about Lemon Cove?"

"He never bloody stops going on about it. I don't think I'd like the food, dear."

"Well, if I know Jack, he'd make sure you have all the Eat Well sandwiches or whatever it is you like. You could always go there instead. They have some great lemonade."

Elizabeth looked down. "I do like lemonade. I've been thinking about it, I must admit."

"So, what about we get you booked in?"

"I tell you what, I'll think about it, if you let go of my hand and go for a nice walk. There's someone behind you who is pretending he's not happy to see you, and I'd like to eat my sandwich in peace."

"So, how have you been?" Grace asked as they walked in a nearby park.

"I've been okay," Harvey said. He wasn't able to look at her, and she didn't like this at all.

"I haven't," she said as she looked at him. This time he looked back at her.

"I'm sorry to hear that."

"I'm so sorry, Harvey. I should never have left like that."

"No, you shouldn't have."

"I was afraid, I can see that now. But it's no excuse. You deserve better." She reached into her handbag and brought out a brown paper bag. "I bought chocolate croissants, from Dave."

She saw a glimmer of a smile.

"The coffees are on me too." She nodded to a small van in the corner of the park.

"Too right they are," he said, but this time the smile reached his eyes.

They sat on a bench next to a blooming rose bush, its scent filling the air.

"Do you know what's funny?"

"What?"

"When I worked all the time, I never gave these spots any thought. The paths, the benches like Peggy's, the parks like this one. But they've been here all along, all these little places – and I've never noticed them at all."

Harvey nodded. "I like it here; I come to escape. Don't tell Elizabeth because she'll tell me not to visit, but that place…brings some bad memories." He nodded in the direction of the hospital.

"But you don't run away."

Harvey shrugged. "I don't want her to be alone. She's not as tough as she makes out she is."

Grace took a deep breath. "Again, Harvey, I'm sorry."

He didn't reply, and he didn't look up. Grace didn't like that either.

"I was a mess. I'm still a mess."

"Please stop saying that," he said. And this time he did look up.

"You keep saying this. But Grace, you're not a mess. Look at you – you're nothing like a mess. You've stood up to your husband, you've proved what was going on with your friend. You've been a CEO of a television company, so you've proven you can do just about anything. You have a wonderful daughter in Pearl. You are not a mess. But even if you were, this is never an excuse to treat me how you did by running away like that."

She wanted to argue, but she couldn't.

"You see – I do get angry; I'm human. We all get angry; we're all human and there's no point pretending otherwise. But it's still never a reason to hurt someone else."

"I know," Grace said, her voice quiet. She knew now better than she'd ever known. There was no point to any of this – walking around, being in chaos. She needed to move on – but in a world where she could find as much peace as possible. Yet she had to face her pain first.

"I know it's awkward to have difficult conversations – but you could have just said you weren't interested."

"Is that what you think?"

"Please, Grace." He raised his eyebrows. "We're not teenagers. There's no need to play games. Running away like that – is hardly code for 'I'm interested'. I said I'd give you space."

The two of them sat back on the bench.

"What if I am interested?"

He looked back at her – she could see a curiosity in his eyes. This was better – much better. Then he looked flustered.

"Well, I don't…"

Her heart sank again. "It's okay. I'm big enough for an awkward conversation."

Harvey shook his head. "It's just…I wasn't expecting that."

She was feeling more confused by the minute.

"I saw you, you know – with your husband. I came to the hotel to find you. I'd guessed that you were scared and ran, and although I was really angry, I just wanted some kind of closure I suppose. But then I saw you both."

"So, why didn't you say anything?"

"When I saw you together, I thought at first I'd been kidding myself. That this was all some sort of a marriage problem and I'd got caught up in it. You sat there looking at him and I thought, that's where she wants to be."

"But it isn't," she whispered.

"I ran into Penelope after; she told me the truth. Then Elizabeth had her fall and I didn't want her to be on her own. But the more I thought about it, the more I realised I had put pressure on you turning up in Antigua like that. It was all too much too soon."

"No, it wasn't."

"I understand – you need your space, and I will give it to you. Jack's looking at opening another place – maybe Thailand. I can get someone else to oversee Elizabeth's house and we can all just get on with our lives."

"I've asked Eric for a divorce."

"You have?" Harvey looked at her.

She nodded. "Leonard is taking care of everything."

Harvey shook his head. "You never stop surprising me Grace Leven. I was not expecting that."

"I wasn't either – any of it. If you'd told me six months ago I'd be here now, sitting on a bench in Somerset in the middle of the week, with no job, no home and no career prospects either, I would have said you'd just described my nightmare."

She leant forward. "But this is everything I want – I just didn't know it. Strawberry House and Strawberry Village have given me everything. But most of all, they've given me a fresh look on my life – to see my old life and what was wrong with it, and that a new life filled with love could actually exist. So my nightmare was actually a dream come true in disguise – I just couldn't see it."

"But you do now." Harvey did a small nod.

"Yes, I do. It's clear now, in a way it's never been. Beatrice said to me the morning I ran away from you, anyone can build a house or decorate it, but it takes someone filled with love to create a home. This is what you do, and Jack does too, that's what makes your hotels so different. It's what my parents did too. All those years I lived in an expensive house, with the best of everything, but it felt cold and empty, and I hated it. Yet my mum and dad's tiny cottage I loved. It was filled with love. That's why I love the cottage at Strawberry House so much, everything is done with love. All of it, even in a hotel. I want this for Pearl now. She may have left home, but I can still show her what's possible. I don't have to keep proving myself now, or chasing. So, if you would be by my side as someone who is a master in his craft of homemaking, I'd love that. And I'll always buy the coffees." She nudged him.

He nudged her back, then he sat back and rubbed his hair.

"Can I ask you a question?" she said.

"Is it a good one?"

Grace smiled. "Why didn't you come back again, after you'd spoken to Penelope?"

Harvey rubbed his head again, and then leant forward, his elbows on his knees. He looked back at her, with his big blue eyes and sandy hair. He looked so warm and full of love. "Because I'm human too, and I couldn't stand to be hurt again. So I suppose you could say I ran away too." He sat back again and folded his arms, then nudged her. "I thought if you were serious, you'd come and find me."

"And I have."

"Yes, you have."

He turned around and took her hands.

"You've been through so much, Grace."

Grace felt her eyes sting again.

"So have you. That's what being a grown-up is, I suppose. Are you really going to leave Strawberry Village?"

"Well, I still haven't finished that cabinet yet, so technically I shouldn't."

Grace leant towards him. "Well, just so long as it's the cabinet you're going to take care of."

"You've been strong and brave for so long Grace – you don't have to be alone."

"I know," she said, as she felt him wrap his arms around her. "It can get really lonely being strong."

"I know it can," he said. His lips were getting closer to hers, as her heart began to race.

"That's more like it," a far-off voice interrupted them. Grace turned to see Elizabeth holding a man's arm.

"That's Derek, the security guard. He's taken a shine to her and walks her on his breaks," Harvey explained.

Elizabeth waved a sandwich in the air – "I said I'd rather have one from the Co-op." She blew them both a kiss then disappeared.

Grace felt her cheeks go bright red.

"Are you blushing, Grace Leven?"

"Maybe." Harvey's lips were getting closer to hers.

"I suspect I won't be able to leave Strawberry Village now either," Grace said.

"Absolutely not. You're one of us now and we've got no plans to let you go," Harvey said as he leant forward and his lips met hers.

SIX MONTHS LATER

Midlife Murders & The Lost Path
25

Dear Reader

My name is Grace Leven. I'm fifty-four years old and I love my life. (And to celebrate this, I've decided this column will no longer be anonymous.)

It sounds nauseating, doesn't it? I love my life. But I've come to accept it's just as important to celebrate what's good as it is to acknowledge when we're falling apart.

When I say I love my life, I don't mean that I'm skipping around in some sort of happy dance, day in day out. But I've lost the numbness I'd once simply thought was a natural part of adult life.

I've discovered a love for paths and benches I never knew I could have. I take deep breaths and treasure a magic moment which in a few seconds will have passed. But I capture it like a gem, and I'm building quite the collection now. I've given up straightening my hair and wearing clothes that make me look like I'm going to some sort of fashion funeral.

However, best of all, I've given up my habit of blame.

Giving up blame isn't letting everyone off the hook. Giving up blame has provided me with a freedom and power I didn't know I could have. It's given me the confidence to make decisions, create my own life, buy a house and begin my own business. I feel in love, not just with a wonderful man, but with friends who love and support me too. I spend more time with my daughter than I ever have, I even have become the person everyone wants on their team for darts. (I've become rather good at hitting the board, even if I say so myself.) By giving up the blame I found me again – it gave me my guidepost home.

I also include the blame I placed on myself. All that shame and self-pity was keeping me somewhere I no longer had to be. There's no reason to treat others badly, and there's no reason to do the same to ourselves. We are of course only human – but we're a rich tapestry of good and not so good. When we become off balance, it's time to reassess, or even leave.

The only person who was keeping me trapped in my misery wasn't the board, or my ex-husband or the friend who wasn't a friend – it was me.

I don't blame older versions of me either. They were all doing their best at the time and I'm so proud of them.

But when we stop the blame – we can grow and flourish with time.

It's daunting, isn't it? That it's just us in charge. But my goodness, it's also wonderful too. Nobody to blame and we can make the change. We are powerful and free.

But if you find yourself in a similar situation to mine (or Jack's or Penelope's), don't think any of us would judge. Please know that you're not alone. Since I've been writing these columns, so many women (and men) have been in touch. There'll be someone in your world who'll understand, and if they don't, then you always have me. There's a bench too, where you can sit, or even a pretty path – somewhere quiet enough where you can listen to that inner knowing but also know: you are never, ever alone. You're still in there, even if you think you're not. I know this, because I found me again. What really happened to me? I lost myself. But if I can find me again, I know you can too.

Epilogue

Harvey: Your chariot, will arrive in five minutes, Grace Leven... I've missed you and can't wait to see you. x

Grace laughed at the message. She'd seen Harvey just the day before, but he and Josh had wanted to spend the night with Jack ahead of his big day – his last night as an officially single man. She took one last look at herself in the mirror. She hadn't been to a wedding in years and the butterflies were fluttering around inside her. She wore a bright yellow trouser suit, which they'd spotted when they were out celebrating Pearl officially changing her name.

Grace thought of Pearl as she applied a last coat of lipstick to her lips.

Pearl was with Iris and Lulu. Grace loved how easily the three of them had become friends. She thought of Pearl, tanned and relaxed from a month in Thailand. She'd gone to look at potential sites for Jack's next hotel, and to spend time in the community to see what they needed. Grace had made a special effort the night before not to show too much excitement when Pearl had said she wanted to settle and make Strawberry Village her home. They'd even discussed taking a cookery course together.

Her phone beeped again.

Matilda: The contracts are all sent. Just enjoy your day.

When Grace had first set up Grace Leven Productions, she'd been nervous to get in touch with her old assistant. She'd invited her to Strawberry Village to see her new office, the first floor of a Georgian building just along the square from Jack. But most of all, she wanted to apologise for how cold and distant she'd become. She offered Matilda a job and a relocation package as her assistant and they'd bid for their first commission. Filming for their first documentary, 'The Warnings of a Perfect Marriage', was beginning in two weeks.

Matilda had been delighted to move to Strawberry Village – she'd been wanting to leave London for a long time. She'd told Grace she was fed up with all the men in London, and was convinced she'd run out of options there. Grace had introduced her to Pearl and Lulu and the three of them were out dancing most weekend nights.

Greg: I've just received the contract. I can't believe it's happening. See you at the wedding. X

Grace was thrilled when Greg had agreed to be the expert therapist on the documentary. He still kept his eleven o'clock slot free, but these days they were talking more about their new project than anything else. She knew he had the right amount of warmth and authority to touch the most closed of hearts. She'd also insisted he get a great agent as, although this was his first television appearance, she suspected it wouldn't be his last.

Grace looked around at her bedroom. She'd bought one of the mews houses near Greg's therapy rooms, choosing every colour, paint, carpet and picture herself. It was a cosy blend of creams, pinks and whites. She'd even bought a strawberry chair from Jack. It sat in her bedroom, and filled her with love every time she sat on it. Harvey had built all her cupboards, and had managed the building work in the house and the office – but he'd consulted Grace on every single decision. "This home is all yours."

Her phone beeped again.

Harvey: I'm just outside. X

She turned her phone off, smiling as she did so. She was no longer a slave to it, and she'd be seeing everyone she loved that day. She'd changed her number a few months before, and only a few people in her old world had the new one. When you live in a world like Strawberry Village, the phone loses its power – she planned to write about this in her next column, but now she had to go.

She picked up her bag and spritzed her perfume – a fresh floral one she'd chosen with Anne Wakefield. They'd both bought new perfumes after they'd met for lunch. The recently-separated Anne had taken Grace up on her offer to get in touch. Grace had offered her a position as production manager on the new documentary and she was hoping she'd say yes.

Still, today wasn't a day to think about work – this was one to celebrate love.

She blew a kiss to her parents, whose picture sat at the side of her bed. Then, as she walked down the stairs, she waved at the others. Photos of five-year-old, eighteen-year-old, twenty-six-year-old and forty-year-old Grace.

"Come on my lovelies," she told them. "Let's go and celebrate – I hear there'll be singing." She collected them in her heart one by one, and took them with her as she opened the door to find Harvey waiting for her, his arms open wide.

More by Ellie Barker

The Cherry Blossom Park Series

vinci-books.com/pinkcoffeeshop

Rosie Nash's life is built on order—her demanding TV job, her safe haven at The Pink Coffee Shop, and her treasured list.

But when the list vanishes, chaos takes over. Forced into the spotlight and confronted by an intriguing stranger, Rosie's life changes in ways she never expected.

Turn the page for a free preview…

The Pink Coffee Shop: Prologue

Lilly's List of Rules

It's up to you (and only you) to discover the joy in your life.

Decide what you want to do, then do it, because if you don't, you won't. But don't dilly-dally, your time won't wait forever – not even for you.

Think positively and the magic will come.

It's far easier (for you) to see the best in people.

However, should above rule prove impossible, use failsafe People Filing System: The Good Person Box & Bad Person Box. It's simple. Keep close to the first, and the other locked tight.

Moments are precious, so save them as memories. (Give yourself a little pinch if you think you might forget. It doesn't have to hurt.)

Never let a dance floor be empty. Ditto a karaoke machine.

What Really Happened To Me?

Beware of The Takers – they won't just have your money, but your thoughts and spirit too.

Smiles and moods really are contagious.

Be polite enough to listen when someone is talking.

Guilt and anger are pointless, they'll feed on that joy you worked so hard to find.

Look out for The Climbing Ivy. Don't let it get you too.

The Pink Coffee Shop: Chapter One

MONDAY 7TH MAY

4.30 am & 0 seconds

Open eyes. Check

Take deep breath. Check.

Reach for list. Check.

Sit up and prepare for twenty-seven glorious seconds of reading list. Yes, please, check.

There was, frankly, no better way to start the day. So, what if she knew the rules off by heart? Nothing could ever beat that first morning look. The squiggly handwriting, the musty smell, the tatty sides showing how useful it had been. It really did make the next step of putting her feet on the floor all the easier.

Cold shower. Check.

Pull on black shorts, t-shirt and trainers. Check.

Tie hair in ponytail and leave house at 4.46am & 26 seconds. Check.

Excellent work, Rosie Nash, she told herself. She'd earned a whole thirty-four seconds for a bonus read.

What Really Happened To Me?

But just as she took the list out of her pocket, a gust of wind snatched it away. She counted three seconds as she watched it and she felt her breath stop too. There it went, dancing around like a leaf caught in the wind.

But it wasn't a leaf, was it?

It was her life.

What was she doing? She grabbed it and put it back in her pocket, her hands shaking as she pulled up the zip. She really must stop this bonus read, outside like this. She should know better by now.

She looked at her watch and started to jog. Thirteen minutes and fifty-two seconds left to get to work. She was cutting it fine now, thanks to the seconds lost on the list-dance.

Rosie was quite aware, as she ran along the path, if a normal person could somehow hear her second-counting in her head he or she would suspect she was being ridiculous. But with all due respect to this normal person, they no doubt also had a normal job, maybe even in one of those offices where you have a whole hour off for lunch and finished at five. But it wasn't like that in the land of television, was it? Oh no. Every single second counts.

When their daily television show went on air in eight hours, fifty-eight minutes and thirty-seven seconds' time, Max Marlow the presenter could hardly say to their very nice and loyal viewers, 'Can you just hold on for forty-four seconds while we just finish off?'

Well, of course not.

Besides, Colin would be waiting for her and Colin's eyes were like those of a hawk. One hint of a fluster, a second too early or late, and it was bound to trigger him. Colin was a Question Asker, and while she hated questions about herself just about more than anything else in life, she could just about forgive Colin. The Security Guard-slash-Odd Job Man-slash Receptionist had a top place in her Good Person Box and besides, it wasn't his fault he was a Question Asker. It was just the way he was designed, maybe it was in his genes? But still, whatever the reason, it was best all round not to set him off.

She looked down at her hands, which were clammy and clenched. She flapped them around in the air, waving heartily at him, hoping the breeze would cool them.

There he was beaming back as he waved back through the glass.

It's up to you (and only you) to find the joy in your life.

Well, coming to work here and seeing Colin six days a week really was a joy, she thought as she walked through the door.

"Rosie love, everything okay?" His eyes were straight on her hands.

She attempted to lounge in a leisurely way next to the pile of newspapers sat on the counter between her and Colin, but his eyes were narrowing. "Yes, all good. More importantly, how did it go?" she asked, wishing her red cheeks would stop burning.

This weekend had been Colin's wife's 60th birthday. She hadn't wanted anything fancy, just fish and chips down on the coast in Cornwall. When Colin had announced this in front of their colleagues at their end of the week meeting on Friday he had been met by a rare silence.

"It was bliss Rosie love, and the sun shone down on us in Padstow. What lovely weather we are having. It's a bit warm out there this morning, you're a little flushed. Extra strong as you like it." He put a mug down in front of her, then frowned. "Would you rather a cold water? Are you sure you're okay?"

There it was.

Colin wasn't just a Question Asker, he was a Multiple Question Asker, the very worst kind. He was the only one of her colleagues who was, which, although unexpected, given the number of journalists she worked with, suited her perfectly. She watched his brow furrow further, and she told herself to stop shuffling.

"Of course, I am Colin, never better."

He nodded but looked unconvinced.

Think positively and the magic will come.

"I am so pleased you had a lovely time, right, must crack on… thank you." She picked up the pile of newspapers and her cup. Colin was also the only colleague who made her coffee and he had done so every morning since her first day here three years, three weeks, two minutes and ten seconds ago.

"You'll need it with that lot," he said as he did every day. Colin was a stickler for routine. "Now don't let them boss you around."

"I never do," she called over her shoulder in a rather unusual high pitch which she hoped Colin wouldn't notice. She balanced the papers and coffee to press number 4 on the lift. She felt slightly encouraged when she turned around to see Colin had moved on from question asking to his usual morning stretches.

Rosie sat down at her desk and allowed herself three seconds to rest her head in her hands. Really, what had become of her? Nearly losing her list and not telling the truth to Colin.

This behaviour had to stop instantly, or else she was at risk of ruining everything. She decided to send a text instead, in an attempt to change the track of the day.

Hope you are feeling better today x

She then remembered the time.

Hope this does not wake you x

Both texts were as ridiculous as the other, and she was never going to answer them anyway.

It's up to you (and only you) to discover the joy in your life.

Focus, she told herself. But her mind felt as if it had been filled with heavy fog. She took a gulp of Colin's coffee.

Think positively and the magic will come.

The warm liquid ran down her throat. She looked around the office, even though she knew she was all alone, before pulling the list out of her pocket. It was still there, she told herself and breathed out.

She began to place the different newspapers accordingly on her colleagues' desks. The front page of one of the tabloids caught her eyes as she lay it down. A beautiful woman Rosie recognised as a model, her hands in her hair, her face crumpled with pain. The headline read 'Because She's Not Worth It?' Rosie didn't bother to carry on reading.

One person's unfortunate moment but still delicious fodder for the miserable eye.

Stop it, Rosie, not now.

She pushed the thought away, along with the newspaper and the nausea which came with it. She unzipped her pocket and felt her list in her hand. Just touching it helped calm her breathing for now, but it didn't take away the thought.

What would the headline be on the front of that paper if her own secret ever came out?

The Pink Coffee Shop: Chapter Two

1 pm & 22 seconds

"One hour until we are on air, people," Rosie shrieked as politely as she could manage as she delivered scripts. It wasn't strictly true but the twenty-two seconds she hadn't told them about wouldn't bother her colleagues as much as they did her.

"All right, keep the noise down," George Bright The Producer growled as he kicked the photocopier.

"George, please, let me help you."

They had to call Services three times last week thanks to George and his lively foot, and she didn't have time to add their round of teas to her already-extended drinks list.

"Isn't it the runner's job to fix this?" George hissed at her.

No, she thought, it wasn't. It was the job of Services, but they had been too busy asking if there were any of Colin's custard creams knocking around when they were last down.

"Let me have a look." She put her scripts down. She counted seven seconds before he began his daily moan.

"How did I ever end up working on a show called PMTV? I promised my mother I'd be working on Newsnight by now."

"But PMTV is the best show on television." Rosie dared yet again, as she opened the printer door. She knew this would set him off further, but she couldn't let anyone speak badly of PMTV, not even George Bright's mum, who in Rosie's humble opinion had it all wrong. Didn't she realise PMTV was an agenda-setting, award-winning afternoon magazine show? Frankly she wished she could tell George Bright's mum, 2pm on a weekday was one of the best times of the week.

"Oh, stop with your perky ways, Nash. Nobody watches."

"What about the four million viewers who tuned in on Friday?" She knew better than to engage, but really.

"That was a one-off."

"It was the same every day last week, you can't deny it, they're huge figures." She tugged at the offending piece of paper.

"I was all perky once, when I was at the bottom like you, when I wanted the next step up," George said.

As she glanced over at him, his hands in his hair, his brow wrinkled, his foot poised ready to kick again, she struggled to imagine there was ever once a perky George Bright.

And to think today was one of the better days. His mother had let him go back on the carbs again. Thank heavens, the office had sighed.

Think positively and the magic will come.

"Remember the breathing expert last week. Think of a square."

"Shut up, Nash," he said.

If she were being perfectly honest, she hadn't really understood the square thing either, but it was worth a try.

"Don't speak to Rosie like that, Bright. Have a bit of bread, why don't you?" the Rons from Sound called.

"And hey, Rosie, where's our tea?"

Rosie did a final thrust, removing the jammed paper, before slamming the door shut with a triumphant smile.

"Shouldn't you be printing out my running order anyway?" he snarled as he marched off.

Rosie sighed as she printed the running order, waving at the Rons from Sound who were now making T signs with their hands and doing gagging impressions. Despite his rudeness, she couldn't help feel a bit sorry for George Bright. His mother sounded quite the tyrant and what was the universe thinking giving them a surname like Bright? She had suggested once he and his mum take part in a feature for the show, 'What's in a Name?', just to try to get them back on track at least, but he had replied succinctly with two words, the second being "off." But she also couldn't help but think he was just in the wrong profession and was only doing this to please his mum. So, for this very reason she kept him in her Good Person Box, albeit at the very bottom.

"And Nash, don't forget my chai latte, I was gasping through the show on Friday," he shouted as he sat back at his desk.

1.16 pm & 19 seconds

Rosie was just running towards the kitchen, when a foot stuck out of the dressing room door.

Fortunately for Rosie she had seen the door open. She knew who was in there and therefore could predict exactly what was coming next, given the number of times it had happened before.

She swerved, pretending she hadn't seen it, and carried on towards the kitchen.

"Look at you, missing my foot like that. Aren't you the clever one," Sophie Smith, the show's correspondent, snarled as she prowled into the corridor.

"Stop when I'm talking to you."

Remember she's in your Bad Person Box.

"Hi Sophie. Sorry, I don't know what you mean. Anyway, must dash." Rosie carried on walking, trying not to run.

"Look at you all busy and important. You're only the tea-maker, you know. It's not like you're on air or anything special."

Rosie looked at her watch. After the photocopier incident she really didn't have time for a Sophie Smith rant too.

"You look nice," Rosie tried. It wasn't a lie. With her immaculate blonde hair, her Louboutin shoes, and figure-hugging dress which clung to a shape Rosie could never even dream of, she did.

"Don't gush. It makes you even more ridiculous."

She may be in her Bad Person Box, but still, Rosie needed to get away.

"Your car's ready." Rosie turned, and ran towards the gallery. She'd be safe in there.

"Is it black? It had better be black," Sophie hissed as she ran through the doors.

Rosie stopped when she was in the cool, darkness of the

gallery. She reached in her pocket, touched her list and breathed a sigh of relief.

"Rosie. Come on girl. Our biccies are getting cold. Those teas won't make themselves."

1.59pm & 46 seconds

Rosie's heart began to beat a little faster just as it always did when they went on air.

She stood in the back of the gallery. It was her very favourite time of her working day, and she never missed it. It never got boring or normal. She was certain the thrill of live television was unlike anything else in the world. A rollercoaster. A bungee jump. A 100 mph drive in a fancy sports car. They wouldn't come close.

Rosie looked around, and allowed herself a little nod of triumph. Everyone was where they should be, drinks perched on the shelves far away from the enormous desk of controls. There had been a slight drama when Harry the Director had announced he was back on bags instead of leaves for his peppermint tea, they were getting stuck in his teeth. However, as luck would have it, she had kept a box of bags in her bottom drawer just in case this change of mind happened. Harry often altered a habit after seeing an item on the show, only to revert it again a few days later.

Rosie watched the steam rise off of George's chai latte and she could smell the bitter aroma of Dickie the PA's espresso from where she was standing. Harry and Dickie were a real-life couple, and Rosie was often concerned about their marriage bliss during one of their heated caffeine debates. But, when she watched them like this, working side by side, she breathed out. Harry's arm was flying in the air as if he were conducting an orchestra, Dickie was counting down every second, making certain the hour-long show was never a millisecond too far from where it should be and Rosie admired their perfect harmony. It was as though they were flying a plane.

"Phone off now, Max," Harry called to the presenter and Rosie's insides tightened. Over the last few weeks, Max Marlow had started taking his phone into the studio, deep in conversation, engrossed by whoever he was speaking to, just seconds before they went on air. It was highly unprofessional and Rosie didn't like the way he disrespected the studio's rules.

She had never been able to make up her mind about Max Marlow. Sometimes she thought it would be easier all round if he just went in her Bad Person Box. But then he did that job, the job she admired and feared the most, both at the same time. She was in awe, every time she watched him do it, so, for this very reason, he was one of the few people she kept in Pending.

She looked at him as he sat upright, smiling now as the final seconds ran out, his face lit by the countless lights shining down on him. She looked as she always did at Tracey the Floor Manager, who stood nearby. Rosie had counted it once. Their positions were six of her steps apart. Just six steps between two different worlds. One, in front of the camera. One behind. They worked in same room, on the same show and with the same people, but in one spot, strangers would call your name and in the other, they wouldn't. The viewers didn't even know Tracey was there, except for the odd times she popped up in the back of shot.

Rosie watched Max as he read the words rolling on the

camera in front of him. Just the thought of sitting in his seat made her throat begin to hurt.

Look out for The Climbing Ivy. Don't let it get you too.

She reached in her pocket and touched her list.

Yes. She was more than happy in the shadows of television, making peppermint tea and fixing photocopiers, and she had every intention to stay there, despite what George Bright might think.

3.12 pm & 16 seconds

"But I wanted chestnut. This isn't chestnut. This is bright red."

Rosie had a feeling the makeover guest wasn't happy when she had seen George scurrying away from the gallery, instead of coming into the studio to check on his guests.

"But you look lovely, so young and fresh," Rosie tried. She didn't want to appear rude, but she still had to check the boy band's car had arrived.

"Young and fresh? I'm eighty-four."

"Well, there you go. I would have thought you weren't a day over sixty. The red, I mean chestnut, suits you."

"I look like a jam tart. Mutton dressed up as lamb. I'm going to have to take myself off Tinder now, I'll be giving them the wrong idea."

"Never, you look great. Would you mind if we…?"

"I had a date tonight too, I'm going to cancel."

"But why? You mustn't. You look beautiful."

The woman looked at her. "I bet you go on lots of dates."

"Not really." If only the woman knew.

"The thing is, I am just so lonely." The woman's shoulders dropped. "I'm a fool trying to work this dating app, I'm always swiping the wrong way. I didn't even mean to say yes to this chap tonight. I should just give up. I'm too old."

Rosie looked at the woman, with her red hair all flicked, her face covered with lines showing a life well-lived. She may not be smiling, but her eyes still sparkled.

Don't dilly-dally, your time won't wait forever – not even for you.

"Never. You're still here and life is for living. Who knows, he could be the man of your dreams. And you really do look lovely," Rosie said.

"Alright gorgeous. You look a right knockout." It was one of the boyband members calling over. She really should check on their car.

The woman touched her hair. "Did he just call me gorgeous?"

"He did indeed, and he is going out with a supermodel." Rosie winked at her. She wasn't a hundred per cent certain the last bit was strictly true, but the woman was smiling at least.

"I tell you what, do you need to rush off anywhere?"

"Where to? My house is empty, even the cat keeps going out because he's bored with me."

"Then I think there's a place you should go to and I promise you, by the time you leave you won't be able to wait for that date tonight."

3.46 pm & 19 seconds

What Really Happened To Me?

"Ah, there you are Rosie. Any chance of a 'between you and me'?" Oscar poked his head and around the door of his office, tapping his nose as she scuttled by.

Her heart sank. She had been hoping to escape. All guests had been dispatched, all members of the boyband were being driven off to their next gig and she had forty-six minutes before she had to start printing tomorrow's briefs. Besides, she wanted to check on the makeover lady.

"Sorry to bother you Rosie, but I am gasping." Oscar was doing a V sign at his lips, as he looked around to see if any of the team were watching, which they weren't.

"Of course, just coming."

Still, Oscar was her boss and next to Colin in her Good Person box, she reminded herself as she returned to her desk to pull out the box. Once she was safely in his office, he opened the door to his balcony and out they both went. She gave him his cigarette and the lighter, she watched as he inhaled for twelve seconds before he finally exhaled. She saw the relief wash over him.

"Ah, that's better." He inhaled again.

Rosie hated watching her boss smoke, but even despite all the rather graphic YouTube videos she'd 'accidentally sent him by mistake' he continued with this life-threatening habit. She knew too if his wife Jasmine knew, it wouldn't just add to his troubles at home, as he called them, it would spell The End. Rosie was his trusted ally.

"Jasmine has a sixth sense," he had explained. "She knows if I so much as walk past a shop selling them. But she'll never trace it back to me, if you buy them and keep them too."

As much as Rosie hated the idea of her boss putting his life in jeopardy, she could not deny there was something she rather enjoyed about balancing on his little balcony on the side of the building. They were high enough that, should Jasmine ever happen to walk past, or anyone else who could blow the secret, they were out of sight. Also, they had a magnificent view of Bristol docks here. The studios were built so the backdrop of the show was the river, and the Neapolitan coloured houses which peppered its banks. Up here, watching the boats tootle along the river, the air was somehow easier to breathe, even with Oscar's cigarettes.

"That was a close one, I thought the makeover woman was going to make an official complaint. George did well to calm her down," Oscar said after several long drags.

Guilt and anger are pointless, they feed on that joy you worked so hard to find.

"Yes, didn't he," Rosie said.

It's far easier (for you) to see the best in people.

"Now, Rosie, I fear I've got myself in a spot of bother which is only going to add to my troubles at home." He took another puff.

Rosie felt a flash of panic. "Jasmine hasn't found out about this, has she?" She pointed at the cigarette.

"Christ no," he spluttered. "Can you imagine?"

Unfortunately for Oscar, she could.

"She says I don't listen enough. Do you think I listen?" He puffed again.

"Of course, you do. You're a brilliant boss."

It was true, he was.

"No, no, I don't mean just work stuff, I mean, *really* listen. Do I listen enough to you about you?"

No, Rosie thought, and this was exactly how she liked it. He never normally asked personal questions, which was one of the many reasons he was her perfect boss. Even though he was the father of three teenage daughters, he was remarkably awkward at discussing anything remotely related to feelings, so they tended to avoid such conversations, much to her relief.

"Absolutely," she replied.

"I mean, I... I... just." He was stuttering, this was never a good sign. Her throat began to hurt again, she had a horrible feeling he was about to...

"What I want to say is, how are you, Rosie? I mean how are you really?"

There it was.

A Question. Oscar was never normally a Question Asker.

"Would you like another one?" She held the packet in front of him. They normally had a strict rule of one max, two only if there had been a disaster on the show. But this was question asking and therefore in the disaster category.

"If you insist." He had taken it and lit it, before she had put the box back in her pocket.

"Sorry, I am really rather rubbish at all this." He puffed again.

"No, really, you're not," Rosie told him. She looked at him, his face filled with worry.

Oscar Hook was such a kind and thoughtful boss that at first, staff at PMTV had taken advantage of him, calling him Off-The-Hook, behind his back. He had later confessed after too much Friday fizz, that he had thought she had a lisp, when he first met her. The truth was, thanks to nerves she had blurted out his nickname, by mistake.

But then slowly they all realised he wasn't weak in the slightest. He solved problems without being panicked, and the Off-The-Hook nickname hadn't lasted long, thank goodness. He really was treasured by the staff, most of all by Rosie. She waited for him to take another drag, and tried to think how she could get him out of this misery.

Smiles and moods really are contagious.

"How did your golf tournament go yesterday?" she asked and his face lit up.

He then spent the next six minutes and eleven seconds telling her all about his near-miss hole-in-one. He demonstrated his swing with such vigour, the balcony began to wobble and she nearly dropped the packet of cigarettes.

The Pink Coffee Shop: Chapter Three

4.06 pm & 19 seconds

The warmth which greeted her when she opened the door melted away all the tensions and worries of her day. Just like it always did.

It was twenty-six and a half of her steps from the door of PMTV to the door of The Pink Coffee Shop, but it felt like a different world.

It's up to you (and only you) to discover the joy in your life.

Every time Rosie opened the door, it was as though she was arriving home, only when she did arrive at her actual proper home, it never felt like this. Not these days anyway. If she lacked colour in her life due to her black ensemble every day, this place provided the injection she needed. It also gave delicious food and a giant hug to everyone who stepped inside.

The perfect blend of cinnamon and coffee wafted over her and she admired, as she always did, the ease of the place. It was stylish without being stuffy, welcoming but chic. The pink walls, covered partly with planks of wood painted off-white, the white chairs and high-backed stools covered with pink and white gingham cushions, the same napkins placed next to the pink mugs serving the best coffee in the city. Little jugs of seasonal pink flowers placed on every one of the tables, all overlooking the bustling harbourside and the shimmering river.

That it was owned and run by two of her favourite people in all the world was the icing on one of its most fabulous cakes.

"Ah, here she is, now," Wanda called from the side of the coffee shop. Rosie saw the makeover lady sat on a table behind her.

"That lot kept you longer than normal, did they?" Millie walked out of the kitchen carrying a freshly baked quiche which she placed on the counter. The smell of it drifted over Rosie and she heard her stomach rumble.

"Oscar."

"Say no more."

They knew the rules of a between you and me.

The makeover lady waved at Rosie.

"So, you came." Rosie smiled, and the makeover lady smiled back. "Doesn't she look great?" Rosie said to Wanda and Millie.

"Great? She looks awesome." Millie pointed to her own hair which she had been dying pink since they bought the coffee shop. "Puts mine to shame."

Wanda turned back to the makeover lady. "My daughter rarely gives compliments, Mavis, you are honoured."

"I feel it. Now, don't let me keep you any longer," Mavis said, getting up.

"Not at all, I've loved our chat. But we mustn't hold you

up. You've only got a few hours until the big date," Wanda said.

"I know. Ooh, I'm getting all tingling inside. I must be excited," Mavis said. She touched Rosie's arm as she walked past. "You were right about this place, young lady, I think tonight could be the night." She winked. "I'll be back to report the details," she called as she walked out the door.

It's up to you (and only you) to discover the joy in your life.

Rosie sat down at the counter in her favourite spot, the same one Millie and Wanda always reserved for her at this time of day.

"Don't tell me, it was Bright who had something to do with the red hair," Millie hissed once Mavis had closed the door.

"I'm not sure it was strictly him," Rosie tried, although as the show's producer it wouldn't have done any harm for him to keep across the colour tones.

"I don't know why you always defend him," Millie said, placing Rosie's americano in front of her. "He's such a…"

"Now, now, Millie," Wanda said as she carried a tray of empty plates and cups into the kitchen. "Remember, Calm is Power." She nodded at one of the signs on the wall. She returned and placed her hands on her daughter's shoulders.

Rosie smiled and sipped her coffee. Every afternoon her visit began with a Millie moan about George Bright. It was all part of their wonderful routine. Just sitting here meant she could finally breathe properly and her throat never hurt here. She watched Millie disappear into the kitchen, and return carrying a basket of scones.

"I've just taken them out of the oven," Millie told her. "Cinnamon, let me know what you think." Rosie picked one up, blowing on it, realising she hadn't eaten all day.

"Oh Rosie, please tell me you have actually eaten something today?" Wanda stood in front of her behind the counter, crossing her arms. Wanda too was a Question Asker but in the twenty-two years she had known her, Rosie had come to accept this in the same way Wanda had come to accept Rosie almost always avoided them now. Besides, Wanda used to be a psychotherapist, so she couldn't help herself.

It's far easier (on you) to see the best in people.

Besides, Wanda was Wanda.

"I thought Mavis would like it in here," Rosie said.

"Nicely avoided," Wanda said.

"Have you got any of Mr Chapman's jam?" Rosie tried again.

Wanda placed a mini jar on the counter in front of her. "Have you really not eaten all day?" Wanda's voice softened. "I'm not going to give you a lecture, but you know I promised her…"

"Is that a new sign?"

On the left wall there was a collection of signs, all with inspirational quotes or rather gentle reminders as Wanda called them. She was used to Wanda and Millie adding to them, but this one was different.

"Not all storms come to disrupt your life, some bring the change of breeze you need," Wanda read out.

Rosie shuddered at the idea of any storm disrupting her life. No, thank you. It was disrupted enough as it was.

"Yes, Sid sent it with his last lot of jam."

"Mr Chapman?" Rosie said. Knowing it was from him did make it a little more appealing. Sid Chapman was not only her very big boss as the owner of PMTV and a billionaire, he was also an excellent jam maker which he regularly sent over from his home in America, and they sold it here in the coffee shop. He was well and truly in her Good Person Box sat next to Colin and Oscar. But still, there was something about the sign.

"You're avoiding my question. I do wish you would look after…"

Rosie's phone began to ring inside her pocket.

"Rosie Nash. You know the rules." Wanda pointed at another sign which read No Phone Zone.

Mobile phones were forbidden inside The Pink Coffee Shop, along with laptops and everything else which could possibly connect customers to the outside world. When Wanda made this controversial decision, she was told by those who thought they knew better, the place would not last a week. But she and Millie had proved them wrong. It was the busiest coffee shop in Bristol by a long stretch and was regularly written about in national newspapers and magazines.

Rosie quickly pulled the phone out of her pocket. It was Sophie Smith.

"It's Sophie Smith," Rosie said out loud.

"Even more of a reason to turn it off," Wanda replied.

Rosie pressed decline. Wanda was watching, and other customers were turning to look at her.

The Pink Coffee Shop wasn't just her special place, she knew, as much as sometimes she wished she didn't have to share it. People travelled from all over the country to come here. Wanda and Millie were the perfect blend of ingredients, a former psychotherapist and an award-winning baker. Customers often left with a lighter mind, and fuller insides. Rosie could still remember when Wanda had arrived home from work four years ago and made her declaration.

"That's it, I'm done." She then opened the bottle of Moët she had bought on her way home. "I'm fighting a lost cause, I'm wasting their money and my time. I tell them one way, then off they go on another. They just want a quick fix. I'm banging my head against a social media brick wall. So, I'm going to do it. I am going to open a haven for them instead, a place of tranquillity, where they can come and have a chat with a slice of my daughter's delicious cake."

Millie, who had recently qualified from catering college, was delighted. A few weeks later, a former patient of Wanda's had tipped her off about the prime premises on Bristol Docks becoming available. The rumours were circulating back then that a television studio was going to open next door, so Wanda and Millie jumped at the chance.

"Your quote is still my favourite." Rosie tried to change the subject again. She pointed to the first sign she had helped them put up the day the coffee shop opened.

Wanda laughed. "Well it's true. Everyone does need a bit of pink in their life, and you can never beat a decent cup of coffee."

Rosie's phone rang again.

"I thought you had turned it off," Wanda scolded.

"Sorry, sorry." Rosie rummaged in her pocket. She could feel her hands shaking. This time she turned it onto silent, but she couldn't get rid of the unease in her stomach. Not answering twice was only going to make it all worse. She picked her scone up and put it down again.

Remember the Bad Person Box.

"Her section on veganism was cut," Rosie said in a low voice.

Wanda let out a slow whistle, while Millie returned for another Millie moan. Who cared what Sophie Smith thought about veganism, anyway? Rosie sipped her coffee and pointed at the Calm is Power sign, but Millie wasn't having any of it.

What Really Happened To Me?

It didn't really matter. Sophie Smith was in her Bad Person Box, and she couldn't hurt her from there. She put her cup down. She was about to open the zip of her pocket just to feel her list but saw Wanda was watching her.

"You are wasted on them, Rosie, you really are," Millie said, as Wanda ushered her daughter back into the kitchen as customers started looking up from their books.

"Is everything okay?" Wanda looked at her through those same narrow eyes Colin had done eleven hours earlier. This was the problem with the Question Askers.

"Yes, of course," Rosie replied.

"It's just you seem a little edgy." Wanda peered over the counter and looked at Rosie's hand moving towards her other pocket. "Are you still carrying that list? I thought you were going to try for a bit to do without it," Wanda said in a hushed voice, her eyes filled with worry.

Rosie looked around to see if anyone had heard this, but all the customers were back reading their books. She felt the familiar tiny prickles in her throat. She wasn't supposed to feel like this in here.

"Oh Rosie, it's just not right. It is after all only a piece of paper with words written by your aunt."

"I know, I know it's just…" Rosie stopped.

"I know too." Wanda's cool hand touched hers. "It's just like I was saying, I promised her I would take care of you, and this is worrying me."

"I know," Rosie said. "I'll try harder. I promise."

"It is after all, only a list, written years ago."

It was time for her to go.

"I have a lot to do."

Wanda went into the kitchen. Rosie knew what she was doing and she returned holding a pink box tied with a pink checked ribbon.

"For later." Wanda placed tonight's dinner in front of her.

"Thank you," Rosie replied. "I do appreciate it." She really did.

"And we appreciate you. More than that lot over there anyway," Millie said, coming to stand next to her mum.

"Will you text me later?" Wanda asked. "When you get home from seeing her?"

Rosie nodded.

"Say hello from us, won't you?" Wanda said, her voice still quiet.

Rosie nodded again.

"Bye then and thank you." Rosie tried to sound as cheerful as she could as she turned and walked outside. She looked at her phone. Fifteen missed calls. She leant back against the small bit of wall between the Pink Coffee Shop and PMTV and breathed in for ten seconds.

"Right, come on then. One, two, three…"

She looked down at her trainers and counted their steps as they took her back to her other world again.

5.46pm & 18 seconds

"Flipping heck, it's not her again is it, Rosie, love?" Colin took the phone off her.

Rosie had stayed down working next to Colin since she had returned from the Pink Coffee Shop. She often did this, she got more work done that way, and Colin's pottering felt like a warm comfort blanket around her, especially when she was on a Sophie Smith phone call.

The first one had lasted for eight minutes and twenty-seven seconds, which was much shorter than Rosie would expect given the veganism cut.

Colin was as used to Sophie Smith's rants as Rosie was, not that Sophie Smith knew. But with his razor-sharp hearing (vital for a blackbelt holder, he would often remind her) he had heard them so often, they had a well-oiled routine to deal with the calls.

A knowing nod from Rosie and Colin got out her laptop, the one he kept for her in his office. Then, he took the phone off her, while she made a few calls on the landline. He would hand back the phone once Sophie Smith was finally quiet, which normally took a while. The second one, which was a complaint about the car which had picked her up had gone on for a whopping twelve minutes and sixteen seconds. Yes, it was black, but it was a BMW and not a Mercedes. It was crystal clear, according to Sophie Smith, Rosie was trying to sabotage her day.

And now the phone was ringing again.

"Are you really sure she should be allowed to talk to you in this way?" Colin asked.

"She's under a lot of pressure," Rosie replied. She could hardly tell him the truth, that Sophie Smith was shut nice and tight in her Bad Person Box, so she couldn't hurt her from there.

"What's it this time?" he mouthed at Rosie, holding the phone at arm's length.

"She wants me to book her a fish pedicure," Rosie mouthed.

Colin rolled his eyes. "Best make it a shark and it might gobble her up."

Rosie laughed.

"Are you laughing at me?" Sophie Smith spat.

"No, no, of course not," Rosie said.

Colin rolled his eyes and did a side kick, followed by one of his blackbelt chops.

"The runner doesn't laugh at me," she hissed this time. "Text me the details, and get the right car this time. It's not that difficult, or is it, for someone like you?" She hung up before Rosie could reply.

Think positively and the magic will come.

"I don't know why you put up that girl," Colin told her, putting down his Black Belt magazine he was now reading. He said the same every day when she called.

"She doesn't bother me, really she doesn't," she told him. She was after all firmly locked away.

"If you say so Rosie, love, if you say so. Right, while I've got you down here, I am going to make us a cup and how do you fancy a nice custard cream?"

6.31pm & 54 seconds

Rosie stayed as long as she could, working next to Colin, writing her briefs and fixing transport for the next day. She called out goodbye to each of her colleagues as they trickled out the door. She didn't mind in the slightest they were going home and she wasn't. Rosie still had twenty-seven minutes and six seconds before she had to set off and she was in no rush to get where she was going.

"I hope you've sorted that photocopier, Nash," George Bright said as he walked past.

"Night, George," she replied. "Have a good evening."

It's far easier (on you) to see the best in people.

Poor George. He no doubt had another evening with his mother ahead of him, watching Newsnight, reminding him how he had failed. Rosie could only hope she never found out about the chestnut.

"Bye then, Rosie," Oscar said as he walked past, the man-bag Jasmine had bought him to make him look more youthful at Christmas, draped across him.

"Bye, Oscar."

"Thanks for the talk earlier." Oscar said.

"You're welcome, thank you," she said. She saw the worry in his eyes again and her insides sunk. She hoped his troubles at home would get better soon. "Any golf tonight?"

"Not tonight," he said. She felt heartened, at least, when he did a fake swing, although he did only just miss Tracey the Floor Manager.

"Watch it Oscar, I'm late for drum practice as it is."

Rosie stayed working next to Colin, until he finally got his keys out from the drawer.

"Right now, Rosie love, that's us. It's that time again. You must get yourself home now, too," Colin told her as he started to lock up the desk.

Rosie looked at the clock. He was right. But she wasn't going home, not that she ever told him that. If she so much as hinted she wasn't, to a Question Asker like Colin, it was bound to set him off, and not even Colin could ever know the truth.

About the Author

Ellie Barker is a television reporter and presenter for ITV West Country. *What Really Happened to Me?* is her fifth novel and second to be set in the fictitious Strawberry Village in Bristol, the city where she also lives.

Ellie is also the host of The Next Chapter podcast. She interviews all sorts of inspiring people, hoping it'll encourage you to live a life you love too. She gets tips and advice as she navigates from journalism to author, and everything she learns, she passes on to you. She truly believes if more of us lived lives we really loved, it might not change the whole world, but it would change ours – which is a really good start.

Ellie lives with her husband and fellow TV journalist Rob Murphy. He tends to cover the darker side of life at the top of the running order, while her stories are more likely to be before the weather. But at home, neither are in the pecking order really. Their two sons, labrador Cookie, endless muddy floors, and abandoned socks see to that.

Acknowledgments

My first thanks must go to the brilliant people behind Vinci Books – Jane Harris, Mark Smith, and James Blatch. When I started writing this book, I had no idea it would be published by you. Thank you so much for believing in my writing and welcoming me into your family. After learning from James through the Learn Self Publishing for so many years, it's an honour to work with him now. To be part of this exciting new adventure of combining the worlds of traditional and independent publishing is a Next Chapter dream come true.

Thank you also to my brilliant editor, Scott Pack, who not only helped me with Grace Leven's story but was there the very moment I needed some life advice too. I'm so happy we can keep working together – if only so I can find out what you're cooking next. To Clio Mitchell for your proofread and copyedits. Apologies for my commas too.

To Susan Lewis for being not just a brilliant role model and mentor but an incredible friend too. I will never forget how you tried so hard for me. To Louise Ross for answering my questions and showing me so much support. Thank you to Mel Sherratt for all your inspiration and belief too.

I'd also like to thank those who've helped make my first dream – working as a television journalist – come true. Hi-TV is *not* ITV. I've worked for ITV on and off for more than twenty-five years, and I love it even more today. I'm so proud to be a tiny part of such a magical machine – because I still think television really is magical.

Thank you, Sarah Clarke, for your wisdom and advice. I watch in awe as you juggle an enormous job with your family and do it in such a humble way. Thank you also to Michael Jermey for supporting my writing and podcast as much as my television work. I'm very sure not many bosses are like you. I've not quite forgiven you for leaving, but I will never forget Monday 16th January 2006 at 12 noon. It was one of the best moments of my whole television career.

To the rest of my ITV family, because we really are a family.

To Vicky Slade, for everything – always being by my side (or in our ears). To Lucy Key for being, well… just lovely. I appreciate you both so much.

To Julie Ebbs for our WPT team talks. To Jacquie Bird for always being one of the first to read my books and calming my nerves. To Lady Claire Manning – forever our Lady Gold. To Kate Haskell for showing us what true Next Chapter living is. I am so lucky to be in your gang.

To Naryan Branch for always caring and showing up. You're so engaged and brilliant, and I know all your dreams will come true.

To Jacqui Bradley for always reading my books and following my work. To Jim Stevens – don't worry, you still don't have to read my books – but thank you for believing in what I do.

To Clare Green for giving me a confidence boost just when I dipped. For passing my books on to Victoria Davies, who sent me one of my favourite messages ever, which came at just the right time. I know you two would only ever tell me the truth, so thank you for giving me the confidence to carry on.

To Julia Reid/Bray – you are amazing. You read all my books, listen to all the Next Chapter episodes, and I cannot thank you enough. To have someone like you in my corner, so engaged and supportive, especially when you have so much in your own life – well, it's impossible to fail.

To the friends in my life who are my own Strawberry Village.

Thank you to the Lunchtime Lovelies – Little & Big Mel. Two of the best humans in the whole world and one of the best wedding presents ever. Thank you for everything – especially the cheese. Harvey is for you two (and Mr Hunter, whom we love so much too).

To Trinske Driscoll-Antonides/The Other Iron Lady. No matter what's been happening, you always believe. Thirty-two years of friendship; I can't wait for our next adventure soon.

To Tashie Amponsah and the gorgeous Astrid & Inez (my two wonderful goddaughters). Thank you for being my sister from a different mister and to all of you for your wonderful advice.

To Jenny Russe and Lee – for always being by our side. The ups and downs and the ins and outs. Stollen, marzipan, and the marble jars – your kindness is the best kind in the world.

To the lovely Jane Drummond-Wilson and Tom for believing in my books. You've listened and supported for so many years. Thank you for all your love and warmth.

To Melissa Law for our coffees, dinners, and endless chats about what I'm doing in the Next Chapter world. I love our time and our conversations.

To the Rogers: Abigail, Dave, Reuben, and Poppy. Thank you so much for your continuous support. It's wonderful to be side by side in our Next Chapter world, watching you bloom and grow, and we cannot wait to see what happens next.

To my Swedish Princess Kristin Magnusson – for taking my books with you around the world. I am so lucky to have such a supportive friend.

To Jessie Watts (yes, Jessie), Fran Clamp, and Jo Dineen. I watch in awe as you juggle your own worlds, yet somehow you always make time for my work too.

To Lesley Hannah, Kate Rajakaruna, and Tina Snowden. My Safari-turned-Supper-Clubbers. Thank you for your belief from the very beginning, for reading and listening, and always helping me feel I'm on the right track.

To Suze and Rosie Anderson. Thank you for all your incredible support. Rosie, I think you are one of my most dedicated readers; I feel honoured to be on your shelf.

To Maddy Hennah for your endless support and belief. I always think of you when I have a blank page, and I never feel quite so afraid.

To my mum and dad, Joyce and Roger. For bringing me up in a home where I could tell my stories. For the days spent making them up with our dogs in the garden - while my dad pottered and my mum made delicious food. You showed me what a home really is, and I'm grateful for this every day.

And to Rob, Arthur, Herbie and Cookie – for being my home today. You teach me so much, not just how to re-stack the dishwasher but how to live life too. I've watched how you tackle your next chapters, and I'm always in awe. I love how a Monday night snuggled with you is one of the happiest times of my life. Thank you for not eating my marzipan and showing me there's always another way.

Printed in Dunstable, United Kingdom